THEY WISH THEY WERE US

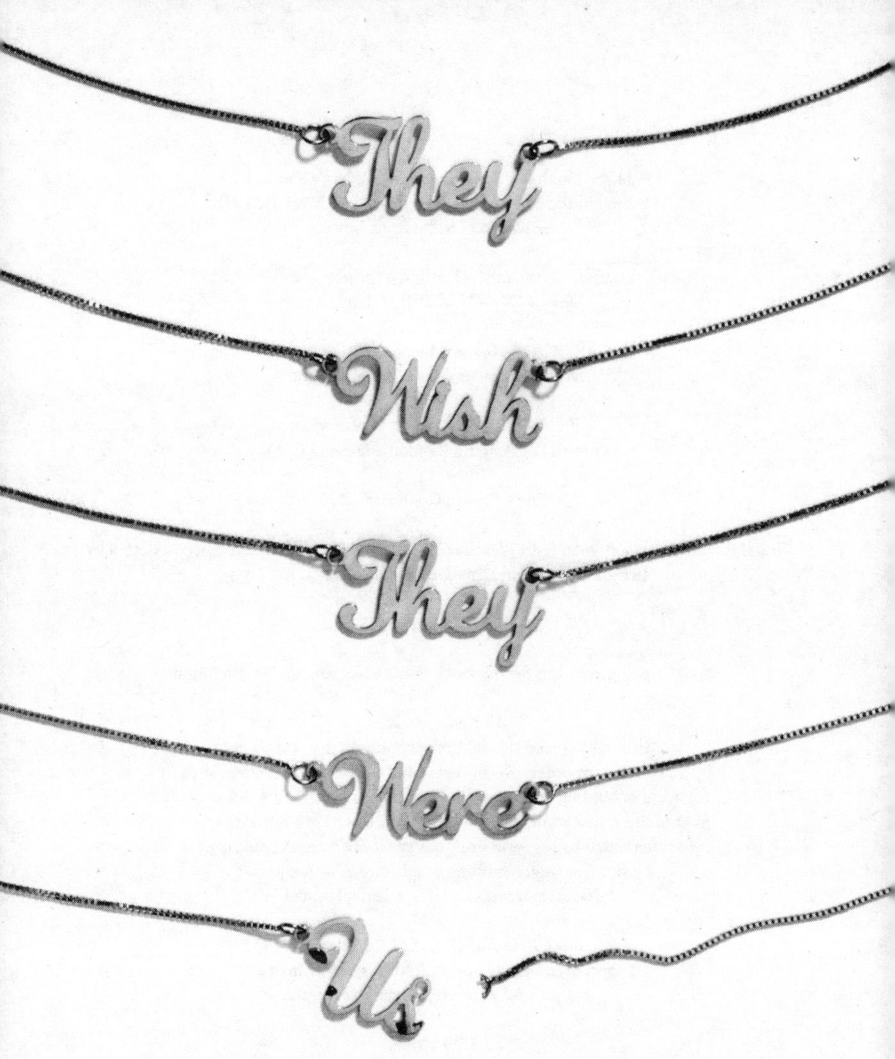

They Wish They Were Us

JESSICA GOODMAN

SCHOLASTIC

Published in the UK by Scholastic Children's Books, 2021
Euston House, 24 Eversholt Street, London, NW1 1DB, UK
A division of Scholastic Limited.

London – New York – Toronto – Sydney – Auckland
Mexico City – New Delhi – Hong Kong

First published in the US by Razorbill,
an imprint of Penguin Random House LLC, 2020

ISBN 978 0702 30803 1

A CIP catalogue record for this book is available from the British Library.

Printed by CPI Group (UK) Ltd, Croydon, CR0 4YY
Papers used by Scholastic Children's Books are made
from wood grown in sustainable forests.

1 3 5 7 9 10 8 6 4 2

www.scholastic.co.uk

To Mom and Dad,
for the roots and the wings.

PROLOGUE

IT'S A MIRACLE anyone gets out of high school alive. Everything is a risk or a well-placed trap. If you're not done in by your own heart, so trampled and swollen, you might fall victim to a totally clichéd but equally tragic demise—a drunk-driving accident, a red light missed while texting, too many of the wrong kinds of pills. But that's not how Shaila Arnold went.

Of course, technically, her cause of death was blunt force trauma at the hands of her boyfriend, Graham Calloway. With trace evidence of sea water in her lungs, drowning may have been the easiest assumption, but upon closer inspection, the bump on her head and the puddle of thick, sticky blood that matted her long honey-blonde hair was unmissable.

Blunt force trauma. That's what her death certificate says. That's what went down in the record books. But that's not *really* how she died. It can't be. I think she died from anger, from betrayal. From wanting too much all at once. From never feeling full. Her rage was all-consuming. I know this because mine is, too. *Why did we have to suffer? Why were we chosen? How had we lost control?*

It's hard to remember what we were like before, when anger was just temporary. A passing feeling caused by a fight with Mom, or my little brother Jared's insistence on eating the last piece of apple pie at Thanksgiving. Anger was easy then because it was fleeting. A rolling wave that crashed ashore before it settled down. Things always settled down.

Now it's as if a monster lives inside me. She'll be there forever, just waiting to crack open my chest and step forward into the light. I wonder if this is how Shaila felt in her last moments alive.

They say only the good die young, but that's just a line in a stupid song we used to sing. It isn't real. It isn't true. I know that because Shaila Arnold was so many things—brilliant and funny, confident and wild. But honestly? She wasn't all that good.

ONE

THE FIRST DAY of school always means the same thing: a tribute to Shaila. Today *should* be the first day of her senior year. Instead, she is, like she has been for the past three years, dead. And we are due for one more reminder.

"Ready?" Nikki asks as we pull into the parking lot. She throws her shiny black BMW, a back-to-school present from her parents, into park and takes an enormous slurp of iced coffee. "Because I'm not." She flips down the mirror, swipes a coat of watermelon-pink lipstick over her mouth, and pinches her cheeks until they flush. "You'd think they could just give her a plaque or start a charity run or something. This is brutal."

Nikki had been counting down to the first day of senior year since we left for summer break back in June. She called me this morning at 6:07 a.m., and when I rolled over and picked up in a hazy fog, she didn't even wait for me to say hi. "Be ready in an hour or find another ride!" she yelled, a hairdryer blowing behind her into the speaker.

She didn't even need to beep her horn when she showed up. I knew she was waiting out front thanks to the deafening notes of Whitney Houston's "How Will I Know." We both have a thing for eighties music. When I climbed into the front seat, Nikki looked as if she'd already had two Starbucks Ventis and a full glam squad appointment. Her dark eyes glimmered thanks to a swatch of sparkly eyeshadow and she had rolled the sleeves of her navy Gold Coast Prep blazer up to her elbows in an artful yet sloppy manner. Nikki's one of the only people who can make our hideous uniforms actually look cool.

Thank God my nightmares stayed away last night and the near-constant bags under my eyes had disappeared. Didn't hurt that I'd had a few extra minutes to apply a thick coat of mascara and deal with my brows.

When Nikki pulled out of my driveway, I was giddy with anticipation. Our time had come. We were finally at the top.

But now that we're actually here, parked in the Gold Coast Prep senior lot for the first time, a shiver shoots down my spine. We still have to get through Shaila's memorial and it hangs over us like a cloud, ready to rain all over the fun.

Shaila was the only student to ever die while attending Gold Coast Prep, so no one knew how to act or what to do. But somehow, it was decided. The school would start the year off with a fifteen-minute ceremony honoring Shaila. The tradition would last until we graduated. And as a thank-you, the Arnolds would donate a new English wing in Shaila's name. Well played, Headmaster Weingarten.

But no one wanted to remember Graham Calloway. No one mentioned him at all.

Last year's assembly wasn't so bad. Weingarten stood up and said something about how much Shaila loved math—she didn't—and how she would have been so thrilled to be starting AP Calc if she was still with us—she wasn't. Mr. and Mrs. Arnold showed up, as they had the year before, and sat in the front row of the auditorium, dabbing their cheeks with cotton handkerchiefs, the old-fashioned kind that were so worn, they were almost translucent and probably held residual snot from decades before.

The six of us sat next to them, front and center, identifying ourselves as Shaila's survivors. We were chosen as eight. But after that night we became six.

When Nikki weaves into the spot reserved for class president, Quentin is already waiting for us. "We're seniors, bitches!" he says, and slaps a piece of notebook paper against my window, flashing a hastily drawn doodle of the three of us. In it, Nikki holds her senior class president gavel, I grasp on to a telescope twice my size, and Quentin's covered in flaming-red paint to match his hair. Our little trio makes my heart melt.

I squeal at the sight of real Quentin and fling the car door open, throwing myself at his middle.

"You're here!" I say, burying my face into his doughy chest.

"Aw, Jill," he says with a laugh. "C'mere, Nikki." She launches herself into our hug and I inhale the dewy scent of Quentin's laundry. Nikki leaves a sticky kiss on my cheek. In seconds, the others appear. Robert, with his slicked-back hair, takes the last puff of a mint-flavored Juul and shoves it into the pocket of his leather jacket. He *should* get a handful of demerits for wearing it in favor of his blazer, but he never does. "I can't believe we have to do this again," he says.

"What? School or Shaila?" Henry comes up behind me and rests a hand on the top of my butt, nipping my ear with his teeth. He smells overwhelmingly male, like freshly cut grass mixed with expensive French deodorant. I blush, remembering this will be the first time we're seen at school together as a *we*, and inch closer to him, tucking my shoulder into his armpit.

"What do you think?" Robert rolls his eyes.

"Shut up, you idiots," Marla says, whipping her platinum-blonde braid over her muscled shoulder. Her face is tanned from a summer spent training at the best field hockey camp in New England. Her stick hangs low over her back in a tie-dyed canvas bag, its taped handle peeking out the top. The ultimate sign of varsity realness. She wears it well.

"Whatever," Robert mumbles. "Let's get this over with." He walks ahead, leading us onto the grassy quad, manicured and untouched after a summer without students. If you stand in just the right spot, below the clock tower and two steps to the right, you can glimpse a sliver of the Long Island Sound just a mile down the road and the tall sailboats swaying carefully next to one another. The salty air makes my hair curl. There's no use owning a flatiron here.

I bring up the rear and gaze at my friends' backs. Their perfect silhouettes set against the sun. For a moment nothing exists outside the Players. We are a force field. And only we know the truth about what we've had to do to get here.

Underclassmen—Nikki calls them *undies* for short—trot along the paved walkways, but no one comes close to our little unit. They keep their distance, tugging at their too-stiff white button-downs, tightening belt buckles, and rolling up their pleated plaid skirts. None of them dare to make eye contact with us. They've learned the rules by now.

I am sweating by the time we reach the auditorium, and

when Henry opens the door for me I'm filled with dread. Most of the velvet-covered seats are already taken and big bug eyes turn to see us walk down the aisle to our places in the front row next to Mr. and Mrs. Arnold. They're both dressed in black. When we approach, they stand and dole out pursed-lipped air kisses to each of us. The smacking sounds echo through the cavernous room, and the scrambled eggs I had for breakfast curdle inside my stomach. The whole thing reminds me of my grandfather's funeral when we stood for hours, receiving guest after guest until my puckered mouth wilted like a flower. I am the last to greet Mrs. Arnold and she digs her crimson nails into my skin.

"Hello, Jill," she whispers into my ear. "Happy first day of school."

I manage a smile and wriggle my arm from her grasp after a moment too long. When I squeeze in between Henry and Nikki, my heart beats fast. Shaila stares back at us from a gilded frame, sitting on an easel in the middle of the stage. Her golden locks fall in full, beachy waves and her deep green eyes have been made more electric with some help from Photoshop. She looks the same as she always did, forever fifteen, while the rest of us have acquired additional pimples, more painful periods, nastier dragon breath.

The theater smells like freshly xeroxed paper and sharpened pencils. Gone is the musk that had settled in by the end of last spring's school year. This place was the one thing the Arnolds got right for her memorial. The auditorium was Shaila's favorite spot on campus. She starred in every class play she could, emerging from afternoon rehearsals on a euphoric high I couldn't understand. "I need the spotlight," she said once with her deep, full laugh. "At least I can admit it."

"Good morning, Gold Coast," Headmaster Weingarten bellows. His bow tie is slightly askew and his salt-and-pepper mustache looks recently trimmed above his pointy chin. "I see many new faces among our ranks and I want to say welcome from the bottom of my heart. Join me."

People turn to the newbies, kids who had spent their previous lives in public schools and up until today thought the first day of school meant homeroom and roll call, not saying what's up to a dead girl. Now, in this new and strange place, their bewildered expressions betray them. They are obvious. I was one of them once, back in sixth grade. My scholarship came through only a week before classes started and I came to Gold Coast Prep not knowing a single soul. The memory nearly gives me hives.

"Welcome!" the rest of the auditorium says in unison. Our row stays silent.

"You may be wondering why we are here, why we start every year in this very space." Weingarten pauses and wipes a tissue across his forehead. The air-conditioning whirs on overdrive, but his brow still glistens with sweat under the bright stage lights. "It is because we want to take time to remember one of our best, one of our brightest, Shaila Arnold."

Heads turn toward Shaila's portrait, but Mr. and Mrs. Arnold keep their focus on Headmaster Weingarten straight ahead.

"Shaila is no longer with us," he says, "but her life was radiant, one we cannot forget. She lives on in her family, in her friends, and within these halls."

Mr. and Mrs. Arnold nod their heads.

"I am here to tell you that Gold Coast Prep is, and will always be, a family. We must continue to protect one another," he says.

"We will not let another Gold Coast student be harmed." Nikki's elbow presses into my rib cage.

"So take this as a reminder," Headmaster Weingarten continues. "At Gold Coast Prep, we strive to do good. We aim to be grand. We see ourselves as helping hands."

Ah, the Gold Coast motto.

"Join in if you know it," he says, smiling.

Five hundred and twenty-three Gold Coast Prep students, ages six to eighteen, raise their voices. Even the new kids, who were instructed to memorize the stupid words before they even set foot on campus.

"At Gold Coast Prep, life is good. Our time here is grand. We see ourselves as helping hands," the chorus says in a creepy singsong.

"Very good," says Headmaster Weingarten. "Now, off to class. It will be quite a year."

We are no longer mourners when lunchtime rolls around. Paying tribute to Shaila is a hurdle we have cleared.

My stomach flips when I catch a glimpse of the senior Players' Table. The juniors and sophomores have already assembled, but the perfect table, the one reserved for us, is empty and beckoning.

It occupies the best real estate by far, nestled smack dab in the middle of the cafeteria, so everyone has to pass us and bear witness to the *fun* we can have, even at lunch. The tables that ring around us are saved for the other Players, the undies, and then from there, how far away you sit from us determines everything.

My feet tingle with excitement as Nikki and I weave

through the salad bar, dropping massaged kale, marinated feta, and hunks of grilled chicken onto our plates. When we pass the dessert table, I pluck a piece of raw cookie dough from the glass bowl. Having the little buttery ball on your tray has been a sign of cool girl vibes for decades. Shaila ate it every single day she was here. A bunch of freshmen let us cut them at the cashier, as they should, and we make our way to the table we always knew would be ours. Even now, I'm still surprised to find my spot empty, waiting for me. Seeing that open chair, the one that's undoubtedly mine, still elicits a weird thrill. It's a reminder. After all this, I belong. I deserve this. I survived.

Nikki and I are the first ones here, and when we slide into our seats, the familiar feeling of being in a fishbowl begins to take over. We know we're being watched. That's part of the fun.

Nikki flips her long black hair over her shoulder and unzips her backpack, retrieving a neon paper box. "I came prepared," she says. The lid pops open, revealing dozens of mini Kit Kats in flavors like pumpkin, green tea, and sweet potato. Her parents must have brought them back from their recent business trip to Japan—without her, of course. A few sophomores crane to see what glamorous treat Nikki Wu has brought to school.

"Another gesture from *Darlene*," she says, motioning to the brightly colored wrappers. Nikki rolls her eyes when she pronounces the second syllable of her mother's name.

Nikki's parents are textile magnates and they moved here from Hong Kong when we were in seventh grade. During her first semester at Gold Coast, she was mostly seen hunched over her phone, DM'ing with friends back home. She was totally disinterested in this suburban life. Her indifference to us gave her an untouchable chill factor. That spring, she became besties with Shaila while they were working on the middle school musical. Shaila had scored the lead role as Sandy in *Grease*, to no one's surprise, and Nikki had signed up to work on costumes. That's when we learned she was basically a fashion prodigy, designing slick leather leggings and poodle skirts that looked ready for Broadway.

When it became clear that I would have to share Shaila as a best friend, I tried to stomp out my jealousy. I was determined to navigate their newly shared tastes ("Bravo, not Netflix") and catch up after they drank for the first time at the cast party ("beer before liquor, never been sicker!"). It worked, mostly, and by eighth grade, we were fused together.

But throughout Shaila's last year, Nikki and I silently battled for Shaila's attention, orbiting around each other. It was stupid though, because Shaila didn't play favorites. She was loyal to us both. When she died, Nikki and I went from frenemies to inseparable. Our link to one another had been severed, so we forged a new one. It was like all that tension evaporated and we were left with just each other and the hungry need for intimacy. Ever since then, Nikki became my Shaila. And I became hers.

"Red bean's my favorite," she says now, unwrapping a bar and popping it into her mouth. I reach for the box and tear into a bright pink one. It's sweet and sticky in my palm.

"Nuh-uh," I say. "Strawberry forever."

"Only when it's paired with matcha."

"Pfft. Snob."

"It's called having taste!"

"What about dark chocolate?"

Nikki chews, mulling over the suggestion. "Simple. Classic. I'm down."

"It's iconic."

"Just like us." Nikki flashes her megawatt smile then swipes a lavender-colored wrapper. "Life's too short to have just one."

"Too real."

Behind me, the buzzing hum of the cafeteria becomes a roar. I turn to see the boys amble toward us. Freshmen and sophomores scatter, making a path for them. Robert's a few steps ahead of the others, barreling through the room. Henry's not too far behind. His backpack is slung over one shoulder and his thick sandy hair flops neatly to one side. His tie hangs loose around his neck and he fist-bumps Topher Gardner, a stocky, acne-prone junior Player thirsty for his attention. Quentin brings up the rear, winking at some cute sophomore on the baseball team as he strides by. The kid turns the color of a tomato. Robert crashes into his seat first and rips the cap off a soda, chugging half the bottle at once.

"Hey, babe," Henry says, sliding into the seat next to me. He presses his lips to the little triangle where my neck meets my collar bone. It sends a shock through my limbs and I hear a gasp from the table behind us. A group of wide-eyed freshman girls with their skirts hanging a bit too long have grabbed front row seats. If they think they'll lay claim to that table for the entire year, they're wrong. That one's reserved for us, too. We'll give it to the freshman Players like a present. They'll see.

But for now, the girls break into giggles, whispering behind cupped fingers, their eyes darting in our direction.

Marla collapses into her seat and, like that, we're all together again. It's roomy since the tables are made for eight. Shaila and Graham made us fit. But we've learned to spread out and take up more space than we should. It helps. And now since all of us Players are here, the game is on.

The air between us is frenetic with fractions of conversations meant to propel us toward the weekend, always the weekend.

"I heard Anne Marie Cummings will give you a hand job if you say you like her shitty band."

"Reid Baxter promised he would bring a handle tonight. Don't let him in if his connect pulls out."

"Well, if you didn't want to get Sharpie all over you, don't get so wasted next time!"

Little clips of conversation float over our heads and disperse throughout the room, carrier pigeons, sharing the most important news with the rest of the school. Some days, we lean in so close, I imagine our heads look like they're going to touch from overhead. But other times, we curl inside ourselves, forming partnerships and alliances. *Who is on my side? Friend or foe?*

"Ahem!" Nikki smacks a knife against her can of seltzer.

Robert groans but smiles in her direction. If it's a good week, they usually spend lunch mouthing filthy phrases to each other over their trays. If it's a bad week, she pretends he doesn't exist.

"Turd." Nikki sticks her tongue out and presses her arms to her sides, making her chest perk up so her boobs sit right under her chin. Robert leans back and raises his eyebrows, impressed. Already, this week seems to be excellent.

"Fine, Miss Wu," Quentin says. "Spill."

Nikki leans in and lowers her voice so we have to crane to hear, although none of what she says will be new information. She will throw tonight's party. (No shit.) Her parents are gone, jetting off to Paris for the weekend. (Sounds about right.) There will be a keg. (Of course.)

Henry turns to me and his hand finds my thigh under the table. His thumb rubs my bare skin in small circles. "I'll pick you up at eight thirty," he says.

I fit my mouth into a smile and try to ignore the heat between my legs. His skin glows like summer, and I swear I can still make out the tan line his sunglasses left on the bridge of his nose the day he asked me to make it official. It was one of the hottest afternoons in June, sweltering on land but cool on his parents' boat in the middle of the Sound. The group text was dormant. Everyone else was on vacation before their elite summer programs began. I still hadn't started my counselor stint at the local planetarium. We were the only ones around.

You like stars, right? Henry texted off-thread.

Everyone knew I was obsessed with astronomy. Well, astronomy *and* astrophysics to be exact. It had been my *thing* for so long. I became fixated with everything up above when I was five and Dad started taking me out to Ocean Cliff after every rainstorm, when the sky was the clearest, to point out constellations, galaxies, planets, and stars. It was the highest point in Gold Coast, an enormous stone formation that extended out over the water. "This is how to make sense of the chaos," Dad would say as we sat on the rocks. He said he had always wanted to be an astronaut, but instead became an accountant for some reason I could never really understand. When we got home that first night, he stuck a bunch of glow-in-the-dark stars on my ceiling in spiral configurations.

Being able to spot *things* up there, little miracles that have been around forever and ever, puts me at ease. It makes the nightmares go away, the darkness easier to deal with. Well, sometimes.

Duh, I responded to Henry.

Sunset ride on the boat?

I waited a beat before typing back. Henry doubled down.

I have a telescope we can bring.

Henry had been chasing me like this since school let out, dropping by the house, offering to give me rides to parties, sending me bizarre news clips that he thought would make me laugh. I was sick of saying no, sick of waiting on someone else. So I said screw it and agreed.

I'm there. But I've got the hookup. No scope needed.

The travel-size Celestron Dad got me for Hanukkah last year sat tall on my nightstand.

A few hours later, we were halfway to the Connecticut shoreline, aboard his small runabout, *Olly Golucky,* named for Henry's twelve-year-old golden retriever. The sun had gone down and the heat was finally starting to let up. A breeze puckered, and the first little stars began to break through the clouds. I breathed in the salty air and lay down on the damp deck. Waves crashed around us as Henry delighted me with surprisingly funny stories about his first week as a summer intern at CNN. His face grew flushed when talking about seeing his idols in the halls. It was totally adorable. Then he grabbed a bottle of rosé and a tin of Russian caviar he found in the little hideaway fridge. He presented them to me with the question, his eyes wide and hopeful. "So, do you want to do this? Us?"

The answer was obvious. He was the captain of the lacrosse team and anchor on the school news channel. More eloquent than most of our teachers. Sweet when he was drunk, that awful time when most of the other guys became monsters. It didn't hurt that he was also beautiful in a totally obvious

Nantucket J. Crew model kind of way. Thick blond hair. Green eyes. Nearly perfect skin. He was bound for greatness. He was a Player. Being with him would make everything so easy.

Plus, the person I really wanted to be with, the guy who had inadvertently led me to this exact place, was hundreds of miles away. It was a no-brainer. Henry was here and willing. Adam Miller was not.

"Of course," I said. Henry dropped the tin and wrapped his sticky hands around my waist. Fish eggs clung to my bare back. He never could have known that while his tongue was in my mouth I was willing Adam to see me, to know what he had let go.

The bell rings and Robert kicks Henry under the table. "C'mon, man. We've got Spanish."

"English," I say, turning to Nikki. She throws her head back in despair but links her arm in mine and pulls me out the double doors and into the quad. The sun shifts as we walk, and if I squint, I can see past the staff parking lot behind the theater, and all the way to the oyster stalls pulling down their canvas curtains and packing up crates, closing up shop for the day.

Nikki and I make it across campus just as the bell rings and slump into our side-by-side desks. I pull out my copy of *The Great Gatsby*, a classic, Mr. Beaumont promised in his summer reading assignment.

"Hi, girls," Mr. Beaumont says as he walks by our desks. "Good summer?"

Nikki cocks her head and looks up mischievously. "Great summer."

"Excellent." Mr. Beaumont smiles and pushes his thick-rimmed glasses up his nose. He looks more bronzed than last year, like he spent the entire summer swimming in the

Hamptons, like he's a grown-up version of one of us, which, I guess in some ways, he is.

He came to Gold Coast three years ago, starting just after Thanksgiving when Mrs. Mullen left on maternity leave. He had Nikki, Shaila, and me for freshman English, right when we learned about the Players. On the first day of class, he won us over with a dare.

"Don't screw with me and I won't screw with you." He said it with a smile. A joke. He said *screw* so he must be cool. He must *get it*. My phone buzzed with a text from Shaila right in the middle of class. *OBSESSED*, she wrote with a few red hearts. I looked up and caught her eye.

"Dreams," I mouthed.

After he arrived, it only took a few days before we all found out he grew up in Gold Coast. Graduated ten years ago now. He's goofy as hell on his yearbook page, with a wild mop of dark hair and a dirt-stained lacrosse jersey. Henry thinks he used to be a Player. There were even rumors that he started the whole thing. I never quite believed them, though.

Headmaster Weingarten was so pleased with his work that year that he hired Beaumont full-time and gave him the AP English Lit class, reserved only for seniors. Now he calls our class his "firstborn."

As he launches into a monologue about East Egg and West Egg, I scribble furiously trying to take down everything he says. "I don't know why you do that," Nikki whispers, pointing at my notebook with a ballpoint pen. "It's not like you need notes."

She's right, obviously. There's a fat stash of *Gatsby* info in the Player Files, alongside hundreds of insanely thorough study guides for Gold Coast midterms and finals. There's also a slew of past SATs, copies of AP exams, and off-the-record college essay advice from the deans of admissions at Harvard and Princeton. I saw those little manuals last spring sandwiched between a bunch of college-level organic chemistry finals, sent back from a Player whose name I didn't even recognize.

They never change the questions! he had written. *Get that fucking A!*

The Files are our entry into the elite within the elite. A way for us to excel, even if we could have on our own. They are passed down as a reward for our loyalty, a way for us to enjoy everything that comes with being a Player. The parties. The fun. The privilege. They alleviate some of the stress, the pressure. The Files make everything easy. Golden. Never mind the crushing guilt and shame that creeps into my stomach whenever I open the app that houses them. The Files are our insurance.

Especially for those of us whose parents can't afford the fancy private tutors and the private college counseling that cost nearly as much as Gold Coast Prep tuition. Or who have to maintain a 93 average to keep our scholarships. The others don't need to know that little detail, though.

"Miss Wu," Mr. Beaumont calls out to Nikki. "What is Miss Newman writing about that is so interesting to you? I'm surprised to see you looking at something other than your phone."

Nikki sits up in her seat, her straight dark hair falling over her shoulders. "Mr. Beaumont, you know I loved this book so much, I was just seeing what Jill thought about it."

"And Miss Newman, what do you think about Gatsby?" He asks me like he really wants to know.

"Well—"

The bell sounds.

"Another time, Miss Newman. Have a good weekend, everyone. Be safe." He says it to everyone, but I feel his eyes on me, like he knows our secrets, like he knows what happens to the Players. Everything we had to sacrifice. Everything we had to do to survive. Especially the girls.

TWO

"JILL!" HENRY LEANS against his car, a nearly new Lexus that he lovingly calls Bruce. "Let's get outta here." Warmth blooms in my chest and I make my way to him, feeling every pair of eyes follow us.

I climb up into Bruce and set my bag at my feet, next to a stack of hardcovers.

"Oops, don't mind those," he says, waving his hand at the books. "New haul." They look bleak as hell with words like *war* and *democracy* printed on their covers. Henry flicks the radio to NPR, his favorite, and I bite back a smile. It's too cute when he nerds out on journalism.

"We invited some freshmen to come to Nikki's tonight." Henry turns sharply out of the school parking lot, waving goodbye to Dr. Jarvis, the elderly physics teacher who always has food on his tie but low-key adores me.

"Already?" I ask. "Isn't it too early for new undies to be hanging around?" I try to remember when I first started going to Player parties, when Adam told me to come along with him. It smelled crisper, more like crunchy leaves than leftover sunscreen. We're still firmly planted in SPF season.

"Robert started scouting the little dudes at lax preseason," Henry continues. "He says we got some winners already."

I chew my lip. "It's still too soon, though, don't you think?"

"Maybe," Henry says carefully, like he's actually thinking it over, like my voice matters. "But we gotta start thinking of pops early. That's what every senior class always says, right?"

Ah, the pops. Also known as pop-quiz-like challenges. Also known as the bane of my existence. I was sentenced to my first one a week after being tapped to be a Player. That asshole Tommy Kotlove instructed me to break into the middle school chem lab after tennis practice and swipe a beaker for his girlfriend, Julie Strauss, to use as a flower vase. I almost started crying on the spot. I didn't know then that would be one of the easier ones.

"Still seems early," I say.

"You know, Bryce Miller could be pretty good."

"He would," I say slowly.

"Adam say anything to you about it?"

The truth is that Adam *had* texted me this morning before school. It was short, but stuck with me all day: *Watch out for my bro, will ya? I know you've got my back, Newman.*

"I'm sure he's expecting it," I say.

Henry rolls his eyes. "Yeah, well, Bryce will have to get in on more than his brother. Being related to Adam Miller doesn't just guarantee you the world."

"True," I say, willing the conversation to stop. Adam's name always sounds chewed-up and poisonous in Henry's mouth.

"We'll see if it's a fit. We always do." Henry pulls to a stop in front of my house.

My skin is crawling and I'm itching to get away from his questions about Adam. I plant a quick kiss on his cheek. "See you later, babe."

"Jilly! Is that you?" Mom says as I push the door open. "I'm in the kitchen. C'mere!"

She does this often, greeting me at home in boxy linen tops and wide silk scarves, her artist hands always pulling something out of the oven or her paint box. Today, she wraps a generous tray of lasagna in tinfoil. She makes it every year as a back-to-school tradition. "How was it? First day of senior year!" she nearly squeals. Her excitement turns her blossoming wrinkles into craters.

"Great!" I say, smiling wide so she has no reason *not* to believe me.

"That Henry's car?"

"Yep."

She shakes her head and laughs. "What a guy."

On the depressing side of fifty, Mom is still the most dazzling woman in the cul-de-sac, active in three book clubs, the temple sisterhood, and Gold Coast's various community service projects—all while throwing elegant pots and twisty-turny vases that land her in the pages of *Vogue* and *Architectural Digest* once a season. Her *cool* factor makes it seem like we can keep up with everyone else at Gold Coast Prep, but the reality includes long hours teaching ceramics at the community college and giving private lessons to the uber-privileged Mayflower crowd. She says it's all worth it, to do what she loves and give us the childhood she never had. Her parents were hippies, strung out at the end of the seventies, selling merch for B-list bands while driving around in an RV.

Being able to send Jared and me to Prep is a badge of honor for her, even if the whole situation makes me feel like I'm carrying her and Dad's hopes and dreams around like a precious 8,000-pound weight.

I didn't really register their intense desire for my excellence until fifth grade, when Mom and Dad not-so-subtly suggested I apply for Gold Coast Prep's Alumni Merit Grant for Students in STEM. It was given out in secret every year, and afforded one lucky student full access to the school's multimillion-dollar science wing, AP classes, and extracurriculars. Dozens of alumni have ended up in the best undergrad science programs, to no one's surprise. I've never seen Mom and Dad as happy as they were when I got in.

It's not like *scholarship* is plastered on my forehead, but sometimes I swear it must be obvious. No designer loafers to offset the pleated plaid skirt. No car of my own. No summers in the Hamptons. "Who needs a beach house when you *live* near the beach!" Mom said when I told her Shaila invited me to the Arnolds' place out east back in middle school.

The grant doesn't cover everything—there are still extra expenses like uniforms and textbooks and Science Bowl dues. And all of Jared's tuition, of course. All of Mom and Dad's resources go into making sure we can stay at Prep with the hope that it will somehow pay off. That my baby brother and I will get into better colleges—Ivies, ideally—than if we went down the street to Cartwright Public High, where only half the class graduates.

How we would pay for college was always a sticky subject, one I tiptoed around on purpose. I pretended not to hear them fighting about it late at night in hushed tones after they thought we were asleep. "Just let her get in first," Dad always whispered. "We'll find a way."

But is it worth it? The long hours Dad spends crunching numbers in a soulless office? The fake smiles Mom puts on when she has to pretend those awful wine drunks are brilliant artists? To be determined. And, that's where the Player Files come in. I need to do well. For me, but mostly for them.

But here in Gold Coast, Mom is forever optimistic. She's the mom who trusts just about anyone, *because people are inherently good, Jill, they just are*. Even after Shaila, she still says that.

It's that same motto that made her say yes one day during a temple sisterhood meeting when Cindy Miller suggested that her eighteen-year-old son tutor Jared in English on the cheap.

"You're off the hook," Mom said when she told me I didn't have to listen to Jared read aloud anymore. "Adam Miller is going to do this with him."

"What?" I was shocked. Everyone at Gold Coast Prep knew Adam. Sure, he was unbelievably gorgeous, with long, lean arms, swoopy dark hair, and blue eyes that could melt ice. But he was also brilliant. Adam had won the National Young Playwright Award three years in a row and was rumored to be shopping scripts around to different regional theater companies . . . as a *high schooler*. Colleges were practically begging him to join their writing programs. He was also, obviously, a Player.

So, why the hell did he want to spend Friday nights reading chapter books with a sixth grader?

Mom smoothed her chunky knit sweater over her jeans and fastened a heavy ceramic necklace behind her head. "Cindy suggested it. He wants some *real work experience*, or something. Probably for his college applications."

They were going out to dinner that night and I was supposed to go to Shaila's for a movie marathon, but my brain basically short-circuited at the idea of getting to hang out with Adam.

Outside of school.

Alone.

Well, after he was done tutoring.

I quickly texted Shaila an excuse. *Sore throat. SORRY!!!!!*

She responded with a wailing face, but I was in the clear. When I told Mom I was feeling sick and staying home, her mouth turned up into a small, knowing smile. "Sure, Jill."

Dad laughed and ran a comb through his hair. "Classic."

Then the bell rang.

I tried to be cool and only sort of rush to the door, but Jared beat me there.

"You're the tutor?" he said, eyeing Adam with a grin.

"Indeed, I am, buddy. You must be Jared." Adam flashed a wide smile that hugged his cheeks. It was lopsided and formed a J shape, pink and full. He crossed his arms over his chest, causing his thin white T-shirt to ripple over his biceps. They were so perfectly round and smooth and strong. He looked so much older without the blazer and khakis all the boys at Gold Coast had to wear. My neck flushed with embarrassment. I fought the urge to lick his skin. "And you," he said. "You must be Jilly."

"I—uh," I said. "It's Jill."

"Jill." Hearing him say my name was intoxicating. *Say it again,* I willed. "Jill," he said, like he'd read my mind, "I didn't realize you'd be here, too."

Before I could respond, Mom burst into the foyer.

"Adam! We're so glad you're here to help Jared. We're heading out for the night, but our numbers are on the counter next to your check. Pizza's in the kitchen. Help yourself to whatever you want." She and Dad were off.

Adam threw me another one of those body-melting smiles and then turned to Jared. "Ready, dude?"

Jared groaned but then disappeared with Adam into the kitchen. I plopped down on the couch and turned Bravo on the lowest volume possible, to make it seem like I was busy and definitely not eavesdropping.

An hour passed before Jared tore through the room. "My turn." He grabbed the remote and switched it to some stupid superhero movie.

When Adam didn't follow, I tiptoed into the kitchen, curious if he was still there.

"Hey," he said when I appeared in the doorway.

My face instantly flushed. "How'd he do?"

Adam stretched his arms overhead, revealing a thin strip of skin and a faint trail of curly, feathery hair between his jeans and his shirt. I had to suppress a sharp inhale.

"Pretty good. Kid's a sweetheart." He gestured to the half-empty pizza box on the counter. "Join me? I hate eating alone."

He didn't wait for me to answer. Instead, he picked up the box and walked toward the back of the kitchen, leading to the deck that jutted out over our backyard. I followed him through the screen door. He dropped the box down on the glass table and disappeared back into the kitchen. When he returned, he was holding two glasses full of ice and two cans of soda.

"Thanks," I said when he handed me a cup.

But before he took a sip, he dug into his pocket and pulled

out a metal rectangle. He unscrewed the top and poured a dark and shiny liquid into his cup. "Want some?" he asked, his eyebrows raised. "I won't tell if you won't."

I nodded. The first taste made me cough.

"It gets easier," he said with a laugh.

I wanted to tell him that I'd done this before. I was cool, too. But I just brought the glass to my lips and sipped again, listening to the ice crackle beneath the booze. It burned in a way that ignited the nerves in the tips of my fingers. Then I did what I always did when I was anxious. I looked up. The stars swirled overhead and I could spot my favorites with ease. My dad's instructions played on a loop in my head. *Find the North Star. Look down to the left. Then tilt your head just a little more. Bam. Big Dipper.* A calm settled into my skin.

I took another sip.

"So, Jill," Adam said, holding out the last letter of my name. *Ji-llllll.* "Who are you?"

I laughed. "Excuse me?" The nerves came flooding back. I forced myself to find Orion's belt and focus on the three blinking lights instead of Adam's question.

"You heard me," he said. "Who are you? Who is Jill Newman?"

I chewed the inside of my mouth and looked down, then back to him.

"I'm no one."

"That's not true."

"No?"

"No. You're just still becoming."

My bottom lip fell. It was so precisely true, it stung.

"That's okay. I am, too," he said. Adam held out his drink as if to meet mine in a toast. "We'll find out together."

Then he reached over and slipped my phone out of the pocket of my jeans, a motion that made my insides turn to jelly, my toes curl. "Here," he said, typing with flying fingers. "I'm texting myself so I have your number."

Later that night, hours after we had finished the last of the cold pizza crusts and he had gone home, my phone buzzed.

I know who you are, Adam wrote.

Oh yeah? Do tell.

My new critic. His typing bubble paused, but then Adam sent an enormous block of text followed by an explanation. *The first scene from my next play. You're the first to read it. Tell me what sucks, Newman. I can take it.*

My heart thumped as my eyes decoded the words. I bit back a smile and responded.

I'm honored.

That's how it started.

Soon, he was over once a week to read and do worksheets with Jared. And then hang out with me after. Fridays usually. Sometimes on Wednesdays when Mom taught evening classes and Dad had late nights. Never Saturdays. Those were Player nights.

At first, I told no one. I wanted to keep my time with Adam secret. I was greedy for more of it. At school, I watched him flit between classes and occupy his place at the senior Players' Table. He wasn't Toastmaster but he anchored their unit. Everyone turned to him for approval, to make sure he laughed at their jokes, to hear his wild, winding stories.

We had an unspoken understanding. My house was safe. School was not. Instead, we exchanged secret smiles in the halls only once in a while. Then, one Thursday, when I walked by him in between second and third period, he changed the rules.

Adam stuck out his index finger and pressed it to the back of my shoulder just for a moment. His touch traveled through my veins, zapping me into an alternative reality.

That's how Shaila found out. "What was that?" she said, gnawing at her cuticle, a gross habit she was always trying to kick. I picked it up too after she died. "Why does Adam Miller know who you are?"

I tried not to smile. "He's been tutoring Jared. I think our moms are friends."

"Huh," Shaila said, her eyes trained on Adam, who was gliding down the hall, turning into the math wing. A wake of students rippled behind him. "He's dating Rachel, you know," she whispered. "Rachel Calloway." My heart sparked and cracked. Rachel was Graham's stunning older sister. Captain of the field hockey team. President of their class. She was a towering goddess. A senior. A Player. That made it all so much worse.

"I know," I lied.

"I saw him over the summer once or twice," she said. "With Graham."

I stayed silent, seething that Shaila had yet another thing to show me up. First a boyfriend, then Adam's attention.

But perhaps she picked up on this because she quickly ceded the power. "He never really wanted us around, though," she said.

I had always been jealous of Shaila, of the way her clothes smelled like summer and were super soft when you rubbed them through your fingers, and how she seemed so comfortable with her long legs and her growing chest. She never had oily little pimples on her back or weird fine fuzz growing above her lip. Even her hair stayed in place, unbothered by the Gold Coast mist.

I was jealous that things were so *easy* for her. That she could be the number one student in our class, run miles, star in plays, and dazzle anyone without much effort at all. She claimed to have only one real fear. A totally benign, normal one. Heights.

"Nope. No way," she said back in seventh grade when I begged her to join me on the Ferris wheel at the annual Oyster Fest. It was always set up right at the mouth of Ocean Cliff, so when you reached the top you felt like you were falling into the abyss. "You *know* I don't do heights." She grimaced as her eyes scaled the metal monstrosity.

Otherwise, Shaila could make everything seem glamorous, mysterious, an adventure. Like if you stuck with her, you'd never be bored again.

She even looked special. Her eyes were a grassy shade of green that grew brighter when she was excited. Shaila was the first one in our class to wear a bra. Mrs. Arnold even bought her the ones with extra padding that pushed everything up and out. Her body always looked like it was morphing into itself at conflicting speeds. I was still terrified of myself and the power I did or didn't have. But I must have had *something* Adam liked, *something* that kept him hanging around, even if he did have a girlfriend. My ability to listen, maybe. My willingness to say yes. For forever, I'd wanted to have something Shaila didn't. Now I had access to Adam. It was a weird imbalance, one I could milk.

"Maybe I can come over one time," she said quietly. "When he's at the house?"

"Would that be weird with Rachel?" I said, trying not to let my annoyance show.

Shaila shrugged. "Nah. Rachel's like my big sister. She'd be psyched. Plus, it could help us get into the Players. Rachel said she couldn't guarantee anything."

She knew I couldn't fight her on that one but I made her promise not to tell Nikki. Three would feel like an ambush, I argued. We didn't want to seem like we were fishing for invitations to parties. She agreed.

That Friday, when Shaila came home with me after school, I was anxious. Concerned he would like her more than he liked me. Worried there was only room for one of us in his freshman-girls-who-I'm-friends-with crew. I spent the nights he was here on stilts, trying not to fall over, to misstep. Adding another whole person to the event felt like narrowing the platform.

The doorbell rang and Shaila bolted for the stairs. I was a few steps behind her but she opened the door, pushing her body into the frame, between Adam and me.

"Shaila," he said. A surprised smirk took over his face.

"I'm spending the night," she said.

"Fun." His eyebrows shot up at me, amused. "Graham out of town, too?" he asked.

She nodded. "One last weekend out east."

"Rachel was *pissed*," Adam said.

"Graham, too." Shaila wrinkled her nose.

I tried to follow their chatter but it sounded like a different language. One spoken by people intimately in the know about a certain family's quirks, the things they keep behind closed doors. But as my unease came to a boil, Adam moved past Shaila and brought me in for a bear hug, resting his head on top of mine.

"Hey, Newman," he murmured into my hair. I wrapped my arms around him, feeling his heat. That was the first night I knew for sure that Adam and I were friends. And Shaila saw it firsthand.

For the next hour, Shaila and I watched YouTube until Adam emerged from the kitchen and Jared rushed down to the basement to play video games.

"Deck?" Adam asked us. He didn't wait for a response and instead headed for the door. By then he knew which wooden board was creaky, where to step to avoid the sticky patch of sap. He took his seat, the one under the apple tree that had never produced a single piece of fruit, and fumbled in his pocket.

Shaila and I sat on either side of him. She nibbled her fingers and tore her skin with her teeth.

"I've got a surprise," Adam said, setting his hands on the table.

"Bourbon?" I said, trying to find the line between knowledgeable and desperate, hoping not to step over it.

He shook his head. "Better." Opening his hands like a magician, he revealed something small and oblong, rolled up like a messy straw wrapper and pinched at one end.

Shaila giggled. "Yes!"

"You blaze before?" he asked her. I shot her a look. It was a line we hadn't yet crossed.

"Once with Kara," she said. "She had dank shit from the city." *Dank shit.* Two words I'd never heard come out of Shaila's mouth, especially not when referring to her chic family friend who also summered in the Hamptons.

Adam nodded and raised his eyebrows at her, impressed. "*Et tu*, Jill?" he asked, jabbing the little cigarette my way. I shook my head. "Well, then. Big day." He gave my knee a squeeze and my stomach clenched. The joint dangled from his mouth, so pink and full, and he flicked on a lighter, inhaling deeply.

"Ah," he breathed out. The air smelled of musk and dirt and

faintly like Mom's pottery studio, and I wondered if my parents had done the same back there, if I was the one who was slow, always catching up. I took the nub from Adam and followed his lead, inhaling until I thought my brain would combust. My lungs expanded and I wondered how long I was supposed to hold this odd air inside me. Adam nodded, and I let it go, releasing smoke. My limbs were heavy and I felt good. Another task completed. Another line crossed.

We passed the joint around and around, and when that one was finished, Adam revealed its twin. Soon, we polished that one off, too. We were starving and silly. Adam made nachos and we danced around the kitchen to Motown music. Shaila and I sandwiched Adam between us, holding hands as he jumped up and down. We collapsed onto the couch and Adam cackled furiously when I insisted we watch a clip of pandas rolling down a hill.

"Jill! I can't, I can't!" he said, gasping for air. Tears rolled down his cheeks, he was laughing so hard. And through the haze I felt accomplished and satisfied. I had made Adam Miller laugh. It was I, the funniest freshman at Gold Coast Prep.

Shaila soon fell asleep on the couch. When Adam noticed, he turned to me and said, "Let's sit outside."

I followed him to the deck, but this time he walked down the stairs and to the white woven hammock on the edge of our yard, hung between two cedar trees. He motioned for me to join him. Slowly, I sunk down next to him so we were lying side by side, head to toe. His mouth was so far away but I could see it taunting me.

I tilted my head to the sky, trying to spot something I recognized. But a fog had settled over the inky night. There were only clouds. I was alone with my tangled nerves.

He rested his head against my feet and I said a silent thankful prayer that I had painted my toes a bright canary blue earlier that morning. The breeze from the bay picked up and I nuzzled into his legs. They were warm and the little hairs tickled my chin when I got too close.

"You're not like everyone else," he said.

"Neither are you."

He stroked my feet, closing his fist around each toe. "You should come hang out with me and my friends sometime."

"Okay."

"They'd love you."

"Maybe," I said.

"I've been telling people about you," he said.

A lump formed in my throat. "What do you say?"

"That you're the shit." He laughed and wrapped a whole hand around my foot. I bent it at the arch so he knew I was there. "That you're one of us."

I mulled over his words, unsure of what he meant.

"I see you looking at lunch," he said. "The table will be yours one day. Don't worry." I felt a tiny prick of moisture and snuck a look at Adam just as he planted his lips on the tender side of my foot. The movement sent a spark through my body and heat rushed to my thighs. I flinched and in an instant, we were both on the ground in a pile of limbs and hair and blades of grass. Adam's eyes found mine. They were fiercely blue, bloodshot. He wrapped his hand around my wrist.

"I have a girlfriend," he whispered.

I inhaled sharply as my heart cracked open. "I know." I ducked my head so my hair shielded me from his gaze.

"We're friends. You and me." The way he said it, the word

friends, had a cosmic, tender pull, as if there were no greater honor he could bestow.

"Friends," I said.

Adam touched his forefinger to my chin and raised my face to meet his. "Friends." His lips softened into a smile. Headlights flashed, a signal Mom and Dad were home, and Adam released me. He entered the house and I was left alone.

THREE

"BIG PARTY TONIGHT?" Jared leans against the doorway in my bedroom and reaches into his hair, wrapping one of his curls around his pointer finger. They're the color of ink, just like mine, and in photos we look like twins even though I've got three years on him.

"Over at Nikki's," I say, turning my attention to the overflowing sack of makeup in front of me.

"Yeah. I heard some kids in history talking about it. Your boyfriend invited them." His voice cracks with the word *boyfriend*.

"Henry? He mentioned that."

Jared looks down at his hands, and I wonder for a moment if I should stay home with him instead. We could put on pajamas and flop down on the couch with Mom's extra-cozy blanket, reserved only for movie nights. He just started reading *The Catcher in the Rye* for Mr. Beaumont's freshman English class and I really want to convince him Holden is a straight-up asshole before he starts to glorify the smug little guy.

"Can I ask you something?" Jared says.

"What's up?"

"Can I come one time? To a party?"

"Why?" I ask. The question pops out before I can stop it and it sounds a little harsher than I meant it. But why would Jared want to come to a Player party? Most of his friends are in the school band with him. They spend Saturdays digging through stacks at the old comic book store downtown or rewatching NBA highlights on YouTube. It was a relief that he hadn't shown interest in the parties, the desperate, hungry need to let go in the darkness, the urgency that we all felt to destroy something and prove ourselves. I wanted it to stay that way, to keep him safe. "I mean, why do you want to go?"

A stray curl falls down over his brow. "I don't know. It sounds fun."

"Maybe."

"Really?"

"Sure." I regret it immediately. I don't ever want him to see a Player party. He doesn't belong there. But Shaila did belong, more than any of us, and look how that ended.

His face lights up and when I stand, ready to go, he hugs me tight. He is now taller than me and his shoulders are bony where they were once soft. My baby brother is no longer a baby.

Henry walks in front of me, pushing us through the crowd like a bodyguard. A mix of Players and hopeful wannabes scatter as we pass, and a few cocky boys offer him half-hearted high fives or fist bumps. Over the summer, Henry told me Anderson Cooper was his hero because of the way he ingratiates himself with sources, gets them to trust him, and then goes in for the kill, pulling out the best, most shocking pieces of information. Now I wonder if that's Henry's strategy for dealing with high school and everyone here.

Deafening hip-hop streams through the stereo and Nikki's house already reeks of sticky spilled beer and stale air. Red plastic cups cover the entire dining room table, just barely hiding the chip that Robert kicked into it last summer. Nikki's parents never said anything, even though it's made of crystal and was a gift from some famous Swiss artist. She's not even sure they noticed.

Now Nikki is hard to miss. Suspended over a keg with her legs up in the air, she's upside down, grasping the metal handles. Tyler Renford, a quiet kid on the golf team who's been obsessed with Nikki for years, holds her feet and someone else shoves the spout into her mouth.

"Ni-kki! Ni-kki! Ni-kki!" the crowd shouts. She'd been a keg stand natural since freshman year. I guess she had a lot of practice, though. She had to do one at every single Player party for an entire semester. That was one of her recurring pops. I slip out of Henry's grasp and find Marla at the kitchen counter, now covered in half-full bottles and plastic cups.

"Thank God," she says when I hug her tight. "This place is overrun with undies. We needed backup. Drink?" she asks, holding up a handle of vodka. It looks deadly.

I nod and she splashes some into a red cup, topping it off with seltzer and pineapple juice.

"Bottoms up," she says.

"To the final year." I raise my eyebrows and she lets out her tiny, warm chuckle.

"At last."

The first sip is sharp against my throat. Before I can decide otherwise, I gulp down half the cup. It won't be long until the familiar feeling of electric warmth courses through my blood. I peer around the dark living room for Nikki, who's now standing upright.

"Where've you been?" Nikki wraps me tight, resting her cheek against mine. She's strapped stilettos to her feet so she has to stoop to be at eye level with me. "This vibe is nuts!" she shouts over the music. "Come on. Let's go upstairs for a bit. Grab everyone."

I catch Henry's eye and motion toward the spiral staircase planted in the middle of the room. Marla points to it and mouths, "Up?" I nod and she grabs Quentin and Robert from the dining room, where they had been trying to organize a game of flip cup.

The six of us bound up the stairs, leaving the party to itself. Nikki throws open the door to her bedroom and we file in, just like we've done hundreds of times. At first it was weird to be down two whole people after nine months of nonstop hanging out. But slowly, we started to fill in the blanks. Nikki began speaking with Shaila's unfiltered, dry sarcasm and when I got stressed, I tied my hair into a loose knot, just like Shay did when she was buried in a script during rehearsal. Marla even borrowed Shaila's clomp-style walk that could be heard throughout the Gold Coast halls.

The boys took nothing from Graham. Not even Robert, who was his best friend. It was like we erased him completely.

Quentin takes a running leap toward Nikki's California king bed and lands in the middle, ruining the neat duvet. Nikki turns on her disco ball, giving the room a perfect, cheesy feel.

"There are tons of people here," Henry says as he plops down in the velvet purple armchair in the corner. I perch on his lap and he wraps his arms all the way around my waist, hugging me to his hard torso. "I saw the freshmen I invited on the back porch. Think they're having fun?"

"Yeah, dude. How could you not enjoy this? It's all fun and games until we crush them with pops," says Robert.

"It's barely September. We've got all the time." Nikki shoves his shoulder and Robert sinks down next to her against the pillows, heaving an arm around her shoulders. "This is going to be the best year of our lives," Nikki says, and I really want her to be right.

"I hope so," Marla says. "We're finally at the top. We run this shit." Quentin elbows her and they tumble into Robert.

Henry rolls his eyes but jumps on top of them, dragging me with him, so we all collapse into a big dog pile. If it's true that we *run this shit*, it means we can change it.

"I love you guys!" Quentin yells, tapping his head to mine.

"You are way too emo for me right now," Robert says. "Let's goooo!"

Robert moved to Gold Coast from Manhattan in sixth grade and he never really shook the slick city kid vibe. His image was aided by the fact that he could get anyone into any club in SoHo—or so he said—and that he was the first one of us to have a fake ID, copped in some basement in Queens. That's why he was picked to be a Player. Didn't hurt that he had an insane streetwear collection or that his dad owned a bunch of resorts in the Caribbean while his mom was a former Miss USA winner. He was overconfident and pretentious, a know-it-all who somehow charmed us into friendship.

All of this made Robert unpredictable and wild at parties, a feral animal testing the limits of those around him. How far could he push us suburbanites? It's probably why he volunteered to demonstrate last year's All-Player Winter Pop.

"So, it's gonna go like this," he'd yelled from the top of Derek Garry's parents' staircase. Robert slid a couch cushion under his seat and propelled himself forward, head-first. But before swinging his feet around, he'd slammed his skull straight into the wall with a too-loud *thwack*, landing himself a sorta-serious concussion and a trip to the hospital. "Fell off my bike," he told the doctor with an asshole grin.

"Uh, let's take a break," Derek had yelled over the blasting music. For once, we didn't make anyone else attempt it.

Robert had appeared at school the next week without a scar. "No pain, no gain!" he said when set his tray down at the Players' Table. It took us a few weeks to realize he was a little foggy and more cruel than before. The Players brushed that one under the rug. Never spoke about it again.

Now he leaps up from Nikki's bed and makes a break for the stairs, bumping into the banister and sloshing liquid onto the rug as he descends.

Henry and Quentin follow him, racing back to the party. Marla breaks the silence. "Wanna Juul?" She whips her head around and flashes a sly, toothy smile. "Don't tell Coach."

Nikki pretends to zip her mouth. "Colleges don't want athletes who partake," Marla said once last year after her habit kicked into high gear. "Star field hockey forwards with 4.0 GPAs on the other hand? Golden."

Out on Nikki's balcony, the three of us stand side by side, our shoulders kissing in the night. The party has spilled out into the backyard and I watch as a few underclassmen dance barefoot in the grass. Nikki's house sits right against the water and beyond the yard, there's a rickety wooden walkway that leads down to the beach. When I squint, I can make out two bare butts running into the sea. They must be freshmen trying to prove they'd pass their pops. My eyes move back to the deck where two female undies kiss on a lounge chair by the pool while a group of guys cheer them on, holding their phones up to document. The salty wind picks up above our heads and I lift my eyes to the sky. The Bull. She's right where I expect her to be, just above Orion. I picture her spindly legs galloping through the darkness, doing cartwheels above her friends. It's the perfect night to see her.

"I don't wanna pick freshmen," Nikki says. She sips her drink and fiddles with the sliver of rose quartz that hangs around her neck. She got super into crystals after Shaila died. "I'm not ready to be the oldest."

"I know what you mean. It doesn't feel like it's time," Marla says, blowing faint vape smoke into the air. It floats above her like a halo.

The liquor buzzes in my ears. "Jared wants to be a Player," I say.

"And you're surprised?" Nikki asks, turning toward me. A stray leaf catches in her hair.

"Your brother?" Marla asks. "So what? He's kind of cute."

"Gross, dude," I say softly. I wonder if I should have told Nikki alone.

Marla is one of us, chosen after she made varsity as a freshman and the senior boys dubbed her best ass when she arrived at Gold Coast Prep that year. She grew up with four older brothers and a near-perfect complexion, both of which made her enviable. But she was always a little aloof, off in her own self-contained world. I've never even been to her house, don't even know where it is. She rarely joined our sleepovers, since she preferred, she said, to stay at home with her brothers, who all went to Cartwright and were strictly off-limits. That's what Marla told us when she caught Nikki drooling over them after a game. They wouldn't have been interested anyway. They were totally unfazed by Prep, probably because they knew they would never lose her, that Marla just joined the Players to ensure she'd get into Dartmouth. Field hockey would help, she said. So would her stellar math skills. But she's shockingly bad at standardized tests. The wildly accurate study guides in the Files helped her get a near-perfect SAT score last year.

As did the morally questionable doctor who diagnosed her with ADHD so she could get extra time on the test. His kid was a Player a few years back.

Sometimes Marla's brothers would all come to pick her up from parties, speeding down the winding, wooded Gold Coast roads in their red Jeep Wrangler. When they came to a stop, they would call out in unison from the car, never setting foot inside.

"Mar-la!" they'd howl until she emerged from whatever hazy doorway she had been inside. "Mar-la!" With a quick wave, Marla would be gone, her white-blonde hair blowing behind her as she sat nestled in the back seat of her protectors' ride. They were ghosts to us, phantom drivers who rode in on chariots and disappeared into the night. But they couldn't protect her from everything.

I wondered if the allegiance I felt toward Jared was burrowed inside of her, but multiplied by four.

"I don't know," I say. "He's not like us. This isn't for him. I mean, imagine him dealing with the pops?" I picture his worried little face, confused and distraught.

Nikki puts her arms around me, hugging me from behind. "It doesn't have to be like that for him. We're the seniors. We're in control now."

"I know. I just . . . He's my brother."

"It's going to be fine," Marla says. She draws one final deep drag before pocketing the plastic pen. "Like you said, we're in control." She pauses. "We're changing everything."

My phone vibrates once, and then again, burrowing itself into my thigh. Jared, I bet. Adam, I hope.

"I gotta pee," I say, and slip past them back into the bedroom. I close the door behind me in Nikki's en suite bathroom and plunk down on the toilet. My phone pulses again and then for a third time. I pull it out, expecting to find a familiar name. Adam, Jared, Mom, Dad. Instead, it's a number I've never seen before.

I open the text and scan the words quickly but they don't make sense.

I know you probably never want to hear from me again, but I have to tell you something.

Graham didn't kill Shaila. He's innocent.

It's all so fucked up. Can we talk?

My stomach is in my throat and Nikki's bathroom spins around me. The walls are on the floor and the sink is flipped upside down and I think I'm going to puke. Another text appears and my heart nearly stops. I grasp my phone so hard my knuckles turn white.

It's Rachel Calloway.

FOUR

THERE WAS NEVER going to be a trial. I knew it as soon as I saw Graham Calloway in handcuffs, his face red and puffy, blown up like a balloon. Maybe it was the shock of it all, but he didn't look like Graham then. He looked like someone disguised as Graham in pricey basketball sneakers and a Gold Coast Prep lacrosse hoodie. But when the police led him in front of us, so close that I could see the faint little cluster of moles behind his ear, the ones I stared at all through seventh grade history, I knew it was him, that he had killed Shaila.

Graham and Rachel had both been at Gold Coast since preschool. They were lifers. All the teachers, even the ones they never had, knew their names and their parents. Graham was well-liked in middle school, not because he was kind or funny, but because he just *was*. His last name guaranteed him entry into everything. When he asked the other boys to come over to his indoor swimming pool or ride sand buggies on the dunes, no one said no. He had big meaty hands that felt vaguely menacing, like he could knock you over with one finger if he didn't like what you had said. In class he'd make fart noises and blame it on whichever girl had been assigned to sit next to him. He'd knock over test tubes full of chemicals just for fun. Once he even bragged about skinning a dead seagull he found on the beach.

But all that shit seemed to disappear the summer before high school. That was when Graham and Shaila started dating. I had gotten into an all-expenses-paid science camp in Cape Cod but was feeling unbearably guilty that all I really wanted to do was be at home with Shaila. She sent me handwritten letters diligently. "It's so much more *intense* than email," she said in her first one. "Plus, what if I become famous? Then someone will want to know all about *Shaila Arnold: The Early Years.*" I devoured those notes like they were Mom's triple chocolate cake.

Her letters made it seem like I was away at the exact moment when everything seemed to shift. She and Kara Sullivan, her chic family friend who spent the school year on the Upper East Side, were enrolled in a Model UN course in the Hamptons. When the Calloways found out, they threw Graham in there, too.

At first Shaila's letters were filled with stories about Kara, how she was obsessed with artists like Yayoi Kusama, Dan Flavin, and Barbara Kruger, and how Kara showed her how to eat steamers without getting butter all over your face. She seemed impossibly cool. It didn't help that Kara's dad grew up with Shaila's and Graham's dads, too. They had all spent summers together since birth. They were the same. I was the one on the outside.

It wasn't until July that Shaila started writing about Graham, peppering her letters with little stories of them eating lobster rolls on her parents' dock, slipping nips of whiskey into soda cans, and sneaking into the locals bars meant for yuppies escaping summer in the city.

In one note, Shaila wrote that Kara had begun making out with some other kid named Javi from Manhattan, which basically forced Shaila's hand. She and Graham were dating now. That was that.

By the time I got home in August, they had become inseparable. Even Nikki was shocked. It was as if Graham had become a different person. He had shed his kiddie skin like a snake. All of a sudden, he was sweet, asking me questions about the bioluminescence in Cape Cod or suggesting I tag along with him and Shaila to play mini golf. He was nicer, too, actually calling me Jill instead of the nickname he coined back in middle school, Newmania, because he once saw me cry after bombing a bio test. I hated that so much. But his good streak only lasted a year.

The morning they took Graham away, we were still at the beach outside Tina Fowler's house. His sister, Rachel, trailed behind him. She was a horrified tornado, aware of her complicity. I remember her outstretched arms reaching toward Graham and the tears streaming down her face. Her voice alternated between a warble and a wail. I shivered when she shrieked. The police pushed Graham's head deeper into the back seat of the car and he was gone. That was the last time I saw him.

After the car drove away, Rachel turned to us and pointed a shaking finger. "You all believe this?" she screamed. Her eyes were red and her hair was a frizzy mess. It was the one time she looked less than perfect.

No one said a word.

Rachel pleaded with Adam to come with her to the station. But Adam shook his head. He was the one who called the cops when Shaila disappeared. They found Graham half a mile down the sand, almost at the entrance to the Ocean Cliff lookout, with

Shaila's blood still sticky on his fingers and stained all over his chest. Flecks of sand clung to him like sprinkles to frosting.

"You're a coward," Rachel snarled, trying to pierce his skull with her eyes. "You're a coward!" She screamed it that time. And with a quick crack of her hand, Rachel slapped Adam across his cheek, leaving a bright red patch on his pale skin. I gasped.

He blinked but said nothing.

"After everything I've done for all of you . . ." Rachel whispered. "Fuck you."

No one moved. Not Tina Fowler, her best friend since kindergarten, nor Jake Horowitz, who she drove to the hospital the night his appendix burst during one Player party. No one followed her, and soon the Calloways were gone.

Rachel didn't walk at Gold Coast graduation. Instead she left for Cornell a few months early, and the Calloways sold their house on Fielding Lane for $6.2 million, according to the listing I saw online. Their Hamptons house went for more. They traded up for a duplex in Tribeca. No one knew exactly where Graham went. We all just heard he was sent away to some place for Bad Boys who did Bad Things but were too young and too rich to go to real jail.

Rachel and her parents didn't come to Shaila's funeral, obviously. Not that the Arnolds wanted them to. It would have been *gauche*, as Mrs. Arnold liked to say.

Shaila was buried during a frenzied, testy storm, the kind that could only happen at the start of summer when the ocean crashes violently before sputtering to a halt. It was almost too on the nose. A funeral in the rain. How sad.

I woke hours before my alarm bleated and stayed in bed until I heard a faint knock on the door. I pulled on the black sheath dress Mom picked out for me and tried to stand up straight in my small frame. My chest was still so flat, there was no way I would fill it out.

Jared coughed. He stood in the doorway dressed in a dark suit.

"You coming?" I asked, and turned back to the mirror. He'd only seen death up close when Grandpa Morty kicked the bucket two years before. But he was eighty-nine. Old people are supposed to die. Children are not.

"I want to, but Mom won't let me," he said, fiddling with a button on his dress shirt.

"For the best, probably."

Jared padded toward me in his socked feet and wrapped my stomach in a loose hug. I was still taller than him then, but only by a few inches and only for another year. Even with my new identity, my new label, I wanted to be young like him, to shield him from all of this. But I felt old and tired. "I'm sorry," he said, his voice soft and quivering.

My guts ached and there was a strange tug in my chest, as if my heart were trying to free itself from my ribs. "Me too," I said. His shoulders were putty under my touch. Jared held me tighter and I could feel the wetness from his face spreading over my dress. His body heaved just once.

The service was short, no more than thirty minutes, and ended with "Somewhere Over the Rainbow," which Mrs. Arnold said was Shaila's favorite song. Maybe when she was six.

The church was packed with hundreds of people from Gold Coast and out east. Dozens of people in fancy suits stood in the back, clutching their Blackberrys. Analysts at Mr. Arnold's hedge fund probably. Kara Sullivan, dressed in all black all designer, sat off to the side with her art dealer mom. She wept silently into her hands, clutching a piece of paper, likely Shaila's last letter to her. Shaila was always writing letters. That must have been how she kept in touch with Kara during the school year, when she was in Manhattan and Shaila was here. I wonder if Kara's letters would be included in *Shaila Arnold: The Early Years*, too.

More like *The Only Years.*

I took my place in the second row with Nikki, Marla, Robert, Quentin, and Henry. The first time we were together as six. Quentin sniffled into his shirtsleeve and squeezed Marla's hand every now and then. I sat still with my gaze down, drilling polka dots into my lap, just trying to ignore the guilt swelling in my heart.

We were there. We were all there. And we didn't save her.

At the funeral, Adam was right behind me, sandwiched in between Tina Fowler and Jake Horowitz. I sat up straight and looked forward, trying not to fidget in front of him. During Mr. Arnold's eulogy, Adam reached up and squeezed my shoulder, his fingers spreading over my bare skin. I was raw and cracked open, filleted like a fish and ready to be devoured.

The morning after Nikki's party, I wake with a start, my face cold and sweaty. Another nightmare. They used to be predictable. Teeth falling out. Being paralyzed during a test. All stress-related, Mom told me. But after Shaila died, I started seeing her all the time. Her bitten nails, her face, her long limbs. They all crept in. So did visions of that night. Wind whipping. Bonfire roaring. Her golden hair swinging as she marched into the moonlight. The stars on my ceiling helped sometimes, when I woke in the hours before dawn. But I always kept the desk light on, too.

Last night's horror show was new, though. I squeeze my

eyes shut and Rachel Calloway's perfectly symmetrical face barrels toward me with narrowed eyes and a stretched-out mouth. My chest seizes and I flutter my eyes open. *It was just a dream.*

Rachel's reappearance in my life, however, was not. I pat around the comforter until I find my phone nestled in between the pillow and the headboard. I open her texts.

It's Rachel Calloway.

That one is almost worse than the others: *Graham didn't kill Shaila. He's innocent.*

Almost.

"Knock knock," Mom says from behind the door. "Can I come in?"

I stuff the phone under my pillow like it's contraband. "Mm-hm," I say.

The door swings open. "You really shouldn't be sleeping this late. The day awaits," she says. In a few quick strides, she's at the window, pulling the gauzy curtains open. The sun is hot and sticky, especially for September.

"I'm a teenager. Teenagers are supposed to sleep." I roll over onto my stomach.

"Can you take Jared to band practice today? Your father and I are going to run a few errands."

"Sure."

"He's got to leave in five. Car keys are by the door."

I groan but heave myself off the bed, slipping my phone into the pocket of my flannel shorts.

When I get downstairs, Jared is already waiting by Mom's hatchback, chewing on his cuticles. He's picked up my bad habit. Shaila's bad habit.

"How was last night?" he asks.

"Fine," I say, and reverse out of the driveway. "Wait. Where's your bass?" The back seat is noticeably empty.

"They have one there for me."

"But you always play *your* bass. You're gonna get all hunchbacked from carrying that thing around."

"Not this kind. It's electric."

"You don't play electric, dummy."

"Make a right here," he says, ignoring me.

I eye him across the seat. He's practically dug a crater alongside his middle finger.

"For real. Where we going?"

"Bryce Miller's."

I can't hide my surprise. "Really?" Adam and I tried to get them to pal around for years but Bryce was always kind of a shit, pushing kids around the basketball court, snapping girls' bra straps. He had a wicked playfulness that made him harmless to me, but scary and unapproachable to Jared.

Jared nods. "He plays guitar. Invited me to jam with him."

"All right." I smile and compose a text to Adam in my head. "Does Mom know?"

"Yeah. She was *just thrilled* to tell Cindy Miller that their *youngest ones were finally becoming buddies!*" he says, imitating Mom's over-the-top affect.

A laugh bubbles up in my chest. "This'll be good for you."

Jared rolls his eyes. "Whatever."

I sync my phone and queue up my favorite playlist. All eighties pop. Madonna blares through the stereo and I feel my stomach settle as I follow the route to Adam's. I know it by heart, could trace the curve along the brick-lined driveway with my eyes closed. Adam isn't due back from school until fall break next month but just being near his house, his stuff, makes my brain buzz.

"Thanks," Jared says when I make a full stop.

"Where's Bryce?" I ask. "I wanna say hi."

A wooden swing sways back and forth on their porch, creaking in the breeze. I remember how it sags when you sit on it, and how it sinks even lower with two people's weight.

"Lemme text him." Jared's fingers fly over the screen and within seconds, Bryce swings the front door open and walks toward us over the manicured lawn. A rust-colored bathing suit hangs low on his hips. He looks older than Jared and if I squint hard enough, he could be Adam.

Jared leaps out of the car, slamming the door behind him, and they high-five.

"What's up, Jill?" asks Bryce, leaning into the passenger side window. "How've ya been?" Confident and composed, just like his brother. A senior Player doesn't scare him at all.

"Can't complain. How was your first week of high school?"

Bryce smirks. "Love it, obviously."

"Naturally."

"You talk to Adam today?"

I shake my head. "Not yet."

"I'm sure he'll hit you up," Bryce says. "He just called Mom. He's coming home next weekend. Some National Young Playwright workshop thing at the county theater. I think he's teaching kids how to write stage direction or some shit."

"Nice." I try to conceal my excitement and bite down on my lip but Jared rolls his eyes. He's picked up on my not-so-subtle crush.

Bryce slaps Jared on the back. "Ready to jam?"

Jared beams. "Let's do it."

"See ya, Jill!"

I wave and wait until they head inside to retrieve my phone.

Just dropped Jared off at your place . . . I guess he and Bryce are finally friends.

Before I can rev the engine, I hear a vibration.

FINALLY!!! Knew our master plan would work out someday.

My face burns and I tear at a cuticle with my teeth.

He says you're coming home soon?

Yeah. I meant to tell you. Make time for me? Breakfast at Diane's? Saturday?

My heart swells and I nod my head up and down as if he can see me.

Def.

I close out of our conversation but before I can look away, I see the last message from the night before, the one I had been avoiding.

It's Rachel Calloway.

But this time, I'm not scared. Adam will know what to do. He always does. We'll figure it out together. Saturday.

FIVE

I HEAR ADAM before I see him. Some old punk band blares from the speakers of the same vintage Mercedes he's been driving since his sophomore year at Prep. The sound is so familiar, I'm dizzy with déjà vu. When I climb in next to him, it feels so different from Bruce. Cozy and lived in.

"Hey, kid," he says. Adam's dark hair curls and swoops in a tousled, adorable mess. I brace myself for my favorite Adam trait, his left dimple. It only pierces his cheek when he smiles wide. Thank God it emerges as soon as I buckle my seat belt.

I beam back at him and he wraps me in a hug across the console. He still smells like lavender soap and the faint trace of tobacco.

"Diane's?" he asks.

"Please. I'm starving."

He starts the car and dials up the stereo, making swift turns as we head up the Cove. I used to go to the diner every Sunday morning after Hebrew school with Mom, Dad, and

Jared when we were little. We'd split mountains of blueberry pancakes and overstuffed bowls of hash browns. Hot chocolate for me and Jared, mug after mug of coffee for Dad, who loved to tell us stories about growing up modern orthodox in Williamsburg before it was cool. We'd listen patiently as he went on and on about his grandparents who only spoke Yiddish and died before we were born and before Dad became less religious. Going to Diane's alone still feels like riding without training wheels for the first time. An adventure of epic proportions.

"So, senior year?"

"Senior year," I echo. "It's chill."

Adam laughs. "That's my Jill. Totally unfazed."

I flush at the notion that I'm his. "It's probably all so boring to you now."

Adam laughs. "Nothing you say is ever boring, Newman."

The hair on the back of my neck tingles and I turn to him and take in his profile. His arms bulge just slightly out of his heathered T-shirt, and the muscles in his forearm stiffen when he reaches one hand to push his clear plastic glasses up the bridge of his nose.

I lean back in the seat and try to relax. I take note of my limbs and my posture, how I sit and how my arm fits just so on the window ledge. *Is this right?* I wonder as we pass the vacant Mussel Bay tollbooth, the skinny one-lane road that's bordered by water on both sides, the tiny fisherman's dock that sells the best stuffed clams in the summer. I can almost make out Ocean Cliff through the fog. It's all so familiar.

Adam pulls into the tiny parking lot, only six spots deep. The bell chimes when we push through the door and a waft of cinnamon and sausage grease smacks me in the face.

"Well, look at you two! My favorite babies!" Diane tucks a pen into her firetruck red bouffant and skips over, wrapping both of us in a giant, sugary hug. As usual, she's wearing bright red lipstick and an old-school white waitress uniform that's been neatly pressed. She looks like one of the servers, even though she owns the place. "Any seat in the house!" She winks, already knowing our booth is free. Adam makes a beeline toward the one with the thick crack down one side.

"Good to be home," Adam says when we sink into the red leather.

"Nothing like this in Providence?" I ask, pulling open the laminated plastic menu. It's as thick as a book.

"No way."

Thank God, I think.

"What'll it be, dawling?" Diane asks in her heavy Long Island accent. "The usual?"

"You know it," he says. "And a coffee. Black."

"For you, dear?" She turns to me.

"I'll have the same."

"Coming right up. You two enjoy yo'selves." She winks and heads to the kitchen.

"I fucking love this place," Adam says. His eyes settle on a point on the wall right above my head. "It feels like home." I turn my head to follow his gaze, though I already know what's there. Tucked into a blue Gold Coast Prep frame, our faces smile back at us. The photo was taken freshman year, the last time I came here with Shaila. Adam had driven us, Rachel, and Graham here after our last final of the year, the week before initiation. I had been grossed out by my own singleness, horrified to fifth wheel their double date. But Adam assured me I belonged. He wanted me there.

We had all expected Diane to chuck the photo after everything. But the Arnolds never came here. And neither did the Calloways, obviously. "So what's it matter?" she said when Adam asked her about it last year during his winter break. "It was a moment in time. Just because it's over doesn't mean it didn't happen."

"So," I say. "What's this playwright thing?"

Adam sighs. "I promised Big Keith I'd come back this semester to teach a workshop to the kids. All fourth and fifth graders from the city. Low income. They come out for a full weekend of script-writing seminars."

"That's so cool," I say, not even trying to hide my awe. Big Keith was Adam's mentor. He ran the theater department at Gold Coast Prep and had put Adam up for all the awards. He was legendary in the tristate area. The fact that he invited Adam back to teach was sick.

"Let's not talk about it, though. It's probably so boring to you."

"You know it's not." I roll my eyes at him.

Adam tilts his head and raises an eyebrow, like he doesn't believe me. "Fill me in on Player drama."

I laugh. "There's no drama."

Adam smirks. "There's always drama."

"Nikki and Robert are on and off, you know that."

"Eh, boring. Next. Have you come up with any good pops yet?"

My heart tightens. The pops are my absolute least favorite thing about being a Player. Everyone else thinks that they're *necessary*, that they set us apart and make us tough. A way to break you and then put you back together, to prove you can follow the Players' rules, that you're worthy, you deserve everything the Players can offer you. I think they're a means to an end. "Not yet," I say slowly. "We gotta personalize them, you know, so I think we're waiting to see who gets in."

Diane comes over and pours long, dark streams of coffee into our mugs, then disappears again. Adam takes a sip and nods. "Sure," he says before pivoting. "How's *Henry*?" Adam cocks an eyebrow and I instantly blush.

"The same," I say. "He's gonna apply early to Wharton. His dad is making him. He really wanted to go to Northwestern for journalism, but . . . you know." The decision had been plaguing Henry all summer but after an epic showdown with his dad over Labor Day, Henry told me he decided. Wharton it is. Business school or bust. He could always parlay it into business of media or something. Run a network, he said half-heartedly. Save the industry, maybe. But I could tell he was devastated by the idea of sitting in a cubicle in some skyscraper instead of reporting live from South America or sub-Saharan Africa.

Adam shakes his head. "That kid needs to learn how to make a decision for himself. Just because his last name is Barnes, doesn't mean he *needs* to become hedge fund royalty or whatever. I mean, look at me. My dad was obsessed with the idea of me being a neurosurgeon like him, but I said fuck that. I'd be miserable as a doctor. You know that. I bet he'll regret it."

Adam's right. But agreeing with him feels like a betrayal to Henry. I try to stay neutral.

"You still applying early to Brown?" He raises an eyebrow.

I nod. "Sent in the app last week."

"Phew," Adam says, and lets out a sigh of relief. "Gonna need you up there with me senior year."

I bite my lip to hide a smile.

Ever since Adam got into Brown, all I could think about was

applying there, too. At first, I wanted to be there because *he* was there. I pictured us away from Gold Coast, with the rest of our lives stretched out before us in parallel lines. Brown would be just the beginning. We would sit together in the corners of dark parties wearing fishermen's sweaters and downing cups of shitty jungle juice, our foreheads almost touching as we got lost in conversation. We would walk through the grassy quad, leaves crunching underfoot, as we made our way to a tailgate.

But when I actually started doing research, I found that there was so much more there that I wanted. Last year, when I told our guidance counselor, Dr. Boardman, that I was thinking about Brown and that I wanted to study physics and astronomy, her face lit up in delight.

"Oh, darling, this will be fun." She stood from behind her oak desk and reached up to the highest shelf in the office, pulling down a slim pale yellow pamphlet. "They have a Women in Science and Engineering program. It's just perfect for you," she said, her dark brown eyes wide and bright. "They offer full rides to the top two students. First you get in, of course, but then you take a test in the spring to determine the money."

I flushed, embarrassed that she knew I was a scholarship kid, though of course she did. It was her job to know.

"You have a shot," she said. "A good one." She thumbed through my transcript and then leaned in close to her laptop, scrolling through my resume. "Science Bowl captain for two years. Math Olympiad Scholar all four years." She kept scrolling. "Ah, look, you've even tutored middle school students in physics! Do you ever sleep?" Dr. Boardman joked and threw her head back with a chuckle, her graying bun bouncing up and down.

Butterflies hummed inside my stomach. This was what I had

hoped for, for all those late nights racking up extracurricular activities, all that risk to get to the top, to be worth it. To make me, as Dr. Boardman liked to say, "marketable" to the admissions boards.

Dr. Boardman slid the shiny brochure over to me, and on the front, I saw beautiful young women laughing and sitting together on benches and in classrooms, textbooks splayed open in front of them.

Brown invests in our female scientists and technologists, said one caption. *Join twenty-five incoming freshmen on the journey of a lifetime.* The words sat under a photo of a group of women staring up at the aurora borealis on what looked like a class trip to Norway. I brought the pamphlet close to my face and peered at the girls. This could be me.

Everything solidified when I visited Adam last year. Mom and I had driven up early one Friday morning so I could sit in on an Intro to Astronomy class with Mallika, a tall, dark-skinned, impossibly confident sophomore from Wisconsin who *adored* the Women in Science and Engineering program.

"I'm so glad you're here!" she squealed when we met in front of the lab. "Showing prospectives around is my all-time favorite thing. I'm basically the ambassador to the program. Plus, I hear you're super into astronomy, too, so it's perfect. I just did a summer at NASA." Mallika raced ahead and threw open the doors to a small auditorium where students were already beginning to gather for class. We grabbed a pair of seats just as the lights dimmed, signaling the professor was about to begin.

"She just got back from doing research at the Keck Observatory in Hawaii!" Mallika whispered in my ear.

As the hour raced by, my heart swelled. I wanted so badly

to be there, to be among these brainy kids, learning and growing and becoming a fuller me, one who knew everything there was to know about the stars, the sky, and the magic up above. I wanted to be friends with people like Mallika, who were obsessed with what I was obsessed with.

After the class ended, I followed Mallika into the hallway as she smiled and joked with just about everyone who passed. "Keep in touch!" she said, squeezing my arm.

I met Adam outside on the quad so he could show me, as he put it, "all the fun stuff they leave off the tour."

"Hey, Newman," he said as he appeared and wrapped me in one of his amazing bear hugs. "Let's go." Adam grabbed my hand and we started walking. I tried to stay in the moment with him; I'd wanted to be alone with him here for so long, but my brain was still spinning with diagrams and theories and constellations.

"Ta-da," he said, after a short walk through campus. We stood in front of a dilapidated townhouse. Shingles were falling off the side and the front porch looked like it was about to cave in. "College life."

"It's perfect," I said. And it was. It was exactly the kind of place that I pictured for Adam. We spent the rest of the evening playing beer pong with his roommates—three other guys in the English department who took turns ripping hits from a two-foot bong. It was so much like everything back in Gold Coast. So . . . normal.

My head started to spin and when I looked at my phone, I saw a text from Mom. *It's about that time* . . . she wrote.

"Shit," I said. "I think I have to go back to the hotel."

Adam nodded and set the bong back down on the cracked coffee table. "I'll walk you."

"You don't have to," I said, embarrassed.

He laughed. "Come on."

We walked together in silence until we reached the sleepy bed and breakfast Cindy Miller had recommended. This time, I was totally aware of every centimeter between us. I wished this were our default. That this was my life, permanently.

Adam stopped and turned to me. "So," he started, his clear glasses slightly askew, making his blue eyes shine brighter than I ever remembered. "What do you think?"

"I love it," I said.

"I knew you would."

I braced myself for something magical. For a cosmic moment that would ripple through my veins. For our mouths to find one another. For everything to collide and make total sense. I closed my eyes and waited. But nothing happened. Instead, Adam hugged me with such a gentle grace I wanted to cry. He rested his head on top of mine and breathed in deeply. "See you soon, kid." Then he was gone.

That night I resolved not to be the girl who followed a boy to college. This wasn't about him, I told myself. Brown was the best. It was the right fit. Everyone said so.

It had the program of my dreams but it was also the perfect place to burst the Gold Coast bubble, to challenge everything I thought I knew, to meet people who grew up in areas that were diverse and interesting and not painted with the same brush. Where people acknowledged how insane it is to have multiple houses and cars, where the administration actually wanted students to have an array of perspectives and backgrounds, didn't just pretend to.

So I put everything I had into that application. I spoke to Mallika and a handful of professors in the astrophysics department, gathering as much information as I could for my essay. I tried my best to explain why studying space was the only thing I could picture myself doing, and why I would be a worthy investment. I could have combed through the Files, looking for Brown contacts or help from the uber-exclusive college counselor who saw Players for free (his daughter was one five years ago). But I didn't. Every time I went to open the app, something stopped me. I wanted to do this on my own. I wanted to see if I could. So instead, I submitted my application and prayed.

At Dr. Boardman's insistence, I also sent in an app to State's honors program, which, if accepted, would guarantee me free tuition.

"Plus, doesn't their physics department have an exchange program at that observatory you love in Hawaii?" Mom asked when I told her.

They did, I admitted begrudgingly.

"Well, okay then."

Now at Diane's, Adam stretches his arms behind him and leans back against the booth. I feel a pang of disappointment as he pivots the conversation away from college and to the Players. "So, when *are* you picking newbs?" he asks.

"In a few weeks, I think."

"Our bros gonna do it?"

I fight the urge to chew on my fingernail. I don't want to have to explain to him why I don't want Jared to be involved. Even with ensured grades, the entry into another world, the deafening fun, I don't want him to go through it, to jump through a bunch of stupid hoops just to prove he can.

Part of me, though, knows the real reason why I don't want

him to be a Player. I don't want him to know what we've done.

"Maybe," I say. "We'll see." Diane plunks our plates down in front of us and my stomach growls at the beige mountain. Pancakes flop on top of hash browns and eggs. Sticky logs of browned meat poke out from beneath the pile.

"Your highness," Adam says, folding his hands in a prayer formation. "I'm not worthy."

"Oh, shut it," Diane says, swatting his palms down. "I'm impervious to that Millah charm."

When she walks away, I know it's time. "I have to tell you something."

Adam takes a bite and swallows. His lips are shiny with grease and I want to lick them clean. He cocks his head to one side, permission to continue.

"I got a bunch of weird texts," I say. My heart beats at a threatening pace. "From Rachel."

Adam drops his fork. "What?" He swallows. "Show me."

I pull out my phone and hand it to him, watching as he scrolls through the messages.

"This is so typical," he says, shaking his head.

"It's nothing, right? There's no way she's telling the truth. This is batshit."

Adam slides my phone across the table and leans back against the booth. "Rachel is nuts." His voice cuts the air between us like a knife. "I didn't want to tell you this but she sent me a text like this over the summer."

"Really?" I ask, stunned. "Why didn't you say something?"

"I didn't want you to get upset. I know how this stuff affects you. Shaila and everything."

My eyes sting and I shake my head. Her ghost is everywhere, even between us at Diane's Diner. Adam reaches out and puts his hand over mine. "Just don't let her get to you, okay? She's looking out for her brother, not you."

I nod. "You're right."

"Gotta pee," Adam says sheepishly. He slides out of the booth and disappears into the bathroom.

I blink back tears and spin my head to face Shaila. Her wide, freckled face smiles out from the frame. She had no idea what was coming, what we would be asked to do, or how it would all end. I didn't know that would be her last night, that it would be marked by crashing waves and warm vodka. Flecks of sand settling on my lips. A crackling scream. Fists clenched around sheets. My frizzy hair, unruly and alive. Darkness. Absolute darkness.

"You okay?" Adam returns and rests a hand on my shoulder. I manage a nod. "It's going to be okay, Jill. I promise."

He's never let me down before. He's always saved me in the end.

"Let's just leave it in the past, okay? You've got the best year of your life in front of you."

"Okay." I offer him a small smile.

I don't want her to fade, but Adam is right. It *is* in the past. Shaila is gone. And a bunch of insane texts from her killer's sister won't bring her back.

The day Shaila died, the cops took us all to the station. They handed out stale crackers and Styrofoam cups of sugary orange juice before asking a few softball questions. Then they called everyone's parents to come pick them up. First Marla, then Henry and Quentin, and finally Robert. Nikki's parents were in Singapore, so Mom said she could stay with us. She didn't yell at us for lying about where we'd gone. We had promised we were staying at Nikki's. Instead, she was silent in the car.

When we got home, Mom made grilled cheese sandwiches, demanded we shower, and split a Xanax in two, placing half in my palm and half in Nikki's. "Call your mom, dear," she said.

"They're staying over there for another week," Nikki said to me when she hung up. "Slumber party until then?" She smiled weakly. We were sitting on the couch in my living room side by side, stiff and awkward. We had never had a sleepover just the two of us. Shaila was always there. I hugged my arms around my stomach.

"I haven't cried yet," I said, and closed my eyes. But then everything came rushing back. The shut door. The bewildering darkness. The moment we realized we were all on our own.

Bile formed in my throat and before I could cover my mouth, my hands were coated in a sticky, green sludge. Tears finally formed in my eyes and I smelled like how I thought poison tasted.

"Shit, Jill." Nikki went and got a roll of paper towels, dropped to her knees, and started wiping the floor.

"I'm sorry," I said, my voice thick.

She looked up at me. Her eyes were no longer sparkly and rimmed in pink eyeshadow, like they had been the night before. "You have nothing to be sorry for."

I turned away from her on the couch and wondered if we were allowed to grieve what we had lost, or if that right was only reserved for everyone else. Were we being punished for what we had done, too? We were complicit after all, weren't we? Nikki must have wondered, too, because she shivered and curled up next to me. Her bare feet pressed up against mine so our bodies formed the shape of a heart. We stayed that way all day.

Nikki was so different from Shaila, hard where Shay was soft, in her collarbones, her hips. She'd cower in fear at the times when Shay would laugh in hysterics, during horror movies and while she was stoned. But they had two similar traits. They were both stubborn and loyal like puppies.

Being with Nikki was like looking in a funhouse mirror where one minute she was me and the next she was Shaila, until she finally morphed back into her own self, no longer the Nikki I knew in the months before. It was jarring but tender, like a dog with only three legs. I was fascinated in a way that made me only want her presence more.

She was a constant presence in our house, and we got in the habit of sleeping like spoons, alternating at hourly intervals so that her knees were pressed into the backs of mine, and then mine would be against hers. I slept with my fists balled against her, and when we flipped, I could feel her little hands in the middle of my spine. Whoever woke first would retreat a few inches to her side of the bed until the other stirred and it was time to turn over and face each other.

In that first month without Shaila we spent the early mornings whispering while the summer fog rolled in, warm and weighty. We talked and talked until our voices grew hoarse, about how Nikki was desperate to apply to fashion school, which of Marla's brothers was the hottest, and how to get the best possible tan by September. I traced the constellations on my skin, drawing imaginary lines from freckle to freckle until Nikki would say, "Do mine. Do mine."

But there were unspoken things, too. I didn't tell Nikki about the nightmares, how visions of Shaila haunted me more nights than not, or that I often woke in the middle of the night, sweaty and panting, a scream caught in my throat. And she never knew that I could hear her crying in the bathroom to her mom, begging Darlene to come home from whatever business trip she was on.

Neither one of us could admit that we were scared of forgetting Shaila. Sometimes we would start sentences with "remember how . . ." just to test our memories.

"Remember how she walked like she was on a mission? Or how she always farted when she sneezed? Remember how she she ate her pizza backwards, crust first?"

We were desperate to recall the details of her, but we were also desperate to move on. The forgetting was nice sometimes, because we started laughing again, too, first by accident at stupid reality TV shows, then on purpose, until our stomachs ached.

That was the odd summer, the black mark on our perfect records, the one three-month span we just had to push through so everything would be all right when it came time for college applications. Just get through this now, everyone said, and you will be fine.

And so, I had been given the summer off for the first time in my life. No science camp, no job tutoring middle schoolers, no girls in STEM program at the community college. At the advice of Headmaster Weingarten, Mom and Dad just let me be, and that is how I learned what boredom was, and how it mixed so devilishly with grief. Together, they became a thick, silky slime that was only remedied, it seemed, by vodka cut with splashes of flavored fizzy water, and joints as thick as my pinky finger, rolled by random Cartwright boys who claimed to have the *dankest* shit in the tristate area. What an enormous relief to realize that everyone else's parents had also agreed to this non-treatment of trauma.

Together the six of us were quarantined to the beaches of Gold Coast. Only Henry had a job, being a stringer for the *Gold Coast Gazette*. Instead we felt like *normal* kids, riding bikes over rocky gravel and searching for horseshoe crabs stranded on the sand. We would beat this infectious disease, everyone decided, and by September we would return to Gold Coast Prep bright-eyed and ready to ace our AP classes. And even though we had suffered such a loss—*What a tragedy! What a terrible, terrible horror!*—this was all we needed. One summer of dicking around with no consequences and no stress.

Just get it out of your system, Nikki's mom said to her when she finally returned from Singapore. Then we would be back on track and ready to grab the futures that dangled in front of us. All of us but Shaila.

Adam had been in London that summer, studying at the National Theatre with some Pulitzer Prize–winning playwright I'd never heard of, but he came home for a week before leaving for Brown. He said I was his first call when he touched down on American soil.

"Such bullshit," he said. "Expecting you all to just *get over it*."

I mumbled my agreement, but turned away. We were stretched side by side on the pebbly beach next to the Bay Bridge Lighthouse, where the coast makes a hard right angle before it retreats into the brush. The waves in front of us were more like gentle ripples and the water was so clear, you could see tiny fish from where we lay.

"Come on." Adam stood and pulled his shirt off in one motion. Little rocks rained down. He held his hand out to me and I grabbed it with reluctance.

I peeled off my shorts and tank top, leaving no time to be self-conscious of the rumpled bikini I'd thrown on that morning—or to ogle his clearly defined six-pack. I staggered behind him to the water. Within seconds Adam was gone, sinking below the surface.

"Screw it," I said out loud, and waded in, dunking my head completely.

The water was warm like a bath from the August sun, and for the first time since Shaila died, I was alone. It was exhilarating. I opened my mouth and screamed into the silence, letting moss and dirt and sediment flow in and out of my body. I imagined Shaila there with me, clenching my hands in hers and shaking her head back and forth, shrieking with rage and delight.

When I bobbed to the surface, Adam was already back on the beach, the sand around him damp and dark.

"Feel better?" he called out.

"Not really," I yelled.

"It helps though."

I swam to the shore and flopped down beside him. The ground stuck to my wet skin like Velcro.

"It's fucked," I said, though I wasn't sure what I was talking about—Shaila's death, Adam's imminent departure, or the idea that we're supposed to live and die all in the same life. Doesn't that seem like too much for one person to bear?

"What do we do now?" I asked, trying to silence the screams in my head.

"We go on," Adam said. "We keep going."

I nodded but I did not ask my next question. *How?*

SIX

YOU SURE YOU *don't wanna come to Quentin's tonight?* I type, trying to find the line between obsessed and friendly, desperate and chill. Adam never wants to come to Player parties now that he's in college, but after seeing him at Diane's, I wish he would.

Nah, you do your thing. Not sure those guys need me hanging around anymore. See you next time.

My stomach sinks. I miss him already and he's not even gone.

I shove my phone into my pocket and push the lock down on Quentin's front door. The house sits on a tiny, tree-lined street straddling the border between Gold Coast and Clam Cove. Everyone calls this area Gold Cove for short. The houses here are smaller, painted in the same four colors—navy, crimson, birch, or gray—because they're registered as landmarks with the historical society. They all date back to 1825 or earlier.

Each mailbox on this street has a little gold plaque nailed to it, a signal that these homes are *special*, they are *old*. And in Gold Coast, *old* doesn't just mean dusty or unkempt. It means you were here when big things happened, that you appreciate the historical distinctions the town has been awarded. Or that you were able to suck up to the right real estate agent twenty years ago when the town sold them off one by one. If you own one of these historical houses, it means you belong, no matter what.

It makes sense that Quentin lives here. He's beyond obsessed with Gold Coast history and can recite every single mayor since the Revolutionary War. His fascination transferred over to Prep in middle school, too, when he learned that the school's founder, Edgar Grace, quite literally came over on the Mayflower and eventually settled the area as a beachside oasis. I think the weird colonial vibe inspires his art or something. Otherwise why would he know that Grace's lineage died out in the early twentieth century when all of his descendants tragically caught scarlet fever? So random. He's basically become the keeper of Player history, too. He was the first of us to successfully memorize the Player packet, able to recite the chant backward and forward, and spew basic info about every single Player when called on during lineups.

At the house, it's just him and his mom, a Welsh novelist who drinks her scotch neat. His dad died of cancer before we became tight and Quentin never brings him up. Their place always feels cozy, like a cabin in the mountains even though it's only a few miles from the beach. Every other stair creaks just a bit, and the front door is so short that Quentin has to duck his head when he enters.

Their *stuff* is everywhere, not put away by a cleaning service twice a week like at Nikki's or Henry's. Even the shed out back is comforting. It once belonged to a blacksmith or something but Quentin's mom converted it into an art studio for him. Now it smells like turpentine and charcoal pencils. The last time I was in there, he had tacked up portraits of all the Players. Even Shaila.

"Fucking finally!" Nikki throws herself into my arms and I

wrap myself around her, burying my face in her jean jacket. It's so thin and soft, like leather.

"Sorry," I say, sheepish. "Got held up. Adam's in town."

"Oooh!" Nikki coos. "You're like the Adam whisperer. Come on." She takes my hand and weaves through the living room, past the reclaimed wood end table and over a woven basket full of fleece blankets. But before we make it to the kitchen, she stops. "Heads up," she says, tossing her hair over her shoulder. She's parted it in the middle so she looks like an indie princess. "Robert made the jungle juice, so . . . you know." She feigns passing out and her voice drops to a whisper. It's hard to hear over the booming music.

I grimace. "I'll make my own drink, then."

Before she can respond, I feel someone move up behind me. "There she is." In a beat, Henry spins me around to face him and slips a warm hand onto the small of my back. His fingers press into my skin and I shiver.

"Here I am," I say. Henry's face is flushed, but he's steady and his eyes are locked on mine, like he's actually, for real, happy to see me. A bout of sweetness blooms in my chest, and for a second, I forget that I spent the whole day drooling over Adam.

"Missed you today, J," Henry says, his mouth forming a tender little pout.

"Oh yeah?" I lean into him, letting myself be enveloped.

"Maybe just a little. Want a drink?" I nod. Henry turns and shouts into the kitchen. "Make way! Make way! Jill Newman has arrived! And the girl wants a drink!" Like that, the crowd parts, leaving a little aisle for me to shuffle down toward the kitchen island. But I hide behind my hair as everyone stares. Being in the Player fishbowl sometimes sucks.

I take my time mixing a cup of whatever's available as Henry leans up against the wall, scanning the room. He thrusts his drink toward Avi Brill, his producer on the Prep News channel, who's standing near the TV. Looks like he's trying to queue up some sad-ass documentary to play on mute.

"Classic," Henry mumbles. Then he turns to me. "Heard you were with Adam."

The muscles in my stomach tense. "Yep."

Henry groans.

"What?" I ask, my jaw clenching. "You know we're friends."

"I know," he says, wrapping his hand around my waist again. "I just get jealous sometimes. I feel like he's been into you forever."

Has he? My face flushes and I hope Henry doesn't notice.

"I mean . . . I get it." Henry smiles a lazy grin, as if his mouth is too heavy to hold up, and slips a finger through the loophole of my jeans. "You're the best." Henry takes a sip. "He knows we're together, right?"

"Of course." I raise my hand to scratch the back of his neck. Henry really is one of the good ones, I have to remind myself, even if he's clearly downed a few cups of Robert's juice. "He's only in town for the weekend. I won't even see him tomorrow. It's no big deal."

"I know, I know." Henry pulls me to him hard and his body feels like a slab of concrete.

"Promise you like me more than him?"

"Promise," I whisper into his chest. I will it to be true. I want it to be true. And saying it now, out loud, is easier than the truth. The truth is unnecessary. The truth is dangerous. "Let's find Quentin."

Henry follows me into the backyard. The music is quieter out here, and string lights rim Quentin's lawn, giving the whole party a softer feel. I finally spot the host sitting on his childhood slide with Barry Knowlton, the sophomore who made the state swimming team last year. Barry sits between Quentin's legs with his eyes fixed on Quentin like he's the most beautiful creature in the world. Quentin drags his forefinger down Barry's chin and they smile like dummies. Wrapped in a private moment, they're totally oblivious of all of us making a hot mess in Quentin's backyard. Envy flares in my stomach, for their intimacy, the sweetness. I wonder if people are jealous of Henry and me, of what they think we have.

No, wait, of what we *do* have. We do.

Quentin's eyes suddenly meet mine and he whispers something into Barry's hair. In a few steps, Quentin's at my side.

"We have to talk," Quentin says, inserting himself in between me and Henry. "You too, man," he says to Henry. His voice is tinny and urgent. We follow him behind a bunch of bushes, out of view of the rest of the party. Henry and Quentin keep looking at each other, seeming to exchange whole sentences with their eyes over my head.

Their moms were college roommates who moved to Gold Coast together to ensure their families grew up side by side. Quentin and Henry's friendship is obvious. It makes them fight like brothers, with iced-out silence or by wrestling in the mud. But they always make up easily thanks to an unwavering understanding that they are bound together not by choice, but by Mom-ordained duty. Another bond I can't break. No matter how many inside jokes Quentin and I make, or how many times I feel Henry's bare skin above mine, I'll never worm my way inside their brains, like they have done with each other.

I admitted this once to Henry when we were lying on the

dock behind his house over the summer. "I wish I had what you and Quentin have," I said lazily.

"You have Nikki," Henry said, dragging his fingertips over my goosepimply stomach. His touch tickled and I suppressed a giggle.

"Not the same. It was like that with Shaila, though," I said. It was the first time I had admitted that out loud, that Nikki wasn't enough to replace Shaila. It dawned on me that I probably wasn't enough to replace her, either.

"I was always jealous of you two, you know," he said. "Of the way girls get to be best friends with each other in such an obvious way. It's so much weirder with guys."

What an odd thing to say, I thought. The boys had it so much better in just about every way. Especially in the Players. But Henry's admission made me like him more. He was delicate, breakable. Before I could press him, Henry stood and galloped to the end of the dock, folding his body into a cannonball and launching himself into the water below.

Now Henry and Quentin jostle each other in one of those aggro-chest-bump ways. "Yeah, man," Henry says, shoving a shoulder into Quentin's side. "I'll get the others."

"C'mon." Quentin motions toward one of the massive weeping willows lining the yard. We race to part its stringy leaves like a beaded curtain.

"Some 007 shit, huh?" I say.

"You didn't check your phone all day, did you?" he says.

"Not really." When Adam and I were together, I usually forgot.

"There's something you have to see." Quentin reaches into his pocket and pulls out a folded piece of newspaper. It's flimsy, from the crumbling *Gold Coast Gazette.*

"Where'd you get one of these?" I laugh. My family is the only one I know who still gets the Sunday *Times* and even that is archaic. Dad says he could never give it up.

"Just read it." He crosses his arms, impatient.

My eyes try to focus in the darkness and it takes a few seconds for the letters to come into view. It's short, just a couple of paragraphs, but the words drain all warmth from my body.

Notorious Local Killer Seeks Appeal

Graham Calloway, the boy who struck a deal after confessing to killing fifteen-year-old Shaila Arnold, seeks to exonerate himself three years after her death. Calloway, who is scheduled to be transferred to New York Federal Prison when he turns eighteen in June, has released a statement through his lawyer confirming the news:

"In light of new evidence, I, Graham Calloway, believe I was wrongfully blamed for the murder of Shaila Arnold. I will be seeking a new trial to prove my innocence. I aim to clear myself of all wrongdoing. I did not kill Shaila Arnold. I withdraw my confession."

The Arnold family could not be reached for comment but the Gold Coast Police Department issued their own statement, standing by their original detective work: "We will review all new evidence but support our detectives who investigated Ms. Arnold's horrific death. We have no additional comment at this time."

I look up, dazed and nauseous.

"They're over here!" Nikki shouts. She bursts through the leaves, causing them to rustle around her. Marla, Henry, and

Robert are quick on her heels and they all tumble into the circle beneath the willow. Nikki's eyes dart to the clipping in my hand. "He showed her."

My head spins and I find the ground with my hands. "You all knew?" I stammer.

"I tried calling you earlier today, but . . ." Nikki's voice trails off.

"When she couldn't get you, we thought it'd be better to talk about it in person," Marla says softly.

"You okay?" Henry whispers. He rests a gentle hand on my shoulder and his boozy breath is hot on my ear.

"What does this mean?" My voice is hoarse and I can't make sense of the words.

For a beat no one says anything, and all we can hear is the party raging on without us.

"He's a liar," Robert finally says, his fist wrapped tightly around a cup. "We were there. We all know he did it."

Everyone is quiet for a moment. I wonder if they're trying to push memories of that night away, too. How the fire smelled like burning rubber. Shaila's hard, steady gaze before everything started. My hands around her wrists. Her fierce gait as she walked away for the last time.

"Such bullshit," Nikki says, toeing the dirt with her combat boots. "Of course he has to come back and ruin our senior year." She wrinkles her nose like the whole thing smells like shit, which it does. "As student council president, I'm going to talk to Headmaster Weingarten about this on Monday. No way this is going to interfere with the rest of our semester!"

"We can't get involved. It's not worth it," Quentin says. He shakes his head and picks up a stick, dragging it over the ground. "Not with college applications coming up."

"But what if Graham's telling the truth?" I say under my breath.

Five pairs of eyes turn to me. "You can't be serious." Henry laughs.

"You're the journalist," I say. "Aren't you the least bit curious? Don't you want to know what happened?"

Henry's mouth forms a straight line. "We already do."

"Can we all just agree *not* to think about this?" Nikki pleads. "Let's just drop it, okay? If we ignore him, the rest of Gold Coast will, too. That's just how it is and you all know it."

Heads nod around me and one by one, they stand and leave.

"C'mon, babe," Henry says, extending his hand.

I shake my head. "Just give me a sec, okay?"

He nods and walks back to the house. Huddled against the tree alone, I can almost forget about the party around me, the other Players, the undie wannabes, the countless vile pops we completed to get here. I watch as my friends trail back inside. We're all we have. I want to wrap my heart around them and hold them close. I want to tie them to me to keep them safe. To do what we couldn't do for Shaila.

Maybe they're right. It's not worth rehashing the past.

But there's something I just can't shake.

I reach for my phone with an unsteady hand and pull up Rachel's texts.

Graham didn't kill Shaila. He's innocent.

My phone feels heavy in my hand, too heavy to hold, and the sky begins to swirl above me.

"Jill, you okay?" Henry returns and kneels down next to me. His hand slinks up the back of my shirt. It burns my bare skin.

I muster a nod. "Just drank that too fast," I say, pointing to my cup.

"I'll get you some water."

"Thanks," I mumble.

The ground is wet and hard under my hands and I push myself up to stand, taking one last look at what Rachel said.

It's all so fucked up. Can we talk?

The first time I spoke to Rachel I thought it was unfair that she had to breathe the same air as me. She was striking, with cheekbones too high for someone who wore a high school uniform every day and eyes that were so dark you could barely see her pupils. She always wore her hair in soft waves that waterfalled down her back. When I got a haircut that year, I showed the stylist her class picture as inspiration. But my mane was never as smooth, always a little too unruly.

She found me in the library one day in early October of freshman year, with *The Odyssey* open in front of me. I tapped my fist against the desk, hoping that by some miracle I would absorb the final two hundred pages in thirty minutes flat before our midterm. My GPA was about to take a nosedive and for the first time, I could feel my scholarship slipping away, everything spiraling out of my control.

I had planned to stay up until 3 a.m. to cram, but I fell asleep with the thick book splayed out on my chest and all the lights still on. I woke up in a panic when my regular alarm sounded at 6:07. It took a Herculean effort on my part not to break into sobs right there in the stacks.

"You look like shit," Rachel said. She rested her hands on the book and leaned down low so I could see the top of her cleavage peeking out over a lacy black bra. "Beaumont?" she asked.

I nodded. A ball sat in my throat. I swallowed hard.

"You know Adam, right? You're Shaila's friend?"

I nodded again.

"Cool." Rachel disappeared and my face grew hot, mortified that she would run to Adam to tell him how awkward and gross I was. What loser screwed up this epically? A minute passed and then another, and then Rachel was standing in front of me, holding out two pieces of paper. "Here," she said. "It's a pattern. First answer's A. Second's B. Third's C. Rinse and repeat. You get the picture. He's just using Mrs. Mullen's test from last year. And the year before that. She never changes it."

"What?" I whispered, incredulous that she just *had* the answers.

Rachel smiled. "Trust me. Look it over, then destroy this. If anyone catches you with it, we're done for, got it?" I thought about how disappointed Mom and Dad would be if I got caught cheating, if I was suspended or worse. How would I be able to live with myself? But then I pictured failing the test, losing my ride to Gold Coast Prep and all the college connections and the status and . . . the most precious pieces of my life would be gone. My chest pounded as I grappled with what I was about to do. I took the papers in my shaking hands.

"You owe me one," Rachel said with a wink before she skipped away, her hips swinging with every step.

The next week, when Mr. Beaumont dropped a graded paper back on my desk, he stabbed at the red numbers proclaiming 98. "Well done, Jill." I had purposely messed up one answer to throw him off my trail. I should have been elated, but instead I couldn't feel a thing. I stuffed the exam way down into my backpack and tried to forget about it, about what I had done.

Rachel was right, though. I would pay her back throughout that year with various pops, like picking up her favorite donuts from Diane's and researching her history term paper on the Vietnam War. I even steamed her prom dress so she could pose for perfect pictures with Adam.

It would be months before I knew the full scope of the Player Files, how there were only straight-up answer keys for small tests like this one. It would be the only one I ever used.

The real power lay in the gray areas, where former Players passed down access to an elite and explicit network of tips, like which local doctors would write you a note proving you needed extra time on standardized tests (Robert and Marla employed that one), and which college departments were partial to Players (a grad from the early aughts now works at Yale's art program; Quentin has been emailing with him regularly for months). There was even a script on how to ace a case study given by the dean of admissions at Wharton (Henry freaked when he found it).

If Gold Coast Prep's whole schtick was to set you up for life, the Player Files took it one step further. They made you untouchable.

We didn't get the password to the app that housed them all until we were fully initiated, but throughout freshman year, we got flashes of its muscle, like when a senior felt pity toward us.

Shaila never touched the app. She didn't need it.

When I got that English exam back, Shaila craned her neck to see my score. She smirked in approval. "Next time maybe you'll get 100." She gritted her teeth and pulled at a stray cuticle between her thumb and her forefinger. "Just don't go beating me," she said. "First in class is *my* shit."

I managed a smile and waited for her to break into giggles, but she held my gaze in a frigid standoff before turning away completely.

It was obvious that Shay was smart. She'd been in honors classes since middle school, and the homework packets that took me days took her just a few hours. English was her favorite. She often skipped study hall to go to Mr. Beaumont's office hours, though she called him "Beau" for short. He was assigning her Shakespeare on the side to prepare for the SAT Subject Test, she said. She'd emerge from his classroom with weathered, worn copies of *The Tempest* and *King Lear* and a small, secret smile.

After a particularly grueling pop where we had to stand in the ocean in November, wearing only bikinis, while singing Marvin Gaye's "Let's Get It On" for an hour, I asked Shay why she wanted to be a Player, why go through with all the hard stuff if she wasn't going to reap the real rewards. She wrapped a terry towel around her body and looked at me with a baffled expression and quivering lips that had turned a pale shade of blue.

"It's the most fun we'll ever have," she said.

She died with a perfect GPA.

Shaila was destined for Harvard. It was basically in her blood. Mrs. and Mr. Arnold had met right there on Harvard Yard. I'd heard the story just once from Mrs. Arnold after she downed a few martinis on Shaila's fourteenth birthday.

Shaila's mom, formerly known as Emily Araskog, was a sweet girl who had moved to Cambridge to attend Harvard from the Upper East Side of Manhattan, where she had lived her entire life in a penthouse that overlooked Central Park. She'd grown up with an elevator operator who wore white gloves and a smart gray uniform, complete with a little hat that he tipped to her when she walked through the ornate wrought-iron doors.

Old money, Mom had whispered to Dad when she met

Mrs. Arnold. *A grade-A WASP.* And it was true. The Araskogs' lineage dated back to the Liberty Bell, Mrs. Arnold said.

One day, Emily was sitting on a bench in Harvard's leafy quad when a football hit her square in the face, knocking her onto the ground. When she looked up in shock, a blond man in a crimson sweatshirt was standing over her.

"Gil Arnold," he said after apologizing profusely.

He took Emily out for a drink, and then dinner, and then the rest is history. They married the week after graduation and the Krokodiloes, Harvard's oldest a cappella group, performed at the reception. Within just a few years, Gil built a multibillion-dollar hedge fund in Manhattan and the Arnolds decided to plant roots in Gil's hometown, Gold Coast.

Emily was hesitant to leave Manhattan and her and Gil's close friends, the Sullivans, whose daughter Kara had started crawling around with baby Shaila. But Gil's other childhood friend, Winslow Calloway, had just moved back home and snagged a plot on the beach. Wouldn't it be so nice to join them and be near the ocean with all that space? The fact that their kids could go to the best private school on the East Coast, which would only be a few miles away from their home, sealed the deal for Emily.

And so, Shaila was indoctrinated with Crimson pride from the moment she emerged from Emily Arnold née Araskog's womb. Swaddled in a ruby red blanket, little baby Shaila was told it would be her destiny to follow in her parents' footsteps.

Twenty-four hours after the news about Graham broke, I'm lying in bed staring at my phone. I scroll through the texts, past Adam's *adios* message before heading back to school and past Henry's *night, babe* note, until I find Rachel's unfamiliar number.

I wonder if she's thinking about me as much as I'm thinking about her. She had to know that we would see the article in the *Gazette,* but did she know that no one would want to deal with it?

I type out what I want to say and stare at the letters dancing on the screen. I picture Shaila on the morning of initiation, sipping from a mug of coffee while she laughed, nervous energy coursing through her limbs. I can see her so clearly when I close my eyes. Her sunny face and long, thick lashes, daring me to betray her by responding to Rachel. But I also see the Players, and all of us promising just last night that we wouldn't get involved. I hear Adam's comforting voice. "Rachel is nuts," he'd said at Diane's.

But what if she's not?

I bite my lip and close my eyes, shoving Shaila, my friends, and even Adam from my mind. I make a decision. I turn my back on them.

Let's talk.

I hit send.

SEVEN

"I CALL THIS meeting of the Players to order!" Nikki announces, smacking a plastic gavel on the coffee table. The six of us are sprawled around Nikki's living room for the first official tribunal of the year. Piles of bagels and schmear, courtesy of Nikki's parents' credit card, are stacked on the table. But no one's ready to start just yet.

Henry sits between my legs on the floor and furiously scrolls through Twitter, reading some thread by his favorite *New Yorker* reporter, who just published a new investigation.

"Man, this dude is a legend," Henry murmurs. "I'd kill to interview him about sourcing."

I pat his head like a puppy.

"Dude, I can probably hook it up," Robert says. "My dad knows all those writers."

"Your dad knows all the writers at *The New Yorker*?" Quentin asks, skeptical.

"Uh, yeah. I grew up in the city, you know."

"No! Really?" Nikki says, feigning shock. "None of us knew that!"

"Just remember who got you fakes this summer," Robert says. "I'm the one with that connect."

We all grumble and roll our eyes, shoving each other with elbows and pillows. I check my phone, more out of hope than necessity, but there's nothing there. Waiting for Rachel to respond has been torture.

No one brings up Graham or the article in the *Gazette*. Instead we're pretending like nothing happened, like we could still go about our normal Players' rituals as usual. Glossing over things is a Gold Coast tradition and I am happy to follow suit. No one needs to know I texted the enemy.

I avert my attention to Marla, who stares intently at the screen in her lap, the Dartmouth admissions portal open in front of her. She applied there early with hopes of walking on the field hockey team.

"You know we won't hear for a few months, right?" I whisper. Acceptances were still so far off, I had to force myself not to think about them.

Marla throws her head back against the couch. "Ugh, I know. I'm obsessive."

Quentin grumbles next to us. "Don't I know it." He's submitted his portfolio to Yale's art program and is dying to hear back, too. "Cannot believe we have to wait eons for this."

I rest my head on Quentin's soft shoulder and try to push thoughts of being at Brown with Adam out of my head, of crushing that Women in Science and Engineering scholarship exam I'd only get to take *if* I got in. It's too much to wrap my brain around. "Uh, hello!" Nikki yells before banging her gavel again. "The Toastmaster is talking here." As president of the student council *and* Toastmaster of the Players, I think it's safe to say the power has gone to her head just a little.

Quentin groans and tosses a pillow at her.

"It's time. We gotta pick freshmen," she continues.

Marla drops her phone and sits up straight.

Robert claps, throwing a fist in the air. "Fresh meat! Let's do it!"

Nikki opens a frayed green binder and pulls out a stack of papers containing photos and bios of all the potential freshmen. The binder had been handed down from Toastmaster to Toastmaster for who knows how long. Hell, maybe Mr. Beaumont even saw it. It holds all the official Players rules—how to nominate freshmen, specific songs and chants we had to learn, guidelines for creating pops, and, of course, the initiation rules. Only seniors are allowed to see the binder, and when last year's Toastmaster, Derek Garry, passed it to Nikki before he left for Yale, we spent hours poring over its contents. When we reached the initiation section, we scanned it desperately, seeking answers for what had happened, but there was nothing.

Today, we're stuck on the nominations chapter. We'd heard the whole stupid process could take hours. I remember Adam told me it took them the entire weekend and they pulled two all-nighters in a row to pick our squad. But Derek used the same line last year.

"You guys ready for this?" Nikki says, a grin spreading across her face. She'd been memorizing the binder all summer, preparing to lead us into a new year. She was ready to finally control the Players. *This year will be different.*

"First up, Sierra McKinley. Quentin, she's your nom. What's her deal?"

"Sierra's in my AP drawing class—as a freshman, which is amazing—and she's actually super talented. I told her so last week and she didn't get all nervous the way the other freshmen do when I talk to them. She just said thanks and drew this insane-looking bird and I was like, damn, that is very cool. Plus, she's got that sick house up near the tollbooth and has like three acres of beach access. Mom went there for Fourth of July last year and they set off their own fireworks. Very good party house."

Nikki smiles. "Anyone dissent?"

"She won't put out!" Robert yells.

"How do you even know that, asshole?" I ask.

He smirks. "Wouldn't you like to know."

"You wish, Robert." Nikki straightens her back and flips her hair over her shoulder. This was a bad week between them. "Next up, Bryce Miller." She points to me. "Your pick?"

"Adam's brother," I say as a way of explanation. Heads around the room nod, but Henry looks down and starts thumbing through Twitter again. "I thought at first he was a little shit but he's been super cool to Jared, bringing him around for band practice and stuff. I'm into it."

Nikki nods in absolute seriousness. "Thoughts?" Her eyebrows shoot up to the group.

"It's a no-brainer," Marla says, and I thank her silently for having my back. "Legendary is in his blood."

"All right then," Nikki says. "Moving on." For the next three hours, Nikki runs through a dozen more names. We debate Gina Lopez's suspicious gluten allergy, Carl Franklin's excessive sneaker collection, Aditi Kosuri's actually-pretty-good attempts at being a style influencer, and Larry Kramer's wild growth spurt that landed him near the seven-foot mark this spring. The boys demand a thirty-minute break to shoot around a basketball, while Marla, Nikki, and I laze next to the pool with a bag of Cheetos and a box of Pocky.

"We're almost at Jared, Jill," Nikki says, wiping cheese dust off her fingers. "What do you want to do?"

Marla nods. "Like I said, he *is* kind of cute." She giggles.

"Mar, I swear," I say, and swat at her arm. I try to think. "We decided that things would be different. We would be different. Nikki, you're Toastmaster now, the first girl *ever*. So we're in charge."

They nod. "I want him here, if we're still in on that promise," I say. "Nothing bad can happen to him or any of the others. We can change everything. We can make this fun, the way it's supposed to be."

"Hell yeah," Nikki says. "I'll make sure of it."

"If that's the case, if that's really the case, I'm all in," I say.

Everything is going to be different.

Jared is voted in, obviously, along with Sierra, Bryce, and a few others.

I let Adam know the good news.

Fuck yeah, he responds in an instant.

Keep it cool, tho. We want it to be a surprise.

Obvi, Newman. I got this . . . wish I was there to celebrate with you.

My heart flutters.

Same.

Have the most fun possible. Ever. Period. All the time.

You know it.

We end the day with pizza and garlic knots, eaten on paper plates in Nikki's living room. She puts on an old Adam Sandler movie and we lie like sloths until varsity running back Eli Jaffe group texts like sixty people saying he's throwing a last-minute beer pong tournament. Henry, Robert, and Marla jump up to go, but Quentin, Nikki, and I stay behind and settle in for a *Real Housewives* marathon.

"This Toastmaster shit is exhausting," Nikki says, splayed out on the couch, the tiny gavel still by her side. "Even more so than student council. At least there, no one questions me."

"You're ridiculous," Quentin says. His stomach is covered in stray pizza crust crumbs. "You love this."

Nikki sinks deeper into the couch. "Damn right, I love it. This time next year, we're going to be pond scum, back at the bottom after years climbing our way to the top. You're nuts if you think I'm not going to savor every second. I'm not ready to go back there yet."

I reach for her hand and squeeze it.

"Intro night is gonna be amazing," Quentin mumbles.

He's right. It's always my favorite, ever since we had ours. It's a big party on the beach, the only one that is filled with hope and anticipation instead of dread.

Our intro happened on a warm night in October, just as the weather was starting to turn. Shaila suggested we all gather at Nikki's since her parents would be away and Nikki jumped at the chance to host for the first time, to be a leader.

She broke out a bottle of tequila and we all took swigs, sizing each other up. I was close with Shaila, Nikki, and Graham, of course, but it was the first time I had really hung out with Robert or Marla outside of school. Robert had secretly always intimidated me. And Marla was still new, unattached to any solid friend group. At that point, Henry was just the cute, lanky kid on the school news channel. He had yet to make varsity lacrosse or fill out his six-foot frame. And Quentin was his best friend, the artsy guy, whose paintings hung in the middle school hallways. But somehow, for some reason, Adam, Jake, Rachel, and the rest of the senior Players had picked the eight of us and changed our lives forever.

That night, I looked around at the weird group and wondered what we each had to offer. I wondered what made me special. Why I had been plucked, instead of one of my eighty-two other classmates. Everyone else looked so ready, so alive, that my heart swelled with affection. I hoped they would become family or something like it.

After an hour, Graham's phone buzzed with the go-ahead from Rachel. He whispered something into Shaila's ear, and they both erupted into a fit of giggles. Nikki rolled her eyes at me, and we shared an annoyed smirk. *Classic couple shit.*

Then Graham cleared his throat. "Let's go."

He led us in a single-file line behind Nikki's house, where the grass kissed the sand before it became beach. From there, her house looked like a UFO, dropped down to earth by chance. The eight of us continued silently, guided by the inky sky and a million little stars.

I looked up to find Orion and then Aries, the Little Dipper, too. Each one set me at ease, more signs this was all so *right*. My stomach flipped and I felt like I was on the brink of greatness. I knew that this was the night I had been waiting for my entire life. It had to be. It was the brightest I'd ever seen the Milky Way. We continued marching across the sand in silence for another mile until we heard the sounds of drunk people who thought they were whispering. "Shhh! They're coming."

A blazing bonfire came into view and soon we could hear the grainy sounds of some house song coming from a portable speaker. Graham stopped as two headlights approached. *Shit,* I thought. *The cops.*

Shaila grabbed at his hand in the dark, and they glued their shoulders together as the brightness grew bigger.

But there were no uniforms or sirens. A sand buggy stopped and someone stepped out. I squinted into the darkness. It was Adam. His eyes met mine but he didn't smile, didn't show any sign of recognition.

"Be quiet," Adam said, his mouth in a hard line. "Follow me and do as I say. If you don't there will be consequences." He looked at me again before turning the buggy around, heading back toward the flames.

We ran after him, breathing heavily to keep up. The fire grew taller as we got closer and when we were standing right in front of it I felt like we had found the center of the earth. "Line up!" Adam yelled.

We scrambled into a row and I found myself in between Nikki and Shaila, standing so close that my fingers grazed theirs. My eyes adjusted and I made out familiar faces. Rachel. Jake. Tina. Derek Garry. They stood by class, a handful of sophomores off to the right, a smattering of juniors to the left, and the seniors in the middle with their arms crossed, holding bottles. They looked ready for a fight.

Adam cleared his throat. "Players."

The voices rose in unison and I made out the words, crisp and clipped.

Gold Coast Prep, hear our cries
Born and bred until we die
For years and years, our fair sea
Has held us up and kept us free
From brush to waves and dusk till dawn
We rise and fall, like kings and pawns
We've read the rules, we've learned them well
We're Players till the end, we yell.

A chill ran down my spine and the sand stretched before us, echoing the chanted words. Wind rustled the tall grass of the dunes and waves crashed onto the shore.

And then Jake spoke. "You have been chosen by this year's senior class to be Players. But that doesn't mean you *are* Players. It just means we think you could be. This year you'll be faced with challenges, some fun, some . . . *not*. If you make it through, if you choose to continue, then you *will* be Players. You'll get access to things you never dreamed about."

Along the edge of the circle, the other Players nodded their heads in solemn motions. It sounded like Jake was offering us the world.

But what would we have to do to get it?

"You'll need to prove yourself first," he continued. "You'll have to show us you're worth it, that you deserve this. Those standing before you have gone through it all." He gestured behind him, eight in each cluster. Shadows danced on their faces. "We've worked hard to make this group what it is, to uphold the values and foundation of the Players before us." He paused and flashed a devilish smile, one that made the hairs on the back of my neck stand at attention. "We've also had a fuck ton of fun."

Cheers erupted all around.

"Do as we say, listen to me, your Toastmaster, and you'll be fine," Jake continued. "Are you ready?" He raised a plastic cup.

"Yes!" Shaila said. Her voice rang out alone, solid, and bounced against the crackling fire.

"Very good!" Jake said. "You get first sip, then." He winked at her and I felt the tequila sloshing in my stomach. I snuck a peek at Adam standing next to Rachel, huddled against her for warmth. His cheeks were flushed and I willed him to look my way, to remember we were in this together. But his eyes lingered on Shaila, curious if she would take the bait.

Jake walked toward Shaila and brushed his moppy light brown hair out of his eyes. He handed her a glass jug full of clear liquid. She took a hearty sip but didn't cough or burp or make any noise at all. "Pretty good," she said, sending giggles around the circle.

Who is this freshman? The one with courage, they must have thought. I wanted that freshman to be me.

Shaila passed me the jug and I finally felt Adam's gaze. I sipped and held back disgust as best I could. It smelled like the inside of an ear piercing, and tasted like sweat and salt and my own fluids. I handed it off and felt fire in my lungs. Later, I learned this was our first pop. We had passed.

"Now," Jake said. "Let's have some fun. The real shit starts tomorrow." He lit a sparkler and the Players broke from their rigid lineup. Someone sent a tiny firework into the air and it exploded overhead. The beach was silent for a minute and then a sophmore yelled, "Let's do it!" Right on cue, the music grew louder, blaring into the night.

"Ready for this?" Adam said into my ear, suddenly by my side. His hair was damp and sand had stuck to the tips. He was the real Adam again. My Adam, with his big, dimpled smile. I nodded and sensed the liquor make its way through my limbs.

"I'm so excited for you," he said. "C'mon." He grabbed my hand and led me to a circle of juniors. I was enveloped in a hug so tight I could barely breathe. Before I was released, Adam had retreated to Rachel's side and slid an arm around her waist. She danced in front of him and laughed as he spun her around. When she saw me staring, she ran over and wrapped her arms around me tight.

"I knew you'd get in," she said, her voice smooth and electric over the music. "Welcome to the rest of your life."

"Thanks," I managed. Her eyes searched mine, and her lips were chapped from the wind. She had tied her hair into a high pony so little wisps of her dark hair fell neatly around her face. She was magnetic.

"Wanna know a secret?" Rachel whispered, leaning into my ear. Her breath was hot on my skin.

I nodded.

"You're just like me," she said softly in a maternal voice. "Scared. Young." My stomach sank. Those didn't sound like good things. "You'll survive, though," she continued. "We're the strong ones."

Her words didn't make any sense at the time, and in an instant she was gone, flitting across the sand to Shaila. They had known each other practically since birth and that night Rachel hugged her like they were sisters. I wondered what secrets they shared.

It was too intimate a moment to watch. I averted my eyes and looked to the sky. The full moon hung as high and big as a ship, directing stars to shine their spotlights brighter on us.

As a kid, I would come to this stretch of beach with my parents to make sandcastles with Jared, pretending we were deep-sea creatures just looking for a gritty new home. We took turns sucking in our cheeks and turning our faces into little fish mouths, pressing our palms out like flippers. We waved to the teenagers in Gold Coast Prep windbreakers arriving just as we were packing up our pails and shovels, dusting the sand off our butts with damp towels. *They look so old,* I thought. "You'll be them one day," my mom had said as if she read my mind. But at the time, that seemed impossible.

EIGHT

"JARED!" I YELL when I swing open the door. It's almost noon and I'm famished, even after polishing off half a pizza at Nikki's last night, and another slice this morning. When no one answers I run up the stairs and knock on his bedroom door.

"Come on!" I call. "Wake up."

I hear a muffled groan through the door. "No."

"I'll take you to Diane's."

More heavy sighs. But within a few minutes, Jared has somehow managed to pull on jeans, slap a baseball hat over his matted hair, and look presentable enough to be seen in public.

"Good enough?"

I throw my hands up. "Good enough. Let's go."

When we get to Diane's I grab my and Adam's booth, the one with the thick crack down the middle of one seat, and shuffle all the way in so my shoulder knocks the wall. Jared does the same.

"Well, what did I do to deserve *both* Newmans today?" Diane asks, grinning. Her red mountain of hair is particularly voluminous today, nestled against her waitress's cap, and her skin is dewy and flushed, like she's been rushing around since dawn. "Such a delight, you two!"

Jared's face turns red and I laugh. "You know you're the best person in this town, Diane?"

"Don't I know it!" Diane throws her head back and shimmies her shoulders. Someone behind the griddle lets out a guffaw. "What'll it be?"

"Diane's Home Plate for me," Jared says. "And a coffee."

My eyebrows shoot up. "Since when do you drink coffee?"

Jared shrugs, his face still pink.

"Look how sleepy he is," Diane says. "He needs it. The usual, dear?"

I nod and Diane winks as she walks away.

"I can't believe you have a *usual* here," Jared says, lifting his fingers to form air quotes. "Guess you're here a lot."

"Sometimes." A silence extends between us and I glance up above Jared's head, where Shaila smiles back at me from inside the Gold Coast Prep frame. Her head rests on Graham's shoulder and he's smushed up against Rachel's side. He and Rachel look so obviously related with their hair parted the same way, their angular jaws.

Jared turns to look, too. "Must be weird, huh?" he asks.

Before I can respond, Diane comes back with our mugs. While she pours the coffee, I peek out the window. The sugar maples that line the parking lot have turned a deep cherry red. They're so bright they look fluorescent. Neon, maybe. Even in here, the air smells like fall, crisp and biting.

"Thanks, Diane," I say. She tips her little white cap and disappears into the kitchen.

"I saw that article about Shay," Jared says. His voice is small.

"Is that why you wanted to come here? To talk about it?"

My chest tightens. I never even thought to talk to Jared about Graham or Shaila or Rachel's texts. I shake my head but can't figure out what to say.

"You must miss her," he says.

"I do. So much." I blink back tears. This was not how I wanted this to go. "But don't worry about all that," I say. "The police are on it. We have to trust they'll figure everything out."

"I guess."

I take a deep breath and tuck my hair back behind my ears. "So, how's school?" I ask.

"Fine," he says. "But . . ."

"But what?"

Jared sighs, letting out a whoosh of air, like a balloon being deflated. "I feel like I'm gonna fail bio."

"What?" I lean in closer. The edge of the table digs into my ribs.

Jared looks down and taps his fingers against his mug. "I don't know. It's just so hard. Not my thing."

"Did you have your first midterm yet?"

He nods. "Sixty-eight."

"Jesus, Jared. Why didn't you tell me?" I hiss. "I could have helped you."

Jared lolls his head back and half closes his eyes. "Come on. You're like perfect at this stuff."

I shake my head. I want him to know the truth, the *real* truth. I was always deemed the smart one by Newman children standards. We had both been at Cartwright Elementary through fifth grade. The classes were big and the expectations were low. But I was labeled *gifted* back in kindergarten with Miss Becky, when I had moved up a reading level before anyone else. So when Jared announced that he, too, had Miss Becky for kindergarten, I clasped my hands together at the dinner table. "You are so lucky," I had whispered to him. "Miss Becky is the best."

But Jared had a harder time with letters and numbers, at first. It would be another few years before he was actually diagnosed with dyslexia. He got into Gold Coast as part of their learning disability outreach program. No reduced tuition for him. Just the promise of being taken care of with small classes and specially trained teachers and tutors. My parents jumped at the chance. They never talked about how they found a way to pay for it. My guess was a second mortgage and a shit ton of debt. But back then in Miss Becky's class, he just couldn't keep up at the rate I had.

"Miss Becky doesn't like me," he said one day after school. His huge eyes filled with tears and spilled down his cheeks in big wet plunks.

"Of course she does!" I said to him, holding his hand and petting his hair.

"She doesn't," he said. "I'm not like you."

I didn't know what to say, so I just hugged his warm little body to mine, trying not to cry, too. We were not the same, I learned. That was the first time I realized there was actually a possibility that we could grow up to not have the same favorite foods or the same taste in books or the same grades. It was a horrifying thought, that our little lives could diverge at any point without warning. *Was this only the beginning?* I wondered.

But we were so similar with our saucer-size green-brown eyes and our shared hatred of mayo. We both loved the stars, thanks to Dad. As we grew, we began to look more and more alike, too. The only thing keeping us from being considered twins was our age. Our dark wavy hair curled in the same places. Even our arms sported the same freckles we turned into constellations every summer. *Cut from the same cloth,* Mom would say. *Two sides of the same coin.*

I look at him across the booth at Diane's now and I see all those years he spent trying to catch up to me, jumping over hurdles that seemed too high for him to reach in order to impress teachers like Miss Becky, to get into Gold Coast, to be friends with kids like Bryce at school. It's then I realize it must be exhausting trying to keep up with Jill Newman. Just like it was exhausting trying to keep up with Shaila Arnold.

"You'll bring it up," I say. "You're not going to fail. Maybe a C, sure, but that'll straighten itself out by the time you graduate." My brain starts calculating, trying to figure out what his average will be if he aces this semester's final with a little help. There's gotta be a bio answer key, or at least a study guide, in the Files. The C won't affect his overall GPA too badly by the time he's a second-semester junior. That's when it really counts.

"Easy for you to say," he mumbles as Diane drops giant plates in front of us. Jared lifts the sticky glass bottle of syrup and drenches his stack of pancakes in a thick, sweet stream.

"Not easy for me to say. I had so much help, you don't even know."

"Oh yeah? From who?"

Suddenly, I'm not hungry anymore and the eggs in front of me start to look like barf. "The Players . . ." I start, trying to figure out how to explain this to him. "It's just . . ."

I pause. I swear I feel a vibration in my pocket. *Rachel.* I whip my phone out under the table to check, but there's nothing. Phantom sirens. *Where is she?* I wonder. *Why hasn't she responded?* I slide my phone back into my pocket and look up at Jared, remembering what we were discussing, why we're here.

"C'mon, Jill. What?" He looks at me with one brow raised.

Something turns inside me and I feel the need to tell him everything, to fill him in on what's to come even though it's totally against the rules. But fuck the rules. Rachel broke them and it worked for me—at least for a little while. The fact that she hasn't answered my text, even though it was an arrow of pity lobbed her way, makes no difference right now. My brother needs to know what's coming. Maybe not everything, but at least the beginning. "Next week," I say. "You're gonna get invited to join the Players. It'll all make sense soon. But . . . it's more than parties and the best lunch table. It's a lifeline. A . . . group. I'm in it. So is Nikki. Shaila was, too. It's been around Gold Coast for decades and every year we bring in new freshmen. It's your turn now. You got in."

He crosses his arms and leans back, trying to hide his excitement, but not connecting the dots. "How's that gonna help me with bio?"

I sigh, exasperated. I'll have to show him. I pull my phone from my pocket and swipe until I find the app I'm looking for, the encrypted one that's only knowable by its green-and-gray icon. Within a few taps, I'm in. I set my phone down on the vinyl table and spin it around so the screen faces Jared. I drag my forefinger up. The titles are endless. Bio. Chem. AP US History. Calculus. French. Past SATs. Admissions officer database. African History. Nutrition 1. Nutrition 2. East Asian Studies. College-level Russian Literature. The list goes on forever.

Jared's eyes grow wide and his mouth drops open. I can see a piece of half-chewed pancake flop against his cheek. "This is the Players?" he asks, his voice a whisper.

I nod. "This is the Players."

By the time Nikki, Marla, and I get to the beach, the boys have the fire going a few feet in the air. A massive pile of wood sits next to the pit and they're passing around a bottle of Jameson.

"Jill!" Henry runs to meet us as we tread down the sand. It's damp and cold, squishing between my bare toes. We're all bundled up in our finest gorpcore attire. For some weird reason, expensive fleece half-zips and comfy beanies are the ultimate status symbol at Gold Coast. "You guys excited?" Henry asks.

"Yes," I say. "Gonna be the best intro night ever." And I mean it. I am ready to start fresh with a new class. With my brother. *Things are going to be different this year.* The bonfire burns higher as the rest of the Players file in and soon it's time. More bottles appear and our voices grow louder. My phone buzzes and my heart stops. *Of course Rachel would respond now.* I sneak a peek at the screen. It's Adam. A slow smile spreads across my face.

Have so much fun tonight. Take care of B.

Wish you were here, I type but then delete. *Always,* I say instead.

He responds in a second. *Thanks, Newman.*

A warmth spreads through my chest and I watch the sophomores light sparklers, making the whole beach look like a birthday cake. Henry's hand catches mine. His eyes shine with wonder and mischief, and I lean closer to him, shoving my shoulder under his armpit and burrowing my face against his fleecy chest.

"I wish Shaila was here," I whisper, surprising even myself.

Henry pulls me closer. "I know, babe."

My throat starts to burn and I'm desperate to test my luck.

"Henry, what if . . ." I start. "What if Graham didn't do it?"

Henry drops his arm from around my shoulders and shakes his head with a slow stoicism. "Come on, Jill," he says. "I thought we decided this was bullshit."

Before I can respond Nikki climbs onto a cement block near the fire. "They're here!" she yells. "Everyone, shut up!"

A hush washes over us. I glance quickly at Henry, trying to read him, but he turns away, toward the path that leads to the beach. Out they come. Like little ducklings, the eight freshmen ascend from behind tall, thick reeds. Jared walks in the middle, standing in between Bryce and Sierra. Her eyes are wild and unfocused, and she tries to smother a smile. They reach the fire and fan out in a line, facing us. The seven-foot kid, Larry Kramer, launches into a quad stretch, like he's preparing for sprints at basketball practice. I try to make eye contact with Jared, but he keeps his focus on Nikki, his gaze unwavering.

"As you may have guessed," Nikki says, taking her spot at the front, "you have been chosen by this year's senior class to be Players." Bryce nods and grins. He must have spoken to Adam. I wonder what he said.

"But that doesn't mean you *are* a Player," Nikki continues, echoing Jake Horowitz's words from three years ago. Coming from her they sound gentle and stern, not menacing or scary. It's the same voice she uses when speaking at all-school assemblies. She'd be an insanely good politician and she knows it. "It just means we think you could be. This year you'll be faced with a series of challenges, some fun, some . . . not so fun. If you make it through, if you choose to continue, then you'll be a Player. You'll reap the rewards and you'll endure the losses. You'll become part of a group that will have your back for life." Quentin shifts awkwardly on his feet next to me and lets out a puff of air. I grab his hand and he squeezes back.

"Are you ready?" Nikki asks, raising an eyebrow and her plastic cup.

Robert steps forward and hands Bryce an unmarked clear bottle. The little Miller takes a swig and coughs. He doesn't do as well as Shaila did but he passes it down the line until they're all nearly in fits.

"I remember my first beer," Robert shouts, his body lurching forward toward the freshmen. Sierra flinches.

The wind picks up and I shiver. Finally Jared looks over at me and his shoulders relax. Relief fills his face. But my excitement disappears when he brings the bottle to his mouth. It's already too familiar, seeing him like this. It feels wrong, torturous. I fight the urge to knock the jug from his hand and instead suck in my cheeks, turning my mouth into a fish face, just like we used to do when we were kids. His lips curl into a smile and he takes a sip from the bottle.

Shaila Arnold was one of those people who went by both her first and last name. *Shaila Arnold.* There were no other Shailas at Gold Coast. I don't even think there were any Arnolds. But nevertheless, when she was alive, that's what everyone called her. Mr. Beaumont, when he said her name in roll call. Big Keith during cast announcements. Only those close to her called her Shay, and only sometimes, when the moment was right. People who didn't know her, but speak of her now, often smush her name together like it's all one word. *Shailarnold.* That's how Sierra McKinley says it tonight during the first senior-freshman girl sleepover at Nikki's house a week after intro night. We did the same thing when I was a freshman. Back then it was a size-up-the-competition thing disguised as a get-to-know-you thing. A pre-pops slumber party to gain our trust before they broke us. *This year will be different,* I say over and over again to myself. *This year will be different.* It has to be.

"Shailarnold was your best friend, right?" Sierra asks while we sit at Nikki's kitchen island. Her legs are bare, save for a tiny pair of flannel shorts with lace detailing around the edges. Her oversize tee makes them nearly invisible when she stands.

"Yep," I say, trying not to show my disgust at hearing her name come from Sierra's mouth.

"I knew her, you know." Sierra brings her knees up to her chest and her eyes flit around Nikki's great room. From our perches on the bar stools, we can see everyone. "Westhampton Beach Club," she continues. "She and Kara Sullivan were my swim counselors."

Shaila and Kara had spent so many summers there, sailing and perfecting their backstrokes. It was where Shaila got her period for the first time in the summer between sixth and seventh grades. She described it in obsessive detail in one of her longest letters to me.

It's BROWN some days, she wrote. *It's so disgusting and I feel like a monster. I can't even talk to Kara about this. CAN YOU GET YOURS TOO, SO WE CAN BE IN IT TOGETHER?!?!?! PLEASE. I'M BEGGING YOU.*

Her wish was my command. The day after I opened her letter, I pulled down my cotton shorts to find a pool of thick, dark goo matting my underwear. It had seeped all the way through my shorts and I cried in the stall, thinking about how I had been walking around science camp with *blood stains* on my butt, in front of boys, while extracting samples from the pond, standing in the dining hall. I stayed there until my own counselor came over with a maxi pad as big as a diaper.

When I told Shaila, she was thrilled.

I'm going to buy us bright red headbands to wear on the first day of school so everyone knows we are WOMEN, she wrote in her next letter.

And she did. I wore mine begrudgingly, annoyed that I was forced to display my deep, dark secret like a badge of honor when really it seemed like a curse. Graham, who was still just a middle school asshole who hadn't murdered anyone yet, lost his shit when he saw us in the library. He pointed at our matching hair and laughed. "What are you? *Blood* sisters? *Gross!*" he called. "Don't get your bloody shit all over me!"

Shaila just laughed at him, waving at him like he didn't even matter. "Sorry, Graham. Guess you can't handle a *real* woman. Sucks to suck." Graham shuffled off, mumbling something under his breath. I wore that stupid headband with pride after that day. Any shame I had felt about my entry into adulthood disappeared, too.

They both seemed to have forgotten the whole incident by the time we entered high school, but for the rest of that year, Shaila was the fairy godmother of periods. She invested in dozens of red velvet headbands and whenever a classmate made the transition, she gifted them one. She even gave them to the quiet girls, the ones who got their PE credits fulfilled in badminton, and the horse girls who sat together in the library during lunch, playing with those creepy figurines. Shaila made it cool to go through that rite of passage. But she didn't realize what it would do to the girls who weren't there yet. Neither did I until I found Nikki crying in the locker room in the middle of eighth grade, devastated that everyone had a red headband but her. It took her until ninth grade to earn one.

All of that feels so far away now in Nikki's kitchen with a whole new set of girls to watch over. The responsibility feels like too much to bear. I look at Sierra and bite my tongue, forcing myself not to ask if she had already gotten her period, if she needed her own red headband. But it's hard to picture. She's small like a child, her skin taut against her bones.

I'm desperate to find a way out of the conversation. Nikki and Marla are spinning and dancing in front of the TV, leading a few desperate freshmen in some butchered Beyoncé choreography. Their giggles make me recoil.

"Can I ask you something?" Sierra asks. She leans in close like she's about to tell me that she has, indeed, begun to bleed this very second.

"Sure," I say.

"What really happens?" she asks, her eyes wide. "The challenges—"

"They're called pops." The condescension drips from my voice.

"Right," she says softly. "And all the rules. Initiation. The binder."

"What do you mean?"

"We all know about the good stuff—the app and everything, the parties, the connections—but . . ." She trails off. "I've heard stories."

My heart beats fast, a quick rhythm that hurts my chest.

"I just want to know what I'm getting myself into."

Guilt pumps through me. She's defenseless. Like a baby deer learning to walk. She can't be more than five feet even. I think of all the other girls, the juniors and sophomores who had asked the same questions. The ones who I had laughed at and whose concerns I had waved off. How they looked at me when they learned the truth. When the Toastmaster, always a guy, told them they had to do something, or else. How they came out either hardened or cracked after the fact. Then, how they looked at the next class of girls when it was their turn.

"You're going to be fine," I say with feigned disinterest. "This year will be different."

Sierra doesn't break her gaze, but her fingers clench around her thighs. "What does that mean?"

"Nikki's in charge," I say slowly, carefully. "This year will be different."

Sierra releases her skin and leaves behind little nail marks. She leans back and I hope she knows that's all she's going to get from me, at least today.

"I'm gonna get a drink." She hops off the stool and pads to the refrigerator. I look around the room again, at the nervous freshmen trying to impress us, my sweet friends trying to seem cool, elegant, old. I wonder how Jared's faring with the boys. Henry promised to look out for him and Bryce. I wonder what our friends are saying about us, how they answer when they're asked that same question. I hope they tell the truth.

My phone erupts without warning, a startling presence against my leg. I glance down and my breath hitches. Finally. It's the text I've been waiting for, the one I sort of hoped would never come. Suddenly, I'm light-headed and need to get out of this room, away from everyone.

I push open the front door. The cool October air winds through my hair and when I sit, the marble steps are like ice against my butt. I huddle around my phone, putting my body between it and the others, the ones I'm betraying.

Can you come to the city? We need to meet in person.

A bubble emerges, a signal that Rachel is typing, but then it disappears like an unfulfilled promise.

When? I ask.

I clutch the phone close to my chest and resist the urge to gnaw on a stray cuticle. But she responds quickly.

Friday at 8 pm? 425 Ave. D. Buzz 6E when you're here.

It's an almost impossible ask. But my brain fizzles and my fingers feel numb as they float over the screen. I bite my lip so hard I taste blood. Then I punch out the answer, knowing it will change everything.

I'll be there.

NINE

IT'S THE LONGEST week of all time. Every class spans a century. By lunch on Friday I'm a ball of nerves, rigid and flinchy all over. When I take my seat at the Players' Table, Henry plants a wet kiss on my cheek and I jump, nearly sending my turkey club and raw cookie dough flying off the tray.

"You okay?" he asks. His mouth turns into a frown.

I muster a smile and nod. "Just nervous for the French midterm. Last period."

"Did you look in the Files?" he asks, ripping a bite out of his BLT.

I spent the last week cramming but had memorized an old study guide as insurance last night. "Just hoping I have it right."

"You'll do great, babe. You always do." He flashes me a smile and playfully nudges my shoulder.

Robert plunks his tray down and turns to Henry without looking my way. "Dude," he sneers. "Fresh meat are gonna get *destroyed*."

Henry laughs into his sandwich. "Which one?" I elbow him

in the stomach and he throws me his *I'm sorry* face. But I just shake my head. Whenever they talk this way it just makes me think of all the things that were probably said about me over the years. My shoulders stiffen.

"Sierra McKinley, dude. She's totally sucking up, commenting on all my Instas. Shooting me looks in the hall." Robert crams a French fry in his mouth. "I'm gonna make her life hell with pops. She'll do whatever I want."

"You sound like a dick," I say.

Robert rolls his eyes. "What are you, a cop?"

I glance at Henry for support, but suddenly a wilted piece of lettuce becomes super interesting. "Whatever," I mumble. I know I should push back but I'm not looking for a fight. Not today.

"Gotta do one last cram," I say through clenched teeth. I rise and turn my back to them, wishing I had the courage to scream. To tear them both apart. Instead, I walk away.

I've just stepped out in the hall when I see Nikki and Quentin coming toward me. "Whoa, wait up," Quentin says. "Where you going?"

I shake my head and inhale sharply. "Robert's talking so much shit about the freshmen." Nikki's face contorts, pissed.

"Sorry," I say, but she rolls her shoulders back like it doesn't matter, like she doesn't care that he's already forgotten her. She flips her hair over her shoulder and readjusts her blazer.

"That's just how he is," Quentin says. "He'll get bored with it soon."

"We said we would change things," I sputter. "And so far, we've done everything the same."

"We will," Nikki says, her mouth in a straight line. "Just relax for now. We'll figure it out together. We're in this together."

"We are, right?" I say, pleading with them.

Quentin wraps both of us in a hug. "Of course."

I let myself believe him—it's easier than not. Their supportive, sweet faces make me want to tell them the truth. "There's something else," I say quietly, motioning for them to lean in close. "I can't stop thinking about Graham. What if he's, you know, innocent? What if someone else killed Shaila?"

The question hangs heavy between us. Quentin and Nikki glance quickly at each other. "Jill, come on," she says. "We agreed. It's over. Let's let it lie."

"But what—" I start. Out of everyone, I thought she would understand.

"Let. It. Lie," Nikki says through gritted teeth.

Quentin shakes his head. "It's just not worth it to get involved. We don't need everyone finding out what happened that night."

My whole body tenses, but I force my head to nod, to pretend like I agree and that I, too, will let this whole thing go. "Yeah, you're right."

"Come on, let's get you back to the caf." Quentin swings an arm over my shoulder and I let them drag me back to the Players' Table where I zone out for another twenty-three minutes, wondering how the hell I ended up here.

When French rolls around, I breathe easy as I realize the midterm has the exact same questions as the study guide I memorized. I breeze through the first section, then etch out a translation. Thank God I'd actually studied on my own for this part. If I only get a few points off here, I'll land a 96, just what I need to solidify a 95 average for the semester. Perfect.

When Madame Mathias calls time, I drop my exam on her desk and retreat into the hallway.

"Did you see Jill Newman?" I hear a voice say behind me. "She was done like twenty minutes in."

"Always," someone else says. "I heard she and that whole stupid table have all the answer keys from, like, years ago. It's bullshit."

"None of them are actually smart."

"So fucking unfair."

"They're all gonna get into Harvard or Yale, too. They always do. Stealing our spots with fake-ass work."

"Ridiculous." Heat creeps up my neck and I peek around my shoulder to find two girls from the debate team shooting daggers at my back. They clamp their mouths shut when they see me and quickly turn on the heels of their leather loafers, retreating in the other direction.

My skin burns with shame, a reminder that I don't deserve what I've been given. But even if they don't know what I've been through to get here, I know it comes with a cost. I paid my dues. I suffered, too. They don't know I'm here on scholarship, that every day at Gold Coast is a fight.

Tears prick my eyes and I blink them back, eager to get out of here, to do what I've been waiting to do all week.

When the final bell rings, I push the heavy metal doors open and feel the cold wind against my face, sea salt blowing into my hair. It bites. But I'm finally free. Until a heavy arm slinks over my shoulder, throwing me off my step. I fall sideways, right into Henry.

"There you are. I was looking for you after lunch." His fingertips graze my chest, hardening my nipple, even beneath layers of clothes. I shiver. "Sorry Robert was such a shit. You know that's just how he is."

"That's not an excuse," I say. I just want to forget about

Robert's comments, what those debate girls said, and everything inside Gold Coast's walls. "But it would be nice if you could stand up for me."

"You're totally right," Henry says, throwing his head back. "I'm sorry. Next time, okay?" He leans down and his lips touch my forehead quickly, almost chaste, before changing the subject. "What's up for tonight?"

I had hoped to avoid this—lying to him. A trapdoor opens inside me and I will my stomach not to drop through it. "I gotta do some family stuff," I say.

"Really?" Henry cocks his head. "I thought Jared was going over to Topher's. The juniors are throwing that whole Super Pong thing."

Shit. I try to picture my brother standing behind a beer pong table covered in dozens of red cups, as he tries to sink a little plastic ball. It isn't so hard to imagine anymore. "Just a me and Mom thing. Gotta put in some quality time, you know?"

He nods. "Totally. See you tomorrow?"

I swallow hard and force a smile. "For sure."

It's 7:59 p.m. and I'm standing in front of what must be Rachel Calloway's apartment. Only two miles from her parents' fancy Tribeca loft, her front door looks janky, like anyone could walk right in without a key. Weekend revelers shout at one another from the many bars that line the street and notes of piss waft over from a phone booth that looks like it hasn't been used since the nineties. There must be dozens of people laughing out here, smoking cigarettes and huddling close together, but I've never been more alone. I pull my parka closed and peer at the cracked intercom until I find 6E.

Buzz. A deep, instantly familiar voice crackles. "Hello?"

"It's Jill Newman," I say, suddenly feeling my nerves in my throat. Do I sound young? Can she sense the sweat collecting between my fingers?

"You made it," she says. "Watch the steps, they're steep as fuck."

The lock unlatches like a switchblade and I push inside, coming face-to-face with a set of rickety stairs that look like a fire hazard. She wasn't kidding.

I dart up, moving one foot in front of the other, afraid if I stop now, I'll stop forever. And finally, when I reach the top floor, Rachel is standing barefoot, leaning with her back propped up against a purple doorframe. She's wearing baggy acid wash jeans and a thin, nearly see-through white T-shirt. Her hair is wavy and shaggy, with big, voluminous layers hanging around her face. She's somehow prettier than she was in high school, vivid and kinetic with sparkly dark eyes and round pink cheeks. I want to reach out and touch one finger to her chin, just to see if she's real.

"Jill Newman," she says slowly, cocking her head. I wonder how she sees me. If I look older or different. She didn't stick around for the after, to see how everything changed or didn't.

"Rachel Calloway."

"C'mon in." Rachel turns and leads me into her apartment. The space is tiny, and I can see the entire place from the entryway. Stacks of books line the brick wall, and a mid-century maroon couch, covered in thick wool blankets, has been shoved to one side. Her walls are bare save for an oversize watercolor painting of bold, abstract flowers that's been tacked to the plaster with thumbnails. It looks like an unfinished art project. Leafy plants hang in macramé swings on either side of the sofa.

"Welcome to the real world," she says, offering me a smile. "Want some tea?"

I nod and follow Rachel into her kitchen, which is really just a narrow hallway that happens to have both a stove and a fridge.

She squeezes honey into two ceramic mugs painted with outlines of curvy female bodies. Their nipples are just pink points.

"Cute," I say.

"Thanks. My girlfriend made them."

I try to hide my surprise but Rachel laughs. "Yep, queer. Started telling people a few years ago," she says. "I guess no one from Gold Coast would know." She pauses. "My girlfriend's name is Frida. She's a coder. Lives around the block."

"That's cool," I say. I mean it, too. She and Adam never really seemed to fit together. But obviously I thought that.

"It's good to see you."

"You too," I respond because what else is there to say? Standing in front of Rachel makes me long for the past, for the months leading up to Shaila's death and our initiation. I want to burrow inside those weeks when we were all bonded together. Even when it felt like torture, when we were pushed to the absolute brink and I thought I would explode from the adrenaline and the fear, I knew, I hoped, it was worth it. We were holding on to a thread that was always at risk of unraveling.

A sunshine yellow kettle whistles and Rachel turns away. As she pours the hot water into the mugs, I spot faint raised scars, white as stone, lining the backs of her arms and the nape of her neck. Some are thin, as if someone drew a sewing needle over her skin, and others are thick and fat, scary.

She turns and follows my eyes. "Ah," she says softly. "Had a bad year after everything. Coulda been worse."

It never occurred to me that Rachel also suffered, that she

had been a victim of what Graham did or didn't do. Her only crime was loyalty, I guess. And she paid for it, too.

"Come on," she says, picking up the steaming mugs and walking past me to the couch. "Let's get this over with."

The cushions sag with our weight and I wait for her to start, trying hard not to be the one to fill the silence. Seconds pass, maybe a minute, before Rachel stands again, her fingers tangling themselves together. "Wait a sec," she says.

She retreats behind the bedroom door and I hear paper rustling, weight shifting from one foot to another. She finally emerges holding a thick envelope, the old-school kind with ruled lines and little cardboard circles bound together with tiny red string.

"Open this," she says, and hands it to me.

I unwind the thread and slide out a stack of uneven papers. It's a whole jumble of random shit. Rachel stays quiet and I set the folder aside. I pick up the first page. Graham's transcript from freshman year. An 87 average. Good thing he didn't need a scholarship. The next page is a thick piece of cardstock covered in a full-bleed glossy image of Shaila and Graham. Their mouths stretch into wide smiles. His arm wraps around her shoulder and she leans her head against his. Their white teeth glimmer and their navy Gold Coast blazers are perfectly pressed. No grass stains or stray crumbs. I look at their eyes and shiver, dropping the rest of the papers in a mess on the floor.

"Shit," I say. I've never seen this picture. It looks like it was taken at a lacrosse game, like they're leaning against the bleachers. I was probably only a few feet away.

"Never made it into the yearbook," Rachel says. Her lips curl up, her attempt at a joke. "But it was always my favorite."

Shaila stares back at me. She was so young. She wasn't done

yet. My throat is dry and my fingers clench around the edges of the paper. It's all so messed up, that Graham's alive and Shaila's dead. I want to hurl my mug at Rachel and her smug little face, for bringing me here, taunting me with memories I had tried viciously to forget. I pull at the edges of the photo, wanting to rip Shaila from Graham's grasp. Then in one crushing tear the sheet gives, leaving me with just Shaila's smile. I let Graham float to the floor.

"I have other copies," Rachel says.

That fuels my fury and I leap to my feet, knocking my knee against a mug. It wobbles before crashing to the floor, a river of ceramic shards and sticky liquid. I don't say sorry because I'm not. Instead, I open my mouth, ready to spit fire. But Rachel has other plans.

"Sit down, Jill."

And for some reason I do.

"This is what I wanted to show you." She reaches down into the heap on the floor and pulls out a single sheet of white paper. Black letters dance on the page, but I can't focus when she places it in my lap.

"What is this?"

"Look," Rachel says, tucking her feet under her butt. "When they took Graham away, it wasn't like they examined any *evidence*. They took his word for it. One and done. Case closed. They didn't even test his clothes or look at Ocean Cliff, or anything. You think the Gold Coast police were prepared for a *murder*? They're barely able to bust a party up the Cove."

I remember that, how nothing really *happened*. The Arnolds showed up at the station with some man in a black suit, a lawyer. It was all so muffled, so adult. And then it was over.

"There wasn't a question if he did it or not," Rachel says. "Everyone just *assumed* he did because that's what he said. But he was so blackout. We all were, you know." She shakes her head. "He didn't remember any of it. He didn't give any details. No one asked. And now, he still can't remember anything. So how could he have done it? There's just no way."

I look up and Rachel's eyes are red. Her lips are pursed, and her hands are wrapped tightly around her mug. She inhales deeply, not glancing at the blooming stain I've made on the floor. "I just turned twenty-one," she says. "Which means I finally have access to my trust. I can pay for the lawyers my parents decided not to get. I can fund Graham's rebuttal on my own. We're gonna fight it." Her voice is scratchy and raw, full of fire. "We're testing everything. His clothes, some rocks, they've all just been sitting in the Gold Coast station in one of those stupid fucking boxes, taking up space. And we just found out something big. Something that could change everything."

"What?" I whisper.

"You know all that blood on his shirt?" she asks. "That was his. He cut his stomach, deep. Soaked right through. Down to his shorts. But none of it was Shaila's. It was all Graham's. He didn't touch her. Not at all." She points to the piece of paper in my hand and I look down, finally understanding what I'm holding. The results of the blood test.

I open my mouth to respond but I come up blank. It's suddenly hot in here. I'm boiling. If I peel my skin away, maybe another layer will be revealed.

Rachel grabs my hands in hers and clenches them both tightly, bringing her angular face close to mine. Her skin is glowy, her pores tiny. I wonder if she's ever had a pimple.

"He didn't do it," she says. "I know he didn't."

But I shake my head. How can this be true? The past can't be rewritten, it just can't.

"Look," Rachel says, finally releasing my hands. I pull them back to my body and wrap them around my knees. "You don't have to believe me just yet. But think about it. Then maybe you'll want to help us."

"Help you?" I spit. The idea is insane. Ludicrous. "How would I even do that?"

"You were *there*, Jill. You're the only one who would understand. Who would listen. You loved Shaila as much as Graham did." Rachel squeezes her eyes shut and thin lines crinkle down her lids. "Adam always said you were fearless. More than the others. That you were smart and steady and good."

My stomach flips with the thought of Rachel and Adam talking about me all those years ago. What else did he say? Did he really believe all that? Then I remember what he said at Diane's. *Rachel is nuts.*

"You're the only one who would want justice for her," she continues. "Who would be willing to fight for it. Just think about it."

The room feels small, like a dollhouse. Her apartment is closing in on me and I notice for the first time that there are no windows in her living room. I wonder how people *live* in New York City. These homes aren't made for that. They're made for survival. "I need to go," I say.

I push open her flimsy door and start down the stairs. Rachel calls behind me. "Just think about it."

I don't stop until I reach the bottom floor, where I twist the tarnished metal doorknob and suddenly, finally, break free. Her street smells of city garbage and sticky beer, but I breathe in deeply, trying to swallow as much air as I can, to shock my system, to know the last hour wasn't a dream.

I'm miles from the train station, even farther from home, but I start walking. Anywhere that's far away from clinical terms like *evidence* and ragged, hollow half possibilities.

I turn her words over in my head until they become bland mush, and then again until I start to see her motives clearly. Rachel doesn't want justice for Shaila. She wants it for *Graham*. And if I believe her, it means someone else we know is guilty. Which truth is worse?

TEN

IT'S EASY TO pretend that Rachel never hit me up. That she didn't plant life-altering theories inside my brain. That she's still cemented in my mind as Adam's ex, the sister of a killer, the enemy—not a potential coconspirator.

All I need to do is agonize about college decisions, like every other senior. I'm due to hear back from Brown in a week, and the only antidote to the stress, it seems, is to go into full Player mode. Obsess, as I have for the last three years, over the weekly check-ins and insane ideas for pops, all the *work* that Nikki huffs and puffs about now.

After intro night, we told the freshmen to clear their weekends for the rest of the year. They were only exempt from Player stuff if they had a family emergency or a Bat Mitzvah or something. For their first test, they had to memorize facts about the Players and recite them back to us on the beach behind Nikki's house. Wrong answers resulted in being squirted with ketchup and mustard. Rinse-offs in the frigid bay were optional. The next week we made them cook an entire Thanksgiving meal at Quentin's after eating pot brownies. Bryce set off the fire alarm with a burnt turkey but Jared nailed the brussels sprouts.

And last week, on the first Saturday in November, Henry devised a new task. He made them wash the Players' cars while singing my favorite eighties songs on repeat. I threw some Stevie Nicks solo tracks on the playlist. Cher made an appearance, obviously. All along, they were forced to do little things, like carry Player packs—little fanny packs filled with Player essentials: Juuls, mints, tampons, pencils, mini Snickers, condoms, Advil. They were our walking drugstores. "Gum me," I'd say when passing Sierra McKinley in the hall.

They were on call 24/7, available to do morning runs to Diane's, to clean out our gym lockers, to do basically anything we wanted. Nikki even made Larry Kramer sort her laundry one Sunday just to see him blush when he folded her lacy thongs. It was easy stuff, harmless shit that brought them together as a class. Nothing they wouldn't experience in college times ten.

Still, I dreaded these tasks when I was a freshman. I was always so sure I would mess it all up. Shaila's reaction was more annoyed than scared. She would whine like hell when Rachel would text her, requesting a dozen pow-do—those totally addicting little powdered donuts from Diane's—at 9 p.m. on a Tuesday. We'd go together, of course, making up excuses to our parents, and as we rode there on our bikes, Shaila would call out behind her, "Nothing brings you closer than being made to feel like someone's little bitch!"

That was the unofficial Player motto.

There was only one time when I was really, seriously scared by one of the supposed-to-be-easy pops. It was a mild Friday night just before Thanksgiving and Rachel texted, asking for a case of Bud Light and a pack of Twizzlers. Shaila and I rode our bikes to the gas station next to Diane's, which is still famous for selling underage kids beer on the DL.

Shaila made a beeline for the refrigerators, retrieved what we needed, and placed the cardboard box full of cans right up on the counter without uttering a word. The cashier looked her over once, twice, and then nodded. She handed him a crisp bill, smiled sweetly, and said, "Keep the change."

I had been standing in the candy aisle with my fists clenched, holding my breath. When Shaila pulled the beer off the counter, I let out a rush of air. But then the bell on the door chimed.

"Jill? Shaila?"

The voice was deep and familiar. I spun around and my heart sank. Mr. Beaumont was standing right in front of us, his collar askew and his shirt tails untucked. He looked . . . cute. Not like a teacher. Not like the person who was about to ruin my life and get me thrown out of Gold Coast Prep for buying beer.

"Hey, Beau," Shaila said first, casually. She held the cardboard box in both hands and didn't bother to hide it. "How you doing tonight?"

"Not as well as you girls," he said, laughing. His cheeks were flushed and he ran a hand through his hair.

Shaila giggled. "Are you gonna rat us out?"

Mr. Beaumont reached into his pocket and pulled out an empty cigarette pack. "Just here for a refill."

"Weingarten hates smokers," Shaila said in a singsong voice.

"I won't tell if you won't?" Mr. Beaumont cocked his head and his mouth turned into an amused smirk.

Shaila smiled. "There's no one like you at Prep," she said.

Mr. Beaumont laughed again and shook his head. "You too, Shaila."

My heart was beating fast, like it was going to burst out of my chest.

"See you tomorrow." Shaila skipped out of the gas station and I darted behind her, making a run for my bike. My arms were shaking as I gripped the handles.

"Come on!" Shaila shouted as she took off down the main drag toward the water, the case of beer rattling in her bike's basket. But before I started pedaling, I glanced back. Mr. Beaumont stood right outside the storefront. He lit a cigarette and watched us ride away.

When we dropped off the provisions at Rachel's, Shaila detailed every moment of our run-in, amping up the drama and tension. "We were almost expelled!"

Rachel rolled her eyes. "At least for a good cause, right?" She laughed, cracking open a can. She tossed one to Tina Fowler, who sat next to her on the big leather sofa, her strawberry-blonde hair piled on top of her head. "All these pops have a purpose, you know. To make you stronger. To bond you together forever." Rachel would say that over and over throughout the year. They all did. And so we believed it and said it, too. "Nothing brings you closer than being made to feel like someone's little bitch."

Tonight's event is one of the bigger ones, though. When we were freshmen they called it Showtime. But now we just refer to it as "the Show," and it always happens a few weeks before seniors are due to hear back from their first round of college applications. That way everyone is on fire, ready to unleash hell and expend all that frustrated energy. Kind of messed up. Even Henry's a little tense when he picks me up to take me to Nikki's. Neither of us bring up Brown or Wharton.

"Thank God you're here," Nikki says, answering the door

in a rose-colored gauzy maxi dress, even though it's freezing outside. "I need help!"

"With what?" I push past her and into the kitchen, ready to raid whatever snacks she has already poured into bowls. Henry trails behind me.

"This."

I grab a handful of Cheez-Its and turn. "What the . . ."

Nikki has forgone the casual setups of Showtimes past, and has instead turned her living room into an arena, complete with stadium seating. In front of the massive TV, she's built a makeshift stage out of crates, and covered the whole thing in glittery fabric.

"This isn't Broadway, Nikki. They're just reading corny sex scenes we've all heard a million times before." I roll my eyes. The scripts had been handed down for years, laminated in the Toastmaster binder. But every senior class tweaked them just a bit, adding a new line of dialogue here, some dramatic stage direction there. According to Jake Horowitz, they were *actual* scenes from sex tapes Players made back in the nineties when camcorders were a thing. But he only said that when he was trying to convince us that the pops used to be *so* much worse.

Nikki balls her hands into fists and stamps her foot. "I want this to be better! Remember last year, no one could hear the stupid undies because everyone was laughing so hard. It was way too easy."

"Whatever."

The doorbell rings and Nikki just stares at me. "Can you get that?"

"Sure, your highness," I joke. Nikki stomps away, unamused. Henry rolls his eyes.

"Whaddup, Jill!" Robert yells, clearly already a few deep. Quentin and Marla are right behind him.

"Whoa, sick," says Marla.

"At least *someone* gets my vision." Nikki stares daggers at me.

I relent. "What can I do to help?" Nikki's face softens and she starts rattling off instructions for how to set up the bar and which dimmers should be set on timers.

"C'mon," Marla whispers to me. "I'll help you."

I mouth *thank you* to her and we retreat to the far side of the living room to stack plastic cups and dump ice into buckets.

"She in a mood tonight?" Marla asks. Her hazel eyes are rimmed in thick liner and her nearly fluorescent hair is tied into a knot high on her head.

I snort and rip open a bag of ice. "Seems that way."

Marla shakes her head. "Let's just get this one over with." Her gold hoop earrings jangle as she leans over the bar. Marla's always been the steady one, the one who calls us on our crap. Perhaps because she's less invested. She knows this is temporary. Out of anyone, she would be the one to root out the bullshit, which makes me wonder if she would understand why I went to talk to Rachel, if she has questions, too.

"I actually wanted to ask you something," I say, lowering my voice.

"Shoot," she says.

"I can't stop thinking about Shaila," I start. "About Graham. Don't you think it's insane no one wants to talk about how he could be innocent?" I hold my breath and Marla stops lining up bottles on the bar. She turns to face me, her head cocked to one side.

"One hundred percent insane," she says. "But that's Gold

Coast. No one wants to stir anything up. We all just pretend like everything is perfect all the time."

"Aren't you curious?" I ask. I pick at a cuticle on my thumb.

"Of course," Marla says. "But let me be real with you. Nothing you or I say or do will change anything. We're not Arnolds or Millers or Garrys. We're just lucky to be here." Marla's face softens and she resumes stacking cups. "My mom works double shifts at the hospital to make sure I can go to Prep. We haven't taken a vacation in a decade. Why do you think all my brothers went to Cartwright? My parents are investing everything they have in *me*. My mom prays every single night that I'll get into Dartmouth. The last thing they need is for me to get caught up in some *Law and Order* nonsense a few months before graduating."

After more than three years of friendship, I can't believe I don't know this about Marla, that we're both buried under an avalanche of expectations. But something stops me from telling her that. Instead I reach out and squeeze her hand. "You're so right."

"We'll be out of here soon," she says. "But until then, we just have to keep pretending everything's okay."

I nod and try to push images of Shaila and Graham and all that thick, dark blood out of my head. My chest tightens and I clench my fists into little balls.

Nikki's doorbell explodes.

"They're here!" she yells. "Let's get this shit going!"

The door opens and a stream of Players enter Nikki's living room. Suddenly, it's a party. Nikki's smile grows wider every time someone compliments her set design and I can't help but be annoyed. *It's just the Show.* I don't know why she feels the need to go all out.

A tuft of dark hair catches my eye. "Jared!" His eyes grow bright with recognition and I swear the muscles in his face relax. I push my way through the crowd. Bryce stands next to him and they both break into laughter. "What?" I ask.

Jared blushes an ungodly shade of red, but Bryce, with his Miller swagger, leans in close. "Just getting ready for our performance," he says.

"Which one do you have?" I ask.

"The threesome," Bryce says with a smirk.

Jared breaks into giggles. "I may need you to leave the room, Jill. Way too awk." He takes a long sip of beer and I close my fist to stop from knocking the can out of his hand.

"You guys will be fine. Just make a joke out of it. That's all anyone wants to see."

Bryce laughs. "We got this. Right, J?"

"Hell yeah." They slam their beers together, spilling liquid onto the rug.

"Players, assemble!" Nikki's voice rings out over the room, and the undies scatter to their seats. "Move." Her voice is sharp like a razor as she shoves her way to the couch. "Seniors only."

"Ugh. Dictator much?" Topher Gardner says. He had already planted his butt in the best seat, where the two sides of the L-shape meet.

"You heard the lady," Robert growls.

Topher rolls his eyes and runs a hand through his dark buzzcut. But he relents and slides onto the floor. Nikki kicks at him with her wedge heel. "Get me a drink, Toph."

"And I thought I was already initiated," he jokes.

"Do it," Nikki seethes through clenched teeth. Her face is red and splotchy and she narrows her eyes at him. I make a note to keep quiet for the rest of the night. To stay out of her way.

"Sit with me," Henry says, as if reading my mind. "Over here. C'mon."

I follow him to the other end of the couch. We take our seats while Nikki presses a few buttons on the remote, dimming the lights and creating a pseudo spotlight at the front of the room.

"Scene one!" she calls out. "Places!"

Larry Kramer pushes himself to his feet and lumbers to the front of the room. He clears his throat and drains the can in his hand. "Oh shit," he starts. "I'm horny."

Henry erupts in laughter next to me. That didn't take long. "This one is always hilarious," he whispers. I know I should be giggling, enjoying watching Larry be humiliated. But a sinking feeling creeps into my stomach. I want to crawl out of my skin.

Larry continues, reading different "ooh" and "aah" sounds from a piece of paper, while the rest of the group chucks potato chips, crumpled napkins, and empty plastic shot glasses in his direction. I watch through parted fingers and take another sip of my drink, trying to fight the churning nausea deep in my stomach. This seemed more fun last year.

Larry clears his throat again and comes to the natural end of his scene. His face is crimson. "Uh," he says. "Thank you."

Topher erupts from the ground and throws his wide, meaty fist into the air. "Woo-hoo, Kramer! All-star whacker-offer!"

"Seven feet of rawness!" Robert yells.

I take a peek at Nikki but avoid making eye contact. Her eyes are locked on Sierra McKinley, who shifts nervously in her cross-legged seat, whispering to another freshman. Both of their faces grow pale.

"Next!" Nikki calls out.

Sierra stands, and so do Jared and Bryce. "I don't know if I can watch this," I whisper to Henry.

Henry squeezes my knee. "You only have to stay for a sec," he goads. "Then go get a drink or something."

I nod and clasp my hands together, bracing to watch my baby brother embarrass the shit out of himself. Because of me. Because I brought him here.

"Action, losers!" Nikki shrieks.

"Well, hi there, boys," Sierra recites in a small, high voice. "What are you doing here by the pool?"

"We're lifeguards this summer," Bryce says, lowering his voice about an octave. "Wanna take a dip?"

"Oh, definitely," she says. "I'm so thrilled you're here to keep me safe."

The stilted dialogue continues and I begin to relax. This won't be so bad.

"Boring!" Nikki yells, tossing a plastic cup toward the front of the room. Robert wraps an arm around her shoulder and leans into her ear to whisper something. Nikki's face breaks into a smile and she nods furiously. "Act it out!" she cheers. "Act it out!"

To my horror, the rest of the room begins chanting the same three words. "Act it out! Act it out!"

I can't sit still anymore. I reach over to Nikki and put one hand on her bare ankle. "Nikki, chill out," I whisper. "You're going too far."

With a flick of her foot, she shakes me off. She doesn't even look my way as she continues cheering. "Act it out! Act it out!"

Only Quentin is silent beside me, staring in wide-eyed confusion as the rest of the room turns into a mob. Jared, Bryce, and Sierra freeze, unsure of how to proceed.

I shake my head at Jared, hoping he can read my mind. *No,* I think. *You don't have to do this.*

But Bryce takes the lead and moves to stand behind Sierra.

He nods for Jared to shift in front of her. As the room gets louder and louder, so does the throbbing in my head. Sierra's face turns red and puffy and I have to leave.

I heave myself off the couch and push my way through the clump of sophomores in folding chairs, still hollering at what's going down in front of them.

The back door is only a few feet away and the relief I feel when I push it open is so overwhelming. I sink to my knees on the wooden deck and lean my back against the house. I try to steady my breathing and look up. But the clouds are blocking out the stars. I squeeze my eyes shut and try to hear my heart beat. *Breathe,* I tell myself. *Breathe.*

The door opens behind me and breezy fabric passes over my head. Nikki.

"What's your deal?" Her words are loud and sharp. It's a side of her I've never seen. And it makes me want to run.

"It's too much," I whisper. "You're humiliating them. That's my brother."

Nikki takes a step forward, towering over me.

"This isn't like you," I say. But her face is stone.

"Do you remember what happened when we had Showtime?" she asks.

"Of course." I got off easy, reading out some stupid softcore scene with Quentin. We were last and everyone was so wasted at that point that no one even realized we were speaking. They had basically lost interest and it was over in sixty seconds flat.

"It was the absolute worst," she says, her voice softening. I rack my brain to remember Nikki's part, but I can't. I can only picture Shaila hooting and hollering, moaning in her deep, gravelly voice with such over-the-top hilarity that everyone cheered. "I was with Robert," Nikki continues. "We were almost at the end when Jake Horowitz got up from the back of the room." She stops. "You don't remember, do you?" I shake my head and bite my lip. Wind gusts from the ocean in the distance and a shiver runs up my spine.

"Ugh," Nikki says with disgust. "Jake shoved Robert back into the crowd and said, 'This is how it's done, loser! This is how you screw her!'" Tiny tears appear in the corner of Nikki's eyes and the memory floods my brain. He had mimed doing all sorts of things with Nikki in front of everyone, and afterward, she disappeared for the rest of the night. Shaila finally dragged her out of the Calloways' third-floor bathroom when it was time to go home. Nikki never said how much it stung. How ashamed she must have felt. How we did nothing to stop it. We let it happen to her.

"Nikki," I start, stumbling to my feet.

But she cuts me off. "The boys were *always* in charge. It's our turn to make the rules," she says. "If we can take it, so can they. Look how we turned out? Strong as hell. Brilliant bitches. We're doing them a favor."

I know she's wrong. So, so wrong. But looking at her beautiful, furious face, I know there's nothing I can say that will change her mind. She's my friend. My *best* friend now. I just have to stay.

I say nothing and Nikki takes that to mean I'm on her side. She turns her chin up and retreats back into the house, leaving me alone in the cold night. I squeeze my eyes shut and will this all to be over, for graduation to come in an instant, for all of this to wash away.

A small vibration hums against my leg. I pull out my phone and see Rachel's name. My stomach flips.

I know it's been a while, but what do you think? Are you down to help us? We need you, Newman.

I stare at the words turning blurry on the screen. Maybe I need them, too.

ELEVEN

WHEN I GET home that night, I gaze at the stars on my ceiling. I'm so tired, but sleep won't come. I try to remember the moments before everything changed. Before I became scared. Of the Players, and, more so, myself. What were we capable of? How far could we be pushed? How much would we sacrifice? When did my world shift?

It always comes back to one night in November of freshman year. It was a Friday, warmer than it should have been. The day after Thanksgiving. I remember because I had apple pie for breakfast and I could still taste the thick, sweet filling on my lips when Adam texted.

Be ready at 9, Newman. We're having a night.

My skin tingled. I knew he was dating Rachel, but he was planning to hang out with *me*. It didn't matter that the Calloways were in the Hamptons for the holiday. Or that Adam and his buddies had spent the past few weeks embarrassing me and my friends, forcing us to be available constantly. That night he sought me out on his own.

Okay, I responded. *Should I bring my Player pack?*

Nope. Night off. You deserve it.

The rest of the day was a slog and by 9, I had started to freak out. *Where were we going? What was going to happen?* When Mom asked me what I was up to, I just said hanging out with Adam. She didn't ask questions. That was a plus, of course, having my parents trust that Adam wouldn't lead me into something dark and dangerous.

Finally, I heard the familiar notes of crashing guitar chords coming from his Mercedes.

"Bye, Mom," I called.

I skipped out the door and forced myself to slow my walk so I wouldn't sprint to the passenger side. But when I went to pull the door open, Jake was there, too. He rolled down the window and flashed a sly smile.

"Get in the back, Newman."

Shame warmed my neck and my skin felt sticky. I sunk into the leather and tried to catch Adam's eye. But he kept his gaze straight ahead. I leaned forward to make out what they were saying above the music, but it was hopeless. Their voices were drowned out by the wailing chorus coming from the stereo.

So, I sat back and stared out the window, trying to figure out what to do with my hands. It was a short ride, though, and soon we were back at Adam's house.

"Fam's in the city," he said. "Come on." He motioned for Jake and me to follow him to the big wraparound porch.

I took a seat on the swing and felt the floor shift as it rocked me back and forth, floating in space. Adam sank down next to me and the wood creaked.

Jake propped himself up on a wicker armchair and pulled out a bottle of something dark from his jacket pocket.

"Here, Newman," he said.

I took a sip and it tasted like poison. Then I took another and forced myself not to grimace.

"Told ya she could take it," Adam said. He nudged my shoulder with his and I tried to smirk, like I thought this little get-together was so normal that it was boring. Adam reached for the bottle in my lap.

"All right, kid. You must be wondering why you're here," he said.

Before I could speak, Jake chimed in. "We're meeting with everyone individually before we hit you guys with the harder pops."

Makes sense, I thought, though I wondered why I was alone with them, why they didn't wait to do it when Rachel, Tina, and the others were around, too.

"We just want to hang out, see what makes you tick, who you really are," Jake continued. "Adam here has told me all about you, but I want to get to know you myself. So spill it, Jill," Jake said, leaning forward and resting his elbows on his knees. "What's your deal?

Adam tapped me on the shoulder with the bottle and I took another swig. Courage. The taste was getting more bearable and my throat had almost stopped burning. So I started to speak. I launched into some stupid word vomit about how I love astrophysics and how I had spent the summer up in Cape Cod with the best telescope on the East Coast. Adam looked down and kicked against the floorboards, sending us swinging back and forth. The momentum turned my stomach.

Jake shook his head. "Tell me something interesting, Newman. Got any deep, dark secrets?"

"What? No." I laughed. I hadn't done anything worthy of secrecy. I was boring through and through.

"Come on. There has to be something. We won't tell. You're a Player now. Or . . . you might be. We're all in this together," Jake said. Adam nodded along but didn't meet my eyes. "How about . . . what's your biggest fear?"

The wind had picked up and I wrapped my arms around my stomach. I thought for a second, tilting my head to the sky. It was covered in blinking, bright stars. Adam's porch light was on, but we didn't need it. I found the dippers, sitting like nesting dolls, just below the North Star. I took a deep breath.

"I'm scared of the dark," I said finally. I tried to laugh but the sound that came out was chalky and strange. "That's why I love astronomy so much. There's no such thing as absolute darkness in the night sky."

Jake didn't laugh. Neither did Adam. And I finally felt calm. Like I had passed a test. Jake leaned forward. His eyes were black and wide and they held my gaze with a ferocity that scared me. He put his hand on the swing to stop us from moving. "Where does that come from?"

"What are you, a shrink?" I asked. But no one chuckled. I took another sip—rye whiskey, I'd decided—and just said, "I don't know. My dad introduced me to the constellations when I was a kid and they always made me feel safe. I even have those stupid glow-in-the-dark stars on my ceiling. Can't fall asleep without some light, you know?"

"Go deeper, Newman," Jake said. His eyes narrowed and he leaned in further so his fingertips grazed my knees.

"Maybe . . ." I started. "Maybe it's because I've always felt inferior." The words were bubbling now. Things I never even let myself think, let alone say out loud. "Like I don't belong at Gold Coast Prep. Like I have something to prove. Like I have to be perfect." I thought of my anxiety nightmares, the ones that started after I came to Prep and now ruined my sleep on the nights before big tests or presentations. How the thought of not measuring up to my brilliant peers made me want to run and hide.

Jake leaned back into his chair, seemingly satisfied. But I felt like he needed more.

"I know I'm not good enough but I'm scared everyone else will find out."

That made him smile. "Do you think other people feel that way, too?"

I turned over the question in my mind, thinking of Nikki and Shaila. "I don't know. I guess everyone's scared of something," I said. "Like Shaila, you'd think she's not afraid of anything. But really, she can't do heights. Not at all. She wouldn't even go on the Oyster Fest Ferris wheel with me."

"Oh yeah?" Jake asked.

I nodded. "She's a baby when it comes to that stuff. We're all scared of something, I guess. Maybe she has some deeper reason why, too."

Adam kicked the ground again and sent us rocking back and forth. Neither of them said anything for a while and I tilted my head to stare up at the blanket of stars in silence.

After a few minutes, Adam finally spoke. "I'm hungry, dude. Should we get a pizza?"

Their conversation continued as they debated the merits of Mario's and Luigi's, the two competing slice spots in town.

But I stayed quiet, turning over what I had just revealed

about my own shortcomings, and, inadvertently, Shaila's. She would have her own meeting like this, too. Everyone would. What would she say about me? Would it be by accident or on purpose? Had I said too much?

I tried to push the guilt down into the pit of my stomach, to convince myself that I hadn't betrayed Shaila's trust. But I knew, somehow, that I had just given the Players ammo. And they would use it. I just didn't know when. Or that it would somehow lead back to Shaila's last night alive.

I'm sluggish and tired all week, my thoughts scattered. Marla was probably right about pretending everything's fine, but I'm still thinking about Rachel's text, the one I left unanswered, and about the look in Nikki's eyes as she grew more vicious during the Show. When Henry texts me on Friday night, it's exactly what I need to take my mind off things.

Date night? My place? he asks.

A few moments pass.

The parentals are gone.

😉 😉 😉 😉 😉 😉

I bite down on my lip and smile. Henry has been extra sweet since the other night at Nikki's, finding the easiest pops for Jared to complete and looking after him at the all-boys nights. He's the only one of us who refuses to talk about college acceptances—or rejections—which come in next week. Says it's too stressful and we should all just freakin' chill. Seeing him would be such a welcome distraction from Rachel and Graham and Shaila, too. They're all characters in my nightmares these days. I could use a night without them.

Plus, Henry's so *obvious* in a way that's easy, comfortable, reliable. He can so quickly shift between newsboy prodigy and all-American *boy*. His only real fault is the never-ending need to please his parents. That's what he used the Files for, to get those math study guides. It's his weakest subject, but he knew he needed A's in calc, stat, and econ to get into Wharton. And even though he sneers at the idea of working for "the man," just like his father, we all know he will.

Sometimes I look at him and I think I can see his entire future: a business degree, a fancy internship, a spacious apartment in the city. He would be riddled with *what ifs*, consumed by the fact that he gave up on his dream of reporting on the front lines to work until midnight worrying about spreadsheets. But he'd still have it all: the wife with big tits and impeccable taste, the mansion in Gold Coast and a place out east. Sometimes I wonder if that wife will be me and if we will stay together forever simply because of Shaila. How could I be with someone who had not known her? How could you make a life with someone who never knew a whole chunk of you?

But then again, the thought of that life, of having everything pre-prescribed, makes my stomach spasm. I push the idea of grown-up, unfulfilled Henry out of my mind and read his texts again. I only have to think about the *right now*, that's all. My mouth twitches into a smile.

Tonight, when everything else seems to be a question mark, hanging at Henry's for a while isn't my worst option. At least I won't have to *think* about the freshmen, or Graham, or Rachel, or whose blood stained an ugly shirt three years ago.

Be over at 7, I respond.

Yes! he writes. *I'll order sushi.*

Henry lives in the new part of town, close to the water, where families have their own private boat slips, where backyards are basically football fields, and where the pool houses have full kitchens and clawfoot bathtubs. I arrive at the mouth of his driveway and punch a few numbers into the code box, triggering the wrought-iron gate to open. When I get to the front door, a quarter-mile later, Henry is waiting outside, wearing his CNN hoodie and holding a plastic bag of takeout.

"Hey, babe," he says. He envelops me in a hug and plants a wet, hungry kiss on my mouth. I follow him into the house and through the marble foyer into the wide, airy kitchen.

Henry rummages through the bag and pulls out an enormous amount of food—maki rolls and shiny pieces of bright sashimi nestled inside plastic containers, little cartons of seaweed salad and salted edamame pods. My stomach grumbles at the sight.

"Someone went ham," I say.

Henry blushes and shrugs his shoulders up to his ears. "I couldn't remember what you liked, so I just got a little of everything." He hands me a pair of wooden chopsticks and looks at me with those big, sincere eyes.

I pop piece of a spicy salmon roll into my mouth. "It's perfect," I say, without bothering to chew.

"Good." He leans his arms on the marble counter in front of him and his forearms look like tree trunks descending from his button-down, rolled up to his elbows. "Wanna go upstairs?" he asks, a glint in his eye. Hopeful. Confident.

My insides tingle, like I've had too much seltzer, but I need to get Graham and Shaila out of my head. "Definitely."

Henry grabs my hand and we take the stairs two at a time. When he opens his bedroom door, it's clear he has a vision for tonight. Soft music floats from his speakers and Christmas lights twinkle over his perfectly made bed. They bounce off the framed newspapers on his wall, front pages from the day he was born. Even a candle burns on his windowsill, right next to the photo of him shaking Anderson Cooper's hand. It's all so . . . sweet.

"Dork," I say, hiding my pleasure that he did all this for me.

Henry's cheeks turn a little bit red. "C'mere."

His hands are strong and thick, calmer than they should be. He wasn't always like this, not when we first started hooking up. We'd both done stuff with a few other people, other Players in other classes. But neither of us had *been* with someone before. There had never been an opportunity to learn or ask questions in a way that felt safe or free of judgment. So when we were together, every session was a new adventure, a new line to throw ourselves across.

One night, after fumbling to unlatch my bra under the stars aboard his boat, *Olly Golucky*, Henry announced he wanted to get better at this, at all of it. "I want to make you feel good," he whispered in a voice that turned my guts into soup. "Show me," he said, breathing hot air onto my neck.

TWELVE

AS FAR AS Gold Coast parents are concerned, college planning starts as soon as you walk through the brass gates in your navy Prep blazer. During sports practices, students wear sweatshirts printed with the names of schools they consider. Yale, Harvard, Princeton. Penn if you wanted to have fun or make bank. Wesleyan if you were artsy. Stanford if you hated your parents and wanted to flee.

And by the beginning of senior year, if you hadn't figured out where you were applying, you were the loser whose future was uncertain. The admissions board wouldn't let you in based on how badly you wanted to go there or how soon after you exited the womb you realized it was your destiny to be a fighting bulldog or a roaring tiger, or whatever. But in our minds, whoever decided where they wanted to go first was the chosen student, the one who deserved to get in. And if you were accepted over them, prepare for war.

I saw it go down freshman year when Jake Horowitz got into Princeton early decision and Tina Fowler got deferred even though Tina's parents were alumni and she always wore that horrible neon orange sweatshirt during volleyball practice. Her fury nearly split the Players apart when she screamed at him during lunch one Friday. Everyone was relieved she got accepted in the spring.

So it was a no-brainer that my friends entered senior year with polished applications and so much hope. Even Robert, who bombed his SATs despite getting so much extra time, believed he was destined to be back at school in Manhattan, studying music management at NYU. Rumor has it his parents made a casual million-dollar donation to the school.

All of that makes today, December 1, the day we are due to hear back from our first round of applications, torture.

I wake up in a sweat, panting, cotton sheets balled in my fists. I can barely catch my breath. But I didn't dream about Brown, about getting in or not. I dreamed of Shaila, her eyes wide and full of fear, bulging out of her beautiful head. Her mouth open, screaming for help. I inhale deeply and try to shake her from my mind. Just another nightmare. Just stress. That's all. I reassure myself of this over and over, but my heart continues to race at a speed too rapid to calm.

I lean my head back, so it kisses the wooden headboard, and rub my temples, willing Shaila to disappear. I fumble for my phone on the nightstand with shaking fingers, hoping an endless scroll will calm me down. But before I can open Instagram or YouTube, I see a text from Rachel. Of course.

You change your number or something? she writes. *Don't give up on us.*

I throw my phone down into my blankets so hard it bounces onto the floor. My fear is gone and I'm left with anger. Why does Rachel have to stalk *me*? Why not Nikki or Quentin or even Henry? Why can't she just leave me alone, especially today? And why the hell am I actually considering helping her?

Mom pops her head into my room. "You okay, Jill?" she asks, her brows forming a deep V. "Thought I heard something."

"Yep," I say without looking at her.

"Big day, sweetie." Her face softens into a warm smile. "Whatever happens, it's all going to work out."

I grunt and throw the covers off, pushing past her to the bathroom. "Whatever."

For the next few hours, I do my best to not think of Shaila or Rachel or Graham. Instead, I focus on the unbearable agony of waiting for our fates to arrive.

Everyone can feel it. An eerie, electric spear pierces through the caf, and even at the Players' Table, we're barely holding it together.

If Shaila were here, she wouldn't have been worried about getting into Harvard. She would have been sitting next to me, rolling her eyes at how *freaked out* we all were. She would have assured us that we'd all be *fine, guys*. I imagine her in the Gold Coast Prep uniform, chewing on a piece of cookie dough with one foot propped up on my chair so her bare knee was visible above the table. That was the real Shaila, not the creepy ghost who haunts my dreams.

"So, uh, what's up?" Quentin tries.

Nikki offers a half laugh but rubs her thumb against the rose quartz around her neck. She's waiting to hear from Parsons, though she's a shoo-in for their design merchandising program. Her portfolio featured dresses I'd die to buy.

"Robert, you okay?" she asks.

But he stays silent, probably for the first time in his life, and chugs his soda, crushing the plastic bottle in a swift, crunching motion. Guess he's not so confident after all.

"Where's Marla?" I ask.

"Ditched lunch for a workout," Henry says as he sets his tray down next to mine. "A distraction."

"This is hell," I admit.

Everyone mumbles their agreement and turns back to their food. We're mostly silent until the bell rings.

The rest of the day is crap, too. It's as if Mr. Beaumont purposely tries to make his achingly long lecture on *Ulysses* even more boring than it has to be. With only five minutes left in the class, he looks at us with pity.

"How about we just relax for now?" he asks. "Feel free to use your phones."

Within seconds, everyone has their admissions pages and email open even though we all know we won't hear for hours.

When I finally get home, eons later, I fly past Mom, Dad, and Jared, shut myself in my room, and lock the door. I sit on my bed, hide my phone under the pillow, and open the State admissions portal. Might as well get that over with.

I enter my info and chew on a stray cuticle as the page loads.

Congratulations! it reads as confetti rains down the browser.

My heartbeat steadies. Thank god. That bodes well.

I take a deep breath and bring up Brown's page. My fingers are heavy as I key my login and my throat goes dry as the text comes into view.

Suddenly . . . I shriek.

It happened.

I did it.

"Are you in? Did you get in?" Dad yells from the hallway.

I choke out a response. "Yes."

Mom throws open the door and wraps me in a hug. "Sweetie!" she yells. "It was all worth it."

My cheeks are wet and my shoulders shake. I let her embrace me like I'm a kid again. I rest my head against her neck and she compresses me into a tight little ball. It *was* all worth it. My future is set. *I did it.*

Jared bounds down the hallway, panting. "In?" he asks.

I nod.

His smile gets wider. "Knew it." Then he wraps his arms around Mom, Dad, and me and knocks his shoulder into mine.

Mom finally untangles us all and holds my chin in her hands. "Let's celebrate," she says. Her eyes are wet, too. "I made mac and cheese."

After dinner, Mom ducks her head into the refrigerator, rummages around, and emerges with an icy green champagne bottle, wrapped in foil at the top.

"You deserve this, kiddo," Dad says. He rests a large, steady hand on my shoulder, winks, and brings a napkin to his face. "You worked so hard for this. And after everything you've been through . . ." He squeezes my arm at the table and waves a hand to Mom. "You make us so proud. Four glasses! One for Jared, too. This only happens once in a lifetime."

Jared grins. The excitement *is* contagious. He even volunteers to clear the plates and before we disperse, he nuzzles against my shoulder for a hug. "Did you tell Adam yet?"

"Just about to."

He nods. "He'll be psyched." Jared squeezes me again and I'm overcome with adoration for my baby brother. Whatever happens with the Players, with Graham, this moment is ours.

I rush up the stairs and pull my phone out with shaking hands. I punch in Adam's number and wait for it to ring. I try to remember everything I want to say. I want to hear all about the bad improv shows we'll see together, the only place in Providence worth getting bagels, the chunky parka I'll need to wear to battle the New England cold. I want to know what dorm I should live in. Do I need a car?

He picks up on the fourth ring, but I can barely hear him. A thumping Eurodance song plays in the background, drowning out my thoughts.

"Hello?" he yells. "Jill?"

"I got in," I say, breathless. "I got in." Even saying the words out loud feels false, like I'm dreaming.

"What?" he screams. "I can't hear you! Text me!"

The line goes dead. He must be at some party, one that I'd be at, too, this time next year.

I text him with trembling fingers

I GOT INTO BROWN! SEE YOU NEXT YEAR!!!!!!

He responds in an instant. *AAAHHHH!!!!!!!*

I set my phone down and breathe deeply, inhaling and then letting it all go. Suddenly, everything around me feels so unfamiliar, like things from someone else's past. I can see the future so clearly, I want to fast forward through the next few months and forget about Rachel and Graham and whose blood really stained his shirt after all.

But then I hear whispers behind the closet door down the hall, where Mom keeps random things like wrapping paper and extra rolls of tinfoil.

I turn my doorknob slowly, and pull it back just an inch to make out the words.

"We're going to figure it out," Mom says in a hushed, nervous tone.

"I just can't make the numbers work," Dad says, exasperated and depleted. "We won't know if she gets money until the spring. Otherwise, she's going to have to take out loans. She'll get saddled with debt for decades. We can't let that happen."

"I mean, we can pay for *some* of it," Mom whispers. "And she's still up for one of those full-ride scholarships. When has she ever let us down?"

"I know, I know. But . . . what if she doesn't get it?" He sounds guilty for even suggesting it.

"There's always State," Mom says. "Honors."

"But this is her dream."

"She'll get that spot. I know she will." Mom's voice wavers and Dad sighs heavily.

"We'll make it work," he says. "We always do."

I hear the muffled sounds of a hug and silently close my door. My heart thumps a million miles an hour and I clench my fists, fighting back tears and unbearable lashes of guilt. A heavy weight settles on my chest. *I have to be good enough,* I think. *I have to win that money. I have to.*

THIRTEEN

"WELCOME TO ROAD RALLY, bitches!" Nikki stands on the hood of her BMW and shakes bottles of sparkling wine in each hand. Like a pro, she pops them both and sprays them in front of her, dousing the freshman Players who stand cheering at her feet. It's a week after acceptances were announced and every single senior Player got into their top choice school. Even Robert, whose dad's donation seemed to have done the trick. He exploded our group text thread with expletives for hours before taking off with Nikki in an Uber to the city, where they went to some insanely expensive steakhouse under the Williamsburg Bridge. After fam dinner, I sat in Henry's hot tub with him, Quentin, and Marla until our skin became wrinkled like prunes. The stars were particularly bright that night and I tried my hardest to push my parents' conversation out of my head. No luck, though. I couldn't—still can't—forget their desperate tone, the need for me to achieve, achieve, achieve.

Now we're standing in Nikki's winding driveway, ready for the final Player event of the semester: an all-night scavenger hunt we call Road Rally. Here's to hoping it's a distraction.

In the crowd, the younger kids whisper among themselves,

comparing notes for what's to come. Jared's packed in the center of their little crew, a core member of this unit we assembled like Legos. After months of tests and trials, they may think they know what's in store, but tonight is next level. Road Rally always is.

When Jared asked me about it earlier this week, after Nikki spread the word that it was happening, I tried to manage a smile. "It's fun," I said. "Just go with the flow."

"Worse than the Show?" he asked with a smirk. I tried to study his face, to figure out how that night made him feel. If a secret shame burrowed deep inside, or if he brushed the whole thing off like a bug. I couldn't bring myself to ask.

"It's fine," I said instead. But the annual scavenger hunt always makes me uneasy. In the past, this night was a beast that chewed you up and spit you out at the feet of whoever was in charge. The only thing worse was initiation.

When we were called to Adam's house freshman year, I spent the whole afternoon trying to figure out how I could be on his team. But I didn't need to worry. As soon as I walked into the backyard, Adam grabbed my elbow and whispered into my ear, "You're with me." I skipped behind him to his car, where Shaila and Jake Horowitz were already waiting, our team of four decided.

"You guys ready?" Jake asked before banging on the dashboard. "Let's do this thing!"

"You okay?" I dipped my head and whispered to Shaila. Her head was turned toward the window, watching Graham get into Tina Fowler's car.

"Yeah. I just don't get why couples have to split up."

"Just part of the rules," Adam said, turning around in the front seat. "Rachel and I aren't together. Don't worry," he said, patting her on the knee. "This is going to be fun."

I nodded encouragingly and bumped shoulders with Shaila. Secretly, I was thrilled to be grouped with her. It was the first time we'd be together without Graham in weeks.

"Here. This will help." Jake reached down and pulled out an oversized water bottle full of orange liquid. "Drink up."

Shaila snatched it from his hands and guzzled eagerly before passing it to me. "First stop," Adam said, making a swift turn into the ShopRite. I felt the booze give me extra legs. "Grab that bag," he said, motioning toward the trunk. "You guys are wearing bathing suits under there, right?" We nodded. We were always ones to follow instructions. "Good, let's do it."

We threw the car doors open and sprinted inside the store, trailing the boys by a few yards. "The frozen aisle!" Adam yelled.

"Quick!" Jake said. "Strip!" He whipped out two lawn chairs, set them side by side, and handed us matching pink sunglasses and sippy cups.

I pulled off my T-shirt and stepped out of my shorts, leaving no time to feel self-conscious. "C'mon, Shaila!" I said.

She plunked down in the chair beside me and we did our best models-on-the-beach impressions while Jake snapped a pic. *I can't wait to frame this,* I thought. *Iconic.*

"You guys are so sexy," Jake said. I giggled and squinted beneath the grocery store's fluorescent lights. Shaila's skin looked translucent and she stifled a hiccup.

"Let's just check another one off the list while we're here," Jake said. "You guys should make out."

I froze and tried to catch Shaila's eye. But she wouldn't look my way. Instead, she bit her lip and waited for me to make the first move.

I looked at Adam for help. *What do I do?*

"That'd be hot," he said, flashing his dimple at us. He stood with his arms crossed in front of his chest, his eyes encouraging.

I took a deep breath and tried to ignore the insane pounding in my chest. I thought my skin might split open. Then I turned to Shaila and closed my eyes, hoping she would meet me halfway. I parted my lips and thought of Adam, how it felt when he touched my skin in the hammock months before. The phone flashed and Shaila's warm mouth pressed against mine. Her tongue slithered against my teeth, wet and unsteady. My whole body began to shake. Shaila must have known because she lifted her palm to my cheek and held my face steady just for a second.

After a moment, we pulled apart, and Shaila's dark, furious eyes met mine. She brought her hand down and wrapped her fingers around my wrist. "Never let them see you hurt," she whispered. Before I could respond or even nod, she was already standing, pulling on her jeans.

It's only a kiss, I told myself. But, once in the car, I had to sit on my hands to keep them still.

Those two items are still on the list, I think, but tonight when Quentin passes around clipboards fixed with the paper checklists, I can't see them in the dark.

"You have to meet back here at midnight. If you're late . . ." Nikki trails off. A devilish smile spreads across her face and she crashes the two bottles in her hands together. "Disqualified!"

No one had ever been DQ'd as far as I know but we'd heard rumors about one car back in the early 2000s that didn't make the deadline. All of them, even the seniors, lost their Player status and their access to the Files. They were disinvited from every social gathering for the rest of the year.

Legend has it their college acceptances were revoked, too.

"Then you'll present your checklists and your souvenirs to the judges: Jill, Quentin, Henry, and yours truly. You all paid a ten-dollar entry tonight, and whichever car wins gets to keep the whole pot!" People hoot and holler all around us. "A little something extra," Nikki says with a smile.

Henry appears by my side, takes my hand, and throws it into the air. "Make us proud!" he says. I tilt my head up and sneak a peek at the Little Dipper. Then the stars that form two twins. Gemini. I imagine the tiny stick figures dancing around with one another and my stomach settles.

Nikki rolls her eyes and stomps a boot on the car. "All right, Players! You have five minutes to find your teams." She pulls a whistle out from her pocket and puts it to her lips. "Ready! Set! Go!"

"Jill! Henry! C'mere!" Quentin yells from across the gravel. He holds one last clipboard, and I finally get a look at the list.

YOUR MISSION, SHOULD YOU CHOOSE TO ACCEPT IT, IS TO COMPLETE AS MANY TASKS AS POSSIBLE BEFORE TIME RUNS OUT. IF THE ACTIVITY TAKES PLACE OUTSIDE OF THE JUDGES' SIGHT, YOU MUST DOCUMENT THE ACT ON YOUR PHONE. JUDGES WILL TALLY POINTS AT MIDNIGHT.

☐ *Bring us a license plate with the numbers "69" next to each other*

☐ *Jump in the ocean with all your clothes on*

☐ *Jump in the ocean with all your clothes off*

☐ *Get something . . . ANYTHING . . . pierced*

- ☐ *Make an outfit out of trash and wear it for the rest of the night*
- ☐ *Do donuts on the Gold Coast football field*
- ☐ *Put a Gold Coast Prep sweatshirt on the Teddy Roosevelt statue at Cartwright High*
- ☐ *Make out with someone in a different class*
- ☐ *Smash a plate in a public place and yell, "Opa!"*
- ☐ *Juul with Mr. Beaumont*
- ☐ *Make a Dairy Barn drive-thru run . . . naked*
- ☐ *String a bra up to the top of the Gold Coast flagpole*
- ☐ *Make out with someone of the same sex*
- ☐ *Lie in a lawn chair in a bathing suit with a tropical drink in ShopRite*
- ☐ *House 4 pizzas, 15 garlic knots, and 2 gallons of ice cream from Luigi's in 15 minutes. NO PUKING!*

"Jill, you ready to go?" Henry holds Bruce's door open for me and I slide in the back seat with Nikki, our knees knocking together.

He takes off, and we head to our first destination, Diane's. The tiny bell chimes when we push through the door and Diane turns to throw us a look, different than the one I get when I come here with Adam or Jared. Skeptical.

"Look at you, dawlings," she says in her twang. She walks over to the booth by the window and drops a few menus on the table.

"Hiya, sugar," Quentin says. "Don't you look *mah*-velous."

He bows like we're in the presence of royalty. Gold Coast royalty, at least. Diane rolls her eyes.

"What can I get fo' ya? Road Rally tonight, is that right?" she asks.

My head snaps up. "How'd you know that?" I ask.

"Oh honey, you can't hide anything from us. We all know when you have your little pawties." Her accent is thicker than usual, meaning she's probably slipped a little nip into her nighttime coffee. "What'll it be?"

"Mozzy sticks and fries," Henry says. "Please." He flashes her a toothy grin.

"You got it," Diane says. "Just tell yuh buddies no games in here! Last year, that Gardner boy tried to steal all our ketchup bottles. Not cool." She jabs a finger, painted in a bright red that matches her hair.

Nikki leans in and whispers, "We gotta be more chill."

"Everyone knows everything. If someone wanted to shut this shit down, they would," Henry says, stretching his arms out to span the entire back of the booth. His fingertips press against my shoulder.

He's right. Everyone at Gold Coast knows. They're in on it, but they just let it lie. *It's kids being kids. They're just blowing off steam.* The hands-off approach to our social lives kicked into overdrive sophomore year, when our grades were steady, a miracle after what had happened.

By the time midnight rolls around, I am ready for this whole night to be over. My head is pounding from a few too many Jell-O shots, taken at the Mussel Bay tollbooth while we watched Jordana Washington pierce Raquel Garza's soft, fleshy earlobe. Raquel bit down on an orange and winced while the rest of her team howled in delight, checking off one more item on their list.

Nikki's all in on her Toastmaster role, clutching her phone and waiting for updates to come in from Marla and Robert, who volunteered to lead two of the teams. "They're not fucking responding," she says as we barrel back toward her house. "They *know* they're supposed to check in with me every thirty minutes. This is ridiculous." Nikki crosses her arms and grabs at the bottle of vodka between her feet on the floor of the car.

"Chill, Nikki," I say softly, rubbing my temples where a sugary headache has taken hold.

"I don't need to hear that from *you*," she says, her tongue a whip.

Henry and Quentin exchange a look in the front seat but stay silent. I fight back tears and clench my fists together, trying to remind myself that she's just stressed. She just wants this night to be fun.

But when everyone arrives back at her house and the designated drivers hand their sheets to Quentin, I feel relieved, grateful Road Rally is almost over. The teams stand huddled together in little clusters. It's easy to spot the new friendships, little tethers extended between juniors and freshmen. These stories will become inside jokes months down the road, legendary in a few short years.

"Hey," Jared says, out of breath. He knocks his shoulder into mine and when I look at his face, hovering a few inches above me, I see his eyes are dilated, his face flushed. "Wild, huh?" he says, grinning and raising his eyebrows.

He looks strange and off-kilter. "You okay?" I whisper, my breath an icy cloud. But he's already on his way back to his team, trotting like a wild horse left unbridled.

"Judges, assemble!" Nikki calls. I roll my eyes and drag my

feet to where she stands with Quentin and Henry.

Henry swipes through the photos on Marla's phone first, pointing out flashes of naked butts and beer cans, someone drenched in mustard, until he pauses on one image. Henry's mouth falls open and he nudges me. "Uh, Jill . . ."

"What?" My head pounds harder than it did before, and the little area of skin above my eye begins to ache. He hands me Marla's phone. A blur of flesh and platinum hair appears. A boy and a girl, with just a few bits of fabric in between. The photo was taken on the sand, which makes it hard to discern where the beach begins and the boy ends. The two are lip-locked, mid-passion, but there's no mistaking who's in the photo. Jared and Marla.

A flush creeps up my chest. My hands start shaking and I close my eyes but all I can see are naked bodies rolling around in the sand.

I swipe to see the next photo and find the tiny freshman Sierra McKinley in only a bikini, her eyes wide with fear. She's standing in front of the ShopRite alone. I swipe again to find another girl, one I can't make out, leaning down, meeting Sierra's lips in an open-mouthed mess. The girl, some sophomore, I think, looks wasted, her hair stringy, her bikini bottoms sagging. But it's Sierra's face I fixate on. Her eyes are open, her fear obvious. She didn't want this, not in front of everyone, not for their amusement. Her gaze is fixed on someone off to the side, hoping for an acknowledgment. I zoom in on the corner of the screen, trying to discern who she's looking to for help. Jared's face is instantly recognizable. I expect him to look uncomfortable, to at least avert his eyes. To stop Sierra's humiliation.

But instead, he's laughing, cackling, even, and throwing up a hand to high-five someone else. He doesn't look like my sweet, kind baby brother. He looks like someone else entirely. He looks like a Player. I scan the circle for Jared. But he's not there. Instead I find the easier target.

"What the hell?" I nearly scream, charging at Marla. All motion around us stops.

"What's your problem, Jill?" she says, crossing her arms.

"My problem?" I scoff. "You hooked up with my brother! You can't do that!"

She laughs. "Are you serious, Jill? It's Road Rally. It doesn't *mean* anything."

"Marla, he's my *brother*." I spit the word out like it's poison. My head feels like it's about to spin off my neck. A circle has formed around us. We have an audience.

"What is your deal?" Nikki screams. She's come around to Marla's side so they stand in front of me like a wall. "It's a *joke.* It's not like she forced him. Right, Jared?"

The Players turn and face my little brother. There he is, standing at the back of the circle, leaning against the house, next to Nikki's side door. And for the first time I see him for what he is becoming, just like all the others. He is tall, broad-shouldered, and flushed, awakened to what he's been missing. He aches to expend all that pent-up, furious energy, just like the rest of us. But why does it have to be like *this*?

Jared smirks. I wonder if this is when he decides that maybe his big sister Jill Newman isn't so great after all. That he doesn't need to keep up with me or play by my same rules. He can create his own without worrying about the consequences. "Yeah," he says. "Just having fun."

"See?" Nikki says. "Stop being dramatic." I swear I can feel my heart break. My chest throbs and my throat tightens. And, then, suddenly, I don't care. About the Players, about Nikki or Marla, or any of this. None of it makes sense. None of it is real. I see everything so clearly now.

"Jesus, Nikki," I say. "Take a look at yourself. Gallivanting around like you *run* the Players, like you *run* Gold Coast. You know the only reason you're class president is because Shaila *died* and you took her place. If she were still alive, if we had *protected* her, she'd have gotten elected sophomore year. And junior. And senior! She'd be Toastmaster. And you'd just be *regular*."

Someone gasps and the air around us grows still and tense. Nikki's eyes are wet and black, full of rage and fury. Her fists are clenched but she doesn't say a word. She knows it's true. I've struck a nerve and I can't go back.

I know what I have to do.

I steady myself. "You know what?" I say slowly. I scan the circle, meeting eyes of people I've doused in ketchup, forced to perform vile skits, goaded into doing bitch work, into cheating on exams. Something deep inside my chest bursts into a million shards. "This is all bullshit."

I pause and close my eyes, breathing in the cold night.

"We're all just following rules and we don't even know where they came from. We're just trying to feel alive, to run away from everything. But none of this matters. It's all made up. It's all a lie." I pause, realizing tears and snot are dripping down my nose. "We said this year was going to be different." A snort escapes me. "But Shaila is still dead. Graham is off somewhere claiming innocence and we're all just . . ." Gasps ring out around the circle and I catch myself. No one knows about the blood, that someone else could be guilty.

Someone here, even.

I turn my head to the sky. It's cloudy now, ominous and foreboding. I can't see a thing. No one says a word and the only sounds come from the ocean crashing violently on the sand behind Nikki's house. It beats like a heart. For the first time in a long time I am totally sure of the words that are about to come out of my mouth.

"I quit."

They're quiet but echo into the night. Nikki's eyes narrow and she takes a step back. Marla's mouth drops open in shock. Only Quentin speaks and when he does, he just lets out a slow, low "Whoa."

I avoid looking at Henry, whose reaction I can't quite stomach. I wait a beat and turn, walking slowly to the road, away from all this.

I quit.

FOURTEEN

WAKING UP ON Monday morning is like emerging from a fog. It only takes a second before I remember what I have done, the line I have drawn, and who I have to face in just a few hours. No one has spoken to me since Road Rally. Not Jared, who stayed locked in his room yesterday, faking sick. Not Nikki, whose absence I already feel deep in my stomach. Not even sweet Henry, who I thought, out of everyone, might have my back and ask to talk it out.

The enormity of my decision has pushed aside any worries I had about paying for Brown, about Graham, Rachel, or Shaila, and I inhale, sipping shallow breaths. No one has ever quit the Players before. No one has come close. But I don't feel like a pioneer. I feel lost and abandoned, even though I'm the one who did the leaving. I wonder if I overreacted, if the Jell-O shots and the cold made me so mad. If I made something that was just *so* not about me . . . totally about me.

But when I remember the photos, my baby brother's flesh bleeding into someone else's, and then seeing him laugh at Sierra, the sting of betrayal beats into my brain. Marla would freak if we ever made a pass at one of her brothers. Siblings are a no-go. Incorruptible. And Jared is becoming someone different. Someone who scares me, who reminds me of that terrible night and how the boys' presence dominated everything they touched. Someone I recognize and hate.

So instead of making amends, I reach for my phone with shaky hands. I pull up Rachel's texts before I can convince myself not to. I look at our last exchange and conjure the smell of her apartment, of her new life. It feels like a doorway. *Responding doesn't mean forgiving,* I think.

I squeeze my eyes together and hold my breath, trying to summon Shaila, willing her to let me know if she approves, if she, too, would cave to curiosity, the possibility of redemption. I let all the air whoosh out of my mouth and try to find Shaila's voice within my own. *What would Shaila do?*

There's no time to know. Mom beats a fist on my door. "Henry's here! You're gonna be late!"

I exhale and my heart steadies. Someone's still on my side. Henry just needed some time to cool off. But he's back. We're good. So, I pull on my Gold Coast uniform, even though it feels like a straitjacket, and push through the front door, where Bruce idles in the driveway. Just another Monday. *I'm still Jill Newman,* I tell myself. No one can take that away from me.

I heave my backpack into Bruce and climb in.

"Hey," I say.

"Hi."

"For a second I thought you weren't going to talk to me again." Tears prick my eyes. I didn't know I needed this. Him. But I do. I so do.

"I thought about it," he says. His face is round and forgiving and the edges of his mouth turn downward. "But it's okay. Everyone will forgive you. We all say things we don't mean. It'll blow over."

Henry peels out of the driveway but the air grows stale and my stomach drops. My mouth is dry when I open it to speak. "I don't regret it."

Henry furrows his brow but keeps his eyes on the road. His blond hair is still dark at the roots, damp from a shower. "Of course you do, babe. You can't quit the Players." He moves to grab my hand in the console between us, but I keep my fingers limp. His skin is waxy to the touch.

I shake my head. "I don't regret it. If this is the Players, I'm out. I can't watch this happen to Jared. I can't trust . . ."

Henry moves his hand back to the steering wheel, clocking in at ten and two. "Is this about what you said about Graham the other night? Do you actually think he's telling the truth? Come on."

I want so badly to tell him about what Rachel told me, about the blood. But I think back to his reaction when I asked at intro night, the way he recoiled from the article in the *Gazette*. He wouldn't understand. He wants this to go away, just like the others. "No," I whisper. "It's about everything else."

Henry sighs and makes a left turn. "You'll come around."

"You're not listening to me." My voice is shaky but I have to get the words out. I know what I have to do and I brace myself for yet another tie I'm about to sever. "We have to break up."

"What?" A sedan stops short in front of us and Henry slams his foot down on the brake. We're only a block away from the Gold Coast parking lot, but I don't know if I can stay in his presence much longer. I don't know if I can watch him crumble, if I can handle his rage when I have to tend to my own. "You don't mean this, Jill."

I swallow hard. "I do. I don't want to be a Player anymore. And you think you can change my mind. If that's true, you don't know me at all. It's better we just end this now."

Henry turns swiftly into the senior lot and throws Bruce into park in one quick move. He stares straight forward, totally unreadable.

"Henry?" I ask.

He looks back at me with those gorgeous eyes, now glossy and wet. His top lip begins to quiver. I already hate myself for hurting him like this. But then his future flashes in front of me again. The finance job he doesn't want. A closet full of designer suits. A mansion out east. We never would have worked. If it wasn't my quitting the Players, it would be something else.

I blink and when I open my eyes, Henry is slumped over the steering wheel, his shoulders heaving up and down.

"Jill, please," he says, his voice almost a whisper.

Something tugs inside my chest, but I lean back farther in my seat, away from him. Why don't I want to salvage this? It would be so much easier if I did. Everything would be simple.

"I'm sorry."

A gurgle erupts from Henry's throat and his breathing becomes labored. "But I love you," he says. It's the first time he's said it. Words I've dreamed of hearing. Words I couldn't wait to be said to me. But my hands are clammy and I fight the urge to bolt out of the car. I don't feel anything. And I realize I never wanted to hear those words from Henry. I wanted them from someone else.

"I have to go," I say.

"Wait." Henry lifts his body off the steering wheel and turns to me, his eyes red and his cheeks puffy.

But I can't. It's too much to see him like this. Too awkward. Too grotesque. I shake my head and push myself out, leaving Henry alone in Bruce. I slam the door behind me and don't look back. The parking lot buzzes with chatter and muffled sharp words. I force myself to breathe in, then out, to swallow the screams I so desperately want to unleash. I hear Shaila's voice in my head, the line she repeated when we needed it the most. *Don't let them see you hurt.*

The bell rings and I know that nowhere will be safe today. So I keep going, my head down, my skin on fire, and dash through the front door, past the senior lounge, and into AP Physics.

When I get there, my usual place next to Nikki is already taken. Amos Ritter, a pimply-faced junior on the baseball team, leans back in the swivel lab chair and makes himself at home, pulling out two binders and a graphing calculator. He's not a Player, but he's well-liked enough that he gets invitations to parties, slaps on the back when he chugs a beer fast enough. He's a warm body to keep the party going. Nikki only knows him because she made out with him after Spring Fling last year.

I try to make eye contact with her but her dark hair blocks her face from my view. Her skin looks perfect from afar. I wonder if the blackhead she was freaking out about last week is still there. When I take the only empty seat—it must be Amos's usual place—I flip open my notebook and try to focus, recording everything Dr. Jarvis says, even though it just doesn't matter.

For fifty-two excruciating minutes I imagine all the things that Nikki is thinking about me, all of the horrible, cruel things she must believe, that I'm a *loser*, a traitor, that I'm not a friend worth keeping.

I imagine her screaming at me, saying the worst things I think about myself out loud, and press my pencil into my palm, nearly breaking flesh. Her unwillingness to even look at me stings more than if she were to stand up and say, "I hate you."

I already lost one best friend. I can't stomach the fact that I've lost another.

When the bell rings, I want to run to her table and pretend like everything is okay. I want to describe the look on Henry's face when I broke his heart and ask her why the fuck did I not feel any single sliver of remorse? I want my best friend. But instead I'm sluggish to pack up my bag, terrified of an encounter here in the lab. She is gone by the time I look up.

I can't bring myself to enter the caf for lunch, to see my empty seat at the Players' Table, now home to five. Instead, I find a carrel in the back of the library and rest my head on the wooden desk. I'm hidden here and I finally close my eyes, letting the tears fall in silence. The lunch period ticks by, but it's excruciating to sit without purpose. I pull my phone from my pocket and tap on the nondescript app, the one that holds the keys to everything, the one that will save me from Mr. Beaumont's English test this afternoon.

"It'll only be true or false, guys," he'd said last week. "Gotta prepare you for the AP exam."

The screen loads and I type in the password from muscle memory. A spinning wheel turns and then turns again and a message I've never seen appears.

Wrong password. Try again. A sad face blinks below the cursor and stares back at me.

There's nothing to do but laugh. Of course. I should have expected this. I don't deserve this massive, bullshit database. None of us do. All the time and effort and dignity I sacrificed to get access . . . it all means nothing.

Then it dawns on me who made this choice. The only person who could change the password. Nikki.

My hands shake and my vision blurs. I try to picture her lying on her canopy bed with her laptop sitting on her chest, making the decision, loading the page, clicking *Confirm*. Smiling with glee at my presumed failure. She had become a monster.

For the first time since Road Rally, I wonder, *Was it all worth it?*

I try to stop myself. I really do. But my fingers fly over my phone screen faster than I can stop them.

Henry and I broke up. I hit send before giving myself time to reconsider.

Shit, Adam types back almost immediately. My breathing steadies. *U ok?*

I will be. It was my choice.

Never liked that kid anyway.

I laugh into my sleeve and avoid a nasty look from Mrs. Deckler. I type the words that are scarier to say out loud. *I quit the Players, too.*

Double shit.

I want to say I'm sorry, to say he didn't make a mistake when he chose me three years ago. That I'm still on his side. But another text comes in, churning my insides into a jammy, gooey mess.

You're still my favorite. That'll never change.

I straight-up fail the English test. I bomb it like I've never bombed anything in my life, earning a 65, a number I've never even *seen* written in red. Mr. Beaumont drops the marked-up exam on my desk with a note, also in red. *SEE ME.* I stuff the piece of paper, along with my pride, into a ball and shove it deep inside my backpack.

When class is dismissed, I try to sneak out behind the others and escape. But I have to wait a beat for Nikki to leave first. The awkward dance leaves me vulnerable and Mr. Beaumont seizes the opportunity.

"Jill," he says. "Wait up." He stands with his arms crossed, like a disappointed big brother, and walks toward me to close the door. "Take a seat."

"I'm gonna be late for next period," I mumble.

"Jill, you're one of my most promising students. You just failed. I think we need to have a little chat."

"A little *chat?*" I scoff. But when I look at him, he's not joking. His eyes are wide with concern and his hands are clasped in a little steeple in front of him. His cardigan is done up wrong so one button sticks out at the bottom, and another, shiny and round, pokes out at the top, knocking his collar askew just slightly. Dark circles sag under his eyes, like he had one too many whiskeys the night before, and the middle of his brow needs a good tweezing. He looks so different than he did that night at the gas station three years ago. So much more worn down. Back then he was tickled, amused that he had caught his "firstborns" doing something so outrageous.

Now he just looks rumpled. There's no way he was a Player,

no way they would have let him in. Maybe under all this, at some point, he had *something*, but the man in front of me isn't special. *Maybe I'm not either.*

"What happened?" he asks.

"I don't know."

"Yes, you do."

"Forgot to study, I guess." I cross my arms, defiant and childish. It feels wrong to talk to authority like this, but after years of sucking up to teachers to throw them off our scent, it also feels like a victory.

Mr. Beaumont sighs and leans back in his chair so the front legs lift off the ground. I wonder if he'll fall backward. "Look, Jill, I'm not an idiot. You know I went here, right?"

"I've seen the yearbooks." I picture him then, strong and lean, with thicker hair and a varsity jersey. It was only ten years ago. He and Adam would have missed each other only by a few years.

"Listen, Jill. I know what goes on."

Now I wonder if this is an admission, an acknowledgment of that moment at the gas station and all the other little ones in between. What else has he seen from afar? How much does he know about what we've done? For a second, hope creeps into my chest. At least that would mean someone else understands.

"You kids have to deal with a lot," he says slowly. "More than I did when I was your age. I know how much pressure can be placed on you here. And after everything with Shaila . . ." He trails off and I can't tell if his words are coded, if he's trying to tell me something. "I know how close you two were. I miss her, too."

Beaumont leans forward, causing the front legs of his chair

to knock against the floor. I can smell his breath. Mint trying to mask tobacco. Menthol maybe. He places his hand on top of mine and his skin burns. I can feel the calluses on his fingertips. It's too close. I want to run.

But instead, I wait a beat for him to finish, for him to say what I need him to say. That I was right to walk away. That things will be better after I'm out of here. But he doesn't. That's it.

"I'm okay," I say, wriggling my hand out from under his. "Just forgot to study. That's all."

"Okay, then," he says, bringing his hands to rest on his knees. "Why don't you retake the test on Monday? I know you're better than this." He stabs the blood-red 65 in front of me with a thick finger.

"Thank you."

Beaumont smiles wide, pleased with how all of this has gone, that he's played the helpful, supportive teacher so well. "You're so welcome."

I force myself to make it through my after-school Science Bowl and Math Olympiad meetings, and when I finally arrive home, it's a sweet relief. I shut the front door behind me and lean my head against the wood, never more grateful to be away from everything. Safe. Finally. But not for long.

"Jill. Get in here right now." Mom is sitting at the dining room table with a glass of red wine. Dad stands behind her with his arms crossed over his chest. The rumpled sleeves of his button-down are rolled up to his elbows and his tie is loose, hanging limp around his neck. "Something you want to tell us?" Mom says before turning her mouth into a straight line.

"Just tell me what you want to hear. I can't do this today." I drop my bag and slump into a seat next to her.

She sighs and pats my head. "I knew this school would be a lot for you." Mom takes a long sip and sets the glass back down. Dad wipes his face with his hands and I can tell he's exhausted—that he didn't need this tonight. A wave of shame passes through me. "I know how hard you've worked, how you've thrived and excelled beyond our wildest dreams."

My heart sinks with the fraud of it all, the cheating, the grades. I'm exhausted by all the effort to pretend.

"But failing? Jill, this isn't like you."

"Mr. Beaumont called?" I ask.

She shakes her head, her dark bob swinging from side to side. "Headmaster Weingarten."

He only calls when shit gets real. This can't be good.

"He's overreacting, Mom. Everything is fine. It was just one bad test. Mr. Beaumont is letting me retake it on Monday."

"Is there something going on, honey?" Dad asks. "Is everything all right?"

"Yes," I whisper. "Everything's fine."

"Are you sure?" His eyes are pleading. He wants me to know I can tell him anything, but . . . I can't. I don't think that's what they really want, anyway. No parent really means that. They just want me to be perfect. A little trophy they can celebrate and fawn over when things go right. They don't want a cheater, someone who inflicted pain on others without a second thought. They don't want to know how I've corrupted Jared beyond repair, or how I'm terrorized at night wondering who really killed Shaila—and if everything we know is a lie. They can't know the dozens of ways I let them down.

"Everything is fine," I say again.

"Okay, then," Dad relents.

Mom's shoulders tense and she takes another sip, smacking her lips together. "Look," she says. "I don't have to tell you how hard we've worked to keep you and your brother at Gold Coast, how much we've sacrificed. You've done so well under all this pressure and you've already gotten into Brown. You're so close. You've made us so proud. Let's just keep it up, you know?"

She tries to relax, offering a sad half smile, but her eyes betray her. Worry. Doubt. I *know* they're both thinking about the Women in Science and Engineering scholarship and how I desperately need to earn it in order to actually go to Providence. It's not over yet and we all know it.

The lines around Mom's mouth are deeper than they've ever been and I try to think of all the things they didn't have because they decided to send us to Gold Coast. To find the money for uniforms and field trips and fancy meal plans and Science Bowl dues. To make us feel like we belong. To give us the world.

I used to think that by getting tapped to be a Player, I had earned a golden ticket, been given entry into the upper echelons of society. I did what my parents wanted. I became the trophy. I became worthy.

But I didn't. It was all a lie. Fake grades. Fake friends. Dead friend.

I have to make this okay.

"I know," I say softly.

"Good." Mom picks up the wineglass and brings it millimeters from her mouth. She inhales deeply then drains the whole thing.

FIFTEEN

I MANAGE A 93 on my English makeup test and a small burst of pride flames in my chest when Mr. Beaumont drops the paper on my desk. *Better,* he wrote in his thick red pen. *Much better.* I smile to myself, knowing that this time hardcore studying actually paid off. I earned this one on my own and no one can take that away from me. Maybe I *can* actually nail Brown's scholarship test. My brain begins plotting a study guide, spinning through figures and equations I'll need to memorize.

I pass Henry in the hall and resist the urge to reach out and grab his wrist, to share the good news. He keeps his eyes straight in front of him, nodding to the undies as he makes his way to the locker room. I wonder if he's hurting, if he's really wearing armor just to make it through the day, too. He disappears into the gym with his lacrosse gear and I turn the corner, gunning for the front door.

January wind whips my hair around my face. Being so close to the water makes winters here unbearable. It's why so many people escape to Palm Beach or the Caribbean for spring break. Only 4 p.m. and the sun's almost gone.

I rub my hands together in the front seat of Mom's car—she

let me take it this morning—and wait for the heat to kick in before I start driving. Then my phone buzzes.

Please let it be him, I think. It's been a week since I heard from Adam. He went to some school-sponsored writer's retreat in Oregon where, he warned me, he didn't have Wi-Fi. He should be back already. He should have texted.

But it's not Adam. It's Rachel.

So . . .

It's a menacing word, unrelenting with a million possibilities.

Last chance . . . I'm going to visit Graham this weekend. I think you should come.

I inhale sharply. I shut my eyes and try to imagine Graham wherever he is, his angled chin, his sandy hair. He was always broad, not muscly like Henry or soft like Quentin. Just kind of solid, like a wall or a couch. His confidence was in his walk, the cocky way he held his head. He played football in the fall because he said he liked to hit people and see the fear in their eyes when they saw him coming. Lacrosse in the spring, for the same reasons. He wanted to check kids hard in the chest with a metal stick and watch them writhe. But he was always jovial after games, relentless in his need for people to tell him they were okay. "It's just fun," he'd say, shoving Henry a little too hard in the shoulder.

Mr. Calloway never showed up to any Gold Coast game, not a carnival nor a fundraiser, even though he was a student here himself. That school stuff was for his wife, Muffy Calloway. She was the ultimate society woman, turning her nose up at my mom for being a sculptor and a teacher, for not being a member of the Gold Coast Country Club, for being Jewish. She had such a fantastically absurd name that elicited the kind of lewd jokes you'd expect Graham to make. But anytime someone tried—

Robert once—he'd ball his hand into a fist and feign a stomach punch. Fire in his eyes and a crooked smile on his face, Graham wouldn't take that shit. Better to be inside the joke than out of it.

In the middle of freshman year, I learned that Muffy Calloway wasn't always a white-blonde sad sack who only wore monogrammed cashmere, pearls in her ears, and a thick strand to match around her neck. She was once Monica Rogers, just another Mayflower chaser from somewhere outside Philly.

Graham revealed that to me one night at his house when his parents were out of town. Shaila was gone, in another room, somewhere else entirely, and Graham had snagged a bottle of sake from the *good* liquor cabinet. His breath reeked of pepperoni and I wondered if mine did, too. "Let's split this," he said, laughing. "Quick, before anyone finds out."

I giggled and followed him into the study. A few sips later, we had entered some weird alternate universe where our brains had melded and it was normal to share secrets with each other. I confided in him that I was worried Shaila and I were drifting.

"She has you," I said sheepishly.

Graham bumped my shoulder with his fist. "I'll never replace her friends." He took a sip straight from the slim bottle. "You know our Hamptons friend, Kara Sullivan? She said the same thing."

"Really?"

He nodded. "But she's jealous of *you*." He jabbed a thick finger in my direction. "I told her Shaila can have more than one best friend."

I thought of Nikki, too. How we were all just orbiting around Shaila, vying for her affection and interest. How did we determine she was the most deserving?

"You know she couldn't live without you guys." Graham

turned and looked me in the eye. "For real."

The thought comforted me in ways I didn't know I needed. I wondered if Nikki had ever talked to him like this.

The conversation shifted to our families, Jared and Rachel, mostly. Then Graham took another sip and started talking about Muffy. "You should see the hellhole my mom had to claw out of to get her flat, bony ass all the way to Gold Coast. Pathetic."

"She's not so bad," I said, trying to recall a time I hadn't seen her wearing a matching sweater set.

"Only reason she got out is because she met my dad at a Buffalo Wild Wings when he was on a business trip." Graham took another sip. "She could smell his Goldman Sachs business card, I bet. Started calling herself Muffy. Murdered Monica and all her 'trash' relatives, as she calls them," he said, using air quotes. "Ridiculous."

I let out a nervous giggle, but Graham shook his head. His tone had changed.

"Not funny, Newman," he said, staring me dead in the eyes. "Now she walks on eggshells all the time, so scared of making one wrong move and becoming Monica again. We're all just hanging on by a thread."

At the time his words were whatever—weird. I chalked it up to the alcohol, mostly. Now they seem like a premonition.

What do you think?

Rachel's texts beckon me and the little blue cursor blinks over and over.

You in?

I think about the people here, the people I thought were my home. Now Nikki and Quentin avoid me at every turn. Marla's barely made eye contact with me, even though I know she's curious about Graham's innocence, too. Henry keeps flashing his puppy dog eyes at me in the hallway, even when Robert gives me the middle finger. Mom and Dad are disappointed in me, scared I won't deliver on their investment. Jared sneers at me every time he sees me, breathing fire through his nose. Adam's been MIA. What else do I have to lose?

I'm in.

Rachel's a good driver, better than I remember or expect. Assured. Gentle. She lets the silence sit between us as bare trees whip by on the Merritt Parkway and the speedometer climbs past seventy. Snowbanks have frozen over into little mounds of ice, and we're the only car on the road as far as I can see. Saturday, 8 a.m., in the dead of January must be an unpopular time to hightail it to western Connecticut.

"Pass me one?" she says, without taking her eyes off the road.

I reach into the greasy paper bag in my lap and pull out a mini powdered donut, still slightly warm from when I picked them up from Diane's. Rachel's one request. Just like old times.

She pinches one with two fingers and lets the sugar fall on her chest like snow. She makes no move to brush it off. "Ugh," she moans with a mouthful of flour and butter. "Nothing like pow-do." She pops the rest into her mouth. "I miss that place." Even though her voice sounds chipper, Rachel looks like shit. Her skin is pale and her thick wavy hair hangs in stringy ropes down her back. Her eyes are fixated, obsessed, and her sweater is baggier than anything I can ever remember her wearing. Little moth holes prick each sleeve.

"Can I ask you something?" I say.

"You already did." Her mouth curls up into a smile. "Shoot."

"Why aren't you at school?" It's what I've been wanting to ask her since she invited me to her place in the city, so far from Cornell, where she was supposed to be in the middle of her junior year. "Don't you have another year left?"

"I graduated early. Stayed there every summer. Took six classes a semester. Worked myself into the ground. It was the only thing that made me feel better . . . like I was normal," she says, shaking her head. "But everyone knew. They looked at me like *I* was the one who was accused of murder. I couldn't escape this shit there." Rachel sighs and props one elbow up on the window, leaning her head against her palm. "You know, you're the only person I've talked to in three years, besides Graham, who really knew me before, who knew what we were like. But now, everyone I work with, my new friends, my girlfriend, Frida—to them I'm just Rachel. No one knows shit." She smiles. "It's so freeing."

"So, why?" I ask. "Why start all of this now?" I really want to ask, *Is it worth it?*

"What would you do?" she asks. "If your entire hometown assumed you, too, were guilty of *something, anything,* just because of who your family is? If your whole life was turned upside down by the people you trusted most in this entire world? Because that's what this is like."

"But everyone's going to know," I say. "All the new people in your life. You're going to be in the *news,* probably." The original article I saw didn't mention her, but if this was real, if Graham was *actually* innocent, Rachel would be front row center.

Rachel smiles again but her eyes mist over. "He's my baby

brother," she says quietly. "Don't you have a little brother?"

I nod. "Yeah."

"Bryce's age, right?"

"Mm-hm."

"He's a Player?" She asks like she already knows. I nod. "What if this were about him? If your brother was assumed to have *killed* someone, to have taken their life? And if the person who *died* was someone you knew so well, spent so much time with, you felt their loss every single day?"

That person *is* lost to me. Shaila is gone. If Jared had done it . . . I can't even bring myself to imagine what I would do. I shake my head.

"If he says he didn't do it, if the blood evidence doesn't lie, then I want the truth. I want to know who's responsible. And I want them to pay." She grips the steering wheel hard and floors the gas. "We're close," she says.

The final leg of the drive is all twisty-turny roads and poorly marked exits. We pass them in silence. Rachel makes a hard left and a gray wooden sign comes into view, nearly hidden behind a curtain of branches. I'm barely able to make out the dull white letters: DANBURY JUVENILE CENTER. I wonder who else is locked up here, kept so far from the rest of society. Not off the grid, but only just on.

Gravel and salt crunch under the tires and about a half mile down the road, we approach a chain-link fence. It opens as if operated by a phantom guard and I scoot forward, craning to see what's ahead. When we emerge from another narrow path, there sits a concrete expanse the size of a football field, marked neatly by white-painted lines. The lot is nearly full with BMWs, Mercedes, and Audis. Helpful, clear markers hang overhead.

VISITORS LOUNGE THIS WAY, one reads in navy block lettering with an arrow underneath. PATIENCE IS A VIRTUE, another one says in cursive scrawl.

"Knock, knock! Need a hand?" A middle-aged woman with saggy cheeks and graying hair appears, standing just outside my window in an all-khaki snowsuit and an eager grin. Her name badge says VERONICA, VISITOR HOST.

I look to Rachel but she's already out of the car, coming around my side. "Hi, V."

"Oh, it's you, dear! Nice to see you."

"You too." Rachel rubs her gloved hands together and motions to me through the door. "C'mon."

The air is sharp and icy. It burns my throat. I wonder what the hell I've gotten myself into.

"This is Jill," Rachel says when I step down from the passenger side. "She's a frie—" but she stops herself and redirects. "She knew Graham."

Veronica nods, showing no emotion, no sign of recognition. "Welcome to Danbury, then," she says. "Follow me."

We do, but I can barely keep up, shuffling my feet forward to try to catch Rachel. I should have asked her more about this place, about what Graham has been doing for the past three years. But instead I'm totally oblivious to everything around us. Veronica pulls open a metal door and leads us down a wide hallway decorated with collaged dream boards and ink drawings until we come to a pair of French doors and a brightly lit cube that looks more like a doctor's waiting room than the jails I've seen on TV.

"Come right this way. You'll need to fill out some forms as a first-time guest." She click-clacks on the keyboard and a ream of paper flies from the printer. "Here's a pen, sweetie."

Rachel raps her knuckles against the Formica countertop and taps her foot impatiently on the floor. I speed up my work, checking boxes until I reach the final page, where I scribble my name.

"Done," I say.

"Finally," Rachel mumbles. But when I throw her a look, she immediately mouths "Sorry." I guess I can't blame her for being anxious, for wanting to see Graham as quickly as possible. I'd be the same way with Jared.

A big, burly man in purple scrubs motions for us to follow him, and the next hallway is just as strange, cold and lined with tile, like a school. More hand-drawn artwork hangs on the walls.

When we reach another door, metal and massive, the guy stops and turns to us. "Rachel, you know the rules, but just a reminder, you can only stay an hour. No touching. Be positive."

"Thanks, TJ," Rachel says. "Go time?" She looks at me now.

I swallow the lump in my throat and break my fingers apart. I hadn't realized they were clasped together.

TJ pushes open the door to what looks like a cafeteria and makes a sweeping motion with his hand like he's a butler or a waiter at a fancy restaurant. My stomach does cartwheels and I scan the room frantically. I spot him before he sees me.

There, just across the room. Graham.

It's almost too much to bear. But I make myself look, to take him in from afar. He's dressed in light green scrubs, not handcuffed like I expected. He runs his fingers through his hair, a nervous tic that gives me déjà vu. He used to do that before major tests or Player pops. His chin has a faint sheen of stubble, making him look so much older than I remember, so much older than I feel right now. He stoops a bit, though it looks like he's grown at least a few inches taller. He's thin, too. Almost skinny, with sharper angles and darker shadows.

His head turns toward us slowly and his eyes meet mine. They widen as we register each other for the first time in nearly three years. Rachel is already by his side and I force myself to walk, to close the gap between us.

"Hi," he says. It's a mixture of shock and excitement. Curiosity, maybe.

"Hi."

Graham drops to a seat at a small circular table and I follow suit, mirroring his movements.

He throws me a sheepish smile, as if we haven't known each other since before puberty. As if I don't know all of his secrets.

"Um, how are you?" I ask because I don't know what else to say.

At first the words are sparse and he stumbles, as if he's trying to remember how people are supposed to converse or make small talk. He chats about the weather and points out other people around the room, kids about our age, talking to older folks who look like their parents or siblings. He motions to an Asian American boy who sits in silence as his mom plays a recording off an iPhone. "That's from his brother," Graham says. "He refuses to come visit, but Andy misses him so much." Rachel nods and purses her lips.

He doesn't say where these people came from or what they did to get here. He rambles on about the food, and how chicken tikka masala night is his favorite, but he used to look forward to spaghetti Bolognese night. He mentions how he's learned to play cricket from some of the British counselors in his "cohort," and that he's taken an interest in architecture. "I've read just about everything we have about Norman Foster and Zaha Hadid. I can't wait to visit the bridge she built in Abu Dhabi—it's, like, legendary," he says.

"So, you actually think you're getting out?" I say.

Graham's eyes dart to Rachel's and she nods, giving him the go-ahead. It's a ritual I'm not part of. A signal between them. Graham's mouth gets small. He hunches lower in his seat and curls his limbs into his body.

"I didn't do it, Jill." His voice is low and measured, deep and full, like he's practiced this line over and over. He's trying to be convincing. He runs a hand through his hair again.

Rachel leans in and rests her arms on the table. "Why don't you start from the beginning?" she says. Her eyes are wide and nurturing, motherly but urgent.

Graham nods and takes a big breath. He squeezes his mouth shut. Then the words tumble out.

"I don't remember much about everything that happened after," he says. "But I remember everything leading up to . . . that. Don't you?" His dark eyes make direct contact with mine. It's almost too intimate to bear.

A lump forms in my throat.

"You do, right?" he asks again. I nod once.

I do. The light spring breeze coming in from Ocean Cliff. Air so salty it stung my pores. No bugs yet. It was too early for mosquitos. Relief when I realized what I had to do. How every sip felt like poison sliding down my throat. Then, complete darkness swallowing me, filling me with paralyzing fear. It was all so much worse than I thought it would be.

I squeeze my eyes shut and try to make out Shaila in all of

this. I picture her gnawing at her ragged nails when she realized what *she* had to do. The moment her face went from determined to terrified.

"Yes," I whisper.

Graham's face goes cold. "Do you remember my initiation pop?"

How could I forget? Jake came up with all of them, we were told. "You were scared of spiders, right?"

"Tarantulas," Graham says. He shivers. "They brought out a dozen of 'em and I had to stand with them crawling all over me in that glass shower for hours."

"Four," I say. "Four hours." That's how long mine was, too.

"Huh," he says. "Two. Mine was only two."

Rachel mutters something under her breath.

"What?" I ask.

"The boys' were shorter. They were always shorter," she says softly, her head down.

Of course they were.

Graham keeps talking, though. "I begged for something to drink. Anything to take my mind off it. Obviously, they complied."

An image of Graham standing in the shower creeps into my brain. I hadn't *seen* it, of course. I was too busy trying to survive my own initiation. But I imagine they had sequestered him in another section of the pool house, dropping furry, creepy creatures on his head while feeding him cups of cheap tequila over the glass doorframe.

I glance at Rachel, but her face is in her hands.

"After that, I barely remember what came next," Graham says. "One minute I was crying like a baby, the next I was somewhere down the beach covered in blood. Can you imagine what that felt like?"

A little ball of anger begins to build inside me. "Can you imagine how *Shaila* felt?"

Graham's mouth forms a hard straight line. "No," he says, firm. "You know I loved her, right? With everything I had. We were only fifteen. But I would have done *anything* for her. She was my entire world."

His face is puffy and red.

"She was mine, too," I say, fighting back the tears.

"I know." Graham's voice is soft now. "Can I keep going?"

I relent and nod.

Graham inhales deeply. "I just remember commotion, everyone saying something happened to Shaila. Jake and Adam were running down the beach, calling for help. Derek Garry, too. I saw them coming toward me and I waved them down. Then there were cops. Those stupid Gold Coast traffic cops pulling up on their little sand buggies, whipping out handcuffs. They didn't even know how to use them."

I was back at the house at this point, recovering, feeling sorry for myself, worried I had been ruined by something I had no control over. I had no idea what was coming.

"They slapped them on me and drove me right to the station. And then that same night, they brought me here. I haven't left in three years."

"What exactly is this place?" I whisper.

Graham sighs and leans back in his chair. "A facility," he says. "Like juvie, but fancy. We can get our GEDs and do activities like pottery and stuff."

I must look confused because he keeps trying to explain.

"The criminal justice system is totally unfair. If you're rich, it's just easier."

Rachel snorts into her palms.

"It's the truth and it sucks," Graham continues. "Most of us are loaded. The ones who aren't are sponsored by some benefactor or nonprofit or something."

"What . . ."

"I know," he says. "But they're going to transfer me to fed when I turn eighteen in June."

"That's why . . ." I start. "This is your last shot."

Graham nods and his face flushes, like he's embarrassed, almost.

Rachel lifts her head out of her hands. "That's why we went looking for more evidence," she says. "The blood. The shirt. It was our last chance to test everything before they put him away for good." Her teeth look fluorescent as she bites her bright red lip.

"The police questioned me for hours," Graham says. "It was such a long time. Mom and Dad were away in the Cayman Islands, and they wouldn't let Rach in the room with me. Right?"

Rachel nods and bites her lip. "I kept trying to call Dan Smothers. He's our dad's lawyer. But no one answered. Our parents got the first flight out, but by then it was too late."

"I just broke down being in that stupid police room so long without anyone. They fed me the story and I just nodded along after a while. Told them what they wanted to hear. I just wanted to make it all stop. I just wanted to go home. I thought I'd just go home."

"They didn't even test anything," Rachel says softly.

"But your parents didn't fight it?" I ask. I can't imagine Mom and Dad letting me get shipped off to this place. They'd never believe that I did something like this. They'd do anything to protect me. That I'm sure of.

"Dad just wanted to make it all go away," Graham says. "He was getting ready for some big investor call. Smothers said it was easier that way. Thought a trial would make it worse. Too much publicity. Muffy didn't want to deal with it. Too much drama."

"They did some deal with the Arnolds," Rachel says. "Money was exchanged."

A fleeting look passes between them.

"A lot of money," Graham says. "Our families have history. This is just how they deal with things, I guess."

"Such fucking bullshit," Rachel says. "No one has the balls to even confront this. Of course the Sullivans stayed far away from everything."

"I guess you don't talk to Kara much," I say.

Graham snorts. "Good one. She never reached out, ever."

I picture Graham's and Shaila's fathers growing up together, buying plots of land in the Hamptons with their other buddy Jonathan Sullivan. I imagine they were all so delighted when they had children at the same time. They must have been thrilled to dress Graham, Shaila, and Kara in those matching blue seersucker outfits on the beach, to snap photos of them rolling around on monogrammed beach blankets. This destroyed everything.

"The 'rents don't come visit," Graham says. "Muffy says I'm insane, barely her son anymore. Dad's busy."

"So busy," Rachel says, rolling her eyes.

"Do they know you're using your trust to test the blood?" I ask her.

Rachel nods. "But they don't want to get involved."

We're all quiet for a few seconds until Graham says softly, "You never gave up on me. You're the only one." He looks up and his eyes are glossy with tears.

Rachel grabs his hand under the table, out of sight, and I can't help but think of Jared and how I would do the exact same thing for him, no matter the cost, no matter how much he hates me in this moment. You don't give up on your blood.

"So what does this all mean?" I ask.

"Someone else was there," Graham says. "Someone blamed me. I thought I was a monster for three years, but . . . it wasn't my fault. It wasn't me."

His words seep into my brain and begin to spin violently around. I can't make sense of anything.

"But who?" I ask. It's the only missing piece. Who else would have wanted to kill Shaila? And why?

Graham inhales deeply and closes his eyes. "There's one more thing. Something I haven't told anyone. Not even you, Rach." Rachel raises her eyebrows and leans forward. "Before initiation, I found out she was cheating on me."

"No," I say automatically. It's just not possible. There's no way she would have kept that from me.

"It's true," he says. "She'd been acting weird for weeks, avoiding me, making up excuses not to hang out. She always said she was in rehearsal for the musical. Or working on her English papers, or going to office hours with Beaumont. It was always something."

Was that really how she was at the end? Not really, no. A little more aloof than usual, perhaps. But she was stressed about initiation *and* starring in the spring musical. It was *Rent* that year and she had been cast as Mimi. Of course she was nervous. She nailed the performances, obviously, belting out that candle song like Rosario Dawson. And Shaila seemed to chill out after that, didn't she? She must have.

Nikki was working on costumes then, ripping holes in hundred-dollar pairs of sheer tights, sewing leather micro-shorts to fit Shaila's body perfectly. Adam was there, too, tweaking the script so it was more "family friendly."

"They're making me neuter it," he said while we all huddled together at Diane's one Sunday morning.

"Listen to Shakespeare over here," Nikki said.

Shaila and Nikki giggled in delight, as if it were an inside joke they had formed backstage.

Graham and Rachel were there, too. They laughed along with me, like we were also part of it. Like we knew their secret language.

I *did* see Shaila all the time before initiation. I must have. Sure, she was tired from playing Mimi. And she was with Graham a lot, of course. But . . . maybe she wasn't. Maybe she was doing something else. *Someone* else.

"I forgot my phone during spring midterms," Graham continues, "and I needed the geometry guide. She gave me her phone to look it up and, fuck, I knew I shouldn't have, but when she went to the bathroom, I looked at her texts. I couldn't help it. There were hundreds with some dude, talking about all the shit they were doing behind my back." He closes his eyes. "I can still remember one by heart. *Graham will never find out.*" His lashes flutter and he taps his knuckles on the table. "Guess what? I did."

"Who?" I ask.

"I don't know. I didn't recognize the number. It wasn't even a Gold Coast area code. Probably a burner phone."

"Did you ever confront her?"

Graham shakes his head. "I was waiting for the right time. But then . . ."

Rachel cuts him off. "No one can know."

"Why not?" I ask.

"A motive," Rachel says.

Graham nods. "It's even more ammo against me. Jealous boyfriend kills girlfriend after he finds out she's going around behind his back? A tale as old as time."

I snort because he's right. Was Shaila really cheating, though? The idea turns my stomach and suddenly I'm hot and sweaty and a little nauseous.

"Where's the bathroom?" I say quickly.

Rachel points to the corner of the room. When I close the stall door behind me, I sit down on the cold ceramic bowl and turn over Graham's words in my mind, trying to make sense of everything he said. His admission must feel like a relief to him. But Graham didn't look lighter or comforted. He was like a shell of someone I used to know, a fossil discovered from a life I once lived. I wonder if somewhere below the surface, a sociopath sits numb to the pain he has caused, looking for a way out of this cushioned-wall bubble, hungry for manipulation, sick of boredom.

Sometimes it's hard to know which qualities really define you, and which ones have been affixed to you by others so many times that you actually begin to believe them and claim them as your own. Mom always told me I was so trusting, a trait she adored but feared would get me into trouble. Because of that, I came to think of myself as gullible, one who could be taken advantage of. Being so close to Graham, I wonder if that's what's happening now, if I'm ready to trust him simply because he's here, right in front me, when Shaila is not. In this tiny steel stall, it occurs to me that Graham could be lying.

I wash my hands slowly and return to sit across from him and Rachel.

"Why should I believe you?" I ask, looking him straight in the eyes.

Graham shakes his head and looks down at the floor. "You think I'm full of shit."

I keep my face still, holding my cards tightly to my chest. I want to believe him but his truth means someone else I know is guilty. I'm not sure I can stand that.

Rachel slams her hands on the table hard enough that TJ turns toward us. "Jill," she hisses. "Trust him." It's a command, not a suggestion.

"You can believe me or not," Graham says quietly, measured. "But the fact is, I'm going to clear my name with or without you. Which side of the story do you want to be on?" He crosses his arms, now defiant, so sure of himself, more like the Graham I once knew. "You cared about Shaila as much as I did."

TJ arrives at our table and gently places a hand on Graham's shoulder. "Time's up, Calloways." He offers a smile. "You can always come back next week."

Rachel rises and exchanges more secret looks with her brother. They seem connected, tethered to one another. I can practically feel Rachel fighting the urge to hug him. The secret language of siblings is so intimate, I feel the need to look away. Graham glances once more in my direction before turning to retreat, shuffling down a white corridor. His long arms hang by his side, fingers fidgeting at he gets farther and farther away. Soon we can't see him at all.

Next to me, Rachel lets out a long gush of air. "Let's go."

SIXTEEN

I'M STILL IN a daze a week later, thinking about everything that happened in Connecticut, when I first see the flyers. They're tacked to the corkboard at Diane's, covering up an ad for babysitting and another one for piano lessons. Printed on thick cardstock, likely stolen from Gold Coast Prep's art department, the letters scream out at me.

WONDER TRUCK
ONE NIGHT ONLY
THE GARAGE
TONIGHT, JANUARY 25
8 P.M.
$5

"Jared's gonna be a stah." Diane comes up behind me and nudges my shoulder with hers. She throws me a wink. Since it's 7 a.m. on a Saturday, I'm the only one in the diner, save for a few elderly folks eating bowls of oatmeal in silence. I thought I'd be safe coming here so early to start studying for the scholarship exam over pow-do and bacon, but I should have known better. The Players, Jared now included, are everywhere.

"I saw him here the other day with the Millah boy chit-chatting 'bout the show," Diane says. "Should be a treat, right?" She smiles widely at me, her red mess of hair bouncing on top of her head.

I swallow a thick lump in my throat and force myself to agree. "Oh yeah," I say. My mouth feels like it's full of sand. "Can I get a couple pow-do to go?"

"Coming right up." Diane disappears behind the counter and I lean back against the wall and close my eyes. Jared booked a show. *How did I not know about this?*

I desperately want to text Nikki or Quentin to hear what the plan is for tonight. Or ask Henry to pick me up so we can go together. There's obviously going to be a Player pregame, Ubers to the Garage, an after-party to celebrate. I want to ask Jared why he didn't tell me, to scream at Mom that I've been left out of everything, including our family. I want to bitch about it to Rachel, though I know she'll only want to talk about last week's visit to see Graham, something I'm definitely not ready to process.

Instead, I text the one person who hasn't completely written me off. Yet.

Did you hear about the boys' show tonight? I text Adam. If he's around, he'll respond.

Yeah.

You going? I type with shaking fingers. I miss him so much it aches. I want him to wrap me in one of his famous bear hugs.

To read me lines from his new script. To smile at me and reveal that dimple.

Yup.

Wanna meet up before?

Can't, he writes. It stings. But then he starts typing again, those three bubbles drumming along in rhythm. *Working on a thing with Big Keith before.*

I chew on my lip. Can I ask him to bail? Can't he sense how much I need this? Him.

Got it, I say.

I'll see you there, Newman, don't worry. I got you.

My stomach flips and heat spreads through my chest. We're still us.

If you squint really hard, the main drag in Gold Coast looks more like a slice of SoHo than what it really is: a stretch of concrete next to the sand. There's a tiny boutique shilling moisturizers with triple-digit price tags and something called "heart glitter," a cycling studio that caters to the spandex-clad moms drinking twelve-dollar green juices, a sushi bar with an omakase menu the *New York Times* food critic once said was "almost worth leaving the five boroughs for," and the one relic of Gold Coast past, the Garage.

It's the only music venue north of the Long Island Expressway that regularly books acts from farther than New Jersey, and once my parents swore they saw Billy Joel holed up at a back table for an entire night, sipping vintage wine and sending vodka shots to blondes in the front row. But that was back in the nineties. Now it's mostly referred to as a vestige of *old* Gold

Coast, the one that attracted funky potters like my mom and ex-corporate lawyers looking to spend the rest of their days bumming by the beach in a house predating the Civil War. That Gold Coast was filled with people who didn't have closets full of Brooks Brothers polos and kitchens stocked with Waterford Crystal. I always thought the Garage lasted so long because it's a reminder of how far you can fall.

Robert's cousin Luis became the booker there a few years back after he realized there was a whole unconquered nightlife scene outside New York City limits. He always let us in for free. I assume he must have gone out on a major limb for Jared and Bryce, hooking them up with a prime slot on a Saturday night. But when I arrive, there's a line around the block. I recognize dozens of Gold Coast kids and a few Cartwright students who sometimes try to crash Player parties. Stickers and graffiti paper the place's outer walls, a stark contrast to the sea of button-downs, ironed khakis, and two-hundred-dollar fleeces. Most girls are in their after-school best, teetering on tall black booties meant for a Manhattan club or sorority rush week. I silently judge a group of sophomores who clearly got blowouts for the occasion.

When I get to the front of the line, Luis is there taking tickets. I start to smile, knowing he remembers me. "Five bucks," he says, his face like stone. My days of free shit are over. I hand him a crumpled bill and walk inside.

The air is dank and stale and I'm suddenly so aware that I'm alone. I wonder who sees me, who cares, and if my presence will be fodder for the gossip mill for weeks. Then I wonder if that thought is just plain narcissistic. No one really cares. That's what I have to remember. I make my way to the bar, a slimy C-shaped piece of wood nestled under an anarchist flag, and push past the sky-high heels and flipped-up collars. But before I reach the sticky counter, someone touches the small of my back.

"Hey, Newman."

I whip around to find Adam standing in front of me wearing a black jean jacket and his round plastic glasses. He looks tired, his face scruffy and a little sad, but he hands me a cold can of grapefruit-flavored seltzer. I'm secretly grateful it's not beer.

"You're here," I say. "Thank God."

He smiles and puts his arm around me. "Wouldn't miss it." He takes a sip from his matching can and nods toward the corner of the stage. I follow his gaze to find the Players looking back at me. Henry pouts and shoves his hands into his pockets. Robert shoots up a middle finger yet again and Marla averts her eyes. But it's Nikki's and Quentin's reactions that hurt the most. They both just stare at me, their faces unreadable. I want to be in between them again, privy to the secrets, the rituals, our inside jokes. Instead I chug my seltzer.

"You're not scared about being seen with me?" I ask.

Adam nods his head at them and waves. Only Quentin holds his hand up in recognition. "Psh, never," he says. "What did they ever do for me anyway?"

My face flushes as the lights go down, making the Garage a pitch-black abyss. A guitar snare ripples through the room. Cheers erupt and a spotlight shines on the stage. My skin prickles and a bead of sweat drips down my back.

"We're Wonder Truck and we're about to fucking get it!" Bryce yells into the microphone. Behind him, seven-foot Larry Kramer perches at the drum kit, nearly as tall sitting down as Bryce is standing up.

Adam lets out a whoop and yells into the crowd. "Yeah,

Miller!" His body rustles beside me.

The room becomes a tornado, people jumping everywhere, bumping into each other. The Players, even the freshmen, stand near the front and throw their hands up at the stage. A group from the debate team are grinding in the corner, gyrating their crotches against one another about a half beat off time.

I train my eyes on Jared. He stands on the right side of the stage, red-faced and elated. His brow is damp and his bass rests on one knee, which juts out into a lunge. He rocks back and forth setting a solid rhythm for Bryce's janky guitar chords. Sweat drips from his brow and his eyelids flutter. I recognize his hyper-focused face, the one he gets when he's concentrating on a geometry practice set or trying to get through a dense book. But now his mouth extends into an easy smile. This isn't work. It's the time of his life.

When the song ends, Jared tosses his hair and wipes his face on his white T-shirt. He looks up as the crowd cheers and his eyes scan the room. His gaze lingers on where I stand for just a second and I wonder if he can see me through the bright lights. I wonder if he knows I'm here, that I'm rooting for him.

Before I can tell, they rush into another song, just as loud and just as fast. The Garage feels like a bounce house, expanding and contracting with every launched step. The wooden floorboards creak and sag.

"They're killing it!" Adam yells over the music. His voice is warm and wet in my ear. "Jared's amazing!"

He is, I want to say back. He really is. But now I can only focus on Nikki and Quentin, dancing together in the corner, singing all the words, lyrics I don't know and wasn't invited to learn. I miss them in my bones, like Shaila but almost worse because they're actually still here, just across the room.

"I need some air!" I scream back at Adam. I wait a beat, hoping he'll follow me, but he doesn't. Instead he nods and keeps his eyes focused on the stage, pumping his fist in the air.

I turn on my heel and squeeze through the sea of sweaty bodies, until I reach the side door. The heavy metal lurches forward when I shoulder it open and the freezing wind shocks me, whipping my face and tossing my hair. Suddenly I can breathe again. I'm free. I lean back against the brick wall and lift my chin, spotting Aries the ram. I trace his horns and picture him headbutting the other nightwalkers, galloping through the sky. My fingers are frozen from the chill but I don't care. It feels good to not feel them, to let something go numb.

I'm not alone for long. The door heaves open, bringing sounds from the Garage into the alley. Guitar chords carry into the night.

Nikki emerges from the darkness and stomps on the frozen concrete in designer black combat boots. I press myself against the building, hoping she doesn't see me. "I know you're out here," she calls.

I wince. I'm not ready for this. I've never been good at fighting or confrontation. When Shaila was still here she was the one who stood up for all of us. She was the one who slapped Derek Garry's hand away when he tried to reach up my dress during one of the pops. She was the one who told Liza Royland to *suck a dick* after she let the air out of the tires of my bike in middle school. She was the one who reported Assistant Coach Doppelt for staring at us too long in the locker rooms after phys ed. Shaila was our guard dog. I was the puppy trying not to piss on the floor.

I realize, standing here in the freezing cold, I don't want to fight with Nikki. I don't want to be mad at her. I want to hug her and pretend like we're not on opposite teams. I want to know if she'd believe Graham, if she would be as hungry for the truth as I am, if she saw what I saw. If she knew what I knew.

I take a deep breath in. "Here," I say, stepping forward.

Nikki clomps toward me so we're face-to-face, exactly the same height. Her mouth contorts into a hurt frown, a pout. Her eyes are wild. She's had a few drinks. Not too many, but just enough to feel a fire in her belly, to muster up her wannabe-Shaila courage. Maybe I should find mine, too.

"I'm mad at you," Nikki says, crossing her arms and cocking her hip. "I'm really fucking mad."

"I'm mad at you, too." My words are more wobbly than hers. Unstable.

"You said we'd do this together. But then you fucking bailed. You left me all alone!"

I scoff. "*I* left *you*? You have Quentin, Marla, Robert. Henry, even. You have everyone," I counter. "I'm the one who's all alone."

"It's not the same without you," she says. "You know that."

"You went against everything we said we would do." I fight the tears threatening my vision.

"That's not true."

I bite my lip. I want to scream. "You know it is. You made the pops so much worse for them. You have the power now and you're acting just like *them*. Like Derek, and Jake, and all the other boys who put us through hell."

Nikki's eyes narrow. "No, I'm not."

"How can you not see this?" I feel like I'm losing my mind, like she's totally delusional.

"I'm not the queen of the universe, Jill. Anyone can say no. It's not like we're *forcing* them to do anything."

"But you are," I say. My throat is scratchy and raw. "We

have the power. They don't. Did you ever feel once, when we were freshmen, that we could say no? Think of how they feel right now."

"This is so classic, Jill. You're just trying to protect yourself. So if anything goes down, if anything happens to your precious little brother, *you* won't be the one to blame. You always let Shay take the fall for you. You're letting me do it now."

My jaw drops open. I stumble backward, feeling like I've been smacked in the face. I know exactly what Nikki's talking about. The Midwinter Challenge. The night where Shaila almost sacrificed everything for me.

It was an unseasonably warm Friday night in February and we were all called to Jake's basement for a full class pop. I panicked when I got the text. I was supposed to be at the All-County Math Olympiad Challenge at 8 a.m. the next morning. There were only two weekend meets a year, and I had specifically requested to have those days off.

"Sure," Adam had said when I asked. "Won't be a problem."

But I knew there was no way I'd get out of participating. Not if Jake was running the show.

Shit, I texted Shaila. *I can't drink tonight . . .*

Don't worry. I'll cover for you.

I sent her a million heart emojis and prayer hands before leaving to accept our fate.

When we arrived at Jake's, there were a few junior boys there, too. But no Adam, or any of the girls. Jake ordered us into what seemed like a small closet. It smelled of cedar and lavender at first. Two handles of vodka sat atop slim benches.

"Drink," Jake said in his deep monotone. "Drink till they're done."

The guys behind him laughed and shouted out some whooping noises.

Robert scoffed. "That's it?"

A slow, scary smile spread across Jake's face. "Yep," he said. "That's it."

Then he turned and closed the door. A small click let us know it was locked.

"Well, this should be easy," Robert said. He picked up one of the bottles and brought it to his lips to take a swig. But after sipping only a tiny bit, he spit his mouthful onto the floor. "Ugh, gross, it's hot."

Shaila groaned and sat down on the bench. Then her eyes grew wide. "Wait. Is anyone else, like, really warm?" She pulled her fleece over her head to expose a tiny piece of flesh between her pants and her top.

It *was* hot. And it was only getting hotter. Steam rose from the floor. I looked up. It was coming through the slats on the ceiling, too.

"Jesus," Quentin said as he spun around the small room. "You guys, this is a sauna."

We were all silent as reality set in. Jake was cranking the heat up high. Too high. Suddenly, I was so aware of my armpits and the boiling sensation between my toes. I breathed in deeply and swallowed too much hot air. Panic began to rise in my throat and I felt like I was going to collapse.

"Let's get this over with," Marla said. She whipped off her sweater and took a long slug. Her face contorted as she choked it down. "That is vile."

She passed the bottle to Henry and it went around the circle, until Nikki placed it at my feet.

I picked it up and thought about the next day. How I could

get kicked off the team if I performed like shit, how that could affect my scholarship or my shot at an Ivy, how it could ruin everything my parents worked for. Everything *I* worked for. My hands started to shake and I blinked back tears. It was all too much. "I can't drink," I said softly to no one in particular. "Olympiad tomorrow. I can't mess it up."

For a moment no one spoke, and then Shaila grabbed the bottle. "I'll drink for her. Whatever."

Nobody seemed to care and slowly my fear subsided. I squeezed Shaila's hand and said a silent *thank you* as she drank more and more.

Soon, we were all bright red and dripping in sweat. My throat felt scratchy from dehydration. Henry wiped his face on his shirt, though it was already see-through.

"I have to lie down," Nikki said. Her skin had turned the color of a tomato and her long dark hair was matted around her face.

"Come on. We're so close," Shaila slurred. She held up the second bottle, which was still about a third full. It was impossible to know how much time had passed but Shaila was swaying at that point.

"Are you okay?" I whispered into her ear.

"Yeah, yeah, yeah," she said. But when I saw her face, her eyes were cloudy and her mouth was slack. She looked right through me.

Actually, everyone was sort of on that level, dipping in and out of reality. Loopy and growing loopier. But Shaila seemed in a league of her own.

"How much did you have?" I hissed.

"I'm drinking for you, remember?" she said, not unkindly. She smiled a little. "That's what friends are for." Then she lifted the bottle and took another huge gulp. Her throat moved up and down as the liquid slid into her stomach.

Graham shook his head and grabbed it from her hands. "No, babe. That's enough." Then he drained the whole thing and clasped a hand over his mouth to keep it all down.

"Jake!" Robert screamed, banging on the door with the other empty handle. "We're done!"

"Finally!" Jake unhitched the latch and we tumbled out of the sauna in a tangle of wet cotton and limbs. The air was a relief and we all gasped, trying to suck it down as quickly as possible. Shaila stumbled out last and almost immediately sank to the floor, leaning up against the wall.

"I don't feel so good," she said quietly.

"Uh-oh," some junior Player mumbled. "She's looking rough."

Jake squatted down next to her and stared at her hard, then at the rest of us, at me. "She had more than everyone else, didn't she?"

We stayed silent.

Just then, Shaila turned to one side and in one long burp, she vomited a sticky beige stream onto the hardwood floor.

"Aw, gross," Jake said, kicking his leg out in front of him. "She puked on my limited editions!"

Shaila slumped forward and onto her other side. She was passed out.

"Um, guys," I said, my voice shaking. "I think we need to do something."

"Oh shit," Nikki slurred. "We need to take her to the hospital."

The junior boys groaned. "Ugh, this happens every year," one said. I think it was Reid Jefferson, the star of the debate team. "She needs her stomach pumped. I can take her." He started putting on his jacket.

"Are you an idiot?" Jake said. "We're all underage." His eyes were wide with fury. Maybe fear. "Get out of my house. Everyone. Figure it out on your own."

"What?" Henry said. "Are you serious?"

"Do I not sound serious?" Jake asked. "I'm not going to Princeton if they find out I almost killed some idiot freshman girl."

The boys around him nodded as if that seemed like a legit excuse.

I froze, seeing no clear path away from disaster. But Marla took charge. "Come on, guys. I'll call my brothers." She wrapped Shaila's arm around her shoulder. "Graham, take her other side. Make sure she keeps breathing. Jill, grab her stuff."

I followed orders silently, grateful for something to do with my hands, and gathered Shaila's jacket and backpack. I scurried up the stairs, following Marla's lead. Nikki whimpered softly behind me, terrified and drunk. "Come on," I said, grabbing her.

When we stepped outside, the cold shocked us all into reality and the air turned sour with dread. It was so dark, too dark, not a star in sight.

"Those assholes," Graham muttered. Everyone else huddled in silence, waiting for Marla's brothers' truck to come barreling down the pitch-black road. Finally, a pair of headlights careened toward us.

"What the hell, Mar?" James, the oldest, was in the passenger seat and rolled down the window to see what was up. "Are you guys total dummies or what?"

"Not tonight," she said. "Please. Just help me, okay? We've got to get her home." Her eyes pleaded with them as they mumbled their disapproval. Marla turned to me. "Are her parents there?"

I shook my head. "They're in the Hamptons."

"Good. Help me get her up."

Graham, Marla, and I heaved Shaila's dead weight into the back seat as she tried to say something incoherent. I let out a rush of air. She was awake.

"Not enough room for all of us," Marla said. "Nikki, Jill, come with me. We can all stay at Shaila's tonight."

We piled into the back seat and left the boys standing in the frigid darkness. I shoved myself into the far side, so Shaila was propped up in between Marla and me. As soon as we buckled in, Cody, Marla's second-oldest brother, started driving. James turned up the radio and no one said a word as we barreled down the wooded, winding roads toward the Arnold estate.

When we got to Shaila's, we spent the next few hours in her bathroom, as she puked and puked until there was only green bile left. Marla brought her cold compresses, Advil, and Gatorade she found in the Arnolds' downstairs pantry. Nikki rubbed her back and held her hair in a tight ponytail as Shay lurched forward over the toilet again and again.

By the time morning broke, I finally left.

"It's fine," Marla said. "Go. I'd be the same if we had field hockey championships today." Nikki was still sleeping.

"Thank you," I said, trying not to cry.

"You'd do it for me," she said. "We all take care of each other."

I was in awe of her calm, how she kept her fear hidden. I always swore I would thank her again and come to her rescue if the time ever came. But it never did. Marla was always the steady one. She never lost her composure. She was the one we could count on. And we never spoke about that night again. None of us.

The fact that Nikki brings this up now, when the last thing

I want to do is think about how I let Shaila protect me when I never tried to save her, means she's out for blood.

Nikki bares her teeth and I step back, plastering my spine against the wall. "I thought you were my *best* friend," she whispers. "I already lost one."

My shoulders fall. It's so exhausting to fight. I just want to wrap her in my arms and remind her that *we* are the survivors. We need to band together. But there's an anger inside me I just can't let go. I don't know if she gets it. If she understands the damage we could cause . . . *have* caused.

"Jared's already changed," I say. "They all have. Even you. Running around as Toastmaster like you own Gold Coast." I want to breathe fire. I want to make her burn, to feel the hurt. "You know I'm right. What I said at Road Rally. That spot would have been Shaila's if she were here. But she's not and it's yours. That makes you happy, doesn't it? That you took her place. Doesn't it?" Nikki's eyes are red and bulging but I keep pushing, tapping into her deepest insecurities. "Doesn't it?" I say again, louder.

"Shut up!" she yells, covering her ears with her hands. Nikki shakes her head and her eyes grow watery. "Stop saying that!"

I snap my mouth closed. Instead of being pleased with myself, I feel sick.

"We only have a few months left," she stammers. "Are you ready to throw everything away now?"

I shake my head like I'm Aries the ram. Menacing. Unruly. "I already did."

SEVENTEEN

I'M STANDING AT the edge of Ocean Cliff. The wind is so powerful it rocks me back and forth, threatening to toss me over the edge. But I can't move. I can't get to safer ground. I spot Nikki off in the distance and try to wave but my arms stay by my sides. I try to call her name but my mouth won't open. Then, suddenly, she rushes toward me, her eyes fiery and furious, her mouth a black hole, and in one motion, she pushes me.

I'm falling, so far, so fast. I'm all alone, plummeting into darkness.

Until a thundering sound wakes me. My eyes blink open and I rest my hand on my heart. Just another dream. Another nightmare. But the noise goes off again, a thick vibration.

I fumble for my phone. Rachel's name flashes on the screen. *Quick question: Did Shaila ever write you letters?*

Yes, I type back. *Over the summers. When we were apart. Why?*

I found one she sent me back in middle school. I wondered if she wrote to other people . . . told them about ~you know what~

My fingers freeze. I'm still not sure I believe Graham's innocence, but the idea that Shaila was cheating almost seems plausible. Were there any hints in one of her letters? There's no way. She only wrote them when we were away from each other, and we were together for her entire last year.

Not to me, I type.

No duh. Anyone else?

I don't know, I say.

Is there a way to find out?

I mean, probably if we snuck into her house or something, I type, a joke, clearly.

Would you actually do that????? Her parents go to Palm Beach every winter. There's probably no one home! Rachel responds.

You can't be serious.

??????

I drop my phone on my duvet. Would it be worth it? What could I find?

The thought stays with me all through school, while I sit in the library alone, studying for the Brown scholarship exam—my new favorite activity—during the Math Olympiad meeting, and still, at the dinner table, as Jared gives me the silent treatment over salmon and roasted sweet potatoes, while Mom and Dad drone on and on about their work and how awful the weather is this year.

I tap my foot under the table, restless and jumpy. I can't take it anymore. I lift my head. "May I be excused?" I say. "I forgot a book at school and have to go back and get it before they lock the doors for the night."

Mom and Dad don't even look up. "Of course," Dad says.

"Come right back, okay? It's getting late." Dad fishes his keys out of his pocket and hands them to me.

I nod and head for the door. My brain spins, turning over what I'm about to do. If someone's home, I'll just leave. That's what I tell myself.

I haven't been back to Shaila's house since before she died, but I know the route by heart. It's like muscle memory. I drive down East End Street, past the light, then up Grove Avenue, through town via Main Street. I pass the spin studio Adam's mom loves, the Garage, and farther out of town, on the wooded back roads, I drive by the horse stables where Shaila took lessons as a kid. I brake slightly as I make my way over the little bridge that separates the Arnold estate from the rest of Gold Coast and suddenly, I'm at the mouth of their massive tree-lined driveway. I stop and turn the engine off.

I grip the steering wheel to keep my hands from shaking. *Am I really going to do this?*

I squeeze my eyes shut and rack my brain for the millionth time. *What would Shaila do?* She would keep going. I know she would.

My legs are wobbly when I climb down from the car, and the wind whips at the exposed skin along my neck. All the cars are gone. A sure sign the Arnolds fled town for winter.

If Mr. and Mrs. Arnold really were off in Palm Beach, they would have left a key in a lockbox attached to the guest house in the back. Their code to everything was always Shaila's birthday, 0316. I inhale the cold air deeply and let it fill my lungs, give me courage.

Then I sprint. First through the thick-wooded grove that divides their property between lawn and forest, so I'm out of sight, away from the security cameras they installed after

Shaila died. It's so dark, I can barely see my feet below me. Fear pounds in my chest, but I tell myself this will all be over soon. I'm almost there. I can see the glow from the moon spotlighting the house a few hundred yards away. I dart through the trees and emerge in the Arnolds' backyard, an expansive field that fits a pool and a tennis court.

From here, I can see Shaila's bedroom window, pitch-black, just like the rest of the mansion. I take a deep breath and creep to the far corner of the yard where the cottage sits untouched. The lockbox is still there, mounted on the front door. I keep my gloves on as I key in Shaila's birthday with shaky fingers. The light changes from red to green and the latch swings open. I gasp.

The key is right where it always was, just waiting to be used.

I grab it and make a break for the side door of the main house, the one that's hidden and only used for deliveries or the caterers when the Arnolds held fancy cocktail parties. It wasn't for invited guests. When I reach the entrance, I peel off my jacket and my boots and leave them in a heap outside the house. Can't track mud or dirt in here.

The key turns and the door unlocks. I wait a beat, for an alarm or . . . something. But nothing happens. I step inside Shaila's house. The air is stiff and stale and I wonder when her parents were here last. No one has seen them since the first day of school. Not around town or at the supermarket. That's normal, though. They stopped socializing after Shaila died.

I tiptoe through the first floor, more out of curiosity than anything else. Everything is as it was the last time I was here three years ago. The good china is still stacked on display in a large wooden cabinet in the grand dining room. The Steinway piano is polished so well I can see my reflection. The spiral staircase is still decorated with red and green holiday-themed runners even though it's the middle of February.

And Shaila is *everywhere*. Her face, captured at her first communion, peers out at me from a painting in the living room. Her fifth grade class photo hangs in the hallway. There she is in her Easter best, grimacing with her parents, on the stairs.

I start up the steps I know by heart, sliding my hand along the banister. I turn right at the landing and creep down the hall. But at her bedroom, I stop.

I press my forehead to the door and feel Shaila behind me, urging me forward. *You can do this. You should do this. You have to do this.* I twist the hard wooden knob and push, stepping into Shaila's world. It's so dark in here that I can't see a thing. I fumble for my phone and turn on its flashlight, casting a spotlight in front of me. When everything comes into view I gasp. Shaila's room is exactly the same as the last time I was here.

Her dark wooden bed, the one with the carved spiraling posts, sits in the middle of the room, its massive headboard pushed against the far wall. The lilac silk comforter with delicate buttons sewn into every square is perfectly in place. A stuffed pig, the one Shaila adored in elementary school and then tossed aside when she got her period, sits in front of the pillows staring into space.

My throat feels scratchy and I resist the urge to curl up with Shaila's duvet to see if it still smells like her. I have a mission and force myself to stay on track, to look for something, anything, that could tell us if she ever told anyone about cheating on Graham. I move first to her walk-in closet, where she often hid half-full liquor bottles and vape cartridges. I rummage through her stack of T-shirts, her volleyball kneepads. No letters. I shut the doors and move to her armoire, but it's only filled with Shaila's old Gold Coast uniforms, pressed with starch. They don't smell anything like her.

I take a few steps toward her dresser, where we stood so many times, painting eyeliner and lipstick on our faces, watching ourselves transform in her mirror. It is still speckled with flecks of red hair dye from the time Shaila insisted on coloring her tips in middle school, just a little, just for fun. I run my fingers over the glass and try to scratch off the dots, but they stay put, stained. Tucked into the corner of the mirror is a photo, a snapshot of Shaila, Nikki, Marla, and me, getting ready for the Spring Fling freshman year. We wore glittery dresses and too much makeup. Shaila had done our hair that night and I had never felt more gorgeous.

My heart pounds looking at our big smiles. Shaila's arms are wrapped around Nikki and Marla, and I cling to Nikki's side. We all look so happy. We didn't know Shaila would be dead within a month.

I open the camera on my phone and take a photo, wanting to remember it forever. Then I extend a hand and pull at the edges, wiggling it out from the corner of the mirror. But it's stuck, tucked so deeply into the tiny opening. Careful not to tear the picture, I inch it out slowly, bit by bit, until something else comes into view.

A piece of lined notebook paper, folded neatly into a tiny square, over and over onto itself. It was wedged in between the photo and the mirror, causing the photo to stay in place.

But now, with nothing to anchor it, the paper drops. I pick it up and open it with shaking fingers. Shaila's loopy handwriting is so recognizable, I almost lose my breath. My heartbeat pounds in my ears and I have to steady myself against the dresser as I unfold the page. I scan the words quickly but nothing makes sense, not at first. I force myself to breathe in, then out, and start from the very beginning.

April 1

KARA! Something major has happened. I am in love. LOVE!

But . . . it's not with Graham. Please don't hate me. I already hate myself for getting into this situation. It's torture! You're the only person I can tell. He said it would ruin everything and that we'd have to end it if people found out. That both of our lives would be O-V-E-R. That he would get in serious trouble. Like massive, life-ruining trouble.

But, oh shit, I am bursting with excitement and tingling sensations. I don't want to keep this hidden. I want to tell the whole world. My love for him tears through everything. I can't breathe when we are apart and it kills me when I see him in the hallways or walking around campus and I have to pretend like there's nothing between us.

It all began one day after school, in the parking lot behind the theater. He told me I was maddening. It was the most remarkable word I've ever heard and I can't believe he used it to describe me. Then he leaned in and touched his lips to mine. They were so soft and tender. I wanted more immediately. But the thing was, I wasn't embarrassed by my want. He seemed to like it. I guess that comes from experience. Graham always seems so scared by it.

The next time, he asked if I wanted to do it and I said yes. It hurt just a little but he made these moaning sounds in my ears that set me on fire. And then it started to feel incredible. He said I was the softest in the world. That made my brain ache.

I want to tell Jill so bad! She's the only one who would understand, but in some ways that's the reason why she can't find out. We used to talk about losing our virginity constantly, what it would feel like, who we wanted to do it with. She'd be so mad that it already happened and that I didn't tell her.

I thought it would make me feel bad . . . or dirty. But it didn't. It made me feel strong, like I had power, like we were equals. Being drunk is fun, but being with a guy like that is the best high I've ever had.

I know I should break up with Graham, but I just . . . don't want to. I like him, too. I like the way he looks at me and the way he puts his arm around me in the caf. I like what we have, and how easy it is for our families, and how our relationship makes Rachel like me even more, like I really belong. What am I going to do?

I'm rereading the letter for the third or tenth time when I hear a loud screech. The noise sends me lurching forward into the dresser and my heart lands in my throat. I look toward the window. It was just a branch, scraping against the glass. I try to steady my heartbeat, but I know I need to get out of here fast. It's too dangerous to stay. I was so stupid to come in the first place.

I fold the piece of paper in half, and then in half again, and slide it into the pocket of my jeans. I creep to the door and turn around, taking one last look at Shaila's room. The creepy stillness, the secrets she was keeping, it all makes me want to throw up. It's like she could come home and flop down on the bedspread any second. But she won't. She'll never come back. Not to make a mess in here, or to tell me the truth—about who killed her and why exactly she felt the need to keep this massive secret from me. I would have understood. I would have been there for her. Instead she went to Kara Sullivan. Snooty, Upper East Side Kara Sullivan. I blink back tears and bite my lip hard.

I close the door and retrace my steps until I'm on the Arnolds' back porch, shivering as I zip myself back into my parka and place the key back inside the lockbox. I inhale deeply and look up into the sky. It's too foggy to see anything tonight, and the backyard is so black, my eyes start to hurt.

I disappear into the darkness.

When I get home, I read the letter again. And then again. And again and again until I've memorized the entire thing and can recite it by heart, without even thinking. It's late now, past 1 a.m. The only thing I can hear is the howling wind and the slight pounding of rain that might turn into snow. When I read Shaila's letter for a final time, I feel the tears start to build, threatening to fall and ruin Shaila's thick bubbly script. I wipe my face with my sleeve, desperate to preserve her words, her scary, wild, rushing words.

I wish she were here. I want Shaila to annotate each sentence, to explain why she kept her innermost thoughts from me. Why she could share them so freely with Kara.

My head throbs as I try to make sense of all of this, of everything Shaila did behind my back, of who she really was. Did I know her at all?

But I don't want to think about that now. I want to find out who the person she wrote about is and what he knows. What he did.

There's only one person I can call.

Rachel picks up on the first ring.

"Do you still have Kara Sullivan's number?" I ask, not even bothering to say hello.

"Jesus, Jill. I'm sleeping." Her voice is hoarse and groggy.

"Ugh, sorry." I rest my head back against my pillow and close my eyes. Suddenly, I'm so tired, too.

Rachel sighs. "Kara Sullivan? I'm sure somewhere. Why?"

"There's a letter," I say. "From Shaila to Kara. We need to talk to her."

"Wait," she says. "You actually went?"

"Yes," I whisper.

I hear muffling, like Rachel is putting her hand over the microphone part of her phone. "Just a sec, babe." Then the rustling of sheets and a few footsteps.

"Sorry," I mumble again.

"It's fine. Frida wakes easily, that's all." A door closes behind her. "What the hell, Jill? Tell me everything."

"No one was home. So, I just . . . did what I thought Shay might do. Found the spare key. Went inside."

"Bold."

"It was addressed to Kara. Shaila must have forgotten to send it. Or decided not to. It's dated just a few months before she died."

"What does it say?"

"It's true," I say, breathless. "Shaila was cheating on Graham."

"With who?"

"I don't know. She doesn't name him."

Rachel is silent for a second. "We have to talk to Kara," she whispers.

"I know." The last time I saw Kara was at Shaila's funeral. She wore a black silk dress that looked too fancy for the occasion. Her hair was perfectly set, falling down her back in waves, somehow untouched by the Gold Coast humidity. She was clutching a piece of paper. I remember that. Maybe it was another one of Shaila's letters. "You guys go way back, too, right?"

Rachel doesn't hesitate. "I've known her since she was born. Babysat her once or twice."

"Can you find her? Can we see her?"

"The Sullivans cut us off after everything. But let me handle it, okay?"

"Fine."

"I'll keep you posted."

We hang up but I know I won't be able to sleep. Instead I pull up Instagram and try to find Kara. Who is she these days? Is she still as standoffish and pretentious as she was three years ago?

It takes just a few taps before I land on her profile. She has a few thousand followers and posts regularly from sceney city spots. There she is having brunch at Balthazar. Looking at massive installations at MoMA PS 1. Seated courtside at a Knicks game.

I scroll further until I reach a post from June. Shaila's death anniversary.

There they are as kindergartners, sitting together on the beach, with their tanned legs outstretched in front of them. Kara's dark hair fades into Shaila's golden locks and their arms are wrapped around each other so tightly. *To my best friend, my sister. Gone too soon. Forever yours, K. #ShailaArnold*

I gag at the hashtag. What an opportunist. But still, I can't drag myself away from her page. Instead, I scroll and scroll until I fall into a fitful sleep for good.

Meet me today at 11 am. 71st between Madison and Park.

The text comes while I'm downing waffles at the kitchen table and testing myself with flashcards I made for the scholarship exam. The house is empty and quiet since Mom, Dad, and Jared are all out, enjoying whatever Saturday activity Gold Coast has to offer. My fork clatters when I drop it into the sink and within minutes I'm out the door, walking the mile to the Long Island Railroad.

When I emerge from the subway on the Upper East Side, I'm shocked by how different it is from where Rachel lives. Each townhouse is perfectly kept, with beautiful metal gates and window boxes full of greenery even though it's still winter. There's not a piece of chipped paint in sight. Even the dogs are better dressed. Little fluffballs wrapped in tiny wool sweaters and shiny down jackets prance by, dragging their owners behind them. The streets are wide and the storefronts are airy and inviting. No wonder Kara never came to visit Gold Coast. It's shocking how beautiful the city can be. But also how stifling.

"There you are!" Rachel barrels down Madison, clutching a thermos of coffee in one hand. My shoulders relax at the sight of her. With her bright red lipstick, oversize leopard-print coat, and neon beanie, she looks just as out of place as I do in my worn-out leggings and science camp sweatshirt.

Rachel pulls me in for a hug and her eyes are wild with excitement. "Her place is up this way." She motions to one of the perfectly manicured townhouses. It's made of silvery-gray stone, with tall windows that smile at us menacingly.

"Which apartment is hers?" I ask.

Rachel stares at me. "The whole thing. Her mom won it in the divorce settlement."

"Whoa," I breathe.

Rachel pushes a button on the intercom and I clench my fists.

"What?" a brusque voice answers.

"You know who it is, Kara. I know you can see me," Rachel says. She lunges for the video camera on the door as if to scare her.

The door swings open and Kara stands in front of us, her arms crossed. She's wearing a camel-colored cashmere sweater, expensive-looking jeans, and black leather mules with fur poking out the sides. Big round diamonds stud each earlobe. Her hair looks recently blown out.

"Hi," she says curtly.

"Aren't you going to invite us in?" Rachel asks sweetly.

Kara glares at her but turns on her heel and walks inside. Our invitation, I guess. Rachel's eyebrows shoot up as she gives me a look over her shoulder. I follow her into the townhouse and try not to gasp. Artwork hangs on every wall. Not just random paintings picked up at some flea market or at Ikea. Real art. Art that could hang in a museum. Mural-size works depicting mid-century architecture on the West Coast. Huge canvases with swaths of colors that look like the Rothko pieces I saw in an AP Art History textbook.

Kara reads my mind, apparently. "Gifts," she says. Her mouth turns into a satisfied smile. She points to a painting of a man standing in front of a swimming pool. "That one's from David Hockney." She pauses in front of another frame that looks like a poster. Big block letters spell out a phrase. *I can't look at you and breathe at the same time.* "This one's from Barbara Kruger," Kara says. "She was Shaila's favorite."

An uncomfortable silence hangs between the three of us.

Rachel breaks the ice first. "Look, I know you're not supposed to see me—"

Kara snorts. "That's an understatement."

"What?" I ask, looking back and forth between them.

But neither of them even glance at me. Instead their eyes are fixed on each other, like they're preparing for battle.

"My mom would seriously kill me if she knew you were here."

"Where is Mona anyway?"

"Out." Kara collapses onto a plush suede sofa and crosses her arms over her chest. Then she turns to me. "My mom banned me from talking to Rachel, or basically anyone from Gold Coast, after everything happened. She didn't want me getting caught up in anything . . . unsavory." She pushes her shiny hair behind her ears. "Her words, not mine."

Rachel rolls her eyes. "Whatever, Kar."

"Hey, be nice. You're lucky I even agreed to talk to you."

"Well, why did you anyway?"

Kara's face softens. For a second she looks like a normal high school girl, not an art princess of New York City. "I miss her," she says softly. "I miss . . . all of it. The summers out east with everyone. The way Shay snorted when she laughed. How she made the best chocolate chip cookies. How she listened, like, *really* listened. No one in Manhattan is like that. She was my best friend. And now she's gone. Everything that tied us together is just . . ." She inhales deeply. "Mom still sees the Arnolds sometimes, when they come back to town. But they don't want to see me. They say I remind them too much of her. It's too painful."

My shoulders tense. I never thought of Kara having a real relationship with Shay. It always seemed so performative, so superficial. But maybe their bond was real. As real as mine. Which means Kara's been hurting all this time, too.

Kara turns her chin up and her voice becomes clipped and polished again. "But let's get this over with. You have something that belongs to me?"

I fish the note out from my pocket. My fingers tremble as I extend my arm to Kara. She snatches the letter from my grasp and her eyes scan the page, searching frantically. She crosses her legs and wiggles her foot incessantly.

Rachel's eyes meet mine and we wait another minute for Kara to speak.

But she's still silent, reading Shaila's cursive over and over again.

"Well?" I ask.

"Can you guys give me a minute?" Kara asks softly without lifting her gaze. Her eyes are glossy. "Some privacy?"

Rachel purses her lips, like she's trying not to show any emotion. "Fine. I'm gonna get some air. Jill?"

I shake my head. "Can I use your bathroom?"

Kara points to the stairs in the hall. "Second floor, third door on the right."

Rachel retreats to the stoop and I climb the stairs, checking out the photographs that line the wall. They're so stunning, there's no way these were taken by amateurs. There's Kara as a naked toddler, beside her mom in a designer gown and diamonds. And again at her sweet sixteen staring at the camera with a smoldering glare and a perfect complexion. Guess she missed that whole awkward phase thing.

I get to the second floor and count the doors, looking for the bathroom. But I stop when I catch a glimpse of something purple through a door left slightly ajar. It's Shaila's bedspread.

Kara must have the same one. I wonder if they picked them out together.

Before I can think too hard about it, I push the door open with my fingertips.

Kara's room is immaculate. It looks like it belongs to a chic twentysomething. Everything is marble or glass. Necklaces decorated with precious stones lie flat in a jewelry case on top of a massive dresser. Black-and-white photographs hang on the walls. They're signed by Robert Mapplethorpe. I have to stop myself from laughing, it's all too wild.

The only thing that signals she's in high school is the varsity tennis trophy sitting on a top shelf.

I tiptoe around her bed, trying not to make noise against the hardwood floors, until I'm at her nightstand next to the wall. My stomach drops. There in a simple black frame is a photo of Kara and Shaila. They must be in elementary school because Shay looks younger than I ever knew her. The camera is trained on them, but they face each other, sitting on a wooden bench with the beach in the background. They're each holding ice cream cones and smile with wide, messy mouths. They look like two girls who share secrets, who keep them, too.

Kara may seem like she has her shit together, but I'm guessing she's just as messed up from all of this as I am.

"You lost up there?" Kara calls from downstairs.

I inhale sharply. "Coming!" I head for the stairs, trying to leave the door just as it was when I entered.

"Weirdo," she says when I return to the living room. Rachel's back, propped up in a velvet teal armchair.

"So what do you think?" Rachel asks.

"Whatever Shaila told me was in confidence," Kara says, lifting her chin. "It's the least I can do for her now."

"Cut the bullshit," Rachel says. "Just tell us what you know."

"Why should I?"

"Because we have evidence that Graham is innocent, that someone else killed Shaila."

A flicker of shock passes through Kara's face, but it's gone in an instant.

"Because you've known Graham and me just as long as you knew Shaila," Rachel continues, "and you owe allegiance to him as much as you owe it to her. You couldn't save Shaila, but you can try and help save Graham."

"Shit," Kara says, biting her perfect red lip. "My mom would kill me." She rubs her palms over her face and leans back into the couch. "Shaila was cheating," she says with an unsteady voice.

"Do you know who she was with?" Rachel asks.

"She never told me." Kara jabs a finger at Shaila's handwriting. "Just like she says here, he told her not to tell and she didn't."

"That's it?" Rachel asks. "That's all you know?" Her voice is frantic, desperate.

Kara sighs and leans forward. She rests her elbows on her knees and her dark hair falls around her face. "Fuck it," she mutters. "There was one thing. Toward the end of the year, just a few weeks before she died, Shay said this guy was getting a little creepy. He was a little *too* into her. Obsessed, almost."

"Really?" My heart is racing.

"He got her a pair of diamond earrings." Kara pushes her hair behind her own studs. "I guess she told him she loved mine so he found a set just like them. I think that was too much for her. I mean, these are each two carats. My dad got them for me when he left us." She shakes her head. "Some consolation prize. But they made Shaila uncomfortable. She said she could never wear them, that people would ask too many questions. Shay gave them back to him and he freaked out. He said she was ungrateful. I think that's when she wanted to end everything. That's what she told me, at least."

Kara tucks her feet under her. Curled up like that, she looks young, like we live on the same planet at least.

Rachel and I lock eyes again. If Shaila was about to dump this rando mystery dude, then that's a perfect motive.

Kara checks her watch. "You guys have to go. My mom's going to be back soon."

Rachel begins to stand but I'm hesitant to leave.

"Wait," I say. "She sent you other letters, right? Could we read some of them? Just to see if we're missing anything?"

Kara starts to open her mouth, but I know it's my last shot.

"I loved Shaila as much as you did. She was my best friend," I say. "I just want to know what really happened."

Kara's brow furrows and she shakes her head no.

"Why?" Rachel blurts out.

Kara's eyes begin to well and she sighs deeply before speaking. "My mom took them," she says. "I kept them all in a box and after Shaila died she said I shouldn't live in the past, that it would only bring me heartache. I don't know where she put them, if she even kept them."

"Kara . . ." I start. "I'm so sorry." I don't know what I would do if I couldn't have a little piece of Shay left in my life.

Kara shakes her head. "It's fine. I mean, it's not. But what can I do?"

I nod. I know what it's like to feel powerless.

Rachel's about to say something when we all freeze, hearing

the sound of footsteps approaching the front door. Then a key turns in the lock.

"Shit, that's my mom," Kara says. Her eyes go wide with fear. "Hurry, you can sneak out the side door," she says, ushering us through the gleaming kitchen. She opens the door slowly so that it doesn't make a sound. Without warning, Kara hugs us both tight—a far cry from when we first arrived—and presses Shaila's letter into my palm. "Catch him, okay?" Before I can respond, she releases us and shuts the door gently.

"I'll walk you to the train," Rachel says, her voice barely a whisper.

We make our way out of the narrow alley, back to the street, and trudge along the sidewalk silently for a minute or two before Rachel speaks.

"We've gotta show the letter to the lawyers next week," she says. "Can I see it again?"

I unfold the paper and hand it to her. Rachel takes her time with it, reading each sentence once, then twice. She gasps.

"Look," she says. "This line right here." Rachel reads it aloud. "'It all began one day after school, in the parking lot behind the theater.' She also says he's more experienced."

I stop short. "Oh my God. *Shit.*"

"The parking lot behind the theater . . ." she says. "Isn't that the staff lot?"

EIGHTEEN

I NEVER UNDERSTOOD people who didn't want to be liked, who said they didn't care what people thought of them. Of course I fucking cared. I wanted—still want—to be liked and included, respected and admired. That's why I spent freshman year carting around expertly poured cups of beer and buying seniors pow-do from Diane's on school nights. Why I laughed at jokes even if they weren't funny, or were at our expense. Why I stuffed empty bottles in trash bags after parties while the boys continued playing flip cup or beer pong. Why I salivated over nuggets of Gold Coast Prep gossip that weren't about me. Better to fuel the rumor mill than be the subject of it.

So when, one night at the beach during freshman year, Tina Fowler whispered, "Can I tell you a secret?" I nodded emphatically. I was thrilled to be her willing audience. We were lying side by side and Tina rolled over, sending flecks of sand flying into my hair. She leaned in close.

"I heard one of the teachers is sleeping with a student. They did it in his car *at* school, after hours." Her eyes looked manic while she said it, thanks to some clumpy mascara and too-dark liner. She never did know how to apply makeup, but always looked cute thanks to a tiny gap between her two front teeth. Everyone called her adorable.

"Whoa," I said, and looked over at the bonfire that raged a few feet away. The boys stood around the flames in a circle, throwing sticks, cardboard, and whatever else they could find into the heat. Their laughter floated above the crashing waves. It was early April, so we were all wearing flannels, wrapped in fleece blankets toted out from various SUVs to keep warm.

"So messed up, right?" But her face didn't look like she thought it was fucked up. She smiled so wide I could see her canines. They were sharp like fangs.

"Totally," I said.

"I bet it's Mr. Scheiner," she said, scrunching up her nose like she smelled something rotten. "He looks like a pedo with those wire glasses."

I giggled. "Or Coach Doppelt. Shaila reported him for being creepy in the locker room."

Tina slapped a hand over her mouth. "Oh my God! Rachel said he was a lurker, too!" She leaned into me, knocking my shoulder with hers. "Ugh, wouldn't it be amazing, though, if it were Mr. Beaumont? Dude's a fox."

At that time, Mr. Beaumont was still sorta new. He'd slide into class just before the bell rang and chug an enormous iced coffee, no matter the weather, while perched on a desk in the front row. Usually Shaila's. Sometimes Nikki's. Never mine. As he asked us about our weekends, his big goofy grin would spread across his face in a way that made it seem like he *got* us. He was on our side. We were all just there to stick it out together.

"Seriously." Tina took a swig out of the bottle next to her. "I'd die to hook up with him. He's like barely twenty-five. It's doable."

"Maybe next year," I joked.

"*This* year for someone, apparently. Get it, girl!" she hollered. A few pairs of eyes turned to us and we collapsed into a pile of laughter, falling back into the damp sand. I was just happy to be near her, to be included, to not be called a *stupid little undie* or be made to recite everyone's middle names in alphabetical order frontward then backward. Gossiping about the hot teacher didn't matter. It was practically sport. All that mattered was being on Tina's good side, at least for a night. She was a *senior* and I was as tiny as a tadpole.

That little moment seemed totally insignificant then. It was just a stupid rumor. People stopped talking about it by spring break. Moved on to something new. Lila Peterson giving a hand job in the auditorium, I think. That one followed her around until she graduated. Of course, I can't remember who the boy was. Funny how that works.

But . . . what if the Beaumont rumor was true?

There's one person who would know. One person who memorized Gold Coast history like he'd be quizzed on it. But he's also not speaking to me. I need him, though, which is why I wait next to Quentin's hatchback after school on Monday like a stalker. It's the first warm day in months, so sunny I have to shield my eyes with my hands.

Quentin sheds his blazer and loosens his tie as he walks toward me. When he looks up, he stops in his tracks and throws back his head. "Ugh, Jill. What?" The harshness in his voice makes me wince.

"I just want to talk," I say.

"Haven't you noticed I'm not doing that with you anymore?"

"I thought maybe you'd make an exception, just once?" I flash him a smile, a pleasing one, I hope.

Quentin rolls his eyes. "Get in."

I scramble into the passenger side and buckle in while Quentin revs his engine. He makes a hard reverse and peels out of the parking lot like a stuntman. "Scared to be seen with me?" I joke.

"Kinda." His mouth is in a hard line.

"I need your help. It's about Graham—"

Suddenly Quentin slams on the brakes. We're in the middle of Breakbridge Road, a narrow, dangerous stretch between school and Gold Cove, but Quentin rests his head on the steering wheel, making no motion to move.

"Come on, Jill. I don't want to rehash this. We all decided to let it go."

"I know, but . . ."

His hard voice cuts me off. "*Some* of us want to leave this in the past. *Some* of us want to move on, to get the fuck out of here and forget what happened."

His words sting. How could he want to forget Shaila?

"If you could stop being so self-centered right now, you'd see that we're all just trying to make it out of here *alive*," he sputters.

I shake my head. "Self-centered? Are you kidding me? I'm the only one thinking about Shaila right now. I'm the only one who cares about finding out the truth." I feel the hot tears swell in my eyes. The crushing loneliness I've been feeling for the past few months hits me.

Quentin jabs his foot at the pedals and we're moving again,

climbing up the Cove. Ocean Cliff is just visible through the clouds. "Well, while you've been off doing who knows what, quitting the Players, obsessing over Shaila, some of us have been trying to figure out a way to actually get out of here, to go to college."

"What do you mean?"

Quentin had gotten into Yale's prestigious fine arts program back in the fall. He had been thrilled that week, just like everyone else.

"Not everyone at this school is rich, you know? Not everyone has a fancy dad—or even a dad at all. It's not like everyone can just *pay* their way through everything." His voice cracks. "It's like, my life is incredible. I am so freaking lucky to have my mom and the Players. I'm among the most privileged people in the world. I know that. And still, relative to everyone else here, I'm still made to feel like shit because we don't have like . . . six houses. No one here has any goddamn perspective. Marla and I talk about this all time."

My heart splits in two. Those of us who *seemed* to have money never talked about if we *actually* did. With some people it was obvious, like Nikki and Henry. You could usually tell based on houses and cars or vacations and jewelry, and because Quentin's mom was a bestselling novelist, because they owned one of those colonial homes up in Gold Cove, I just thought . . .

He must think the same about me. He doesn't know I've been busting my ass every day, using my solo lunches to study for this stupid Brown scholarship exam.

"I'm sorry," I whisper.

"I don't want you to feel sorry for me," he barks. "But I

don't want to spend senior year thinking about the past. It was bad enough the first time. It's just . . . exhausting. I have to think about the future."

"Now who's self-centered?" I say, hoping it sounds as jokey as I mean it to.

Quentin smirks and turns the radio to the eighties station he knows I love. "Alone" by Heart floats through the speaker and I let out a laugh. It's so on the nose.

"I'm on scholarship," I say. It's the first time I've said it aloud to anyone. A piercing shame burrows deep in my stomach, not for *being* on scholarship but for feeling the need to hide it.

Quentin sits up straighter. "Really?"

I nod. "Merit-based. For STEM. I have to keep a 93 average."

"I got the visual arts grant," he says with a smile. "Full ride since middle school."

"I don't know how we're going to pay for Brown, either," I say softly. "There's a test and if I come out on top, I'll get tuition covered. That's what I've been doing at lunch without the Players' Table. Studying. But I don't know how I can ace it. Not without help."

"You think you need the stupid Files?" Quentin laughs. "You're Jill Newman. You were born to be in that program. You just have to show them." He stops at the red light and turns to face me. "Do the work, Jill. Earn it."

Looking at his sloping splash of red hair and his perfect freckled complexion, my heart breaks for Quentin's kindness and tears prick my eyes. I want more than anything to give him a hug. To rest my head on his doughy shoulder and curl up for a *Real Housewives* marathon. I want to tell him that it's easier to worry about Shaila than to worry about the future and how we were going to live up to everyone's expectations.

Sometimes it's easier to pretend like life ends after high school. Wouldn't that make this all worth it?

Then I remember what I came here to ask him.

"I just want to know one thing," I say. "Do you remember freshman year, there was that rumor going around that a teacher slept with a student?"

"Oh my God, yeah."

"It was about Beaumont, right?"

"Yep," he says without skipping a beat. "I was volunteering in the admin department that year. Once I overheard the secretary, Mrs. Oerman, take a call from a pissed-off parent. Someone who said their kid was talking about how Beau was *with* a student. Mrs. O. was so freaked out she couldn't stop babbling about it all day. She definitely told Weingarten. She had to. I mean, someone claimed there was abuse going on at Prep. That's no joke."

"Did he ever look into it?"

Quentin shakes his head. "Nah. You know our dear headmaster. Always pretending like everything's fine. He didn't want to deal with any drama, make a scene, find out something he'd rather not know."

Quentin's right. That's just another gross fact about Prep. Always sticking to the status quo. It's the same mentality that results in so few people of color getting accepted every year. The administration doesn't like to discuss it, but the swath of sameness is there, glaring and obvious. Sure, there are diversity initiatives, outreach programs, but as Nikki said once, "Those are clearly just for show." If Weingarten wanted more perspectives in our classrooms, wouldn't he have them? Hire more teachers of color, too? Just another reason I can't wait to get out of this place.

My heart pounds in an electric thump that I can feel in the

tips of my toes. I suddenly remember the gas station. The wink Shaila gave Beaumont. How he watched Shaila ride away with a case of beer on her handlebars. A smile danced on his face. Were they speaking their own secret language?

"You okay?" Quentin asks. "You look like shit. No offense."

"Mm-hm," I say. I want to say so much to him, to tell him about Kara and the letter and the earrings. But instead I just ask, "Are we okay?" Quentin glances my way and the corner of his mouth twitches into a smile. He places his hand in the console between us, palm side up. I grasp it and squeeze, holding on for dear life.

When I call Rachel, she's breathless with excitement.

"What did you find out?" she asks.

"Well, nothing," I say. "I have no proof."

"But you have a hunch?"

"Remember that rumor that was going around? About Beaumont hooking up with a student?" My stomach turns even saying the words out loud. I try not to picture them behind the theater.

Rachel goes silent like she's trying to think, to recall the before. When she speaks she sounds frantic, like she's desperate and exhausted. "Well, shit." She pauses. "I'm actually on my way out to Long Island to give the letter to the lawyers. Can you meet me there? They need to hear how we got it."

"I—"

"Look, it's not breaking and entering if you had a key, okay?" Rachel doesn't wait for me to respond. Instead, she rattles off an address and a time but my brain spins. It's all happening so fast. Is it really possible Mr. Beaumont hurt Shaila? That he *killed* her and blamed it on Graham?

But then I remember what he said to me in his office.

I know what goes on.

Within hours, I'm at some boxy, ugly corporate office building. It's a nondescript gray compound just off Route 16 in Port Franklin, eleven miles from Gold Coast. Rachel meets me in the parking lot with huge, unblinking eyes. Her face is thin, too thin, like she's lost a few pounds she couldn't spare since I saw her last week.

I only have to talk to the lawyers for a few minutes. Pleasantries, really. They're tall scrawny guys in expensive-looking suits and slick haircuts. They'll test the handwriting. They'll dig into Beaumont. Apparently, he's had a few DUIs in the area so it won't be hard to bring him in for questioning, they say.

I won't even be named. No one will see me here. No one will know I was involved.

It's only when I get home, curled up on the couch with my study guide, that I start to feel uneasy, like I planted a bomb and am now just waiting for it to go off. To witness the carnage.

My phone explodes and I drop my notes on the couch.

!!!, Rachel writes. Then she sends a link to a tweet from the *Gold Coast Gazette*.

GOLD COAST PREP TEACHER BROUGHT IN FOR QUESTIONING RELATED TO LOCAL KILLING. WATCH NOW!

I tap the link and hold my breath as a video loads. When it does, the picture takes up my whole screen. The clip is dark and grainy. A house or an apartment building, maybe. No, that's not it. It's the Gold Coast Police Department illuminated only by the moon. No street lamps in sight. Just a short stretch of concrete. Some sand in the background. I can hear waves crashing faintly in the distance. Then a chyron appears on the lower third of the screen.

A female newscaster in a pressed pantsuit walks into the frame and I pump the volume.

"What are you—" Mom yells, padding into the living room.

"Shh!"

Mom leans down and looks at my phone. "Oh my . . ." she mutters as she watches over my shoulder.

The reporter's words are crisp and clipped through my phone's speaker.

"The Gold Coast Police Department brought twenty-eight-year-old Logan Beaumont in for questioning tonight after receiving new information that Beaumont may have been involved in the murder of Shaila Arnold, a fifteen-year-old girl who was killed here in Gold Coast three years ago. Her classmate and boyfriend Graham Calloway was convicted of the crime soon after she was found dead. Calloway now proclaims innocence."

Mr. Beaumont's school photo flashes on the screen. His jaunty smile and tousled hair make him look young and hot, like a teacher who was on our side, a teacher whose students *would* have crushes on him. A teacher who might be capable of manipulation, of abusing his power.

Graham's and Shaila's class pictures appear, too. They match in their Gold Coast blazers. Side by side they look like siblings.

"The police have no comment at this time," the reporter continues. "But we're joined now by Neil Sorenson, an attorney who represents Graham Calloway. Mr. Sorenson, how does this affect your client?"

One of the lanky city slickers I met earlier now stands next to her. He's dressed in the same suit, his tie still perfectly in place around his thin neck.

"For some time now, we've believed that Graham Calloway's confession was coerced, that he didn't commit this heinous crime. We've been building Graham's case for appeal and while doing *our* jobs, we stumbled upon new leads that might bring about the truth of what really happened to Shaila Arnold." Mr. Sorenson looks directly into the camera. The dude's clearly had media training. "We just hope the Gold Coast Police will do *their* jobs, whether that means investigating Logan Beaumont or someone else. We all just want justice for Shaila Arnold."

"Thank you, Mr. Sorenson. We have also just received a statement from Gold Coast Prep, the elite K through twelve private school where Logan Beaumont currently teaches and where both Shaila Arnold and Graham Calloway were students. The statement reads as follows: 'Mr. Beaumont is a respected and beloved member of the Gold Coast community. We have never received any credible reports of wrongdoings since his employment began. We will be conducting our own investigation at this time.' There you have it, Gold Coast. Reporting live from the GCPD, I'm Linda Cochran."

The clip cuts off and my screen goes dark.

When I turn to face Mom, her hand is over her mouth and she's scrolling through her phone at a rapid pace. "My gosh," she murmurs. "Did you know about this?"

I shake my head. She slams her phone on the coffee table and eases onto the couch next to me, resting her hand on my shoulder. I resist the urge to flinch or pull away.

"Sweetie," she starts. "Did Mr. Beaumont ever touch you? Did he ever hurt you?" I picture his hand burning mine in his classroom, the way his breath smelled like toothpaste and cigarettes. I feel dinner climbing up my throat.

I shake my head no. Never.

Mom squeezes my bare skin. "I have to call Cindy Miller." She retreats from the room. The silence hurts my ears and my brain fizzes.

I pick up my phone with a trembling hand.

Did you watch? Rachel writes. *This could be IT!!!!!!*

I can't bring myself to text her back but there's another message. This one from Quentin, also sharing a link to the tweet.

Is THAT why you asked me about Beaumont???? he texts.

Yes.

Shit!! Is this for real?

I don't know, I type. *What if . . .?*

FUCK!!!!!!!!!! Quentin responds. *School's gonna be BATSHIT tmrw. Weingarten's gonna investigate. Did you see that???*

Wonder what he'll find.

Wonder what the police will do. If anything.

I bite my lip and type, knowing my next words could smash what's left of our friendship into bits. But I want to know where he's at. I hit send.

Wonder if Graham is innocent.

He waits a beat.

And then another.

Finally he begins typing. The words appear.

He might be.

My brain starts to crackle, like it can't connect the dots fast enough. I shove my phone under the couch cushion, just to get away, but it buzzes again. When I fish it out and look at the screen I see Adam's name. My heart steadies and already I feel calmer, knowing he's on the other end.

Did you see this clip about Beaumont? This is wild . . .

I'm so confused . . . I type back.

Same, he responds.

Then another text pops up. *I wonder if Rachel is behind this. Did you ever end up talking to her?*

My whole body tenses. The one thing I can't tell him. The one act of betrayal. I said I'd drop it so many months ago, that I wouldn't believe a thing she said. But here she is just a few text messages away. Something tugs inside me and I know I have to lie to him. No one can know I was involved.

Nope.

NINETEEN

THE SUN SLOWLY creeps into view through my window, but I've already been up for an hour trying to memorize equations from my Brown scholarship exam study guide, the one I actually made myself. Numbers and facts swim on the page, but I can't concentrate. Not today.

I set down my folder and flashcards and close my laptop for the morning. There's no use in pretending to study. Not when something is nagging me about this Beaumont thing. How was I so oblivious back then? There must have been clues—some sort of sign that Shaila left behind.

I tap over to the photos on my phone and scroll frantically, looking for Shaila's face. *Tell me, Shay. Tell me what I missed.* When I hit my most recent pictures, there we are. Me, Marla, Nikki, and Shaila getting ready for Spring Fling. The photo I saw in her room. The formal was notorious at Gold Coast Prep. We had been looking forward to it since middle school. Adam had told me that the school spirit council would go all out, renting a fog machine and a fancy DJ. That year's theme was masquerade.

Shaila and I spent the entire week talking about what we would wear, what kind of music would be played, and who would hook up behind the risers. She and Graham were still in such a good place at that time. At least I thought they were. The whole night would live up to the hype, we were sure of it.

Shaila dismissed Graham's suggestion for us all to pregame together, and instead invited Nikki, Marla, and me over to her house to get ready.

"Don't you want to show up with your boyfriend?" Marla asked.

"I've got plenty of time to hang out with him," Shaila said. "We only get one Spring Fling as freshmen and I want us to enjoy it together."

My face flushed from excitement and the four of us sat in a little circle on Shaila's carpeted floor, rubbing gold glitter onto our cheeks. Shaila gave us all matching cherry pouts with a Chanel lip gloss she swiped from her mom.

When I asked for an updo, she piled my hair high on my head in an elaborate curly mess. "Audrey Hepburn with some edge," she said wickedly. "So you."

"Do me!" Nikki squealed.

Shaila twisted Nikki's long mane into a low bun and pulled out some tendrils in the front. "Very nineties-chic." Then she coiled Marla's white-blonde hair into a braid crown, making it look like a halo.

When we arrived, Nikki and Marla sprinted into the hazy gym ahead of us, but Shaila looped her arm in mine so we could strut in side by side. When we passed by the trophy case and saw our reflection, she held my gaze in the glass. "Confirmed," she said. "We're fabulous." The gym was dark, and covered in neon balloons so the wooden rafters were just barely visible. Every so often, confetti floated to the floor, making the shiny basketball courts slick. Everyone tied lace masks around their faces, shielding themselves from reality. Shaila marched us to the corner where the rest of the Players gathered in a small section of the bleachers. "Wow," Henry said when we arrived. He had on a charcoal gray suit, his shirttails hanging over the front. He looked adorable.

"Where's Graham?" Shaila asked.

"Over there." Henry pointed to a buffet of punch bowls and cups. "But I'd let him breathe for a bit."

Shaila's pink lips turned to a frown. "Why?"

"Well, for one, he's kind of pissed that you guys didn't come over before this."

Shaila rolled her eyes. "He'll get over it."

"But, two, Jake just gave him a brutal pop." Graham was huddled close to Jake, who seemed to be handing over an oversized unmarked water bottle full of clear liquid.

"What's he doing?" I asked Henry.

"Jake tasked him with spiking the iced tea."

My gaze shifted to the snacks table. The physics teacher, Dr. Jarvis; the librarian, Mrs. Deckler; and a handful of other faculty crowded around it like bodyguards.

"Isn't that kind of risky?" Nikki said softly in my ear.

I swallowed hard and nodded. But everything was risky at that point. A ball of terror had developed in my stomach after the sauna incident and it never really went away. There was always something else coming.

Shaila tilted her head toward the rafters. "His funeral," she said. I assumed she was pissed at him for being pissed at *her*. Shaila then called out to Marla.

"Come on. Let's have some fun." Shaila tossed her hair behind her shoulder and walked ahead to the dance floor. None of us protested.

Shaila extended her hands and we all joined together, forming a circle in the middle of the gym. Her brow softened and she threw back her head, shaking her honey waves down her back. As the song peaked, she pulled us to her and hugged us hard.

"Look around. Look at everyone else," Shaila whispered into the huddle. "They wish they were us."

Marla giggled and Nikki beamed. I loved them all in that moment. I loved that Marla didn't *need* so much. I loved that Nikki just wanted to have as much fun as humanly possible. I loved that Shaila was quick to forgive, and that she did so with her whole heart. I loved that she kept things so wildly interesting, that she kept us entertained, on guard. I loved that there were eyes burning holes into our backs. I loved that we were special. We were watched. We shouted out the chorus and Shaila twirled us around and around, one by one, like we were little ballerinas in a music box. And when I faced outward, toward the rest of our peers, I repeated Shaila's words in my head. *They wish they were us.*

Until my gaze drifted to the corner of the room, where Graham shifted his balance from one foot to the other. The bottle was gone from his grasp. My chest tightened.

Mrs. Deckler then appeared at his side and grabbed him by the elbow. My jaw fell open as she whisked him away, down the hall.

I stopped dancing and turned to Shaila. "Did you see that? I think Graham just got kicked out."

Shaila's eyes followed mine to where Graham had just stood. "Jesus."

"What happened?" Nikki said, breathless.

"Graham got caught," Shaila said with little emotion. Her

voice warbled for only a second.

Nikki's eyes widened. "Do you think he'll get suspended?"

Shaila rolled her eyes. "Don't be dumb. He's a Calloway. He'll be fine."

Nikki's shoulders collapsed and she just nodded her head before turning back to find Marla near the bowls of chips.

"Let's not let him ruin the night for us," Shaila said. She looked worried, maybe even a little sad. "Come on." We kept dancing until the overhead lights turned on, but it wasn't the same. The electric joy had faded and soon we were in Mrs. Arnold's Lexus heading back to Shaila's for a sleepover. Shaila threw open her bedroom door. "I call the outside of the bed," she said, tossing the covers back on her king-size mattress. She usually stuck to the wall, sandwiched between me and the cold plaster.

"But I want my side," I whined.

"Nuh-uh. Mine for tonight. Just in case I need to get some water," Shaila reasoned. Hours later, I turned over onto my stomach and awoke to a sliver of light shining from the bathroom, just off the side of her room. I sat up and saw Shaila's hair through the slit. Her back was to me and she wore a ratty old T-shirt from the Beach Club. She was talking quietly, in muffled tones.

"No," she said, exasperated. "I can't just *leave*. Jill's here. She's sleeping." She sighed and went quiet for a few seconds, listening to whoever was speaking on the other end. Graham, I figured.

"I want to see you, too, it's just . . ."

Another quick silence.

"Okay." Her voice softened. "You're coming here?" She

paused. "Fine. Meet me at the end of the driveway."

She kept the phone to her face and turned to the mirror. I saw her then, pale and without makeup. She looked so young, like the Shaila I first met in sixth grade. She stared intently at her reflection, puckering her lips and smoothing her brow. "I love you, too," she whispered into the phone.

I pretended to be asleep as Shaila tiptoed around the room, gathering a sweatshirt, her wallet, and a pair of flip-flops. I watched as she crept out of the room. I tried desperately to trace her faint footsteps as she made her way to the front door. I imagined her bounding down the driveway, away from me and toward something so much better, so much more alive.

At the time, I thought Graham had snuck over to make amends for getting kicked out of the dance, for being mad at her. They returned to normal when he got back to school after a two-day suspension. I thought, maybe this is just how relationships work. You fight in public, make up in private, and pretend like nothing ever happened.

But now it's so painfully obvious: she was meeting someone else, someone she was hiding from us all along. Someone . . . like Beaumont. Maybe actually Beaumont.

I shiver thinking about his callused fingers and his unshaven face—all of it too close to Shaila.

But now that the truth could finally be coming out, I actually want to go to school for the first time in months. I want to catch whispers, hear the chatter of what people think could be true.

I take my time getting ready. I lather moisturizer on my face, take a tweezer to the middle of my brow, and make my bed with tight hospital corners. I tuck my thick white button-down into my plaid skirt and smooth it over my thighs.

When I look in the mirror, I know I'm still me.

"Wild, huh?" Jared appears in the doorway, half-dressed. His tie hangs loose around his neck and his shirt is untucked, flapping against his baggy khakis. He looks like the older boys, the Players. They're the first words he's said to me in weeks. "Mr. Beaumont, I mean."

"Talking to me now?" I ask, turning back to the mirror. I adjust my collar, curl a strand of hair around my finger.

"C'mon," he says. "Can I get a ride?"

"Topher not picking you up?"

Jared shrugs his shoulders up to his ears. "I don't know. Figured we could hang a little. Take Mom's car today."

I scoff. "All of a sudden, I'm worth your time again?"

Jared groans. "You're really gonna make me work for this?"

"Yup."

"You don't know how hard it's been," he whines. "How many pops I've had to do. Stuff I never thought . . ." His brow furrows.

I fold my arms over my chest and picture the worst. My baby brother streaking through town after midnight. Eating dog food and trying not to cry. Lying to Mom and Dad about where he was going. Cheating on tests just because he could. Everything I did when he was still in middle school. But there's no way his would be that bad. The guys didn't have to do half the stuff we did. They were always tasked with things like bartending and blowing up the pool floats. Never asked to bend over in a bikini in the middle of winter. Never expected to laugh it off when Derek Garry honked their boob or smacked their butt—but, like, as a *joke*. *Relax*, they'd say. Never told to send nudes. Never punished with even more dumb pops when they didn't.

Jared drags a socked foot against the hardwood floor. "I think they're making it harder for me because of you," he says in a soft voice.

I inhale sharply. "Leaving in five," I say. "With or without you."

I push past him and head downstairs, away from his gaze, fighting the urge to challenge him on what he *thinks* he knows about me and about the Players.

At school, the halls are creepy and quiet, only punctuated by the sounds of metal lockers slamming and hushed whispers. Everyone walks like they've just seen a crime scene. Giddy. Anxious. Hungry for information and thrilled just to be alive.

When I get to English class and slide into my seat, the one next to Nikki, Mr. Beaumont isn't there, obviously. Instead some baby-faced sub with greasy bangs pulls down the projector.

"We're, um, going to watch a movie today," she says in a high-pitched squeak. "*The Great Gatsby.* The one with Leo. You read that in the fall, right?" She tries to smile, but when no one returns the favor, she furrows her brow, turns her back, and hits some buttons. The lights go down and the music starts.

Just after the opening scene, my phone erupts and Nikki's name blinks back at me.

Bathroom in five.

I turn around to see her staring at me, her eyebrows raised.

She shoots her hand into the air. "I have to go to the bathroom."

The nameless sub doesn't even turn around. Instead, she waves her hand in our direction and Nikki slinks out the back door. A few beats later I follow suit.

The Gold Coast restrooms are nice, to put it mildly. They all come stocked with little baskets full of peppermints, Q-tips, and tampons. The good ones, too. Not the cardboard kind that stab like knives. Each girls' room is outfitted with a baby-blue leather couch. They're usually reserved for seniors, though sometimes an undie will plop down when they think no one's looking. I did that once freshman year and was promptly caught by Tina Fowler. I had to carry her SAT prep books around for a week after that.

When I shut the door behind me, Nikki pulls me into the stall closest to the couch, the one that's big enough to be a horse stable, and locks the door behind me. "Shaila," she says. Her voice is scratchy, like she's been yelling or crying. Both could be true. "Do you think Beaumont did it?" I turn over what I know in my head. How much I want to reveal. I'm so, so tired of lying. Of trying to hold everything in. And so, instead, I decide to tell the truth.

"Maybe. But there's so much you don't know." I take a deep breath and close my eyes. Then the words tumble out, tripping over one another. I tell her about Rachel's texts. Her cramped, cozy apartment. The drive up to Danbury. The way Graham cried when he spoke about the blood. Sneaking into Shaila's room. Finding the tiny folded-up letter behind the photo of us. The look on Kara's face when we showed her. The sparkling diamonds someone had gifted Shaila. How Shaila only trusted Kara with her secret. How that secret may have gotten her killed.

"I don't know if there's any proof yet that it's Beaumont," I say. "But it has to be. There was that rumor. Shaila wrote that he was older. Maybe the police will find something."

I wrap my arms around my stomach, holding myself together, and sit on the toilet. The porcelain is cold against the backs of my legs. I expect Nikki to run out of the bathroom, to tell on me, to tell the others, to ruin everything more than I already have. But instead she steps backward and slides down the wall to sit on the tile floor, resting her chin on her knees.

"I knew," she says.

"What?"

"I knew Shaila was cheating on Graham. She told me. One night when she was shitfaced. Said we'd never understand." Nikki shakes her head. "It was just like her, always pretending like she knew more than us. Was more *experienced*. I was shocked. I told her to break up with Graham. That it wasn't right. And you know what she said to me? 'Don't be such a baby, Nikki!' She didn't give a shit what we thought. I don't even think she liked me all that much. You didn't either."

Nikki's words sting like a slap. I was always jealous of *them*. It never occurred to me that Nikki wasn't one hundred percent confident about everything—including her friendships.

"Shaila had to *die* for you to be friends with me. It was always you and her against the world. Until she told me her secret. It was the one thing I had over her. Over you, too." Nikki's eyes are wet and glossy. She swallows hard. "She was nicer after that. I didn't know she told Kara, too."

I want to ask her so many questions, to hold her and tell her we have to stick together now. That she has to stop her Toastmaster tirade. Her eyes fixate on the two-ply toilet paper and its perfectly folded triangle edge as she continues talking.

"She never said it was Beaumont, though. Just said it was someone older. More sophisticated. Someone who knew what he was doing. 'You'd be lucky to have someone like him,' she told me." Nikki turns to me, her eyes now rimmed in red. "Guess she was wrong about something."

I sink to the floor to sit beside her and rest my hand on Nikki's knee. She lays her head on top of my fingers. Her hair falls to one side so it skims the tile floor.

"I thought this was all over," she says.

"It won't be over until we know who did it."

"I thought we *did*."

"Me too."

We stay like that a long time, at least through the rest of the period, until Nikki speaks.

"I miss you," she says, so softly I can barely make it out.

"I miss you, too. It's lonely as fuck over here." I try to edge out a smile. A weak one, but still a smile.

"It's not the same without you," she says. "Marla checked out after getting onto the field hockey team at Dartmouth. Robert's obsessed with making the pops harder and harder. He's really going after Jared, you know."

Ugh, so Jared was right.

"Henry's not over you, even though he pretends to be," Nikki continues. "He just sulks around, trying to lecture us about the power of nonprofit journalism. It's like, shut up already, we get it!"

I let out a laugh. "At least you have Quentin," I say. Sweet, loyal, talented Quentin, doodling Nikki's perfectly symmetrical face on paper napkins, cardboard containers, elegant canvases. I wonder if he told her about our conversation in his car. About how we made up, too.

"There's always Quentin."

"And the undies. They all worship you."

Nikki shakes her head. "Not for the right reasons."

"I know."

She reaches for my hands and holds my fingers tight.

"Things are going to be different now," she whispers. "They need to be."

I exhale and squeeze her hands. "Are we friends again?" I ask.

Nikki throws her arms around my neck. Her skin is hot and sticky, comforting like a toddler's. She smells like an expensive candle. Her tears fall in wet splotches on my white shirt and when we untangle ourselves, it looks like I spilled water down the front.

We walk back into the hallway arm in arm, holding back smiles and whispering into each other's hair. I try to ignore the hooded eyes that flick our way. The questioning stares. Here, word travels faster than the breeze.

"What, did she blow you or something?" Robert leans against the cold metal and looks at Nikki with expectant eyes. They must be together this week but he's still such an absolute jerk.

"Shut up, asshole," Nikki says. She squeezes my elbow. "We're cool."

"Just like that?" Robert asks. One eyebrow shoots up.

"Yep," she says, a smile in her voice. "Just like that." She nudges me with her shoulder and I wrap an arm around her waist.

"Whatever. I can't even begin to deal with whatever this is," he says. "Because shit just got weird. Look." Robert whips out his phone and pulls up a news article from GoldCoastGazette.com. Mr. Beaumont's school photo is plastered on the screen and the headline is written in all caps.

BEAUMONT CLEARED OF ALL WRONGDOING IN ARNOLD CASE

"What?" I ask, incredulous. "I thought . . ."

Robert shakes his head. "Wasn't him. Dude was in the

Hamptons that whole weekend with his girlfriend and his parents. Some place in Amagansett. There's even footage of him dancing to some shitty cover band at a bar."

"But . . ." Nikki sputters. "That doesn't mean he wasn't *with* Shaila, right? She was cheating on Graham. She told me."

Robert's eyebrows shoot up. "Really? I mean, I didn't peg her as that type of girl."

"And what type is that?" I say, rage crawling up my spine.

"Relax, Newman," he says, rolling his eyes. Before I can claw his eyes out, he keeps talking. "Even if she was hooking up with Beaumont—which, gross—he didn't kill her. Couldn't have. Case closed."

"At least we know it was Graham for sure," Nikki says. She kicks her leather bootie up against the lockers. "Fucking monster."

But I can't shake the feeling that something still isn't right. "I don't know. What if it wasn't?"

Robert taps his foot against the floor. "Jill," he says. "Let. It. Go." He punctuates each word with a clap, bringing his hands together right in front of my face. People turn to stare. They're obvious and they don't care.

"I can't just let it go," I hiss.

Nikki takes a step back, her eyes flitting up to the ceiling. "This is giving me a migraine." She squeezes the bridge of her nose and throws her head back like she has a nosebleed. "I don't know if I can talk about this anymore."

"You don't have to, but I do. I just . . . do," I say. I spin on my heel and bolt for the door. I can hear Robert groan behind me, but I don't care.

"Let her go," Nikki says, her voice kind but so far away. "She needs to get it out of her system."

I push outside and step into the parking lot. The air around me is suffocating, too stale. Images of Beaumont, Graham, and Shaila flash in front of me. I want to push them aside, to forget everything and be a *normal* person. A Player. So close to the end. But I can only think of Graham and Shaila, how their whole relationship was a lie. And we were just collateral damage.

My phone buzzes right as I climb into the car with a text from Adam.

You okay? I just saw all the news. Beaumont's innocent?

Ugh, I know. Everyone here is freaking out. No idea what's going on.

The words fly from my fingers. I so desperately want to confide in him, to ask him what he knows, but I hold back, unwilling to let him know that I've betrayed him. That Rachel and I have been plotting all along.

I bet Rachel's behind this, he writes. *Just more confirmation Graham is guilty.*

I fight back tears. What if he and Nikki are right? What if I've wasted my time trying to believe my best friend's killer was innocent? What if all of this is straight-up bullshit?

My phone buzzes again and I flinch.

I really thought we had him. It's Rachel.

Me too, I type back. It's the truth.

There have gotta be other leads though. Someone else??? Got any ideas???

I sigh, utterly exhausted at the idea of Nancy Drew–ing this shit all over again. It's just . . . too much.

Can't talk right now, I write. *I gotta hardcore cram for the scholarship exam.*

Don't back out on me now, Newman!

I throw my phone onto the passenger side and it falls to the floor, buzzing again and then again, with more messages from Rachel. But I leave it there and punch in the oldies station. I turn the volume all the way up, letting synthesizers and pop crescendos drown out her pleas for help.

TWENTY

IT'S INCREDIBLE HOW much space freed up in my brain when I stopped trying to make undies' lives hell. When I'm *not* constantly thinking about the Players and the next party or the latest juicy rumor. *Or* who the hell killed my best friend. There's so much time left to study. To let the facts and figures marinate in my mind, to let them become a part of me. So much so that on the morning of the scholarship exam, I'm not even nervous.

I wake at 5:30 a.m. without an alarm. It's already warm for April, and the sky is a mess of pinks and purples. I finally feel calm. I feel ready. Little numbers and symbols dance in harmonious rhythm inside my head and I know, I just know, I've studied as hard as I could have.

I arrive at the physics room at 6:45 a.m. and the AP teacher, Dr. Jarvis, is already there, though he looks like he just woke up. "Early, Jill," he says, offering me a toothy grin. "Guess you want to get it over with, huh?"

"Guess so."

He waves me in and I settle into a desk at the front of the room. Dr. Jarvis reads the directions aloud from a packet, even though I'm the only student here. He looks at me, then at the stopwatch sitting on his desk.

"And . . . go."

I work on autopilot for the next ninety minutes, solving equations, identifying figures, writing analyses, and pounding through the essay about *why* I deserve this scholarship more than the other students taking the exact same test at this exact moment. I fill up little blue book after little blue book, dumping everything that's in my brain onto the page. By the time Dr. Jarvis clears his throat and calls time, I am wrung out like a damp towel.

Dr. Jarvis pulls my exam toward him and scans it quickly. Then he tilts his head up. His eyes are warm and his fuzzy beard makes him look like Santa.

"Whatever happens, I want you to know something," he says. "You have been a joy to have in class. They would be lucky to have you."

I swallow the lump in my throat.

Dr. Jarvis gives my shoulder an awkward, tender pat.

"Students like you don't come around that often. I hope you know that."

I nod and feel the warmth spread throughout my chest. I did this test on my own. I earned this feeling.

"Thank you," I choke out.

He nods and opens the door. "Off you go, then."

The rest of the morning dissolves like a sugar cube. I float from class to class, high on the adrenaline that pushed me through the test. But that all comes crashing to a halt when French class ends.

"Oh, Jill. *Un instant, s'il vous plaît.*" Madame Mathias

stretches her head up from her turtleneck, even though it's springtime and her classroom is about one million degrees. "Headmaster Weingarten would like to see you in his office." The lines around the edges of her mouth deepen as she speaks. *"Au revoir!"*

This can't be good. My backpack suddenly weighs a ton and my stomach sinks. I trudge toward Weingarten's office, with its dark cherrywood doorframe and floor-to-ceiling bookshelves. The waiting area smells like varnish and mint, as if this place is greased down at the end of every day. I sink into a thick wood chair in front of his secretary, Mrs. Oerman.

She looks up, her round gray eyes and a matching bob giving her a grandmotherly air. Her jaw trembles as she acknowledges me. "Miss Newman, of course. He's expecting you."

I've only been in Headmaster Weingarten's office one other time, the first day back after Shaila died. It was the last day of school, so humid and sticky that my skirt stuck to the back of my thighs even when I walked. I felt like a dog, sweating in the heat. He had summoned me, Nikki, and Marla into his chambers and sat in a circle with us, bringing his chair out from behind his desk.

"Girls," he said. "Your time at Gold Coast will never be the same." He was blunt but kind, which was actually sort of refreshing. Everyone else treated us like we were made of glass. The other teachers would barely look at us, just offer tepid shoulder squeezes, knowing head tilts, and sad, sleepy eyes. *Those poor girls.*

Nikki started crying and wiped her snot on the back of her sleeve, leaving a neon green trail slithering up her wrist. Marla clasped her hands together and her shoulders heaved up and down. I wondered just for a second if he knew what had happened to *us*, not Shaila. If he would bring it up, and if he did, how would we respond?

But then Weingarten spoke.

"I had a friend die when I was about your age," he said. "A boating accident in Connecticut. Connor Krauss."

I stared at the crystal-blue centers of his eyes. They looked warm and generous.

"It was the single most important event of my young life," he continued. "It shaped me in every way. His death taught me that life is short and every moment is important, worth it." He held his fist up for emphasis. "I learned to love fiercely and use my time wisely. I wished more than anything that he had stayed alive, but I would not be who I am without that loss." Weingarten looked at all of us intently, his focus jumping from Marla to Nikki to me. "This will mark you. Shaila's absence will change you. But it does not have to *define* you. Do not let it."

The whole meeting was about ten minutes, just enough time to show he cared, but not enough time to ask too many questions or uproot real issues. He didn't ask about why we were all together that night, or what had happened just before. He didn't want to know.

After that he let us go back to our homerooms, where we packed up our stuff and left Gold Coast Prep for three months.

I forgot all about that meeting until today. Nikki, Marla, and I never spoke about it. I don't even know if Quentin, Henry, and Robert had one, or if they did, why Weingarten chose to separate us by gender.

Now I wonder what version of Weingarten I will find. The intimate one who spoke to us then. The formal one who addresses the school every week in Monday morning assembly. Or someone else entirely, the stern authoritarian I had only heard about through whispers in the halls from the *bad* kids. The ones who got detention and were in danger of not graduating on time. The ones who got *suspended,* whose parents donated hundreds of thousands of dollars just to keep them here semester after middling semester. Graham was summoned after the Spring Fling debacle. But he never mentioned what was said.

"Miss Newman, please come in." Weingarten stands up from behind his desk and motions for me to take the chair across from him. "Shut the door behind you."

I perch on the lip of the seat and wait.

"Well, well, well." He smiles, baring all his teeth. "I have to admit I never thought I'd be calling you in here. But it seems like we have something to discuss, young lady."

My legs are heavy and I try my best to cross them, but they stay still. I am paralyzed completely.

"I have to ask you, Miss Newman. You've been digging into the past. Why?"

Weingarten leans back in his chair and his eyebrows shoot up, like he's waiting to be dazzled.

My heart stops. "What do you mean?"

"You've shown great promise while at Gold Coast. Nearly a ninety-six average three years in a row. Well past the requirements of your scholarship. Captain of the Math Olympiad team. Science Bowl champion. Early acceptance into Brown. The Women in Science and Engineering program. Oh, how delightful!" He sucks in a gulp of air then lets it out in one whoosh. "Then why, dear, are you on a mission to ruin the integrity of this school?"

"What? I'm not," I stammer.

Weingarten raises one finger and wiggles it. "But of course

you are," he says. "Pointing fingers at Mr. Beaumont. Digging up your dear friend, Miss Arnold, from the grave." He leans in and I can smell his breath. Musty, like an old towel or the inside of a shoe. "This school was almost destroyed when Miss Arnold was killed. Did you know that? We almost lost our donors, our investments. It could have been a disaster." My stomach sinks. How does he know I had anything to do with Beaumont?

"But the whole thing was handled so swiftly, thank heavens for the Arnolds, and so we were spared," he says. "But now, Miss Newman, you are threatening to dismantle everything we have built."

My head spins as I try to untangle his words and find their true meaning.

"I know you've been having some *issues* with your friends. Maybe you are feeling lost and unwelcome here at Gold Coast Prep. You may have convinced yourself that you found out something dark and dirty swirling beneath the surface of what you *thought* you knew about Miss Arnold. Your *teacher*." Weingarten rubs his temples with his forefinger and thumb. "But let me be very clear, Miss Newman. You will not ruin this school's reputation. After everything we have done for you."

"But—" I sputter.

"Wait, wait, wait," he says, holding up one hand. "I asked you here so we could have a little chat about your final weeks at Gold Coast Prep. About your future." Weingarten leans forward and picks up a hefty manila folder filled with little blue exam books I filled out only hours before. "Your exam." He drops it back on the desk with a thud.

I have to force myself from leaping up to snatch it from his wrinkled hands.

"Did you grade it?" I ask, my voice small.

Weingarten laughs, the sound coming from deep within his belly. "Of course not. That's for the university to do." He gestures to the exam books in front of him. "But I would hate for this all to be a lie."

His eyebrows shoot so far up on his forehead and his blue eyes are icy, no longer gentle. He knows. He's always known.

"They don't look kindly on cheating in the Ivy League."

"I didn't," I breathe. "I studied. I had no help. I did that on my own."

Weingarten holds up a hand. "Maybe this time," he says. "But not all the others." He clasps his hands behind his neck and puffs out his stomach. "You think we don't know what goes on? That we don't know who's a liar, who's a cheat?"

My stomach drops and my mouth grows dry.

"It would be very easy to convince Brown that you had some extra help on this exam, that you've cheated on every exam. Your life would be ruined. All that time and money your parents have spent would be wasted."

I swallow hard and try to force the tears to stay put.

"You have been so *lucky*, Jill Newman." Weingarten stands and walks to his window. From my perch, I can see his gaze land on the lower schoolers, kindergartners maybe, climbing on the pristine jungle gym in their plaid Gold Coast uniforms. They're still fearless.

"But not anymore. You have been ungrateful. Bringing Mr. Beaumont into all of this. Tsk tsk."

"How did you—" I start to ask.

Weingarten laughs. "You think I don't know every police officer in this town? That I don't have people all around Gold Coast just *dying* to share information with me, to trade secrets to get their children into Prep? And that lawyer Miss Calloway hired, Mr. Sorenson? Gold Coast Prep Class of 1991, of course. A star pupil. He gave me a heads-up about Logan that very day."

My cheeks burn and I squeeze my knees together to keep my legs from shaking.

"Miss Newman, I want to be very clear," he says. "You are ruining our reputation. I will not have any more negative attention brought to this school. The past is in the past and you are in danger of blowing up our entire future for a little fishing expedition."

Weingarten's face is flushed and the corners of his mouth are wet with saliva. He sits back down and pulls another manila envelope from the corner of his desk. It's thinner. New. "Let's see. Jared Newman. Looks like he pulled his biology grade up from barely passing to a ninety-two with his midterm. Well done, Mr. Newman!" His eyes linger on mine, playful and menacing. "Wonder how that happened."

His message is clear. If I keep going, if I keep shitting all over Gold Coast Prep, bringing unwanted onlookers to our campus, he will ruin my chances of going to Brown. He will expose me. He will expose Jared. And he will let all the others get away with what we do just to prove a point. If I had doubts about continuing to help Rachel and Graham before, they're all but certain now. I just can't risk it.

"Mr. Beaumont had no part in Shaila's death. Graham Calloway is a murderer. Those are the facts. I need you to drop your little investigation. We can't have any more black marks upon this school. Do you understand what I'm saying, Miss Newman?"

"Yes." My voice is clear and urgent and I do my best to look him dead in the eyes.

"Good girl." He smiles and drops Jared's folder onto his

desk, sending my little blue books flying. "Well, then. Glad we had this little chat. I'll send your exam to Brown this afternoon." He waves his hand and spins in his swivel chair so his tweed-covered back is to me.

I stand with shaking legs and turn toward the door.

"Oh, and Jill?" Weingarten looks over his shoulder at me. "Send my regards to Miss Calloway. Always such a promising young woman. Such a shame. Such a shame."

Mom swings the door open before I even make it up the driveway. Dad's head peeks out behind the frame. "Is that her?" he asks.

My stomach drops and I can't bear to face them. All I want to do is hide.

"Hi," I muster as I push past them through the door.

"Well?" Mom asks. She's wearing a linen tunic and a big chunky necklace. Her face is warm and hopeful. She wants to talk about the test.

"We won't know for a while," I mumble. "You know that."

Dad clasps his hands together behind his back. "Did they say when?" he asks.

"No." I drop my bag with a thud in the hallway and march upstairs to my room, hoping they get the hint. I just can't deal with their questions right now.

I shut the door, collapsing onto my bed. I stare at the stars on my ceiling and notice for the first time that they've faded into a pale yellow, no longer neon against the darkness. A faint knock raps on the door. "Sweetie? Can we come in for just a sec?"

I don't answer but the door opens ever so slightly. "We just want to talk," Dad says softly.

"Fine." I relent. They both come to sit on the foot of my bed.

"We know you have a lot going on . . ." Mom starts to say. But that's when I lose it. A volcano erupts in my stomach and fire rises into my throat.

I sit up. "You have no idea what's going on," I cry. "You have no idea how hard I've worked or how much pressure I'm under." My hands start to shake like my nerves have been shocked. "I *know* how much you've sacrificed so we could be at Gold Coast and all I'm trying to do is make sure that you don't have to sacrifice even more. I'm trying my best and it might not be good enough. You're just going to have to deal with that, okay?" Dad shifts backward, as if I've shot an arrow right at him.

"Sweetie," Mom starts. "I understand . . ."

"No," I say. "You don't understand. You have no idea what it's like every day to walk in there knowing I could lose everything in a split second. And all you've ever wanted is for things to be *better* for me. For me to *succeed*." Snot runs down my face now and I hate myself for digging into them like this. They've done nothing wrong, but I'm so mad. I'm so overwhelmed. I just need to get it all out. "It's fucking hard!" I yell. "And I'm trying. That's all I can do. Just . . . try."

"Oh, Jill." Mom raises her hand to my hair and strokes it. Dad comes to sit beside me and together they gather me up into a hug so tight I think I can't breathe. At first I try to pull away, to free myself from their grasp. But they hold on tighter.

"I'm so sorry," Dad whispers. "This isn't how we wanted things to go." He pulls away and his eyes are wet.

"We grew up so different from all of this," Mom says, motioning outside. "Your father's family lived paycheck to paycheck and my parents didn't care if we ever went to school. We wanted you to have it so much better than we did."

"But maybe it was too much," Dad says. "We put too much pressure on you to be . . ."

"Perfect." Mom gives me a sad smile.

Dad nods. "You don't have to be perfect. You just have to be you."

It sounds like a greeting card, but his words make me cry even harder. "What if I don't get the scholarship?" My words sound soapy and wet, like bubbles ready to burst.

"So what? We'll live."

"But then I won't go to Brown." It's a fact we all know is true.

Mom nods. "Sweetie, you already have a full ride to State's honors program." She smiles wide.

"You won't be disappointed?" I say.

Dad brings me in for a hug that's even tighter than before. "Never."

TWENTY-ONE

"I'M OUT."

The words sound harsher than I want them to. Final. Destructive. But I don't regret them. Not even when Rachel's bottom lip trembles and her eyes reflect a hint of rage.

"You're *what*?" she asks.

"I can't do this anymore," I say. "I'm just a few weeks away from graduation. I'm trying to work things out with Nikki and . . . it's just too much." I shake my head and my hair swings around my shoulders. I decide to leave out the whole *I was threatened by our headmaster* thing.

Here in some overpriced coffee shop in Alphabet City I feel anonymous and a little emboldened. No one knows me except her. I can speak freely. Except my words are really a cop-out. Just like that night in the sauna, I'm choosing to protect myself instead of fighting for Shaila. The guilt will eat at me, but I have to remind myself this isn't just about me. It's about protecting Jared, too.

"So that's it? One false lead and you're dropping this?" Rachel leans back against the rickety wooden chair. The tiny Formica table between us wobbles, causing our lattes to seesaw back and forth in mugs the size of ice cream bowls.

"It's not like we have any other potential suspects," I say. But Rachel doesn't react. "You're not in Gold Coast every day. You don't know what it's *been* like." Weingarten's face appears in my brain, red and furious, wagging a gnarled finger at me.

Rachel narrows her eyes. "Explain it to me, then."

"I'm the one who showed you the letter. Who has to deal with the fallout from Beaumont."

"Just say it," Rachel hisses.

"What do you mean?" My face begins to burn. I've seen this version of her before. Heard this voice. It's how she was when she was a Player, urging us to drink, to dance, to perform. Her rage bubbles to the surface.

"Say it." She bares her teeth.

I shake my head no and clench the mug in front of me.

"You think Graham's guilty. You think Graham murdered Shaila because that's the easy way out. That makes everything go away and you get to go on with your life, pretending like nothing happened. That you once had a friend who died and, boy, did that suck. It'll be something you wow your college roommates with next year, or talk about at parties to make yourself seem interesting. Shaila will just be a blip on your perfectly recorded life. Graham will be someone you used to know who just *snapped*." She leans in so our faces are only inches apart. I can see the tiny little hairs between her eyebrows, waiting to be plucked. "But you know he didn't do it. You know he's innocent. You're just too chickenshit to deal with it."

"Fuck you, Rachel," I whisper through hot, fat tears. "You don't know what I think." The words come up like bile, sticky and sour. There's a real reason why I'm so mad. Why I've been so *angry* for three long years. Initiation changed everything and it wasn't just because someone killed Shaila.

I steady my breath and continue. "You're using me now like you all used us then. Playing God and pulling strings to make us do what you want, just so you can watch." I say it again, letting both hardened syllables land with a deliberate thud. "Fuck. You."

Rachel leans back, her eyes wide. "That's not what happened."

"That's how it always happens," I say.

That was what we were told over and over and over again, as if somehow, that made everything okay. Those little words gave everyone *permission*. But they didn't. No one had permission to do that to us. And we didn't have permission to do it all over again.

Initiation was the last time the eight of us were together.

We gathered at Nikki's at six in the morning and munched on toasted bagels with cream cheese in silence while we waited for the call, the signal that our months of *hard work* would be over soon. Our official entry into the Players was upon us. No more lineups. No more pops. No more Player packs. All we had to do was get through the next twenty-four hours.

A big minivan pulled up to the house and we piled into the car in silence through wide double doors. Two hooded figures wrapped blindfolds around our heads and tied our hands together with zip ties. My stomach flipped and I pressed my shoulder into Shaila's.

We drove for what seemed like hours. The only sound came from the stereo, which blasted the same Billy Joel song over and over. I still can't listen to it. *Only the good die young*. Such bullshit.

Finally we pulled to a halt. Gravel crunched under the wheels and the air smelled heavy and salty, a little like the Fourth of July. Once we got out of the car, our shepherds removed the blindfolds. We were at Tina's house, though we must have driven to the North Fork and back to pass the time. Her parents were gone for the weekend and all the other Players were standing around the massive remodeled farmhouse. We could hear techno music bumping from the backyard. Players' voices rang out until one of our captors yelled for them to shut up.

It will be fun, Adam had said to me the week before. *Just enjoy it.*

We were led into the backyard, to everyone else, and then our drivers pulled off their masks. Rachel and Tina. My stomach settled. I was going to be okay. Rachel was the first person to be nice to me, to hand me the bio exam. She liked me because Adam liked me. And Tina, with her clumpy mascara and that little gap between her teeth, had always been soft. This was her house. She wouldn't let anything bad happen here. I thought back to the moment we shared on the beach, giggling about Mr. Beaumont. I was going to be okay.

But I was so, so wrong.

A chant rang out, so full of elation it made me shiver. It took a minute before I could make out the word.

"Draw! Draw! Draw!"

Jake emerged from the crowd and turned to us, a smirk on his face. "You heard them. Draw!" He held out a stack of thick cardboard playing cards. There were eight of them. "Lowest number gets it worst."

So this was how it would all go down. We each had one final test.

I searched for Adam's steady gaze to anchor me. He was off to the side, whispering to someone else, but then he looked up.

Adam gave me a slowly spreading smile. His dimple was on display. He'd make sure we would be all right.

We each drew one card to our chest.

I snuck a peek at mine and fear filled my stomach. Three. I glanced up and around the circle. Quentin looked calm. Henry, too. Nikki brought her hand to her mouth and started to bite her nails. Shaila's face went white.

"Reveal 'em!" Jake shouted.

We turned our cards toward Rachel and she shouted out our numbers.

"Eight, Quentin; seven, Henry; six, Robert; five, Graham; four, Marla; three, Jill; two, Nikki; ace, Shaila!"

The Players around us erupted into shrieks and whoops, clapping each other on their backs. I'd only find out later that somehow the girls always drew the low numbers. Absolute crap.

"Freshmen," Adam yelled. "You have one hour to prepare yourselves for whatever comes next. We'll be back then with your assignments." But before disappearing, he yelled over his shoulder. "You might need this, too. Courage." He winked wickedly and tossed a handle of vodka onto the lawn. The whole group disappeared and we were left alone on the grass. The sun beat down on us and that stupid Billy Joel song blasted over the speakers.

"What the hell," Nikki mumbled. "What are they going to do to us?"

"Did Rachel tell you anything?" Shaila took the first sip from the bottle and turned to Graham, her eyes like saucers. It was the first time I had seen her scared like this, terrified of the unknown.

Graham shook his head, but he looked a little shaken. I remember his number. Five. He took a swig. "She only gave me one clue," he said. "She just said, 'We know your fears.'"

My stomach sank and I remembered the night I sat with Jake and Adam on Adam's porch. What I had told them about me . . . about Shaila. How I couldn't sleep without a night-light, how Shaila could never ride the Ferris wheel because it was so high off the ground.

Had we all betrayed each other at some point that year? We must have. There's no way I was the only one. Not if they knew everyone here had something that terrified them. But no one said anything as we stewed in our own shame, slowly passing around the bottle. I turned away from the group and spotted Ocean Cliff off in the distance. Shaila saw it, too.

We stayed quiet, mulling over our fates, until the rest of the Players returned to read out what we had to do.

It was clear then that Adam, Jake, and the rest of the boys were running the show. The girls hung in the back, taking selfies and hyping up the whole event. They were never in charge. We never are. I know that now.

"You'll each be given a personalized task," Jake said. "Lower numbers, watch the fuck out. You'll also be paired with a senior who will oversee your challenge, to make sure you complete it correctly." The crowd behind him hollered their support. "Ready?"

Quentin's was first: He had to watch two horror movies back to back since he was terrified of zombies. Tina would hang out with him while that all happened.

"Lame!" someone called out.

"Eat a turd, dipshit!" Jake countered. "Next up, Jill."

I took a step forward from our lineup and held my head high.

"Afraid of the dark, are we?" Jake said.

"Yes," I whispered.

"There's a crawlspace in the basement," he said, motioning to the main house behind me. "You'll stay in there for four hours. Alone." I sighed deeply. I could do that. I would pass. "I'll be the one to come check on you periodically."

My brain rattled as he read off the rest of the assignments, but it was only when he announced Shaila's name that I snapped back to attention. "Ocean Cliff," Jake said.

The group behind him gasped. Even Adam looked a little surprised.

"What about it?" Shaila asked, trying to keep her cool. She shifted her weight back and forth from one foot to the other.

"Jump," Jake said. He smiled sweetly. "And swim back to shore."

Rachel shook her head and Tina covered her mouth.

"That's like a million feet above sea level," Shaila said. Her voice trembled.

"So?" Jake countered. "Others have done it before." No one questioned if this was true or not.

Shaila's eyes hardened. "Fine."

Adam stepped forward as if to appease her. "I'll be there, too," he said, his voice kinder now. "I'll be monitoring yours."

Shaila's face softened and I felt my shoulders relax a little. I grabbed her hand and she squeezed it. She turned to me and her eyes were wide and scared. "Don't let them see you hurt," she whispered. I nodded and then she turned and trotted off behind Adam, toward Ocean Cliff jutting out over the shore. That was the last time I saw her alive.

Suddenly Jake appeared by my side. "Come on, Newman." His voice was deep with no emotion.

He led me to Tina's house, which was bright and airy, decorated with shades of white and gray and blue. "Here," he said, motioning to a set of stairs behind a door in the kitchen. I followed him down into an unfinished basement that smelled like musk and mildew. I scrunched up my nose and tried to ignore the fear churning in my stomach. Jake walked to the back corner and opened a small doorway that only went up to his shoulders. "You might want to get on your knees," he said. A menacing smile spread across his face. I did as he said and held my breath as I crawled into the dark space, feeling my way around the cold cement floor. The whole room was about as big as a full-size bed. Jake knelt down and tossed me a blanket and an unmarked glass bottle. "Provisions."

"Thanks," I whispered.

"I'll be back soon," he said. He shut the door and I heard the lock slide into place with a *click*.

I inhaled deeply, smelling plaster and glue. Then I spread the blanket around as best I could and lay down, trying to pretend like I was in my own bed at home, looking up at the plastic stars on my ceiling. At first, it was okay, just a little uncomfortable; I could barely sit up, the space was so small. But then I started to hear things, or at least I thought I did. Mice crawling through the walls. Banging from the floor above. It was all too much, too scary, too surreal. Then it became torturous, like the walls were caving in around me. My heart raced and my fingers trembled. I shuffled over to the door just to see if I could get it open. I shoved my shoulder against the entrance, but it stayed put, like something was pushed up against the door. That's when I started to panic. My chest tightened and there was only one option, only one way to get through this all.

I sat back on the blanket and brought the bottle to my lips. I took a generous sip. The liquid smelled like gasoline and was harsher than vodka. But I was grateful for something . . . anything to be a distraction. I took a big gulp and then another, letting the vile liquid give way to a numb, tingly feeling. It wasn't just strong, it tasted rancid—chemical.

Then I disappeared.

I came to hours later. I swear I heard a scream—a wrenching, bloodcurdling scream. Was it my own strangled voice? Was it far off in the distance? It didn't matter because I was safe, I figured. I must have been because I had been moved somewhere with a window, though no sunshine came through. I was on a bed, I knew, because there were sheets, soft beneath my bare legs. Above ground, I realized. It had to be because a flame licked the window. A bonfire, I determined, raging just outside in the backyard. It was so close. So was the group. I could hear them. Was it over? Did I pass? I must have. But then why wasn't I with the others? Why was I alone?

Until I realized I wasn't.

"You smell like a s'more." He whispered the words, slurring a bit. Adam must have found me. I felt a pang of relief. Then his tongue slithered into my ear. The warm, wet heat was shocking and forced me to tense, to try to sit up. But I couldn't move.

"Shh . . . It's okay." His face came into focus and in an instant, I realized it was not Adam. It was Jake. Hovering over me. Pinning my arms over my head. Up against me. Waiting. Patient, but not really.

"What . . ."

"You made it through," he said again. "You passed the test." His tongue found its way into my ear again and I shook my head, as if trying to swat away a fly. The room spun around me.

I tried to pull away but Jake was so big, like a giant brick. "I don't feel well," I said, my head swimming.

"C'mon," he said, his mouth moving over my neck. "Let's celebrate."

My limbs were so heavy. I just wanted everything to stop.

"No," I said softly. "No." Jake laughed and moved his hands lower, lifting my sweatshirt. His touch was freezing and I shivered.

"See? It's nice," he said. "Aren't you going to thank me for helping you get through it?" I tried to wiggle out from under him, but Jake tugged my wrists down by my sides. I was immobile, unable to think. I wanted so desperately to leave, to join the group, to go home, to find Shaila. Had she jumped? Had she passed, too? Was it easier to succumb? To let my brain leave my body? Suddenly, the door squeaked open.

"Dude." It was Adam. I recognized his voice. "What are you doing?"

"You know what I'm doing." Jake whipped his head around and in his profile I saw a wide, scary smile. I wanted to run, to use this free moment to crawl to the floor, to get away completely.

"She's wasted."

"What, you're a cop now?"

"Let's just get a drink. It's not worth it." Adam kicked the door open farther so more light streamed in.

Jake rolled his eyes, indifferent, over it. "Whatever." Finally, he rose and retreated from the room. "You're no fun, bro," he called on his way out.

"Adam," I tried to say, but it came out like garbled mush. I reached for him but my arms stayed on the bed, too heavy to lift.

"Are you okay?" he asked. His words were just a tiny bit slurred and a little sad.

"Mm," I said.

"You gotta sleep this off."

"Mm," I said again. The relief was overwhelming. I wanted to cry, to bury myself in these sheets.

"I'm going to lock the door, okay? No one can get in. The key's right here on the dresser."

I nodded.

"Say okay, Jill."

"Okay."

He shut the door quietly behind him and I rolled over, forcing myself to stare out the window and into the darkness. *Look up,* I willed myself. *Find the moon. Just find an anchor.* But all I saw was a smattering of twinkling lights, jumbled in piles like puzzle pieces that I would never be able to put together. It was too beautiful, too chaotic.

Then I fell into a sleep so deep it ached. It was hours later when I awoke to the sounds of sirens and Nikki's sobs. To Shaila's death.

It took until the next day to find out that Nikki had just barely passed her pop. She was scared of getting lost and had been blindfolded, then dropped off five miles away in the woods, forced to find her way back to Tina's on her own with no phone. Marla nearly got caught while completing hers—breaking into the field hockey coach's summer home to steal the county finals trophy. Her biggest fear was getting cut from the team, losing everything. Rachel helped her flee at the last minute.

The boys' tasks were easier, less dangerous, like the seniors had less ammo to use, less to torture them with. Henry had to plant a false story in the *Gold Coast Gazette* that got him a slap on the wrist and fired from his internship. Robert was forced to steal his dad's Lambo and let each senior take it for a ride up and down the expressway. He dropped it off only minutes before his dad came home around midnight. Graham had his thing with the tarantulas and emerged only to find Shaila, wet and exhausted, having survived Ocean Cliff. He coaxed her into going for a walk, when he lost it and killed her. At least that's what we were told.

But we didn't talk about any of it the next day. I never told them about Jake or how Adam saved me. How could I? Shaila was dead by then. There were bigger things to not discuss.

Still, Jake's words seared into my brain. *Aren't you going to thank me?*

As if I owed him some chunk of myself. As if he was entitled to a prize for locking me in a closet with a bottle of something sketchy.

The memory makes my insides crumble and my head pound. What if Adam hadn't found me? I tried desperately not to obsess over the possibilities, over the fear and the blurry reality of what had and had not happened.

That day after initiation, while we were supposed to be grieving, there was one thought I couldn't get out of my head: *Why did the boys have the power? Why did they make the rules while we dealt with the consequences?*

A montage of pops flashed through my brain. Adam and Jake calling out directions. Tina and Rachel standing on the sidelines, cheering and whooping along. They seemed in control, but they never were. Moments flickered in my brain as I remembered all the times the boys took advantage. Humiliating Nikki during the Show. Acting like we were being so dramatic when Shaila almost drank herself to death. It happened all over again this year. Robert zeroing in on Sierra. My own brother laughing at her during Road Rally. The boys always spoke in code when we were present, a secret language not meant for us. We were always kept in the dark.

It spread like a virus to Derek Garry and to Robert. Then passed along to boys like Topher Gardner and, now, my brother.

Had we stood by and let this transformation take place?

Shaila's death should have signaled the end. I wonder if every class thought their initiation would be the last, though. *We'll keep them safe. We'll make everything okay. We'll stop this.* But we didn't. We were complicit in the sick, twisted games we played with each other. *Prove it,* we taunted. *Prove you're a Player.*

And the worst part is that it felt good, really good, to have someone else endure what we did. That next year, when we were sophomores, Nikki, Marla, and I did all the bitch work to set up for initiation, driving out to Derek Garry's Hamptons house the night before, filled with adrenaline. We made vats of neon pink Player Punch, stoked the bonfire, and squealed with excitement when the freshmen showed up blindfolded, shaking, and scared. Robert, Henry, and Quentin had one job: get ice.

And when the Toastmaster, Fieldston Carter, called out the final pops, I stood back as they shouted out assignments: Spend the whole day naked in the sun. Get on all fours and let the seniors walk you on a leash for the rest of the night.

I smiled as we chugged beer until we forgot our reality, that this was the night that killed Shaila only a year before. It's only now I realize I thought I was still on the chopping block. I thought I was up for grabs.

We did it again last year, too, convinced we were only juniors, not quite at the top. That's why I kept telling myself, *This year will be different.* I tried to push the guilt away, to keep it from eating me alive. But now I know that's a lie, too. Initiation will go on as planned. Jared will complete his horrific transformation. Unless something happens. Something big.

Rachel clears her throat and I'm back in the dingy downtown coffee shop. "We were wrong," she says. Her red-rimmed eyes are wet, threatening to spill over. Her mouth crumples. "To go along with everything. To let it happen."

"Why do we do it?" I say.

"It's easy to convince yourself of something if you just pretend it's the truth."

We sit in silence as our lattes grow cold.

Finally she speaks. "So you're really out?"

I think of Weingarten, of Brown, of what I can do to really protect Jared. There's still time for him. "I need to know what happened to Shaila," I say firmly.

Rachel nods and leans in so our foreheads almost touch. "I want you to know something. The Players . . . all that bullshit. That's not who I am anymore." She looks me dead in the eye. "It's not who you are either."

She's right. That Jill would never have responded to Rachel's text back in the fall. She never would have agreed to meet Graham or go talk to Kara. She would have clapped along with everyone else at the Show and cheered when Jared laughed at Sierra during Road Rally. She never would have found herself being threatened in the headmaster's office. That Jill would have graduated with a 96 average and a hole in her heart.

This one will not.

TWENTY-TWO

I NEED YOU.

Those three words are better than any, better than *I miss you* or even *I love you*. They send a rumbling sensation through my body, starting at my toes and ending at the tips of my split ends. And today, on the first Saturday in May, they come from Adam in the form of a text.

Big Keith hated my latest. He says I'm slacking.

The sun streams through my window, hitting my bed, and I squint to read his words again. I didn't even know he was home. He must have just ended the semester.

Want me to come over? I type.

Yes.

My heart is heavy, filled with a desperate need to make Adam feel better. It's the best distraction right now. Rachel and I have been going over file after file in Shaila's case for the last few days and I'm exhausted. And, after what I owe him, I can't imagine ever saying no.

I take a quick shower, pull on a coral-colored sundress and my jean jacket, and drive the route I know by heart. I roll the windows down and crank up Stevie Nicks's first solo album. A warm breeze floats through the car. This used to be my favorite season in Gold Coast. Those few weeks just after everything thaws for good but before the heat becomes oppressive. It used to feel like the only time of year when everything bubbles with possibilities. Now the weather just reminds me of losing Shaila.

Within a few minutes, I turn into the Millers' familiar C-shaped driveway and I throw the car in park. As I begin to unbuckle my seat belt, my phone pings.

Check your email. It's Rachel.

???? I write back.

Kara found all of Shaila's letters. Her mom kept them in some box in her office. Kara went through them and took a million pics. She just sent them over.

Shit! She came through . . . My heart starts to race. What could Shaila have possibly said? *Anything good in there? Any leads?*

Looking, but I can't tell yet. Maybe you can see if anything sticks out? Rachel says.

I tap over to my inbox and see one email from Rachel. It has an enormous attachment. The wait time to download is minutes but it might as well be an eternity. I groan and heave myself out of the car.

I'm still staring at my phone, willing the letters to appear, when Cindy Miller answers the door.

"Oh, Jill," she says through a bright smile. "You must be here for Adam. Rough meeting with Big Keith last night." Her nose crinkles like she's smelled something funny. "I'm sure you'll cheer him up. You always do."

I can't help but flush. "Thanks, Mrs. Miller."

She moves aside and I run up the stairs, shoving my phone in my pocket. The letters will be there later.

I push the door open gently. Adam's room is just like I remember it, wallpapered with little blue sailboats. Two lacrosse sticks hang in an X over his king-size bed. Rows of well-loved paperbacks line two floor-to-ceiling bookshelves.

Adam's flat on the bed, with his legs dangling over the side.

"You came," he says.

"Of course." I close the door and take a seat in his desk chair, the black swivel kind that goes up and down with the pull of a lever. "How are you?"

Adam groans. "Shitty. Feel like an talentless loser."

"You know that's not true."

"Come closer," he says. "You're too far away." My heart races and I stand. Being his person has always meant following his directions. *I need you. Come closer.* I sit down next to him and lie back, letting our whole bodies touch. Every inch of my skin tingles.

"You're always here for me, Jill," he says. "Even when I don't deserve you."

"You always deserve me," I say softly. His skin is so close, I can feel his heat, the tiny hairs on his arm grazing mine. I wonder if he's aware of me, too. If he can sense the nervous humming in my veins. It bleats over and over again. *You saved me. You saved me.*

Adam heaves himself up to sit.

"Jill," he says again. "Promise me you'll always love me."

The words shock me. *How did he know?* But before I can say anything, Adam leans down and the space between us disappears. I inhale sharply as his mouth presses against mine. His lips are soft and he tastes minty and sweet, like a peppermint patty. Every crevice of me is on fire. He slides his wet tongue against mine and I fight the urge to nibble on it. He brings one hand to my neck and rests the other on my knee. My body has wanted this for so long, to mold to Adam's, to relent. To let everything go.

I feel him hard, pressing against his jeans. Something I've dreamed about forever, since the first night he came to my house. I wrap my arms around his neck and run a finger along the prickly baby hairs. They're so real, I want to cry.

But my brain snaps to attention. The room tilts, as if everything is sliding off a table. Adam is suddenly stale against my mouth. It all just feels . . . wrong. Like he could be doing this with anyone. *I* could be anyone. I'm just *here*.

I pull back. "Wait," I whisper. "We can't."

Adam lets out a soft laugh against my neck. "Of course we can. After all this time, we finally can."

But everything is different now. I'm different now.

"It doesn't feel right," I say.

He leans back and flops against the bedspread, bouncing away.

"I don't want it to be like this. If you want this," I say, motioning to the air between us, "I want it to be real. For good. Not because you're upset or sad. I want it to be more."

"You don't want to live in the moment?" He's not looking at me now. His eyes are on the little boats, their white sails flapping in the wind.

I take a deep breath. If I say what I really want to, I can never take it back. I go for it. "I want us to be together next year when I'm at Brown. I don't want to fuck this up."

Adam turns back to me and runs his index finger down my

cheek. "You won't," he says softly.

"Adam!" Cindy Miller's voice rings through the house. "Can you come here for a sec? My laptop's on the fritz."

Adam rolls his eyes but flashes me a smile so wide I can see his dimple.

"Be right back." The bed groans as he retreats and I blink back tears. It only took a minute for me to ruin everything. My phone vibrates against my thigh.

Did you read???? Rachel writes. *I don't see anything usable yet. She mentions Adam though.*

My heart beats fast and my palms grow sweaty.

I tap back over to my email and see the attachment has finally downloaded. I click to open and I'm greeted by dozens of pages of Shaila's loopy handwriting. I scan the words, hoping to find something, anything, that could be a clue. I catch fragments of sentences, of Shaila's effusive, loving prose, her all-caps moments of excitement. But one letter dated mid-March stops me. One word stands out. A name. It's bolded as if Shaila traced the letters twice, maybe three times, without even realizing it. When I see it, my heart drops. I scan back to the top of the page and start reading.

> *KARAAAA!*
>
> *I can't even tell you how excited I am for summer these days. I just want to be back in the Hamps with you and Graham again. I am loooonnginggg for the days of hanging at Graham's house, our feet dangling in the pool while we shove ice cream bars into our faces.*
>
> *Adam says he'll come out for a few weeks, too. Then it'll really be like last year—all of us together again. I promise he and I won't ditch you guys again. You know we were*

just running lines for that play he's working on. He says I'm the only one he trusts here in Gold Coast to do his dialogue justice.

Speaking of, I'm starring in Rent, bitch!!!! Remember when we saw it back in middle school and sang that candle song back and forth for literal months? Now I'm going to get to do that on an actual stage in front of actual people.

Adam has been helping me run lines after school and I cannot tell you how amazing it is. There's seriously no one else here who gets this whole world. Thank god I have him. Anyway, I gotta go. Rehearsal is starting back up in a few. Talk soon, love.

Xo, SHAY

My head spins and I can hardly breathe. Shaila and Adam hung out the summer before freshman year? A lot, it seems. Enough that Kara had called her out for ditching. I knew they had gotten friendly during *Rent*, but why didn't they mention it? Shaila made it seem like she saw him once or twice with Rachel. Never alone. Not that they had their own . . . thing.

"Sorry. Mom's a total dummy when it comes to all things electronic." Adam steps back into the room gingerly and shuts the door behind him. "Everything okay?"

I shove my phone in my pocket and sit on my hands. They need to stop shaking. "Yep," I say, and try to keep my face neutral.

"You sure?"

I nod. I need a moment to myself. Just one more. "Just a little warm. Could I have a glass of water?"

Adam smiles that sweet, lopsided smile of his and backs out of the room.

I let out a rush of air and lie back against his pillows. Images of Shaila and Adam dance in my head. Why had they kept that from me?

I curl over onto my side and my knee knocks against Adam's nightstand, jostling it open. I extend a hand to push the drawer back in its place, but it won't move. It's stuck, as if something is blocking it from shutting all the way. I reach into the drawer and wiggle my hand around, trying to see what's there. My fingertips graze something soft and velvety. But when I wrap my hand around it and try to pull it loose, it stays put. Weird. I sit up to get a closer look and when I do, all the air rushes out of my lungs. There in Adam's nightstand is a slim square jewelry box. My head spins as I convince myself that it can't be what I think it is; it's just not possible.

With shaking fingers, I reach for the box and wiggle it free. It's light and fits completely in my palm. I just need to check, to know I'm not losing my mind. Carefully, I pry the box open.

A flash of bright light. The afternoon sun bounces off of whatever is inside and spreads through the room, blinding me for just a second.

I blink and look again. My stomach drops. Two sparkling diamond studs are nestled in the box. Big and round and shimmering, with tiny platinum prongs holding the stones in place. They look just like Kara's.

Her words ring in my ears.

She said she could never wear them, that people would ask too many questions. She gave them back to him and he freaked out.

My heart thumps so loud, I fear Adam can hear it from the hallway.

They're Shaila's.

"Hope tap's okay," Adam calls from outside the room. "Seltzer's all the way downstairs."

I snap the box closed and place it carefully inside Adam's drawer, shoving it back into place. I leap to the opposite side of the bed. Adrenaline courses through me and I need to escape. To forget whatever I just found.

I try to find words but my throat is scratchy. "Yep!" It's all I can say and it comes out like a cat's howl.

"You sure you're okay?" he asks, appearing in the doorframe. He lets his head fall to one side. Gone is the messy, bummed-out boy who sat beside me before. The real Adam, my Adam, appears instead. But I don't know anything anymore.

"I'm not feeling well," I say. "I gotta go."

"C'mon," he says. "Stay with me. We'll figure everything out."

I shake my head and stand. A rage builds inside me, pulsing through my blood, reaching my fingertips. I want out. I need to go.

I push past him and make for the stairs.

"Jill, wait!" he calls after me. But I'm already out the door, sprinting to the car. My hands shake as I shove the keys into the ignition and reverse, peeling out of the driveway.

It's not until I'm halfway to my destination that I realize where I'm going. The road is open and I gun it. A kelly green sign looms overhead on the Long Island Expressway.

NEW YORK CITY
30 MILES

TWENTY-THREE

I STAND IN front of Rachel's doorway drenched in sweat. The city is so humid the air sags. Was it always ten degrees hotter here than in Gold Coast? My damp hair sticks to the back of my neck and my sundress is a full shade darker than it should be.

"C'mon, Rachel," I mutter. I must have been here for five minutes already, buzzing her apartment. She's not picking up her phone and I'm starting to panic.

I peer into the cloudy glass window in the doorframe when suddenly, someone taps me from behind.

"Jill?"

I spin around to find Rachel standing with her arms crossed over her chest, her hair braided and pulled to the side. She's dressed up in platform sandals and a chambray dress, like she's just been at the farmers' market, or brunch with Frida. "You're here."

"Uh, of course," she says. "I live here. Why are you here?"

"I saw something," I say. My voice warbles in an unfamiliar tone. "At Adam's."

Rachel's eyes widen and she shifts her canvas tote from one shoulder to another. "Let's go upstairs."

It's even more muggy in the stairwell and I start to pant. We take the steps two at a time, and I'm almost out of breath by the time we reach her apartment. Rachel throws open the door and gestures for me to sit on the couch, then slides in beside me. "Okay, what's up?"

I shake my head. I don't know where to begin.

"The earrings," I say. "The ones Kara was talking about. Shaila's diamonds. I saw them in Adam's drawer today. He has them."

Rachel's face goes white.

I watch her eyes as she puts the pieces together. They squint and search and finally she squeezes them shut. "Fuck."

"She wasn't with Beaumont . . ." I say. My face contorts as I fight out the next words: "It was Adam."

"But Graham," she says.

"I know," I whisper.

"And . . . me."

"I know," I say again.

"I always suspected he was cheating when we were dating," she says. Her breaths are labored, sharp. "Honestly? I thought it was you." She laughs. "He always adored you."

My face feels hot and my stomach flips.

"I reached out to him last summer, you know. About all of this." She motions around with her hands. "I thought he might have a soft spot for me after all these years and that he'd want to help me find justice for Graham." Rachel lets out a sad, soft laugh. "He didn't even respond to my text."

I remember what Adam said when he told me Rachel contacted him, too. *She's nuts.*

"Even though I thought he cheated, staying with him was easier than breaking up senior year. Being alone. Trying to figure out whatever *this* was."

She motions to a framed photo on the coffee table. In it, her arms are around a Latina girl with long dark hair and a big red smile. That must be Frida. Rachel's eyes are bright, and together, they seem so alive, so happy.

"It was so much better to be the hot couple," Rachel says. "The couple everyone wanted to be. He made it easy, too. We had fun together. We loved each other. In a weird kiddie way, but still . . . in a way. At least I thought we did." Rachel leans back against the couch and lets out a low whistle. "You know what this means, right?"

I do.

"He could have killed . . ." I hold up my hand to cut her off. I can't hear the words right now.

I wish I could ask Shaila why she did it and if she knew how much this would hurt. I want her to know she had the power to break me, even from the grave. I want her back so we can get over it and hold each other close and say *fuck him!* I want to hear her deep, full laugh and see her written apology scrawled out in her round script. *I'm sorry, J.* I want to scream.

I want to mourn what I thought I knew about the people I love. *Loved.* How do I recover? How do I get over this?

I can't.

Not yet, anyway.

Because it feels like my heart has been smashed open and every truth I ever knew is spilling onto the floor. Rachel starts talking so fast I can barely keep up. She creates a plan, a road map out of this mess. A way to find out the truth. Pretty soon there are papers and pens and details and directions. She makes some calls and opens a bottle of cold brew. Her exhilaration vibrates through the tiny apartment. I swear I can see it in the faded paint slapped on the walls, blowing up little air pockets until they're about to burst.

Through all of this, I clutch a throw pillow and sit still, alternating between listening and zoning out.

Until finally Rachel stops talking. The room is silent for the first time in hours and I wonder how late it is and what my life will be like in a week's time.

I heave myself off the couch and shuffle over to the window. The view faces the East River and across the way, little flashes of light shine back at us from Brooklyn. I know there's no hope of seeing stars here, not with all the streetlamps and the neon billboards and blinking lights aboard the ferries. But like I always do, I look up. Sticking my head all the way out Rachel's window and turning toward the sky, I try to make out just a single star.

The night stretches on forever and the air is clear and warm. I wait a beat and then another, just hoping for one.

Finally, a cloud sails along an imaginary track to reveal a swath of galaxy visible just for a second. My heart slows to a steady, determined thump.

When I finally get home, Jared's the only one awake, seated at the kitchen island, housing the last of Mom's eggplant parm straight from the glass dish. "Where've *you* been?" he slurs.

"Maybe I should ask you that." I pull out a stool next to him and grab a fork. I'm so exhausted and drained that the piece of silverware feels heavy like lead.

"Nuh-uh. Mine," he says, shoving me over with his shoulder.

"No way! I'm starving." Jared relents and makes room for me in his saucy, cheesy minefield.

"Party tonight?" I ask.

He nods. "Just a lineup." I let out a snort. *Of course.*

"Topher's?"

"Nah. Robert's. That house is nuts."

I haven't been there since last year, but I remember it. All chrome corners and glass edges and uncomfortable furniture not made for actual sitting.

"It got broken up, though," Jared says. "Robert took his dad's Lambo for a joyride. Such a show-off."

"Idiot," I mutter.

"No kidding. The group thread says he got caught speeding up toward the Mussel Bay tollbooth. A DUI maybe. He's at county right now."

"Wait, are you serious?" It's not a shock that it happened. Just that Jared says this information so nonchalantly, like it's no big deal, just a bummer they all have to deal with.

Jared nods. "Guess we'll find out details on Monday."

I shake my head at the stupidity of all of this, of Robert and the Players.

"I heard you were at the Millers' today," Jared says. "Bryce told me. He heard you hanging."

I nod and force a forkful of food into my mouth. Jared looks at me with bloodshot, half-droopy eyes.

"You guys a thing?" he asks.

I choke back a lump in my throat and stare back down at the layers of eggplant. The cheese on top has chilled, turning into a flat piece of rubber.

"No."

"For the best," Jared says. "Henry's not over you, you know?"

My heart softens and I picture sweet, sad Henry. He was never right for me, but thinking of the look on his face when I broke up with him still breaks my heart.

"Plus, Bryce says Adam's going through some shit now."

He pauses but I don't speak.

"Weird, huh?"

"Weird," I echo.

"I think he's hanging around for a while. At least until after our finals. Probably through the month. Then he's off to some internship in Los Angeles." Jared slams another forkful of food into his mouth. "At least that's what Bryce said."

Finals. They're all next week. And before then, Nikki had scheduled initiation. Their last test.

I sit with what I know for the rest of the week, bottling it up inside and keeping it close. I decline Nikki's invitation to rejoin the Players' Table for a few last meals, using the awkwardness between me and Henry as an excuse.

"Come on," Nikki pleads. "There's only one week left. Plus, Robert is totally shook from the whole DUI thing. His NYU acceptance was revoked and he has to start court-ordered mandatory rehab after graduation."

"Serves him right," I say.

Nikki's mouth forms a pout, but then she nods once. "Yeah, it does."

Even Robert being put in his place won't make me come back. I shake my head and hug her hard as we part ways in the hall. "I just need a little more time." She knows what's coming—about the plan Rachel and I made—and so she relents. It feels good to share secrets with her again.

I retreat to the library where I read all of *Wuthering Heights* in prep for the AP English final, then go over my flashcards for the physics exam even though I know them all by heart now. I try not to check my email for news about the scholarship. Instead, I run errands for Mom after school, popping in and out of the drugstore and the farmers' market and the art supply shop. I even clean out the boxes in the basement, the ones with all my old quizzes and research projects from elementary school. Anything to avoid reality. To avoid what I know is coming. And, mostly, to avoid Adam's texts.

I need you.

Please.

I can't talk to anyone else here.

Mom's driving me insane.

Why are you ghosting me?

I'm sorry about the other day!

Each one is like a sledgehammer to my heart, a reminder of what I thought we were. Everything I thought I knew was a lie.

Finally I relent.

Caught an awful stomach bug. Super contagious!!!

He responds with one emoji: ☹

When I get to school on Monday, the last Monday before finals, I try to be invisible. I want to soak everything in—how the lockers sound when they're slammed shut, how the desks are always slick with Windex, how the library smells new even though the books are ancient. I want to remember how the morning buzz shifts from sleepy to frenzied in record time. How Weingarten's beady eyes roam the audience during morning assembly, how they linger on mine, waiting to see if I'll break.

I even want to remember how the Players look from afar,

how sometimes the table can feel like a raft in the middle of the ocean, and other times like a shark hunting for prey. How Quentin's easy kindness radiates when he makes his way through the sandwich line, letting sophomores cut him while he decides between focaccia and ciabatta. I want to remember how Nikki's confidence seeps into every interaction, and how that took years to build. I want to remember how Marla drags her field hockey stick behind her like it's a security blanket or an extra appendage. How Henry's lip quivers just a little when he reads the morning broadcast. I even want to remember how Robert's eyes scan the caf, drinking this world in, like he knows this might be as good as it gets for him.

I want to hold this place still in my heart before it changes again for good.

TWENTY-FOUR

EVERYTHING HAPPENS QUICKLY once the positions are in place. The days fly by and suddenly it's Friday, the last real day of school. The halls are maddening, fizzing with anticipation. I am, too, but for such different reasons.

By the time the final bell rings, it's as if someone set the school on fire. Everyone pushes and shoves, sprinting toward *almost* freedom.

I head out to our designated meeting place—Nikki's house—and find Rachel there, already waiting. We share a quick hug and wait for the sun to set.

I sit on the deck, sprawling on the chaise lounge and find as many constellations as I can. It's a perfect night. They're all out, dancing and galloping through the sky. I should be terrified but my breathing is steady and a calm sets in. Maybe it's because we finally have a plan.

"Ready?" Rachel asks. She stands over me in jeans and a ratty black hoodie. Her eyes are tired and her skin sags just a bit around the edges, like she's aged a decade during this fucked-up year. I want to hug her close and say *thank you* a million times over. I want to bottle her smile and carry it with me as I do this next part alone. Without her bravery, none of this would have been possible. I would be floating along like a ship with no course, crashing ashore someday, maybe.

But instead I just whisper, "Yes," and send the text. It only takes a minute for him to respond. "He's coming," I say. "Fifteen minutes." We sit in silence, a nervous current running between us, until I see the headlights of his beloved vintage Mercedes. Bad punk music blares from the speaker and I try to remember what about those notes made me swoon.

"My heart is *racing*," Rachel whispers.

"It's okay," I murmur. Her hand finds mine and we squeeze each other hard.

I kick off my sneakers and walk to the beach where I told him to meet me. With every step, I try to stand taller, stronger, more like Rachel—or Shaila. I shake inside my fleece. Not from fright, though. From rage. Pure, searing rage coiled inside me like a snake. I'm ready to let it out.

When I get to my mark, I turn to the ocean. It's one big black roiling mess, crashing with impatience. Foam peaks glisten in the distance. They provide the only other light aside from the moon and the stars. *How can something this violent be my home?*

"Here you are," Adam says. He gives me that stupid dimpled grin and opens his arms for a hug.

I want to unleash something wretched but instead I walk into his arms and let him rest his head on mine, like we've done hundreds of times before. "You made it," I say.

"So mysterious, Newman."

I let him go and step back. I want to see his face head-on when he has to tell the truth for once. I need to catch everything he says, or none of this will work.

"Look, Adam," I say sweetly. "This isn't easy to say, but I

need to talk to you about something."

He raises his eyebrows and rests his hands on his hips. "What's up?"

I take a deep breath and begin, just like we practiced. "I know about you and Shaila." I try to look sad, like I'm heartbroken and hurt, not seething beneath my skin.

"What do you mean?" he asks softly. His smile fades and his dimple disappears.

"I know that you two were . . . you know." I can't bring myself to say it.

"Huh," he says. "I don't know what you mean."

I shake my head and meet his eyes. "She wrote letters."

Adam's voice becomes a whisper. "What?"

I nod and purse my lips. "About cheating on Graham. About everything. About you." I hold my breath and wait for him to speak next. I need to exaggerate, to pretend like I'm so sure of these facts my brain will explode.

"Well," Adam says. He runs a hand through his hair and shifts from foot to foot. "We both know she was a little out there, though, right? I'm sure she blew things out of proportion."

"Maybe." I turn away to the sea, hoping I look miffed, jealous.

"What did she say?" Adam asks. His curiosity betrays him.

"That she was in love with someone who wasn't Graham. That it would tear the Players apart. That it was you." I bite my lip and hope he believes me.

Adam tilts his head up to the sky and closes his eyes. "I made a mistake." My stomach ties itself into knots and Adam lowers his gaze to the waves. "You're not, like, mad, are you?" he asks. "That was years ago. She's not even . . ." Adam trails off and steps closer to me, just like I planned. "You and I have something special, something different, you know. It's always been you and me."

The words I'd always wanted to hear, now coated in a thick greasy sheen. I want to toss them into the Atlantic and watch them drown.

"Next year, we'll finally be together. We can do all the things you wanted," he continues.

I shake my head. "I don't think so, Adam. Everything is different now."

"What?" His eyebrows shoot up. I don't say anything. My stomach flips. "Is this about Graham? All that bullshit about being innocent?" His eyes narrow and he stabs a finger at me, like I'm in trouble, like I betrayed him, which I guess I did. "You don't really believe him, do you?"

"He makes some good points."

"You've talked to him?" Adam asks. His voice is getting louder.

"Yes," I say, trying to steady my voice. "Rachel, too."

Adam's eyes look like they're about to bulge out of his head. "I told you she was crazy." His fury starts to build. He's almost where I need him to be.

"I believe them," I say, egging him on.

"What's she saying now? That *I* killed Shaila? That we were sleeping together and on initiation I killed her and blamed it on Graham?" Adam blows out air and shakes his head. "Fucking crazy."

"Is it?" I ask, my voice steady and loud. "Is it *crazy*?"

"What are you saying?" he says.

An eerie sense of calm passes over me. "It makes sense," I say slowly. "You gave her those earrings, spilled your guts to her, and she rejected you. Maybe . . ." I let my voice trail off.

Adam's shoulders tense when I mention the diamonds. His

fists clench.

"The earrings," he says, like he's just remembering them for the first time in three years.

"I saw them," I say, trying to hold my voice firm. "In your nightstand."

Adam's eyes go cold. "After all I've done for you? This is how you repay me? By suggesting that *I* killed Shaila? You're out of your mind. Dumb bitch."

"What did you call me?" My rage leaps into my throat, threatening to strangle me.

"A *bitch*. You and all the other little girls. You're all the same. Pretending you're *cool* but ready to fucking snap if something doesn't go your way." Little flecks of spit pool around the corners of his mouth. I need him to keep going. *I can take it.*

"Is that what happened with Shaila?" I ask. "Is that really why she's dead?"

"You don't know what you're talking about."

"Then tell me." I'm yelling now and my voice wavers, but I know each of these words by heart. The truth is so obvious now. I just need him to admit it. "Tell me what happened. Tell me the truth."

Adam shakes his head back and forth and pulls his black denim jacket around his stomach. "No," he says, his voice shaking. "I didn't mean . . ."

Something inside me cracks and my rage boils over. Suddenly, I'm running toward him so fast the air around me turns to ice. When I make impact with his middle, Adam tumbles to the sand. I dig my knees into the ground, straddling him.

"Admit it," I scream. "You killed her." The tears are flowing hot and fast, and I think I'm going to throw up.

"Don't do this, Jill." His voice is tangled in his throat.

"You killed her!" I scream again, so close to his face I can see his stubble growing in.

"Stop it!" he wails, throwing his head back into the ground. I'm knocked off balance. The sky above me shifts. Adam catches my wrists in his hands. His grip tightens and in one swift move he flips me over and pins me to the sand. I'm trapped. "I trusted you," he says. "You were the only thing I had left in this fucked-up town and you betrayed me by going to *Rachel*, by not believing me." His voice is wet and garbled as if the words are caught in his throat. "I saved you that night," he wails.

"But you did it," I whimper. "You did it."

"I didn't mean to," Adam says. A lump forms in my throat even as my wrists go numb. *Keep talking*, I plead. *Keep going. Say it. Say it.*

"You didn't mean to do what?" I scream, sending tiny drops of spittle onto the very tip of his nose. My heart aches inside my chest. I want to vomit.

"It wasn't my fault." He shoves my wrists down farther into the sand and tucks his knees up under my armpits. I'm paralyzed. For the first time all night, I realize that if Adam killed once, he can do it again. I, too, could be just another dead girl in Gold Coast. But in this moment, I need to know more. I need to know everything. The tears are rushing down my cheeks and I find Adam's eyes. They mirror the ocean behind me, wild and unrelenting.

"Tell me what happened," I say through my teeth. "I deserve to know."

Adam lets out a rush of air and for a split second, I think I see my Adam in there somewhere. The guy who forced me to listen to Fugazi and bought me platters of hash browns and runny eggs at Diane's. The boy who sheepishly sent me play after play, just hoping they were *good enough*. The boy with the dimple and the plastic glasses. The boy whose future I had paired with mine. The boy who did, in fact, save me.

But it was all a lie, calculated to get me to trust him. My Adam has been replaced by a monster I'll never unsee.

"We hung out all summer," Adam says softly, though his fingers are still clenched around my wrists. "When Graham and Rachel weren't around. We ran lines together, drank spiked lemonade by her pool. We had . . . a bond."

My heart breaks. I thought that bond was mine. I thought I was the special one.

"We kept it cool, though," he says. "Until the spring musical. Remember that? *Rent.*" Adam's face twists into a weird smile and I wonder if he's picturing Shaila shimmying and singing on stage with thick coats of makeup patted onto her face. "Keith asked me to doctor up the script so I was there a lot. Shaila was . . . amazing," he whispers. "It was easy after that, to sneak around behind the theater after rehearsals, to pull my car into the staff lot, and be together. We just . . . fit."

His grip is still strong, but his knees unclench just a bit. He wants to let it out. I can feel it.

"But then, I gave her those earrings, the same ones Kara had that she was so obsessed with. Shaila told me it was too much." The anger builds in his eyes again. "She couldn't do it to Graham anymore. She couldn't do it to Rachel. She told me I wasn't worth it. That she didn't want to hurt you, her best friend, more than she already had. That *you* were in love with me, as if I couldn't already tell." His mouth curls in a sad little frown, like I'm some pathetic little child who needs his pity.

"The guilt was eating her alive and we had to stop."

I want to spit in his face and rip his skin with my teeth. I want to show him who's a little girl with a crush now. But I bite my lip and wait for him to continue. I need him to press on. I steel myself for what's next.

"I told her she was making a mistake, but she insisted. I was still so fucking mad on initiation. When it came time to pick pops, I chose Ocean Cliff for her. I was never going to make her *actually* jump. I just thought we could have a little time alone and, you know, make up. But when we got there . . ." He pauses and sucks in a puff of air through his teeth. "She rejected me. Again."

Adam looks me dead in the eyes.

"You know what she did?" he asks. "She laughed at me. I tried to kiss her one last time and she laughed." Adam lets out a snort. "That stupid laugh of hers, all deep and raspy, like I was an idiot for even trying. So I told her to just jump so we could get it over with and go back to the group. She refused. She said she was smarter than that. That she'd die and it wasn't worth it."

Adam shakes his head.

"But I needed her to do it. I wanted to see the fear in her eyes. I said we couldn't leave until she did it and then she started walking away. She said, 'You're not the boss of me,' like a petulant toddler. And so I grabbed her arm and . . . pulled."

Tears stream from my face. I can picture this all so easily.

"It must have been too hard. She stumbled back into a pile of driftwood and just fucking lost it. She shoved me. So I shoved her back, right up against those rocks, and then I heard her head crack. Something inside me just . . . snapped. Next thing

I know she was lying on the sand near a puddle of sea water. There was so much blood everywhere. I panicked. I started running. It wasn't long before I found Graham wandering around like a drunk baby, totally blackout. He had cut himself on some glass in the house, I guess, and was covered in blood. It was almost too easy. I pointed him in the direction of Ocean Cliff and told him to find Shaila. When I got back, I went looking for Jake. Then . . . well, you know." His eyes soften as he continues. "I told everyone Shay went to take a shower, but when she and Graham didn't come back, Rachel and Tina got nervous. So I called the cops and told them I saw Graham covered in blood by the cliff with Shaila. That was that. They arrested him on the spot. And when he confessed, no one thought otherwise."

He's relaxed now, comforted by his own admission. Relieved, almost.

"So that's it," I say, trying to temper the vibration in my voice.

"That's it. I've had to live with this for three whole years," he says, like he can't believe he's actually done something this heinous, like I should feel sorry for him for having to carry around this weight. My insides curdle.

"You fucking piece of shit," I say. My fury mixes with a hollow shade of forgiveness. Shaila felt bad. She wanted it to stop. I wish I could hug her now and tell her it's okay.

I open my mouth again but before I can speak, Adam's eyes dart up behind me and his mouth drops open. *She's here. It's time.*

"You're so done," Rachel says. I inhale deeply, letting the air fill my lungs. My muscles tense, waiting for Adam to move, to finally let me go.

But I don't expect what happens next. He releases me and in one swift motion leaps to his feet, colliding with Rachel in a crunch so hard I wince.

"No!" I yell. But it's no use. She's already crumpled on the sand, curled into a ball next to a pile of dried seaweed. She's nearly motionless.

Rachel moans and I hear Adam's foot make contact with her stomach. *Oof.*

"You're not going to ruin me," he yells, bringing his foot back again and again and kicking her over and over. Sand flies in a cloud around them.

"Stop!" I yell. I push myself to stand and stumble over to them, my vision blurry with fear. I have to do something, anything to make this all stop.

My hands are shaking and I grab at Adam, a final plea. *He knows me. He'll forgive me. He'll stop this.*

But instead, he turns to me, with fury in his eyes and a vein throbbing in his neck.

"Adam, please," I whisper. "Let us go."

He bends at the waist and I think finally, *finally* this will be over. He's giving up. Then Adam lunges at me with something cold and heavy and so, so big.

In one sharp crack, my world explodes, then collapses into dust. The stars fall out of the sky and I taste iron on my tongue. I'm back on the sand. I can't move. My vision narrows to a single point and I try to find Adam in front of the murky sea. But I only hear his voice one last time.

"Oh no."

Then everything goes black.

TWENTY-FIVE

THE LAST TIME I saw Shaila—the real last time, the one that I choose to remember—was at Quentin's house just before initiation. His mom was away, giving a lecture at some university in Norway or Wales, or maybe Finland, and he had gathered us all together for one final night before we *actually* became Players. "A goodbye to our youth," he joked. We were still so young.

No one had any beer stashed away, so we were all sober. A relief, I thought.

Nikki ordered a stack of pizzas on her parents' AmEx and Quentin queued up a bunch of old eighties movies. *Ferris Bueller's Day Off. The Breakfast Club. Say Anything.*

Henry hadn't seen any of them and was cackling the entire time.

"You've been holding out on me, Q!" he yelled when Cameron crashed his dad's car. "Stop letting me watch *Spotlight* over and over, dude." He grabbed Quentin in a headlock and gave him a little noogie.

Graham and Shaila sat curled together at the end of the couch. She had tucked her bare feet under his butt and his arm slinked around her shoulder, tickling the skin underneath her cotton T-shirt.

Robert sprawled across the floor, and tried to convince someone, anyone, to wrestle. Henry obliged every now and then, before tapping Marla in for a final go. She pinned him to the floor with ease and Robert finally relented.

"She has brothers!" he whined. "No fair!"

"If you break that coffee table, I will destroy you!" Quentin yelled from the kitchen. He and Nikki had taken on the roles of hosts. They refreshed popcorn bowls, retrieved plates, and sopped up pizza grease from the carpet. They even turned one of those store-bought cake mixes into a chocolate work of art while we all fought about which member of the Brat Pack spoke to us most.

When they presented their creation, a mess of frosting and sprinkles and candles lit for no reason, Marla squealed. "Ina Garten could never."

Quentin blushed but Nikki looked delighted. "The things we do for you guys," she said.

"Hell yeah!" Graham stood to grab a fork and dug right into the middle of the sheet cake, leaving Shaila alone in the corner of the couch.

"C'mere," she whispered.

I scooted over to her so that our toes touched. She wrapped her arms around me and pulled me to her, so we were both lying back just watching our friends, our people.

Her hands were clammy and warm on my shoulders. She reminded me of a sticky little kid. When my eyes met hers, she looked like she was crying.

"You okay?" I whispered.

She nodded and turned her head back to the group, all huddled around the coffee table, eating spoonfuls of cake straight from the pan.

"I love this so much," she said softly. "I want to stay like this forever."

I hear some machinery beep first. Then the rustling of paper, the hushed whispers of worry. Feeling returns to my toes and then my fingertips. The throbbing starts next, on the left side of my head just above my ear. It continues down my face and through my eye socket, inside my mouth, dry like a desert. Everything aches.

When I find the strength to open my eyes, I land in a sea of white. White walls. White cotton. White wires. Gold Coast Medical Center. It must be.

"She's up." Jared's next to the bed. I hear him before I see him. His voice is anxious and high, choked just a bit.

"What . . ." I start to garble.

"Shh," he says.

He's right. Speaking hurts my throat and burns the roof of my mouth. I want to sleep for hours, for days.

"She'll be a little out of it for quite some time," someone says with authority. A doctor maybe. "She just needs rest right now."

But I shake my head. So hard, I think it's going to split in two. They need to know. "Adam," I whisper.

"It's okay, sweetie." It's Mom now. She grabs my hand and holds each of my fingers in hers. Dad rests an open hand on my shoulder. "We know."

I relent. I give way to the pain and the wretched feeling inside, and succumb to sleep.

It was all Rachel's plan. After I told her about the earrings, she put everything into place. Even if Adam didn't do it, we had to know for sure. He was the last question mark.

She told me to avoid Adam as much as I could, planting seeds of doubt in his head so that when I finally called he would come no questions asked.

"Boys like that hate the word no," she said. "But they *despise* being ignored."

She was right.

Then I had to recruit Nikki. I caught her after physics and asked her to meet me at her house after school, where I explained everything about Adam and Shaila, and what we needed to find out the truth for certain.

Her face went pale and she held my sweaty hand in her cold one for a long, long time as we sat on her deck, watching the water lap against the shore.

"My parents are gone until graduation," she said. "Do it here."

I flung my arms around her neck and breathed a *thank you* into her hair.

She bit her lip and nodded. "Let's just get this fucker." Rachel came out from the city later that week with two digital recorders. Her assuredness calmed me, but all I wanted to do was run.

After school on Friday when I showed up at Nikki's, Rachel had her game face on. She was so ready it scared me.

None of us could eat or drink, or even really talk. But before I texted Adam, Rachel snaked one recorder down the front of my fleece, and one down hers. Nikki would listen to the receiver from inside the house, making sure we got every last word, every single piece of his confession.

When she had it all, that's when she would call the cops. Maybe we should have let them handle it without us. Given over the evidence and watched it all play out. But we wanted to do it ourselves. To hear it from him. To take control. For once. For Shaila.

"Hey." I hear a small, soft voice next to my ear. "Are you awake?"

The room is dark and frigid, but a soft hand takes hold of mine. I try to open my eyes, but only one relents. I turn the good side of my head and try to see who's there.

"Nikki?"

"Yeah," she says. "It's me."

"What time is it?"

"Nighttime," she says. "Sunday."

"Oh shit," I murmur.

She laughs a little. "It's okay."

When my one eye adjusts I can finally take her in. Her long dark hair hangs unwashed and stringy, and she's also in a white hospital gown. A little plastic intake bracelet circles her narrow wrist.

"Are you hurt?"

Nikki shakes her head. "Just here for observation." She holds her arms out as proof. She's all right.

"Rachel," I say. "How is she?"

"A few broken ribs. A black eye like you. But she's going to be okay. We all are." Nikki sniffles and squeezes my hand tighter. "You were right," she says. "He did it. Adam did it."

"I know," I whisper. "Where is he?"

Nikki's shoulders heave up and down as tears stream down

her face. "Upstairs."

The rest of the story tumbles out through choked sobs.

When she heard what was happening through the recorders, Nikki called the police and told them to hurry. They were taking too long, she thought. It sounded like we didn't have much time. She panicked and grabbed a field hockey stick from her mud room before running to the beach. She sprinted toward Adam, hoping to knock him off his feet. But when she collided with him, she swung the stick overhead and knocked him out cold.

Nikki shrieked, and was sure she'd killed him, that she'd brought more death and pain and trauma to this town. To us.

When the ambulances came, they found her huddled with Rachel, awake and woozy. They were sitting next to me, telling me to hang on, while Adam lay passed out on the sand. Nikki told the cops the truth, that she hit him to stop him. Rachel backed her up.

They handed over Adam's confession right there on the beach. That's when they found Adam's pulse. He was alive. Alive and guilty.

Nikki watched as they loaded him into the ambulance and handcuffed his wrist to the stretcher. His head bobbed about and he groaned, coming to.

"I hope he rots in jail," I say, almost a whisper.

Nikki looks up at me through glassy eyes. Spit and snot pool around her nose and she wipes her face on her paper-thin hospital gown.

"I know you lov—" She cuts herself off. "I'm so sorry, Jill. I'm so sorry." She rocks back and forth in the chair next to my bed.

I squeeze her hand so hard my knuckles ache. I repeat the words she once told me.

"You have nothing to be sorry for."

TWENTY-SIX

I DECIDE TO return to the Players' Table one last time. Word has spread by now. The details were splashed on the front page of the *Gold Coast Gazette*. Local news trucks swarmed the school. In a way, it's good. We don't have to explain ourselves.

No one asks about the plum-colored bruise under my eye, or the bandage taped to my forehead. No one questions my and Nikki's plastic hospital bracelets we refuse to take off. They're our reminders that this was all real.

Rachel went up to Danbury as soon as she could. She texted me that Graham will be out soon. He's going to live with her in the East Village, reacclimate to real life before taking a few college classes over the summer. I'm not ready to see him. I don't know if I ever will be. Adam was transferred to the county jail where he awaits trial. The Millers were ready to cough up a million in bail, but the judge denied it. It hurts too much to think about him now.

Today, Nikki and I walk together through the cafeteria for our final lunch at Gold Coast Prep. The sea of students parts, but this time the air around us is still. The frenetic energy is gone, replaced by a simmering sense of wariness and disbelief.

I grab a turkey club, a banana, and a piece of raw cookie dough for Shaila. We pay for our food in silence and walk straight toward the center of the room where all eyes turn to watch us sit down. I slide into my seat, nestled in between Quentin and Nikki. I look around, at Henry, whose tender eyes meet mine, at Marla, who cocks her head in sympathy, and even at Robert, who's zoned out completely.

"Well, this is awkward," I start.

Quentin lets out a snort. He wraps his arm around my shoulder and squeezes me to him.

Nikki's eyes are dark and sad, but the corners of her mouth perk up. "One last Players' tribunal?" She doesn't wait for anyone to speak. "I call this meeting of the Players to order." She taps a fork against her tray and a few of the undies turn their heads to listen.

"Tonight," she says, raising her voice. "Bonfire at my house." She turns in her seat to Topher, who leans in so close, he's basically sitting on Quentin's lap. "Spread it around, okay?" He nods.

Nikki faces us. "Let's burn it all down."

When Jared and I push through the front door, Mom is already in the kitchen, puttering around the island, prepping an enormous pot of linguini with clams.

"Jill?" she calls. Her maternal senses have moved into overdrive. For good reason I guess.

Mom appears in the hallway, her hands covered in oil and flecks of parsley. "Something came for you." She gestures to the side table where the mail piles up.

A large, thick envelope with my name on it sits on top of the stack. The return address says Brown. My stomach flips.

"Do you want to open it?" she asks.

Jared inhales sharply behind me.

I reach for it and feel the weight heavy in my hand. The paper is made from fine cardstock, thick and embossed with ink. I stop myself from ripping it apart and instead close my eyes and remember everything that's happened this year, everything that I lived through. *I lived.*

It all becomes so clear.

"Well?" Mom asks.

I shake my head. "It doesn't matter," I say. "I'm not going to Brown."

Mom purses her lips. Dad appears behind her, a worried look on his face.

"I don't want to. I want to go to State."

"Jill, if this is about the money, we'll find a way," Mom says, wiping her hands on the apron tied around her waist.

"We will," Dad says.

But I shake my head. "No," I say. "I don't want it." I set the unopened envelope back down on the table. My voice is firm and my mind is clear. I've already forgotten the hunger, the need I felt to be there. Now that I know the truth, everything has changed. The idea of being around Adam's past makes me want to barf. I have another option. My future exists at State and for the first time in a long time . . . I am free.

That night, I arrive at Nikki's with Jared in tow. The boys have already started the fire on the beach and now they stand together at the edge of the circle with their arms by their sides, not saying much. Quentin nudges Henry when he sees me walk up. A cautious smile spreads on his face. One lock of hair flops over his forehead.

"Hi," Henry says.

"Hi." Before I can think better, I reach for him and wrap my arms around his waist. His body is tense at first but then he pulls me to him in a warm hug.

"We're good, Jill. We're all good," he whispers into my hair. Something inside me releases and I finally feel forgiven.

Nikki appears with the massive green binder that holds everything about the Players. "Hey," she says. Her eyes are wet. "Ready?"

I nod.

"Yes," Henry whispers. "Let's do it." The others follow suit. Even Robert, who crosses his arms over his chest. His leather jacket tightens at the elbows.

I look around the circle now and see Players from all grades. The juniors and sophomores mingle together, shifting from foot to foot. Jared stands with his class in a little huddle. The mood is somber. Tomorrow would have been their initiation.

Nikki clears her throat and holds the binder above her head. The group quiets, expecting her to give a final speech, to pass the rules to the next Toastmaster in line.

But in one swift motion, she throws the binder in front of her, straight into the middle of the fire.

Topher Gardner gasps and a handful of sophomores bring their hands to their mouths.

Jared looks at me from across the circle, a slow smile appearing on his face.

"It's over," Nikki says softly, her eyes trained on the pieces of paper that go up, up, up in flames. The fire rages and grows taller until I can no longer see through its heat. "It's all over." She shouts this time.

"What about the Files?" Quentin asks.

"Gone," Nikki says. "Rachel's girlfriend's a coder. I had her trash the app. It's gone for good."

Marla nods. "Well done, Nik."

The undies stand with their mouths hanging open. I wonder if they wanted the Players to continue or if they're thrilled at the idea of being regular. Of earning what they think they're owed. We forced it on them and it's not fair to take it all away. But something had to change. *This year will be different.*

We stand together in silence for another minute before Robert lifts his head. "Look." He points toward the house. Dozens of people are now walking toward us, emerging from behind the reeds. It takes me a few moments to recognize them. Our classmates. People who never come to parties. The chess team and the jazz club. Marla's field hockey crew. Pretty soon, it seems as if the entire school has assembled to watch the Players burn.

My heart thumps wildly in my chest. This is the way it should be. We're no better than anyone else. We're just the only ones who didn't realize. Now we know.

"Hey." Someone grabs my elbow and I flinch, pulling my body back instinctually. "It's okay. It's just me." Henry appears next to me again. "C'mere," he says. "I want to show you something." He tugs gently on my wrist and I follow him down to where the water meets the sand.

"Close your eyes," he whispers. I do as he says, willing myself to not be scared of the darkness. Not anymore.

"Okay, open," he whispers. "Look up."

I flutter my eyes and turn my head to the sky. It's a wide open galaxy. A million tiny pinpricks of light. The stars twinkle like diamonds. I can plot my entire life on tonight's perfect map.

"Amazing, huh?" Quentin says.

"Breathtaking," Nikki echoes.

They've all appeared, leaving the rest of Gold Coast Prep to itself for one last time.

"That one looks like a dick," Robert says a little too loud.

"Shh, asshole!" Marla says. "You're ruining it."

"Ow, lay off!"

And suddenly, I laugh. I laugh so hard my stomach aches and I have to bend over to hold myself together.

Nikki starts giggling, too, and pretty soon we're all in fits at the mouth of the Sound, staring up at the perfect stretch of sky my friends found just for me.

Henry is the first to get ahold of himself and soon we're all quiet again, looking up. I wonder who we are right now, and how long we'll stay this way. Will we recognize each other in a year? In ten? I wonder who Shaila would have become if she were still alive. What would Graham be like if he were here, too? I wonder what kind of damage we have inflicted on each other and if we will ever learn to heal. I wonder if we are ready to let each other go.

I turn my head slightly and spot the Big Dipper, the Lyre, the Eagle, Taurus. My constants. My truths. A shooting star flies across the sky, explodes, then disappears. Small waves crash softly at our feet.

Together, we stare into the darkness to find the light.

We did it.

We made it out alive.

ACKNOWLEDGMENTS

ACKNOWLEDGMENTS

Thank you first and always to my indomitable agent, Alyssa Reuben. She believed in this story from day one, and she also believed in me. I am so grateful for her tenacity, patience, and guidance.

Additional gratitude to the entire team at Paradigm, who scheduled phone calls, talked me through contracts, and are just, in general, the best: Katelyn Dougherty and Madelyn Flax.

My editor, Jess Harriton, is a gift to writers and a storytelling wizard. She saw what this book *could* be and helped make it so much richer, deeper, and more meaningful. I am in awe of her skill and generosity. Jess, I can't wait to do this with you again.

All the design kudos to the incredible team who came up with the concept for and photographed this exquisite, compelling cover: Christine Blackburne, Maggie Edkins, and Jessica Jenkins.

Thank you to Elyse Marshall, a publicist I knew I would adore as soon as she ordered fries for the table.

And to every person at Razorbill and PenguinTeen who rallied around Jill and her friends, I am so lucky to have a cheerleading squad like this one: Krista Ahlberg, James Akinaka, Kristin Boyle, Kara Brammer, Christina Colangelo, Alex Garber, Deborah Kaplan, Jennifer Klonsky, Bri Lockhart, Casey McIntyre, Emily Romero, Shannon Spann, Marinda Valenti, and Felicity Vallence.

This book has so many additional possibilities because of the people who believe it could extend beyond the page: Meghan Oliver and Matt Snow at Paradigm, I am walking on clouds because of you.

Shoutout to Sasha Levites, my legal warrior. Her unflappability and ferocity are boundless.

Thank you to Sydney Sweeney, who shows me what hard work really looks like, and whose support is unparalleled.

Jill and the Players originated in Melissa Jensen's YA fiction writing class at the University of Pennsylvania (yes, it's a real class; yes, it was a dream). Melissa, thank you for this note in the margins: "I can't wait for you to publish this one day!"

Years ago, I sat in Laura Brounstein's office at *Cosmopolitan* and she asked me, "What do you *really* want to do?" This was a job interview, so the obvious answer was *work here*. But for better or worse, I said, "I want to write YA novels, but like, eventually, you know? Not now." Her response: "Why wait?" Good call, LB.

To my editors at *Entertainment Weekly*, who urged me to keep going and to just keep writing, thank you for always saying *yes*: Tina Jordan, Kevin O'Donnell, and Chris Rosen.

To the members of Team *Cosmopolitan*, past, present, and future, thank you for the memes, life advice, and the endless supply of Cheetos and champagne. Life is sweeter because you're in it. Extra special thank-yous to Faye Brennan, Meredith Bryan, Katie Connor, Sascha de Gersdorff, Mary Fama, Dani Kam, Sophie Lavine, Ashley Oerman, Jess Pels, Michele Promaulayko, Andrea Stanley, Molly Stout, Susan Swimmer, and Helen Zook. Allie Holloway took my beautiful headshot, and damn, she's good at it.

Isabella Biedenharn, Ali Jaffe, and Kase Wickman were some of my earliest readers. Thank you for your thoughtful notes and encouragement that kept me going when there was no end in sight. Colette Bloom and Marley Goldman read many, *many*, many drafts of this manuscript, and I will spend the rest of my life thanking them for their precious time, feedback, and love. Hey, guys, *you* made this book better.

To my friends, who hugged me when shit got dark and celebrated when it all turned around. Man, I'm the luckiest: Maddie Boardman, Gina Cotter, Lisa Geismar, Mady Glickman, Josh Goldman, Katie Goldrath, Mahathi Kosuri, Ellie Levitt, Lora Rosenblum, Jordan Sale, Andrew Schlenger, Derek Tobia, Lucy Wolf, and Ari Wolfson.

Thank you to my sister, Halley, for learning how to Insta Story to mark this occasion, and for being my forever champion. You're my hero. Lots of love to Ben and Leia for keeping the chocolate chip cookies and the cuddles coming (respectively, of course).

I am a writer because I am a reader, and I am a reader because my parents, Candyce and David, brought me to bookstores and libraries as early as I can remember. They let me pick out whatever I wanted and never censored my choices. They celebrated trade paperbacks and literary hardcovers and everything in between. They let me read in long car rides and in the bathtub. They always said yes to books. Thank you for giving me the world and for the infinite love and strength.

I love you, Maxwell Strachan. This is only the beginning.